外研社 高等英语教育学术会议文集

文体学：中国与世界同步
——首届国际文体学学术研讨会暨第五届全国文体学研讨会文选

Stylistics: China and the World
—— Papers from the 1st International and the 5th National Conference on Stylistics

主编 刘世生 吕中舌 封宗信

外语教学与研究出版社
FOREIGN LANGUAGE TEACHING AND RESEARCH PRESS
北京 BEIJING

图书在版编目(CIP)数据

文体学：中国与世界同步：首届国际文体学学术研讨会暨第五届全国文体学研讨会文选/刘世生，吕中舌，封宗信主编 .— 北京：外语教学与研究出版社，2008.9

ISBN 978 - 7 - 5600 - 7854 - 0

Ⅰ. 文… Ⅱ. ①刘… ②吕… ③封… Ⅲ. 文体论—学术会议—文集 Ⅳ. H052 - 53

中国版本图书馆 CIP 数据核字 (2008) 第 152099 号

出 版 人：于春迟
责任编辑：段长城
执行编辑：毕　争
封面设计：张　峰
出版发行：外语教学与研究出版社
社　　址：北京市西三环北路 19 号 (100089)
网　　址：http://www.fltrp.com
印　　刷：北京双青印刷厂
开　　本：787×1092　1/16
印　　张：22
版　　次：2008 年 10 月第 1 版　2008 年 10 月第 1 次印刷
书　　号：ISBN 978 - 7 - 5600 - 7854 - 0
定　　价：46.90 元
*　　*　　*

中国修辞学会文体学研究会
会议论文集编委会

顾　问：胡壮麟　王德春

主　任：申　丹

副主任：刘世生

委　员（按姓氏音序排列）：

董启明　郭　鸿　苗兴伟　秦秀白

徐有志　俞东明　张德禄

序

　　进入新世纪以来，具有跨学科优势的文体学在国内外都呈现出更加旺盛的发展势头。在国外，文体学在英国、欧洲大陆和澳大利亚等文体学的坚固领地不断向前推进。在美国文体学曾一度先盛后衰，但也出现了逐渐复兴的迹象。这主要是因为近年来美国激进的学术氛围有所缓解，作品的形式研究逐渐受到重视，被叙事学所忽略的语言层面也得到了更多的关注。在国内，改革开放以来，文体学得到了长足发展。二十世纪八、九十年代，文体学在西方（主要是在美国）受到政治文化批评和解构主义的双重冲击，在国内则幸运地遇到了适宜的学术氛围：在经历了长期的政治批评之后，中国的学术界注重作品的形式审美研究，欢迎科学性和客观性，教学界（尤其是外语教学界）则看重工具性和实用性，而文体学十分符合这些需求。国内很多大学陆续开设了文体学课程，有的培养出文体学方向的硕士和博士，越来越多的文体学著述在杂志上发表或成书出版。世纪之交，中国的文体学研究者们开始筹备成立全国性的文体学研究团体，得到了中国修辞学会王德春会长和常务理事会的大力支持。2004 年在河南大学召开的第四届全国文体学研讨会上，隶属于中国修辞学会的文体学研究会宣告成立。由中国文体学研究会主办、清华大学、北京大学承办的首届文体学国际会议暨第五届全国文体学研讨会于 2006 年 6 月 16 – 18 日在清华大学召开。来自英国、美国、加拿大、澳大利亚、意大利、中国大陆和香港地区的 130 多名代表汇聚一堂，主要就以下议题展开了热烈研讨：（1）文体学作为学科在国内外的建设与发展；（2）普通文体学/文学文体学/理论文体学；（3）文体学各流派理论模式及方法论；（4）文体学与相邻学科；（5）文体学与文本阐释；（6）语言各语体特征；（7）文学各体裁风格；（8）文体学与外语教学：文体学作为学科的教学和用文体学方法教授外语的教学；（9）文体学应用研究前景等。在外语教学与研究出版社的大力支持下，由刘世生、吕中舌、封宗信三位教授主编的会议论文集即将付梓，可喜可贺。

i

作为中国文体学研究会成立以来的首届国际学术会议，西方知名文体学家的参与构成了这次研讨会的一个突出特色。他们的大会发言带来了国际前沿的新视角和新方法。但由于版权规定的限制，本论文集仅收入了他们三篇论文的全文，其它的则收入了较为详细的论文摘要（其全文请见已经出版或将要出版的相关西方书刊），我们从中可以了解到他们发言的基本内容和主要特点。本届会议的另一特色是"认知转向"。二十世纪九十年代以来，西方文体学、语言学、叙事学等领域均发生了"认知转向"。这两年国内对认知的关注急速升温，与2004年在河南大学召开的研讨会相比，本届会议上认知文体学论文的比例有大幅增长。在本届会议上，功能文体学的论文也为数不少。功能文体学一直是我国文体学研究的主流方向之一，有的研究成果达到国际先进水平。本论文集收录的有的国内学者的功能文体学论文已在西方权威杂志上发表。文体学（各个分支）作为学科的发展和文体学对英语教学的意义也是本次会议上的两个主要关注点。除了诗歌和小说这些文体学的传统关注对象，会上有不少论文探讨戏剧和非文学语域乃至非印刷媒介的文体，关注其语言的审美效果、修辞效果或语言隐含的权力关系。有的论文还注重对不同语言或不同文本之间的文体进行比较。无论是在国内还是在国外，越来越多的文体学家将是否能对文本阐释做出新的贡献视为衡量文体分析是否成功的重要标准。这是面对严峻的挑战而作出的一种回应。有的批评家之所以排斥文体学，主要是认为文体学分析不能带来新的阐释，而只是为已知的理解提供一种"伪科学"的证据。面对这种局面，文体学家旨在证明文体学能够提供有力的阐释模式。会上有不少分析具体文本的论文在阐释方面有可喜的进展。

虽然由于篇幅和版权所限，本文集仅仅收入了本次研讨会上宣读的部分论文，但依然很好地体现了这次国际研讨会论文的前沿性和广阔性。借此机会特别感谢为这次研讨会做出了最大贡献的清华大学外语系。也特别感谢远道而来的国外文体学家对中国文体学事业的大力支持。这次研讨会的成功和本论文集的出版定会对我国文体学事业的发展产生深远的影响。

申　丹

2007 年春于燕园

Table of Contents

Part I

Stylistics Abroad

Literary Stylistics and Systemic Functional Linguistics

Michael Cummings

York University, Canada

Systemic functional linguistics has a great currency in Chinese scholarship, due to the efforts of many direct and indirect students of Michael A. K. Halliday in China. I am therefore very honored to be asked by some of these colleagues to talk about systemic functional literary stylistics and to say something about my own work within it. You can find the names of many of these distinguished Chinese systemic linguists in the article by Huang Guowen, "Hallidayan linguistics in China" (2002), and in the article by Zhang Delu, Edward McDonald, Fang Yan & Huang Guowen, "The development of systemic functional linguistics in China" (2005). Today I want expressly to thank Professor Liu Shisheng of Tsinghua University for his very kind invitation, and Professor Hu Zhuanglin of Peking University for his many years of friendship and support. I also want to thank Liu Nannan and Professor Fang Yan, both of Tsinghua University, the first for her great help in preparing this occasion, and the second for the preparations she is making for the 36th *Annual International Systemic Functional Congress*, to be held here in 2009. My talk today has four parts: 1. systemic functional linguistic description illustrated by an English poem; 2. systemic functional linguistic description illustrated by English literary prose; 3. recent important readings in systemic functional literary stylistics; 4. some recent research of my own into the stylistics of systemic functional Theme and Rheme.

1.0 I will structure the first part of the discussion in terms of the three general functions of language, that is, the systemic functional "metafunctions": the interpersonal function of language, which serves the relating to one another of the reader and writer; the experiential and logical function, which serves the representation of reality; and the textual function, which serves the formation of discourse (Halliday & Matthiessen, 2004: 29-31). In the approach I take, literary stylistics reveals the contribution of a text's language to that text's literary aim. Systemic functional linguistics approaches the language of a literary text by

3

situating the language within its culture and its genre, and by construing its lexico-grammatical form, even its phonology, in terms of its discourse semantics (Martin, 1992: 19-21, 495-496). The English poem which I want to use for illustration is W. H. Auden's "Musée des Beaux Arts" (1976: 146-147). Many of you will have encountered a systemic functional description of this poem in Michael O'Toole's *Language of Displayed Art* (1994: 145-154, 161-166).

Musée des Beaux Arts

About suffering they were never wrong,
The Old Masters: how well they understood
Its human position; how it takes place
While someone else is eating or opening a window or just walking dully along;
How, when the aged are reverently, passionately waiting
For the miraculous birth, there always must be
Children who did not specially want it to happen, skating
On a pond at the edge of the wood;
They never forgot
That even the dreadful martyrdom must run its course
Anyhow in a corner, some untidy spot
Where the dogs go on with their doggy life and the torturer's horse
Scratches its innocent behind on a tree.
In Brueghel's Icarus for instance: how everything turns away
Quite leisurely from the disaster; the plowman may
Have heard the splash, the foresaken cry,
But for him it was not an important failure; the sun shone
As it had to on the white legs disappearing into the green
Water; and the expensive delicate ship that must have seen
Something amazing, a boy falling out of the sky,
Had somewhere to get to and sailed calmly on.

1.1 In terms of its culture, the whole poem is, of course, a cultural allusion: to Pieter Bruegel the Elder's (1525?-1569) painting "Landscape with the Fall of Icarus", hung in the Museum of Fine Arts, Brussels (Hyde, 2003: 67). The first stanza also appeals to certain common cultural values—our sympathies are drawn not only to the figure of suffering, but also to the many innocents: the reverent aged, children, even to doggy dogs and an innocent horse. In terms of its genre, the text offers an appealing literary irony. Irony is an understanding shared between writer and reader which is lost on the characters in between. Here we share an understanding with the speaker and his "Old Masters" which is apparently lost on all the rest. This understanding situates human suffering in relation to various cultural ideologies: myth about justice in the case of Icarus, salvation religion in the case of the miraculous birth and later martyrdom, political power in the case of the torturer, bourgeois capitalism—or political power again—in the case of the expensive ship with somewhere to get to. The second stanza, however, suggests another cultural norm, the imputation of guilt: the plowman may have heard, the ship must have seen. Auden also plays with a classical generic form: the difference in the numbers of lines in the two stanzas, the crazy rhyme scheme that almost comes together, both suggest the sonnet form. As if in a sonnet, the first stanza presents a general situation, and the second stanza encodes it in a particular instance. The first stanza makes use of the present tense to represent the universal present, but the second stanza is mainly in the past tense, as if the painting represents a particular past event. As is usually true of sonnets, at the end we are left with the satisfying feeling that we have been given some kind of answer.

1.2 To describe the lexical and grammatical form of a text is to construe what the text aims at. The first metafunctional perspective on lexico-grammar I want to take up is that of the textual metafunction. The textual metafunction is the secondary, text-forming capacity of structures and meanings which are deployed primarily to achieve interpersonal and experiential meanings. A good illustration here is the meanings associated with the definite article. The definite article in written English typically makes reference to some previous occurrence of a participant in the same text. That is, like 3rd-person pronouns, it is typically endophoric—referring within the text—and anaphoric—referring back. But Auden's poem is distinctively different. There are 8 instances of the definite article in the first stanza, and just a single one barely represents anaphoric endophoric reference: the one in "the torturer", referring back only by inference to "the... martyrdom". All the rest are doing something different. The one in "the edge" is cataphoric, that is, referring ahead to "the wood". The rest aren't even endophoric, but instead refer outside the text altogether, to generic categories which are culture-specific. Michael Halliday calls these "homophoric" references: "The Old Masters", "the aged", "the miraculous birth", "the wood", "the dreadful martyrdom", "the dogs" (Halliday & Matthiessen, 2004: 557-558). These homophoric references create the situational generality of this first stanza. In the second stanza, 8 of 9 other definite articles have anaphoric endophoric reference only by inference from the mention of "Brueghel's Icarus"—that is, they all make reference to what can be seen in or inferred from the painting: "the disaster", "the plowman", "the splash", "the foresaken cry", "the white legs", "the green water", and so forth. From the viewpoint of the imaginary onlooker, they are straightforward exophoric reference—reference to something outside the text. From either perspective they are truly definite, not generic, and help produce the contrasting particularity of the second stanza (cf. Flanagan, 1984: 99-102.).

1. 3 The interpersonal metafunction on the other hand can be invoked to account for different kinds of speech acts, and for modality. Modality in Auden's poem is construed both by modal verbs and by modal adverbs. The modal verbs occur in both stanzas, the modal adverbs only in the first. Modal verbs in the first stanza are exclusively deontic, that is, representing objective necessity: "there always must be/Children", "martyrdom must run its course". Modal verbs in the second stanza are mainly epistemic, that is, representing human judgement: "the plowman may/Have heard", "the. . . ship that must have seen". This fits our impression that the first stanza implies general truth about life, the second stanza a particular instantial situation which is to be decoded or evaluated. (A different perspective can be found in O'Toole, 1994: 162.) The modal adverbs of the first stanza have an interesting uniformity: "never" (twice), "always", "how well", "specially" and "just". The first five of these six form a set whose common meanings involve the universal and the emphatic—chosen it seems to help convince us of universal truths.

1. 4 The experiential metafunction provides a third perspective. Construal of the world-out-there can be seen in the distribution of lexis in a text. The structuring of lexis represents the text's fields of reference. Our very first reflections on the poem would lead us to expect a set of lexical items which involve the field of "suffering"; and this turns out to be the lexical item "suffering" itself, plus "dreadful", "martyrdom", "torturer", "disaster', "foresaken", and "cry". Text lexis is structured by meaningful contrasts among lexical sets. Among the contrasting sets here is one for "innocence", including "innocent" itself, plus "aged", "birth", "children", "doggy", and "boy". Another contrasting set is for high intensity evaluation, including "reverently", "passionately", "miraculous", "important", "expensive", "delicate", and "amazing". Yet another is for low intensity evaluation, including "dully", "anyhow", "leisurely", and "calmly". The contrasting "suffering" and "innocence" sets ironically suggest that the virtue of innocence is just as apt to belong to the vast, indifferent context of suffering, as it is to belong to suffering itself. The significance of the "high intensity" and "low intensity" sets is to contrast an evaluation of suffering that we as witnesses share with "the Old Masters", with a dis-evaluation shared by all the other witnesses of the poem.

1.5 It seems paradoxical at first that the poem's title is not "Icarus" – but rather "Musée des Beaux Arts". What this does imply is that an important field of reference is *being in the museum*. Two lexical sets correspond to this. First is the set of four items: "Musée des Beaux Arts", "Old Masters" "Brueghel" and "Icarus"; and then a much larger set representing mental activity: "wrong", "understood", "waiting", "want", "forgot", "heard", "seen", "amazing". The poem is after all about evaluations: the Museum onlooker's evaluation of an Old Master's painting, the painting's evaluation of innocents' failure to evaluate suffering. But that brings us to another side of the experiential, which is grammatical transitivity. Systemic functional linguistics divides all semantic clause processes into six types, material, mental, relational, verbal, behavioural and existential. The lexical set of mental activity is nearly the same as the set of verbs which represent mental process. Another set of verbs represents material process, and these seem just as crucial to the text as the mental process verbs: "takes place", "eating", "opening", "walking", "happen", "skating", "run a course", "go on", "scratches", "turns away", "shone", "disappearing", "falling", "get to", "sailed on". You will immediately recognize that nearly all of these processes are intransitive. In the systemic functional approach to the ergative, only one clause participant is involved with such processes, the Medium.

7

Just two of them, "opening (a window)" and "scratching (its... behind)" involve two participants. Michael Toolan (1998: 89-90) proposes one version of the scale of empowerment, which orders the types of material process participant. The most empowered participant is the agent, a human acting upon a human or non-human medium. Only one of these fifteen different material processes involves a human agent, and all the rest of the participants rank much lower on or at the bottom of the empowerment scale.

Ironically, the single representation of an agent is "someone... opening a window", the process instanced as a totally trivial act. It would seem that in Auden's moral microcosm, even suffering is inconsequential because nobody is connecting with anybody else.

Empowerment Scale	Nos.
Agent (human)	1
Force (nature)	1
Instrument	0
Medium-initiator (human)	5
Beneficiary/Recipient	0
Medium-target (human)	0
Medium (non-human)	11
Total:	18

Figure 1. The empowerment scale

2.0 The language of a short poem is a system in itself because it is sharply framed. A prose episode does not have the same sharp boundaries as a short poem. Nevertheless it is framed, because it is an episode. In his short-story collection, *Dubliners*, James Joyce represents people morally crushed by cultural ideologies of nationalism, religion, sexual repression and class. At the beginning of the story "The Dead" Joyce uses a single episode to introduce and characterize the protagonist, Gabriel Conroy, a teacher, who has been invited to speak at a party and encounters the servant girl on his way (1958: 178-179):

"O, then," said Gabriel gaily, "I suppose we'll be going to your wedding one of these fine days with your young man, eh?"

The girl glanced back at him over her shoulder and said with great bitterness: "The men that is now is only all palaver and what they can get out of you."

Gabriel coloured, as if he felt he had made a mistake, and, without looking at her, kicked off his goloshes and flicked actively with his muffler at his patent-leather shoes.

He was a stout, tallish young man. The high colour of his cheeks pushed upwards even to his forehead, where it scattered itself in a few formless patches of pale red; and on his hairless face there scintillated restlessly the polished lenses and the bright gilt rims of the glasses which screened his delicate and restless eyes. His glossy black hair was parted in the middle and brushed in a long curve behind his ears where it curled slightly beneath the groove left by his hat.

When he had flicked lustre into his shoes he stood up and pulled his waistcoat down more tightly on his plump body. Then he took a coin rapidly from his pocket.

"O Lily," he said, thrusting it into her hands, "it's Christmastime, isn't it? Just. . . here's a little. . . "

He walked rapidly towards the door.

"O no, sir!" cried the girl, following him. "Really, sir, I wouldn't take it."

"Christmas-time! Christmas-time!" said Gabriel, almost trotting to the stairs and waving his hand to her in deprecation.

The girl, seeing that he had gained the stairs, called out after him: "Well, thank you, sir."

He waited outside the drawing-room door until the waltz should finish, listening to the skirts that swept against it and to the shuffling of feet. He was still discomposed by the girl's bitter and sudden retort. It had cast a gloom over him which he tried to dispel by arranging his cuffs and the bows of his tie. He then took from his waistcoat pocket a little paper and glanced at the headings he had made for his speech. He was undecided about the lines from Robert Browning, for he feared they would be above the heads of his hearers. Some quotation that they would recognize from Shakespeare or from the Melodies would be better. The indelicate clacking of the men's heels and the shuffling of their soles reminded him that their grade of culture differed from his. He would only make himself ridiculous by quoting poetry to them which

they could not understand. They would think that he was airing his superior
education. He would fail with them just as he had failed with the girl in the
pantry. He had taken up a wrong tone. His whole speech was a mistake from
first to last, an utter failure.

2.1 Our omniscient narrator here portrays Gabriel as an insecure and self-
conscious man who does not cope successfully with people, and consoles himself
with little attentions to his personal appearance. Gabriel is acutely conscious of
differences in class, but fears that his social inferiors will not respect his social
superiority. His problems with people are compounded by his problems with
women. We learn elsewhere that his marriage has grown cold. His sexual
inadequacy is mirrored here in the symbolism of his standing on one side of a
closed door, listening to the sounds of other people dancing.

2.2 The distribution of lexis again defines the fields of reference. Prominent
contrasting sets include those for literary culture, mental activity, error, the sexes,
the human body, clothing, and appearance. The appearance set is particularly
important, in that it ridicules Gabriel by making him seem a little kewpy-doll of a
man: "colour", "stout", "tall", "scatter", "formless", "pale", "red",
"hairless", "scintillate", "polish", "bright", "gilt", "delicate", "glossy",
"black", "curl", "lustre", "plump". Also prominent is the error set, although
more abstract: "mistake" (twice), "no", "discomposed", "retort", "gloom",
"undecided", "fear", "ridiculous", "fail" (twice), "wrong", "failure". The
clothing set is important partly because it relates, as we shall soon see, to a
transitivity pattern. This set includes "goloshes", "muffler", "patent-leather",
"shoes", "glasses", "hat", "waistcoat", "skirts", "cuffs", "bows", "tie",
"pocket", "heels", "soles". This episode in Gabriel's mental life has two parts:
the fear of error in dealing with a servant girl, then fear of error in dealing with a
petit-bourgeois audience. Gabriel's reaction to this fear is the same in both cases—
he fiddles with his clothes, the first time as if to hide, the second time as if a kind
of consolation.

2.3 In both these pathetic crises, Gabriel is also betrayed by the interpersonal
metafunction. In the exchange with Lily, Gabriel patronizingly initiates a polite
conversational opening with the modal projecting frame clause "I suppose" and the
question tag "eh?". What wounds him is the shock of Lily's impolite directness,

her very unmodalized retort. Later in his mental monologue outside the drawing-room door, modal verbs pile up: "until the waltz should finish", "they would be above the heads of his hearers", "some quotation that they would recognize... would be better", "He would only make himself ridiculous", "which they could not understand", "They would think", "He would fail". These past-tense modal verbs represent the conventional wording of free indirect discourse. Free indirect discourse has the potential for irony because it makes such an intimate connection between the voice of the narrator and the voice of the unsuspecting character (Toolan, 1998: 116). Here we share with the omniscient narrator his intimate knowledge of Gabriel's mental cowardice, while Gabriel is unaware that we dissect him.

2.4 However it is by grammatical transitivity that Gabriel is most betrayed. There are 35 material process verbs in this episode, and a bare majority, 18, have Gabriel as a participant. In 10 of the 18, Gabriel as subject is only a human medium, either because the verbs are intransitive or passive. In the remaining 8, Gabriel manages to rise to the top of the empowerment scale as agent—but what sorts of mediums is "he" agent to? Once his own hands, and in the rest, only his clothes or things in his pocket. In this portrayal, it is Gabriel who never gets a chance to connect with somebody else. What he can connect with is life's goloshes, shoes, waistcoats, coins, papers, cuffs and bows.

Gabriel as agent	
kicked off	goloshes
flicked at	shoes
pulled down	waistcoat
took	coin
thrusting	coin
waving	hand
arranging	cuffs and bows
took	paper

Figure 2. Gabriel as agent

3.0 In these linguistic analyses of two short texts, I have tried to show a systemic functional approach to some crucial features of literary language. What I want to do now is review a few of the most important and most recent books about the systemic functional literary stylistics. In discussing these six books, I will show you the systemic functional approach to a wide variety of literatures.

3. 1 First I want to take up David Birch's theory of critical stylistics in *Language , Literature and Critical Practice: Ways of Analyzing Text* (1989). This approach has much in common with any systemic functional stylistics. It reviews the principles of the older, formal stylistics, and compares them with alternative points of view. Thus a formal analysis is seen to construct an ideal reality and an ideal of language, and to marginalize social and institutional factors in discourse. But critical and systemic theories hold that language constructs not just a psychological reality but also a social reality. Its meaning is shaped by culture-specific institutions. Again, formal analysis tends to see language as a transparent medium which serves as a neutral vehicle carrying meaning. But critical and systemic theories hold that the interpretation of language concentrates not on what the language is saying, rather on what the language is doing. Language as a performance is central to its meaning. Furthermore, formal analysis espouses the ideal of an objectively, disinterestedly determined meaning which is context-free. However, texts do not have single, correct meanings; rather they have multiple meanings which are mediated by multiple readers representing the multiple ideologies of multiple cultures. Finally, a formal analysis of a text means revealing what meaning has been put into the text by its writer. However, the meaning of the text for the writer should not be privileged over the meaning of the text for the reader—rather the opposite is to be preferred.

3. 2 In her 1985 book, *Linguistics, Language, and Verbal Art*, Ruqaiya Hasan proposes both to demonstrate a systemic functional literary stylistics and to offer her own theoretical framework for it. She begins the demonstration with grammatical and lexical co-patterning in nursery rhymes. From here she makes her way through the analysis of poetry and literary prose, concentrating on co-patterning in clause structures, on the logical relations among clauses, on transitivity patterns and on lexis. Ruqaiya states that her reason for the demonstration is that the analysis of any one work is really for the purpose of exemplifying a general framework of analysis. That general framework has as its core the use of language in verbal art. What is distinctive in verbal art is the operation of three semiotic strata: the outer level of theme, realized by the next level, which is symbolic articulation, realized in turn by the level of verbalization (Figure 3). On the level of verbalization we have language in its natural condition, itself a semiosis. On the level of symbolic articulation, we have the metaphorical meanings which are attached to the patterning of language within verbalization. On the level of theme, we have the most abstract meanings symbolized by the metaphors of symbolic articulation. In addition, Ruqaiya asserts 1) the principle that verbal art is both aesthetic and pragmatic, i. e. , representing truth about humanity, and 2) the principle that verbal art must also be related to the community context which engenders it.

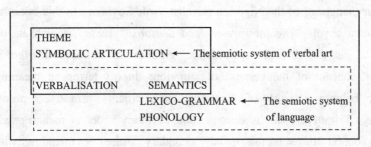

Figure 3. Verbal art and language (Hasan, 1985: 99)

3.3 Many of the objectives of these two approaches are met in the 1988 *Functions of Style*, edited by David Birch & Michael O'Toole. Here contributors share the common objectives of coming at literary text from the perspectives of all the metafunctions, and of demonstrating that a linguistic stylistic reading of a text contributes a meaning to that text not otherwise available, and in so doing, recontextualizes that text in culture. Among those contributors, Michael Halliday demonstrates how the central argument of Tennyson's poem "In Memoriam" is achieved through successive phases established by the grouping of mood choices, by transitivity and by the grouping of lexis (31-44). Ruqaiya Hasan reads the Ann Sexton lyric "Old" in terms of the logic of its clause-complexes, clause structure, patterning of theme choices, transitivity and lexis. She demonstrates in her reading a meaning that goes beyond the "zero-level" of the motifs, and towards meanings found elsewhere in the context of the Sexton corpus (45-73). Modalization and modulation in the earliest 17th century English are systematized by David Birch in an exploration of meaning potentials in a Shakespeare sonnet. Birch is concerned to develop a systemic framework which is diachronic as well as synchronic, and covering applications of all three metafunctions (157-168). In another approach to the literature of a different era, Jill Durey examines the irony of the narrational voice in its presenting the hero and heroine of George Eliot's *Middlemarch*. Durey uses the systemic functional framework to examine the different sorts of irony in the wordings of group, phrase, non-finite and finite clauses (234-248).

3.4 There are three more recent single-volume applications of the systemic functional framework to take notice of, all of which are very individual. In his 1992 book, *Language and Style in Soyinka: A Systemic Textlinguistic Study of A Literary Idiolect*, Oluwole Adejare proposes a systemic functional understanding of the literary language of the Nigerian novelist Wole Soyinka. In this book he covers two Soyinka novels, *The Interpreters and Season of Anomy*, which are popularly understood as difficult prose. Adejare grounds his method in the systemic functional concept of the context of situation. In his terms, a meaning of an utterance belongs to one of three inclusive orders: primitive, primary and secondary. Primitive order is decontextual. Primary order is meaning within the generic context of situation, and secondary order is meaning within the fictionalized instantial situation. On the formal level, Adejare pursues his analysis of Soyinka's prose through its lexical cohesion and its lexical innovations; he uses the framework of systemic functional clause grammar to analyze Soyinka's resort to parallelism and contrast across the elements of clause structure. Much of his description is given over to Soyinka's use of the varieties of English. This includes the prominent dialectal varieties from Nigerian pidgeon through Nigerian interference dialect to Standard Nigerian, as well as Standard British English, American English, and German second-language English. Marked functional varieties include expository, religious and bureaucratic Englishes. His purpose is partly apologetic—he is using systemic functional stylistics to make a difficult prose style intelligible.

3.5 In his 1994 book, *The Language of Displayed Art*, Michael O'Toole generalizes the framework of systemic functional linguistics to the semiotics of plastic art. Each of the three metafunctions, for example, is found to be a principle also in Western painting. The interpersonal metafunction underlies personal assertiveness and attitude in painting, realized in framing, perspective, colour, and many other elements, including even the gaze of characters depicted. The experiential metafunction is realized in narrative, events, character and clothing. The textual metafunction is realized in compositional geometry, rhythm, and other forms of pictorial cohesion. In addition, the rank scale is found to operate in painting. Each of the metafunctions has its own kind of realization in each of the ranks, which are the ranks of the work, the episode, the figure and the member. Each of these elements has a meaning which it takes on from its place in the context of its historical culture—and the discussion can be couched anywhere on a scale of delicacy. This extension of literary stylistics doubles back on itself in O'Toole's discussion of the semiotics of Brueghel's "Landscape with the Fall of Icarus" and that of Auden's "Musée des Beaux Arts". In the latter, O'Toole concentrates on the clause-complex structures which frame Icarus's fall within the description of its witnessing by onlookers. He also takes up the effects of modality and marked thematicity in clauses. The semiotics of plastic art is extended to many other forms as well, including sculpture and architecture.

3. 6 The most recent of these systemic functional approaches to literature is Nina Noergaard's 2003 *Systemic Functional Linguistics and Literary Analysis*. The core of this book is a systemic functional analysis and discussion of the story "Two Gallants" from James Joyce's *Dubliners*. However it is preceded by a thorough summary of systemic functional theory, and followed by an analysis of passages from Joyce's *Ulysses*. Noergaard's approach to the story involves a methodical analysis of the lexico-grammar across all three metafunctions. It is based on a predecessor analysis of the same story by Chris Kennedy in his 1982 article "systemic grammar and its use in literary analysis". But Noergaard goes beyond Kennedy's analysis while accepting his conclusions, and she also applies the more developed systemic functional framework exhibited in Halliday's *Introduction to Functional Grammar* editions of 1985 and 1994. For example she has the benefit of the more delicate six-fold analysis of process types, developed from the less explicit division into material, mental and relational processes (Halliday, 1970). In her approach to *Ulysses*, Noergaard emphasizes the interpersonal relation construed between narrator and reader, but grounds its realization principally within lexical cohesion and the play of genres.

4. 0 At the beginning of this presentation I offered examples of systemic functional reasoning about literary texts. Now, after having reviewed some publications in the area, I want to take up some recent research of my own into the application of the systemic functional theory of Theme and Rheme in literary stylistics. The original Hallidayan definition of English clause theme was that part of the clause which represents its starting point as a message, or what the clause is basically all about (1967: 212). This definition has been significantly reinterpreted by Peter Fries. It is now generally agreed that the theme of the clause is also the part of the clause which is most apt to contribute to the Method of Development of the text. The Method of Development of a text has two main principles: a) the principle of consistency, in which a topical continuity is maintained, and b) the principle of variation, in which the outline logic of the text is represented at points of demarcation. What clause theme typically contributes to consistency is repeated references—that is, "presuming" references—to the same participant. What clause theme typically contributes to variation is any signal of a new departure: often, marked topical themes with a new participant, or conjunctions, as textual themes (Fries, 1981/83, 1995, 2002). What I myself am trying to add to this interpretation is a quantitative analysis of the language of the Method of Development in English texts, and with it, a quantitative understanding of English clause theme and rheme.

4.1 First let's look at the literary function of theme in Auden's poem "Musée des Beaux Arts". It is now commonly accepted that the theme stretch in a clause includes everything from the beginning through a pre-verbal subject element, the unmarked topical theme (Cummings, 2004: 344-345). Each of the two stanzas in Auden's poem starts, however, with a marked topical theme, and then continues to an unmarked topical theme. In the first stanza, the marked topical theme "About suffering" thus announces what the poem is all about, and the following unmarked topical theme "they" announces a secondary topic, "The Old Masters". Each of these topics is maintained in chains of presuming reference items for a while—the "Old Masters" chain even into the second stanza. Another consistency pattern in themes in the first stanza is the succession of themes introduced by "how": "how well...", "how it takes place...", "how... there always must be...". The logical midpoint of the stanza is introduced by a contrast to the "how" themes—the plain "They" theme of line 10.

4.2 In the second stanza, the marked topical Theme "In Brueghel's Icarus" announces the instantiation of the first stanza's prototype. The following "how" component of the theme stretch adds to the consistency of the development from the first stanza. All the rest of the themes chain together referentially with the first theme's evocation of the Icarus painting. Just as in the first stanza, there is a logical mid-point—this time marked by the disjunctive conjunction "But". So even in this short poem we get a Method of Development shown by consistency signals and outline signals in the themes. (A complementary perspective can be found in O'Toole, 1994: 152, 164-165.)

4.3 Similarly, in the Gabriel passage from Joyce's "The Dead", there is a Method of Development, showing consistency and variation. The consistency is signalled mainly by reference chains in themes. These are dominated by two chains, a longer one for Gabriel and a shorter one for Lily. Gabriel's chain is mostly pronouns but Lily's is more often lexicalized because less continuous. The most obvious variation in this passage is its outline division into four parts: 1) dialog between Gabriel and Lily, 2) Gabriel's physical appearance, 3) renewed dialog between Gabriel and Lily, 4) Gabriel's introspection. But this time marked topical themes are rare and disjunctive conjunctions non-existent. The boundaries between each of these four parts are signalled in the clause themes otherwise. The aggregate of themes in each one of these four parts has an internal consistency, but one which differs from the adjoining parts. In part 1 the themes are dominated by reference to Gabriel and Lily. In part 2 they are dominated by reference to Gabriel's features. In part 3 we are back to thematized references to Gabriel and Lily. But in part 4 the themes are dominated by reference to Gabriel alone. Thus the divisions among the parts of the passage are signalled by the contrasting textures of their theme stretches.

4.4 One of the ways of distinguishing the Method of Development from the rest of the text, that is, its "point", is by its language. We've noted that the language of the Method of Development is typically rich in presuming reference. The language of the point of the text is typically rich in lexical variety (Cummings, 2006). But these are statements of proportion, and proportions vary from text to text as a stylistic variation. Such variation can be measured on a quantitative basis. Presuming reference for example can be measured in a text by counting its tokens. I count these tokens in three areas of the clause: the theme stretch, the last element of the clause, and the rest of the rheme (Cummings, 2004, 2005). The last element of the clause is the most important part of the rheme, called by Peter Fries the "N-Rheme", because it is the default or average location of the new information in the clause (1981/83: 128-129). To illustrate this technique, we can look at the second section of the Method of Development in the Joyce story set out in Figure 4.

```
13 He | was [ a stout, tallish young man.
14 The high colour of his cheeks | pushed upwards
                even [ to his forehead,
15 where it | scattered itself [ in a few formless
                patches of pale red;
16 and on his hairless face there | scintillated restlessly [ the polished
                lenses and the bright gilt rims of the glasses which screened his
                delicate and restless eyes.
17 His glossy black hair | was parted [ in the middle
18 and | brushed in a long curve [ behind his ears
19 where it | curled slightly [ beneath the groove left by his hat.
```

Figure 4. Gabriel's physical appearance

Five of the presuming reference groups (underlined) fall into themes (divided from the rhemes by verticals), two of the groups fall into N-rhemes (divided from the other part of the rheme by brackets), and one falls into the other part of the rheme. (Three presuming reference groups are not counted or underlined because they are too deeply embedded to be grammatically significant.) As Figure 5 shows, the themes have 62.5% of presuming reference, the N-rhemes 25% and the others have 12.5%. This association of reference chains with themes is very typical of English text.

Reference element distribution in		
Theme	Other	N-rheme
62.5%	12.5%	25%

Figure 5. Proportions of presuming reference

4. 5 Another indicator is the relative density of presuming reference, measured against the total number of experiential elements in each of these three parts of clauses. For example the five presuming reference groups are among eight experiential elements in themes. But, in N-rhemes, the two presuming reference groups are among seven experiential elements. Themes then have a density of 62.5%, whereas N-rhemes 29%, and the others have only 8%. The density measurement gives a truer picture of the significance of presuming reference in the different parts of the clause because it compensates for the differing sizes of those parts.

Reference element density in		
Theme	Other	N-rheme
62.5%	8%	29%

Figure 6. Densities of presuming reference

4. 6 A third kind of indicator supposes that long reference chains are particularly significant. In the story segment there is just one long reference chain, for all or parts of Gabriel. One index reckons the proportion of the long-chain elements that go into themes, here again 62.5%. Another reckons the proportion of themes that contain long-chain elements, here 71%. For English text in general, both these figures are very high, reinforcing the general impression that the thematizing of long reference chains is especially characteristic of English narrative.

Long-chain distribution	
% in Themes	% of Themes
62.5%	71%

Figure 7. Long-chain distribution

4. 7 All these indicators suggest that the second section of the Method of Development in the Joyce story is very typical of English text in general. However, we get another picture if we expand our view to take in the whole of the Gabriel episode. For the whole episode, the relative proportions for presuming reference shown in Figure 8 are sometimes very different from typical English text. Granted, the density figures are not too jarring: reference elements in themes amount to 80% of experiential elements there, compared with 15% in the other parts of rhemes, and 48% in the N-rhemes. But in absolute numbers, the themes with 49% of all reference elements do not even have half—a bare majority belong to the rhemes instead, which makes the episode as a whole stylistically marked. As for the distribution of the long reference chains, those for Gabriel and for Lily, a bare 52% of their elements belong to the themes, although 59% of themes have them. Both these figures are low. The conclusion to draw is that something is going on in this text which makes the language of the Method of Development less distinctive than normal.

Reference element distribution in		
Theme	Other	N-rheme
49%	15%	36%
Reference element density in		
Theme	Other	N-rheme
80%	15%	48%
Long-chain distribution		
% in Themes		% of Themes
52%		59%

Figure 8. Table for "Gabriel" episode

4.8 So what is going on? If we go back to the text to look at the disproportion of presuming reference elements in the rhemes, we find that elements from both the Gabriel and the Lily reference chains frequently play the roles of Rheme Mediums or Circumstances. In very nearly all cases, these mediums or circumstances are in the same clause with thematized agents or mediums which are also Gabriel or Lily. There are four distinct patterns: a) Gabriel in theme interacting with Gabriel in rheme—15 instances, b) Gabriel in theme interacting with Lily in rheme—7 instances, c) Lily in theme interacting with Lily in rheme—3 instances, d) Lily in theme interacting with Gabriel in rheme—4 instances. But of these four patterns, fully half the instances are the first pattern, Gabriel in the theme interacting with himself in the rheme.

4.9 Earlier in this discussion we noted a significant transitivity cryptotype: Gabriel acting as agent only to the mediums of inert possessions or articles of clothing. My quantitative analysis of the way the reference language is skewed serves to complement and reinforce that earlier conclusion. Gabriel is so consistently present in the rhemes of clauses because he is so constantly dealing with, thinking about, fussing with, or even just being himself.

5.0 In conclusion I should say that there are two other branches to quantitative analysis deserving of mention. One is the quantitative analysis of lexical distribution. The Method of Develop in English texts typically shows a language rich in grammatical items, whereas the point of such texts, that is, the collection of rhemes, is rich in lexis. The degrees of lexicalization in these two parts can be measured as various kinds of lexical density. Texts can have varying degrees of lexical density in their method and point for significant stylistic reasons. Another area for quantitative investigation is texts which absolutely reverse the norms of distribution for presuming reference and for lexis. This sort of text plays in a very overt way with our expectation that topicalization in English is maintained at the beginnings of clauses. I hope, then, that as stylisticians, you may find these procedures useful.

References

Adejare, O. 1992. *Language and Style in Soyinka: A Systemic Textlinguistic Study of a Literary Idiolect.* Ibadan: Heinemann Educational.

Auden, W. H. 1976. *Collected Poems.* Edited by Edward Mendelson. New York: Random House.

Birch, D. 1989. *Language, Literature and Critical Practice: Ways of Analysing Text.* London: Routledge.

Birch, D. & O'Toole, M. (eds.). 1988. *Functions of Style.* London: Pinter.

Cummings, M. 2004. Towards a statistical interpretation of Systemic-functional Theme/Rheme. In *LACUS Forum XXX: Language, Thought, and Reality*, ed. by G. Fulton, W. J. Sullivan & A. R. Lommel, 343-354. Houston, Texas: Linguistic Association of Canada and the United States.

Cummings, M. 2005. The role of Theme and Rheme in contrasting methods of organization in texts. In *The Dynamics of Language Use: Functional and Contrastive*, ed. by C. S. Bulter, María De Los Ángeles Gómez-González & Susana M. Doval-Suárez, 129-154. Amsterdam: Benjamins.

Cummings, M. 2006. Measuring lexical distributions across Theme and Rheme. In *LACUS Forum XXXII*, ed. by S. J. Hwang, W. J. Sullivan & A. R. Lommel. Houston, Texas: Linguistic Association of Canada and the United States.

F. B. Olson. 1984. Nominal groups in the poetry of Yeats and Auden: notes on the function of deixis in literature, *Style* 18 (1): 98-105.

Flanagan, F. J. 1984. Three U. S. G. S. mafic rock reference samples, W-2, DNC-1 and BIR-1. U. S. *Geological Survey Bulletin*, 1623: 1-54.

Fries, P. H. 1983 [1981]. On the status of Theme in English: Arguments from discourse, *Forum Linguisticum* 6 (1): 1-38. Reprinted in *Micro and Macro Connexity of Texts* (Papers in textlinguistics, 45), ed. by J. Petöfi & E. Sözer, 116-152. Hamburg: Helmut Buske Verlag.

Fries, P. H. 1995. Themes, methods of development and texts. In *On Subject and Theme: A Discourse Functional Perspective*, ed. by R. Hasan & P. H.

Fries, 317-359. Amsterdam: Benjamins.

Fries, P. H. 2002. The flow of information in a written text. In *Relations and Functions within and around Language*, ed. by P. H. Fries, M. Cummings, D. Lockwood & W. Spruiell, 117-155. London: Continuum.

Halliday, M. A. K. 1967. Notes on transitivity and Theme in English, part Ⅱ, *Journal of Linguistics* 3: 177-274.

Halliday, M. A. K. 1970. Language structure and language function. In John Lyons (ed.) *New Horizons in Linguistics*. Harmonsworth: Penguin Books.

Halliday, M. A. K. & C. Matthiessen. 2004. *An Introduction to Functional Grammar*. 3rd ed. London: Arnold.

Hasan, R. 1985. *Linguistics, Language, and Verbal Art*. Australia: Deakin University.

Huang, G. W. 2002. Hallidayan linguistics in China, *World Englishes* 21 (2): 281-290.

Hyde, W. J. 2003. The fall of Icarus: A note on Ovid, Bruegel, and Auden's *Expensive Delicate Ship*, *English Language Notes* 41 (2): 66-71.

Joyce, J. 1958. *Dubliners*. Compass Books edition. New York: Viking.

Kennedy, C. 1982. Systemic grammar and its use in literary analysis. In *Language and Literature: An Introductory Reader in Stylistics*, ed. by R. Carter, 83-99. London: Allen & Unwin.

Martin, J. R. 1992. *English Text: System and Structure*. Amsterdam: Benjamins.

Matthiessen, C. 1995. Theme as an enabling resource in ideational "knowledge" construction. In *Thematic Development in English Texts*, ed. by M. Ghadessy, 20-54. London: Pinter.

Nørgaard, N. 2003. *Systemic Functional Linguistics and Literary Analysis: A Hallidayan Approach to Joyce, a Joycean Approach to Halliday*. Odense: UP of Southern Denmark.

O'Toole, M. 1994. *The Language of Displayed Art*. Rutherford: Fairleigh Dickinson University Press.

Toolan, M. 1998. *Language in Literature: An Introduction to Stylistics*. London: Arnold.

Zhang, D. L., McDonald, E., Fang, Y. & Huang, G. 2005. The development of systemic functional linguistics in China. In *Continuing Discourse on Language*, ed. by R. Hasan, C. Matthiessen & J. Webster, 15-36. London: Equinox.

A Voice of Her Own: A Feminist Stylistic Analysis of *Jane Eyre*, *To the Lighthouse* and *Bridget Jones's Diary*

Ruth Page
University of Central England, UK

Feminist Stylistics: Definition and History

Sara Mills defines Feminist Stylistics in broad terms, stating that it "is concerned with the analysis of the way that questions of gender impact on the production and interpretation of texts" (2006: 221). However, as she points out in her earlier work, neither part of the term, either "feminist" or "stylistics," are necessarily used or understood in unified ways. Both terms are contested, have complex histories and incorporate a number of perspectives through their interdisciplinarity. In order to understand the eclectic and diverse territory that feminist stylistics might embrace, I begin by tracing the origins and development of work that might come under this umbrella term.

Feminist stylistics emerged as key trends in stylistics and feminism converged in the 1980s. First, stylistics moved away from the text-immanent approach of the 1960s. Under the influence of sociolinguistics and Hallidayan Systemic Functional Linguistics, stylisticians recognised that context could not be ignored as a determining factor influencing language use. Moreover, context was not regarded as some kind of neutral entity, but drawing on the work of French structuralists, was conceptualised instead in increasingly politicised terms. Second, the focus on "ideology" as a key term of reference stretched across disciplinary boundaries, impacting the evolution of feminist theory and practice during this period. Kavka (2001) argues that this marked a significant turning point away from the material and social concerns of feminism in the 1970s into "the discursive concerns of literary and cultural theory prominent in the 1980s and into the 1990s" (p. xii). With stylistics moving into a more ideologically sensitive, contextualised approach and feminism moving towards the analysis of discourse, the groundwork was laid for the project of feminist stylistics which brought these two elements together.

How political commitment and textual analysis might be combined remains a contentious question for feminist stylistics, raising questions about what the term "feminist" itself actually means in this context. Burton's (1996) landmark paper on Sylvia Plath laid out two central tenets for feminist stylistics. The first point she makes is that all analysis is inevitably selective, and therefore cannot escape subjectivity which in turn unavoidably carries ideological influence. Taking this further, she argues that stylistic analysis itself can be a form of political practice. As such, its impact must be felt outside a discussion of the text alone and result in some kind of change in the "real world". This dual premise has coloured much of the feminist stylistics that has followed, and which I will exemplify in part here. But before doing so, I want to preface this with some caveats that should be borne in mind throughout the following discussion.

First, the selectivity inherent in stylistic analyses generally that Burton points to is a critical issue, and feminist stylistics is by no means exempt from the problematic questions this raises. For example, Mills (1995) states that her work "aims to show that gender is foregrounded in texts *at certain key moments*" (p. 17, my emphasis). Cameron concedes that "Certainly there are areas in the study of language where feminism is unlikely to make much difference" (1992: 3). That being the case, we need to question the basis upon which feminist stylisticians select their texts and moments within those texts as worthy of investigation. To what extent does the feminist agenda impose an interpretation on the text that might obscure other possibilities, or indeed lead feminists to miss interpretations that might be equally salient? The feminist stylistician, then, must be careful to verify their selection (and rejection) of material, particularly as Cameron (1998a) points out, "where the observation and analysis has to do with gender it is extra-ordinarily difficult to subdue certain expectations" (p. 75).

Second, not all stylistic analyses which are gender-conscious need necessarily entail a feminist dimension. The point I am making here is perhaps an obvious one. Simply identifying stylistic features which imply a particular gender identity is not enough to warrant a feminist interpretation, and could be used as the basis for many other kinds of discussion, including those that might be underpinned by patriarchal values.

Finally, we might reflect on what kinds of feminist theory have influenced feminist stylistics. Writing about feminist narratology, Kathy Mezei poses the "question of whether the modifier 'feminist' refers to feminist literary theory [...] or feminism(s)—a movement, an ideology, a political position" (1996a: 6). Although she argues against this dichotomy, the initial separation of these perspectives is a telling one that echoes the opposition of theory and practice. Where the feminist perspectives used in stylistic analysis emphasise theory at the expense of political practice, the feminism of "feminist stylistics" needs to be understood in very specific, if not limited terms. With these issues in mind, I will turn now to three sample case studies in feminist stylistics which problematize these issues in different ways.

Women's Speech

I will focus my analysis on the issue of women's speech. The issue of language, the right to speak and the ways in which women are spoken to (or not) is central to the feminist enterprise of calling attention to women's abilities, agency and socio-political positions. Cameron summarises the feminist perspective thus: "'Speech' and 'silence' have been powerful *metaphors* in feminist discourse, used to figure all the ways in which women are denied the right or the opportunity to express themselves freely" (1998b: 3). The theme of communication is thus politicised as a negotiation between oppression and liberation. One outcome of this is that the analysis of speech, understood within the broader and itself multi-layered field of discourse analysis, has become an extremely prominent area of research in language and gender studies. Over the last three decades feminist analyses of speech have embraced an array of theoretical perspectives and methodological practices spanning anthropology, ethnomethodology, conversation analysis, text analysis, discourse analysis. I cannot attempt a summary of this here, but refer the interested reader to Bucholz (2003) for an initial and helpful survey.

Discourse analysis has also had a significant and multifaceted impact on stylistics (Carter & Simpson, 1989), ranging from the application of models from discourse analysis, to the textual representation of speech and thought to a Foucauldian treatment of the term "discourse". The analysis that follows here weaves together different aspects of this research in language and gender and discourse stylistics in order to illustrate three trends that have developed in feminist stylistics. First, I examine how stereotypes about gendered discourse can be used to interpret characterisation, relating this to the broader socio-historical context in a text-immanent analysis of passages from *Jane Eyre*. I then turn to consider debates about women writers' search for an authentic and distinctive voice through an analysis of the speech and thought presentation in *To the Lighthouse*. Finally, I move on to look at more recent developments in feminist stylistics that take account of the changes in sexism and current research in language and gender. I do this through an analysis of the gendered discourses of the self-help genre as they relate to speech in *Bridget Jones's Diary*. In each case, the strengths and limitations of combining feminist and stylistic perspectives will be critiqued.

Rights and Resistance: Dialogue in *Jane Eyre*

Jane Eyre became a central text for second-wave feminist literary criticism of the 1970s and 1980s. Drawing also on psychoanalysis and Marxism, a wealth of criticism followed which explored the feminist potential of the narrative. On the one hand, the development of Jane's "surprising independence" (Hess, 1996: 16) suggests that there is much in the text to challenge Victorian ideals of womanhood as subservient and self-sacrificing. However, other critics have pointed out that Brontë's interrogation of the dominant ideologies of love and marriage are rather more equivocal. Showalter argues that

> *Jane Eyre* does not attempt to rupture the dominant kinship structures. The ending of the novel ("Reader, I married him") affirms those very structures. The feminism of the text resides in its "not-said", its attempt to inscribe women as sexual subjects within this system (1989: 107).

Indeed, feminist readings of *Jane Eyre* draw attention to the ambivalent way in which it engages with the contradictions inherent in the gender ideology of the time. This ambivalence is manifest in a number of ways, especially focused on the figure of the governess who was central in debates about the model of separate spheres. The reading that I offer in this paper shows how these shifting and ambivalent interpretations of Jane as a feminist figure can be revealed through a discourse analysis of the dialogue in key scenes in the novel, and that these are best understood with reference to its contemporary social context.

My work follows that of Bennison (1993) and Toolan (1989) who use discourse analysis to examine characterisation in fictional texts. I shall focus on turn length and move analysis as a means of tracing the relative power the characters have to express themselves or to control the conversation in three contrasting scenes. Literary criticism has already indicated that speech is an important indicator of character quality in this novel. Freeman (1984) says, "the best way to know anyone in *Jane Eyre* is to pay attention to how he or she speaks" (p. 691). Not only this, but speech is intimately linked to agency, particularly for its heroine, where the "power of speech" is seen as indicator of Jane's "control of her life" (Freeman, 1984: 686). I am particularly interested in how Jane's relationship with Rochester is represented. Thus I have selected three scenes which show key changes in the dynamics of their relationship. The first scene is the initial meeting between the two characters. The second occurs after Rochester's first marriage is revealed and he attempts to persuade Jane to become his mistress (henceforth referred to as the "Refusal scene"). The final scene is Jane's reunion with Rochester following his maiming in the fire at Thornfield, culminating in her acceptance of his second proposal of marriage. I have chosen these scenes because there are clear parallels in content and style in the second two. They both acutely foreground the novel's treatment of marriage and romantic love and the heroine's independence from and compliance with the ideology related to them.

Analysis 1: Turn Length

Bennison notes that turn length, although not statistically robust, may give an initial indication of changes in a character's conversational behaviour over the course of a text (1993: 82). I counted the number of words in each of the turns allocated to Jane and Rochester as direct speech in the refusal and reunion scenes. The results of this calculation are summarised in the table below:

Table 1: Total number of words for Jane and Rochester (as a percentage)

	Jane	Rochester
Refusal scene	7%	93%
Reunion scene	42%	58%

These statistics suggest a fairly stark picture. In the earlier scene, Rochester occupies nearly all the conversational floor. Despite the fact that Jane takes nearly an equal number of terms, the length of those turns means that she appears to have very little ability to speak at all. In contrast, in the later scene, the figures have shifted considerably so that although Rochester is still speaking for longer turns and maintaining the majority of the verbal space, Jane's speech is much more prominent here (now 42% of the words belong to her, rather than the earlier 7%). If the increasing quantity of speech is an indication of Jane's ability to speak out and to express herself, then this would seem to uphold an interpretation of Jane's emerging agency and independence.

Analysis 2: Move Analysis

Of course, the turn length is only a first step in the analytic process and by no means the whole story. We need to examine not only how much is said, but who is speaking to whom and what it is that is being uttered. With that in mind, I turn to look at the structure of the conversation in more detail. I do this by using Burton's (1980) model of move analysis. Burton identifies seven types of move, of which five are conversational. These are:

> Opening moves—essentially topic-carrying items which are recognisably "new' in terms of the immediately preceding talk;
> Supporting moves—may occur after any type of move and involve items that concur with the initiatory moves they are supporting;
> Challenging moves—function to hold up the progress of a topic or the introduction of a topic in some way;
> Bound-opening moves—occur after a preceding opening move has been supported; they enlarge and extend the topic of the original opening move;
> Re-opening moves—occur after a preceding opening move has been challenged; they reinstate the topic that has been diverted or delayed.
> (taken from Toolan, 1989: 199)

In the following analysis I have simplified the framework further, paying particular attention to the first three categories of these moves. I am particularly interested in the ways in which the different moves can indicate the developing power relations between Jane and Rochester in their conversations. Here I take opening moves as indicative of a character's ability to initiate and maintain conversational control. Challenging moves suggest that either another character is trying to wrest control of the conversation or is refusing to comply with the wishes of the other participant. In contrast, supporting moves might indicate a character's compliance, both with the conversational goals and more general wishes of the character who has initiated the opening moves.

Scene 1: Initial Encounter

In this scene, Jane and Rochester meet for the first time. Rochester has fallen from his horse and Jane comes to his aid. Their identities are initially unknown to each other, and although Rochester discovers Jane's identity, he fails to disclose his own. The distribution of moves and their attendant acts are summarised in Table 2.

Table 2: Move allocation in the initial encounter
between Jane and Rochester

		Jane	Rochester
Opening	Question	6%	26%
	Request	0%	18%
	Inform	6%	3%
Challenge	Silence	0%	0%
	Direct		
	Refusal	0%	0%
	Indirect		
	Refusal	0%	6%
	Interruption	0%	0%
Supporting		35%	0%

The initial meeting between Jane and Rochester acts as a base line from which we can measure the changes in their conversational behaviour. In this first encounter, it is Rochester who makes the most opening moves, asking questions (elicitations) or giving commands (directives). For example,

"You live just below—do you mean at that house with the battlements?" pointing to Thornfield Hall, on which the moon cast a hoary gleam, bringing it out distinct and pale from the woods that, by contrast with the western sky, now seemed one mass of shadow.
"Yes, sir."

"Whose house is it?"

"Mr. Rochester's. "

"Do you know Mr. Rochester?"

"No, I have never seen him. "

"He is not resident, then?"

"No. "

"Can you tell me where he is?"

"I cannot. "

(*Jane Eyre*, pp. 130-131)

This fragment of dialogue also indicates that it is Jane who supports Rochester's initiations, providing answers to his questions. Indeed, Jane's compliance continues, even against her natural inclination. The pattern of the discourse thus emphasises the relative social status of the two character, where Rochester's privilege (both in social standing and knowledge of the situation) are in line with his control of the conversation and interrogation of Jane.

Scene 2 : Refusal

This scene occurs in Chapter 27. In the intervening episodes, Rochester has wooed Jane and proposed marriage to her. At the altar, Rochester's existing marriage has been revealed. He now attempts to persuade Jane to begin life with him as his mistress, but she refuses and leaves Thornfield. The conversational and narrative goals of Jane and Rochester are clearly in direct conflict with one another here. In line with this, the move allocation presents a rather different picture from the compliant Jane of the earlier scene. Instead of submitting to her master's demands, Jane here asserts her independence. A summary of the moves is given in Table 3.

The figures in Table 3 indicate that Rochester is still dominating the conversation in terms of the number of moves, and as in the earlier scene is responsible for making the majority of opening moves, only offering minimal support. Examples of his opening moves include informing acts (in which he relates his past experiences which led to his earlier marriage), elicitations (questions) and directives (commands).

Table 3: Move analysis of Jane's refusal

		Jane	Rochester
Opening	Question	3%	24%
	Request	3%	10%
	Inform	3%	15%
Challenge	Silence	8%	0%
	Direct		
	Refusal	8%	0%
	Indirect		
	Refusal	0%	0%
	Interruption	3%	0%
Supporting		18%	3%
Total		48%	52%

These elicitations and directives form a series of acts which in terms of Brown & Levinson's (1987) theory of politeness strategies threaten Jane's negative face. In other words, they seek to impose Rochester's will upon Jane's, indicating Rochester's belief in his position as a patriarchal figure to influence not only the conversational goals but Jane's behaviour also.

Rochester does not soften his face threatening demands with politeness strategies, but instead intensifies them with threats to which Jane responds. Jane's support is perhaps best interpreted here as at least sometimes resulting from extreme coercion, rather than positive compliance.

"Jane! will you hear reason?" (he stooped and approached his lips to my ear); "because, if you won't, I'll try violence." [...] But I was not afraid: not in the least. I felt an inward power; a sense of influence, which supported me. The crisis was perilous; but not without its charm: such as the Indian, perhaps, feels when he slips over the rapid in his canoe. I took hold of his clenched hand, loosened the contorted fingers, and said to him, soothingly— "Sit down; I'll talk to you as long as you like, and hear all you have to say, whether reasonable or unreasonable."
(*Jane Eyre*, p. 341)

Moreover, the extent to which Jane complies with Rochester's conversational goals is considerably less than in the earlier scene. As the figures in Table 3 attest, her opening moves account for only 18% of the conversation now, almost half the proportion from that in the initial encounter (35%). Instead, Jane's moves which are most frequent in this episode are challenging, holding up the progress of the conversation. In these challenging moves, Jane refuses to give in to Rochester's requests. Half of these challenges are expressed as direct expressions of contradiction or negation.

"Jane, you understand what I want of you? Just this promise—'I will be yours, Mr. Rochester.'"
"Mr. Rochester, I will NOT be yours."
"Then you will not yield?"
"No."
(*Jane Eyre*, pp. 354-355)

Such direct challenges to Rochester suggest independence and self-determination on Jane's part. These qualities are those we might associate with a feminist stance of rebelling against a patriarchal figure of authority.

The remaining half of Jane's challenging moves use a different strategy of resistance: that of silence, as in the following examples.

(a) "Solitude! solitude!" he reiterated with irritation. "I see I must come to an explanation. I don't know what sphynx-like expression is forming in your countenance. You are to share my solitude. Do you understand?"
I shook my head: it required a degree of courage, excited as he was becoming, even to risk that mute sign of dissent.
(*Jane Eyre*, p. 340)
(b) Then I should have asked you to accept my pledge of fidelity and to give me yours. Jane—give it me now."
A pause.
"Why are you silent, Jane?"
(*Jane Eyre*, p. 354)

How then are we to interpret these silences? If Jane's ability to speak is interpreted as a metaphor for her increased agency, one possibility is to read her silence as the opposite, symbolising her oppression. Indeed, she is being subjected to extreme emotional pressure in this episode. But to understand her silence as passivity is too simplistic and fails to recognise the significant resistance it represents for Jane.

In terms of politeness strategies, Jane is using what Brown and Levinson term an off record strategy for performing a face threatening act herself (refusing to give Rochester what he wants). While this is less overt than using an on record strategy, which if softened, might signal to Rochester her potential compliance, silence remains a non-cooperative strategy. In terms of Grice's cooperative principles of conversation, Jane is flouting the maxim of quality: she is simply not saying enough. What I want to argue here, then, is that silence is not then a symbol of Jane's passivity, but a highly appropriate form of resistance.

In this scene, Jane's silence is at least, if not more important than the words which she does utter. It represents the feminist subtext that Showalter referred to as the "not said": the expression of women's sexual and emotional desire. To articulate support for Rochester's intentions would make Jane complicit with the role of fallen woman. Indeed, at one point when Jane fails to remain silent and gives in to Rochester's entreaties, she expresses her moral reservation at her response,

> These words cut me: yet what could I do or I say? I ought probably to have done or said nothing; but I was so tortured by a sense of remorse at thus hurting his feelings, I could not control the wish to drop balm where I had wounded.
>
> "I DO love you," I said, "more than ever: but I must not show or indulge the feeling: and this is the last time I must express it. "
>
> (*Jane Eyre*, p. 341)

If to speak is morally suspect, silence here is not only resistance, but also moral virtue. Jane's silence also distinguishes her from the other female figure with which she is linked in the narrative: that of the lunatic. Rochester repeatedly comments on Jane's emotional self-restraint, which he compares with Bertha Mason's emotional outbursts. To express emotional response would not only be morally corrupt, but in this case is also associated with lunacy, needing to be constrained and controlled by medicine.

Jane's silence is thus a critical form of resistance, setting her apart from the two women with whom Rochester has been previously associated (the lunatic, Bertha Mason, and the fallen woman, Cecile Valens). In separating her from the fallen woman, it allows Jane to remain virtuous and so able ultimately to enter into marriage, which as a fallen woman she would forever have forfeited. In separating her from the lunatic, the narrative also rescues the figure of the governess from its subversive erosion of the separate spheres model. As Poovey puts it,

> Jane's departure from Rochester's house dismisses the sexual and class instabilities the governess introduces, in a way that makes Jane the guardian of sexual and class order rather than its weakest point. (1989: 136)

Ironically, then, in this scene where Jane appears to be the most independent and able to assert her will against the demands of Rochester, the strategies that she chooses to do so ultimately reinforce dominant gender ideologies of that period.

Scene 3: Reunion

The final scene from *Jane Eyre* that I examine is the point at which Jane returns to Rochester and finally accepts his now legitimate offer of marriage. Once again, the allocation of the different types of moves indicates a shift in the power dynamics of the relationship between Rochester and Jane. Critics have emphasized the increased mutuality between the characters. Jane is now financially independent through the inheritance of a long lost uncle. In contrast, Rochester is physically and emotionally dependent (blinded and maimed) following the fire at Thornfield, symbolically marking his passage through the castration complex (Showalter, 1989: 107).

The discourse analysis mirrors this change in various ways. Table 4 shows that the proportion of moves in total made by Jane and Rochester is now much more equal than in the earlier scene. However, there are significant reversals in who is assigned which type of move.

Table 4. Move analysis from the reunion between Jane and Rochester

		Jane	Rochester
Opening	Question	6%	28%
	Request	1%	9%
	Inform	5%	11%
Challenge	Silence	0%	2%
	Direct		
	Refusal	2%	0%
	Indirect		
	Refusal	4%	0%
	Interruption	0%	0%
Supporting		27%	4%
Total		46%	54%

For the first time, Rochester is assigned challenging moves. It is he who is silenced in the conversation, not Jane. While these silences do not signal oppression or passivity as such, they are always associated with his dependent state.

> "You should care, Janet: if I were what I once was, I would try to make you care—but—a sightless block!"
> He relapsed again into gloom. I, on the contrary, became more cheerful, and took fresh courage: these last words gave me an insight as to where the difficulty lay; and as it was no difficulty with me, I felt quite relieved from my previous embarrassment. I resumed a livelier vein of conversation.
> (*Jane Eyre*, p. 484)

In contrast, as the quotation above indicates, Jane is now able to initiate conversation. Moreover, when she does refuse to answer Rochester's questions, it is to tell her story on her own terms and not at his bidding, using strategies of deferral and indirectness with the express intention of teasing rather than the contradiction of the earlier scene. The indications of mutuality are neatly crystallized when Rochester hands Jane the ability to choose the future of their relationship, which she in turn hands back to him:

> "Ah! Jane. But I want a wife. "
> "Do you, sir?"
> "Yes: is it news to you?"
> "Of course: you said nothing about it before. "
> "Is it unwelcome news?"
> "That depends on circumstances, sir—on your choice. "
> "Which you shall make for me, Jane. I will abide by your decision. "
> "Choose then, sir—HER WHO LOVES YOU BEST. "
> "I will at least choose—HER I LOVE BEST. Jane, will you marry me?"
> "Yes, sir. "
> (*Jane Eyre*, pp. 493-494)

Thus the relationship between Jane and Rochester seems to have reached some middle ground, no longer that of the power relationship between master and employee in the initial encounter, where Jane made no challenging moves at all, but neither the necessary independence expressed by Jane in the refusal scene.

On the other hand, it is important to situate these reversals within the bigger picture here too. Rochester still retains the majority of the opening moves, and it is Jane who provides the majority of support. Even though he invites her tell the story of her past experience, this is narrated indirectly, not given the verbal space of Rochester's history in the refusal scene. Although Rochester's dependence allows Jane to be in a position of literal and conversational control to some extent, Jane's supporting moves clearly indicate her alliance with the dominant ideology of romantic love and marriage, emphasised most acutely in the supporting moves of her triple acceptance of Rochester's offer:

"... Jane, will you marry me?"

"Yes, sir."

"A poor blind man, whom you will have to lead about by the hand?"

"Yes, sir."

"A crippled man, twenty years older than you, whom you will have to wait on?"

"Yes, sir."

"Truly, Jane?"

"Most truly, sir."

(*Jane Eyre*, p. 494)

Critics debate whether to read Jane and Rochester's marriage as subversive or conservative. On the one hand, Showalter points out for Jane to become a member of the "master class" she must accept "a sexual master whereby her submission brings her access to the dominant culture" (1989: 105). Marriage as an institution was the only means of class improvement. As such, it remains unchallenged in *Jane Eyre*. On the other hand, Poovey argues that the very fact that Rochester marries Jane at all is subversive, for "transforming the governess into a wife extends the series of aberrant women to include the figure who ought to be exempt from this series, who ought to be the norm" (1989: 146). The ambivalent status of Jane and Rochester's union as both supporting and subverting the dominant ideology is reflected in the discourse analysis of this final scene, both reinforcing Rochester's control and Jane's support of this, but tempering it with gestures of mutuality.

The Search for a "Woman's Voice": Woolf and FID

The question of speech and silence is not just a matter of interest to be discussed in relation to matters of representation within a fictional text. Rather, the project of examining actual women's voices and the contexts in which they may have been oppressed or excluded has been of great significance in feminist studies. One such context of relevance here is that of literary culture. Women writer's ability to express themselves at all (for example, to be recognised as published authors, and latterly included in the academic canon) has lead to significant questions about the style of women's writing. Cameron puts it thus,

In these cultural conditions, how can women write "authentically"? Is it enough for women to be able to write as men do? If we are "allowed in" to literature and culture only on condition that we accept the traditional (masculine norms) regarding what is worth writing about and how, are we not simply exchanging one kind of silencing for another? (1998b: 7)

In attempting to establish an authentic "voice", some women have gone to great lengths to employ stylistic devices that mark their writing as different from that of men's, which is perceived to represent a dominant, patriarchal norm. In this way, it is not just the speech within a fictional text that is important, but the ways in which that speech is textually represented that becomes a feminist issue, taking the form of what Furman (1980) calls textual feminism.

Textual feminism is underpinned by the essential assumption that the dominant generic and stylistic norms are inflected with patriarchal values, as these norms are derived from a corpus of primarily male-authored texts. In order to find an authentic voice, the woman writer must then resist, challenge or transform these norms in some way. One author who has been a central focus for this is Virginia Woolf, particularly in relationship to what she terms the "male sentence" which is "too loose, too heavy, too pompous for a woman's use" (p.145). Instead, the sentence the woman makes is "one that takes the natural shape of her thought, without crushing or distorting it" (p.145). While Woolf's gendered interpretation of discourse structure has been enormously influential in shaping the textual feminism that followed, Livia (2003: 143) points out that these descriptions are deeply problematic, "annoyingly vague and impossible to quantify". How can we quantify the stylistic differences that Woolf is alluding to here? One possibility is to examine her use of interior monologue using the stylistic framework of speech and thought presentation, particularly focusing on Free Indirect Discourse (henceforth FID).

In this analysis of FID, I am interested not so much in the actual words that the characters use as indicators of their conversational control within a fictional world. Instead, questions of control are transposed onto the formal features of FID. Mezei describes the power dynamics of FID in the following way:

> The site for this textual battle between author, narrator, and character-focalizer and between the fixed and fluctuating gender roles is the narrative device, "Free indirect discourse" [..] The undecideability inherent in the structure of FID makes it an appropriate space for the complicated interchange between author, narrator, character-focalizer, and reader. (1996b: 67)

Mezei (1996b) goes on to give a rich picture of the various feminist effects that FID might achieve. These include allowing a female character's words greater freedom from masculine narratorial control, thereby creating space for the suppressed "not said" of the female perspective to emerge. Within *To the Lighthouse*, a novel concerned with woman's artistic expression, the three sections of the novel, contrast in their use of FID. The central section, Time Passes, uses pure narration, used to articulate an account of the actual narrative events. In contrast to this, in the two sections which flank Time Passes, there is no central focalizer, but rather a multiple array of perspectives are used to create a double voiced text, especially through the use of FID. This is put to feminist ends. For example, Mr Ramsay, the patriarchal figure is focalized through his wife, child, and the painter Lily Briscoe, as in the examples below.

> But his son hated him. He hated him coming up to them, for stopping and looking down on them; he hated him for interrupting them; he hated him for the exaltation and sublimity of his gestures; for the magnificence of his head; for his exactingness and egotism (for there he stood, commanding them to attend to him); but most of all he hated the twang and twitter of his father's emotion which, vibrating round them, disturbed the perfect good sense of his

relations with his mother (*To The Lighthouse*, p. 42).

Politely, but very distantly, Mr Ramsay raised his hand and saluted her as they passed. But what a face, she thought, immediately finding the sympathy which she had not been asked to give troubling her expression (*To The Lighthouse*, p. 169).

The effect of these choices is to give voice to the marginalised characters in the story (the women, children), allowing their words to be heard alongside the narrator's. In so doing, they turn Mr Ramsay into a "pitiable caricature of male authority" (Mezei, 1996b: 81), ultimately telling the "other story" of the effects of an egocentric and powerful father and husband on his family.

Moreover, the question of authority and gender identity is opened up at the micro-level too. The multiple focalizers sometimes shift almost imperceptibly through the stretches of FID. The effect of this is a sleight of hand where it is not always clear whether it a male or female character whose perspective is being given, or whether this is blurred with the apparently gender-neutral voice of the narrator. I will illustrate this with the following passage. Indications that the narration has shifted into FID are underlined.

[1] And Andrew shouted that the sea was coming in, so she leapt splashing through the shallow waves on to the shore and ran up the beach and was carried by her own impetuosity and her desire for rapid movement right behind a rock and there <u>oh heavens!</u> In each other's arms <u>were Paul and Minta! Kissing probably.</u> [2] She was outraged, indignant. [3] She and Andrew put on their shoes and stockings in dead silence without saying a thing about it. [4] Indeed they were rather sharp with each other. [5] She might have called him when she saw the crayfish or whatever it was, <u>Andrew grumbled.</u> [6] However, <u>they both felt</u>, it's not our fault. [7] They had not wanted <u>this</u> horrid nuisance to happen. [8] All the same it irritated Andrew that Nancy should be a woman, and Nancy that Andrew should be a man and they tied their shoes very neatly and drew the bows rather tight.

(*To The Lighthouse*, p. 88)

In this passage, the gender-neutral narration shades into FID inflected with the perspectives of either the female character (Nancy) or the male character

(Andrew). Thus line 1 opens with Pure Narration, but the exclamations colour the FID with Nancy's perspective, summarised in the Pure Narration of the following sentence [2]. The discourse of Nancy and Andrew is related as a narratorial report in sentences 2 and 3, thus the reader begins sentence 4 with the perception that the opening words, "she might have called him," are being attributed to the narrator. It is only when the reader reaches the final reporting clause that they have to retrospectively reassign the source of these words to male voice of Andrew. This is not sustained, however, and in the next sentence, the perspective shifts once again, this time shared between both the male and female characters, sustained into the FID of the following sentence, as indicated by the deictic marker "this". By the end of the paragraph, the character's attitudes are being reported, but subordinated to the gender-neutral narration once again. My point here is that Woolf's manipulation of the FID is not clear cut, but relies on indeterminacy and ambiguity. Textually, this creates a micro-level effect of non-linearity where the sentence final position of the reporting clauses cause the reader to retrospectively revise their interpretation of the source of the spoken words, sometimes resulting a temporary gender indeterminacy.

As interesting as this might be, I want to stress that it is the effects of FID within this particular text that can be interpreted as feminist. It is not that FID in itself is a feminist form. Indeed, FID can be used to achieve a range of stylistic effects, most of which need not be related to gender-specific concerns in any explicit or fixed way. As Livia (2003) points out, the multiplicity of FID is not used exclusively by women either, and goes on to find similar effects in the writings of Proust. Thus I caution strongly against creating a fixed correlation between feminist value and a linguistic form (Richardson, 2002).

The concept of a distinctively different voice for women's writing has been critiqued more generally. Mills (1995) shows that the metaphorical concept of the "female sentence" cannot hold in the face of empirical evidence. The range of "feminist" features associated with women's writing are also used by male writers, throwing into question the very basis upon which women's writing is differentiated in the first place. Other critics have gone on to point that such an abstracted model of women's written speech is ahistorical, universalising and untenable. It is most useful, not as an empirical means of tracing stylistic contrasts, but rather as stimulating further research questions such as why people might believe that there is a feminine style of writing in the first place, how these stereotypical beliefs might be used as political weapons both for and against the interests of feminists.

Postfeminist Discourse Analysis? *Bridget Jones's Diary* as Feminine Discourse

Since the early 1980s when Burton first began the project of feminist stylistics, much has changed, both in the field of stylistics and within feminist studies. However, as Mills (1998) writes, the impact of liberal feminism and of postmodern feminist theory has yet to be fully felt in feminist text analysis (of which feminist stylistics is a part). As a result, she (1998: 241) argues that we need to move towards an analysis

> which recognizes that the context in which texts are produced and interpreted has been profoundly changed by the impact of feminism and any form of analysis developed must be aware of the context of words rather than analysing words out of context. It must analyse words at the level of discourse as well as at the local level of occurrence.

With that in mind, I turn to a text which clearly shows the impact of feminism, *Bridget Jones's Diary* (henceforth *BJD*). I provide an analysis of the narratorial voice which moves away from the level of the word. Instead I examine the ways in which it interplays with existing discourses (in the broader, Foucauldian sense of the word).

The heroine and narrator of *BJD* (Bridget herself) is a comic, ironic portrayal of a postfeminist woman. On the one hand, Bridget demonstrates many of the attributes available to women after second-wave feminism. She is independent, has a successful career and is sexually agentive. However, contemporary reviewers of the novel deemed her "an insult to feminism". The following discussion examines how and why the narratorial voice might contribute to this ambivalence.

Alison Case (2001) argues that the voice of *BJD* supports many of the conventions of feminine narration, for example acting as a "'witness' who presents experience in a more or less 'raw' and unmediated way" (p. 178). While I might take issue with the implications of Case's description, which seems to imply by default that a masculine narrator produces a more mediated, sophisticated and mature account of events, I do think that the narratorial voice of Bridget Jones plays with gendered conventions in striking ways. This is particularly felt through the evocation of the self-help discourse.

The self-help discourse is interwoven throughout *BJD* in many ways. First, the format of the diary itself initiates a framework where Bridget articulates a number of goals to be achieved in the coming year, goals which will improve herself physically, emotionally and relationally, laid out on the opening pages of the text under the two headings "I will not" and "I will". Each of the diary entries then monitors and evaluates Bridget's attempts to move towards these goals, as indicated in the following example.

Sunday 15 January

9 st (excellent) , alcohol units0 , cigarettes29 (v. v. bad, esp. in2 hours) , calories 3879 (repulsive), negative thoughts 942 (based on av. Per minute) , minutes spent counting negative thoughts 127 (approx.).

(*BJD*, p. 30)

Bridget constantly seeks advice from her close circle of friends about how to achieve these goals. The topics range from how to operate her video machine to matters of physical appearance, but more than anything else, Bridget seeks her friends' advice on how to improve her relationships with men. Moreover, Bridget's speech is littered with references to self-help texts, as in the extract below.

Saturday 25 February

11 p. m. Oh God. Why hasn't Daniel rung? Are we going out now, or what? How come my mum can slip easily from one relationship to another and I can't even get the simplest thing off the ground. Maybe their generation is just better at getting on with relationships? Maybe they don't mooch about being all paranoid and diffident. Maybe it helps if you' ve never read a self-help book in your life.

(*BJD*, p. 60)

The most fully developed reference to self-help literature comes in the form of advice on how a woman should speak at a social event:

Tuesday 11 April

Determined, instead of fearing the scary party, panicking all the way through and going home pissed and depressed, am going to improve social skills, confidence and Make Parties Work for Me—as guided by article have just read in magazine.

(*BJD*, p. 96)

The entry then goes on to describe the interactive skills the woman should have: how long to speak for, how to ask questions, how to introduce people, how to set goals. Although these are set out as work-oriented, "to improve your career", Bridget's next entry transforms these into personal goals to achieve a (hetero) sexual relationship, "To meet and sleep with sex god" (*BJD*, p. 97).

Not only do these references to self-help literature foreground gender, in that they constantly point to Bridget's main focus of self improvement as gaining a heterosexual partner, the discourse is also gendered at a more subtle level. Cameron (1995) points out that self-help literature is a discourse primarily associated with a female audience. Moreover, her account traces the ways in which women's responses to self-help texts produces not so much the empowerment to change themselves or their circumstances, but rather to engender a sense of self-identification between reader and author.

The reading pleasure lay in the familiarity, the banality even, of the scenarios presented in the book... YJDU's success does not lie in its potential to bring about change [..] but in the reassurance it offers to readers that their experience is widely shared: in short, that they are normal (1995: 208).

In this sense, the allusions to the self-help genre collude in both the sense of authenticity and reader empathy that *BJD* is perhaps most renowned for (Case, 2001: 177). What I want to suggest also is that these effects also contribute to the gendering of the narration in that they set up a sense of cooperation and solidarity between narrator and audience, characteristics stereotypically associated with all-female spoken interaction in western contexts.

It is also important to note that Bridget does not draw upon just any kind of advice literature. Instead, as we have already seen, most of the advice is focused on romantic relationships, reinforcing both heterosexuality as normative and a goal

43

which a woman must improve herself for. In its neglect of self-help career literature, Bridget's discourse is firmly located in the private, domestic domain. In fact, most of the speech situations which are recounted in the narrative reinforce this emphasis on the private sphere. The diary contains Bridget's gossip with her friends, small talk at dinner parties, private SMS messages, all embedded within the confessional mode of the diary genre. Each of these speech genres carries gendered associations which locate Bridget's interactions as "off stage", domestic, and trivialised. When she does speak in public situations, she repeatedly fails, utters sexual innuendoes (unintentionally) all of which lead to comic effect. It seems then, that we are not supposed to take this feminine discourse terribly seriously.

However, there are serious consequences for locating *BJD* within relational self-help discourse. Cameron (1995) goes on to debate the feminist potential of this kind of literature. She argues that the literature is an empowering fiction, which instead of leading to collective action replaces political change with personalised progress which reinforces essentialist models of gender difference. Ultimately, at least some self help literature might actually devalue women. In the case of relationship advice, the empowerment to women appears particularly limited:

> Relationship advice grants women authority over domestic life and (hetero) sexual relationships, but all women seem authorized to do within their allotted sphere is to ensure things run smoothly, without conflict and misunderstanding— which entails once again that they adjust to masculine norms. Heads you win, tails I lose. (Cameron, 1995: 197)

The use of relational self help discourse in BFD thus underscores the heterosexual relationship as the ultimate goal to which Bridget aspires, but while it apparently empowers her to reach that which she desires, it also constrains her by emphasising the different sphere in which she has influence. Both male figures in BJD (*Mark Darcy and Daniel Cleaver*) operate in the public domain and have greater socio-economic status than Bridget. Rather than meet them on their own terms, Bridget's feminine discourse maintains and emphasises her separation from and subordinate position to them.

44

Summary

In summary, I have shown three different ways in which feminist stylistics can operate to analyse speech in fictional texts. This may focus on matters of representation, showing how gender ideology shapes the way we interpret speech as a form of characterisation. Second, the analysis may invest the linguistic form itself with gendered meaning, as I showed through the analysis of FID. Finally, the analysis may move above the level of the word and attempt to account for the way in which wider discourses are used intertextually to create gender-specific effects.

To what extent, then, is this *feminist* stylistics? How are these analyses different from stylistics more generally? I have used linguistic analysis to reach a gender-conscious interpretation of each text and related this to the politics of gender ideology in each case. In so far as this has revealed the power dynamics in matters of representation and use of language, then yes, these analyses can be treated as feminist stylistics. However, if we return to Burton's conception of feminist stylistics as politically committed with the ultimate aim of achieving some kind of social change, then it would appear that there is some way yet to go here. Both in terms of data and audience, it may be that feminist stylistics will need to evolve yet further if it is to go beyond these first stages of exposing stereotypes to challenging and transforming them.

It is here that the multiplicity of both feminisms and stylistics point to possible ways forward. Widening the range of texts that are considered and drawing on methodology from other disciplines might be particularly useful. For example, an important next step is not just to focus on the text but the ways in which readership respond to those texts. While this is inevitably more difficult to analyse, and less closely related to the project of stylistics, recent developments such as fanfiction can help supplement our analysis of contemporary texts, while reader response might be augmented by concepts drawn from cognitive science or linguistic approaches like Communities of Practice. What it means to read texts like those I have illustrated here as a woman, or a man, from a feminist perspective or not, could then be opened up to fresh scrutiny. The plurality of feminist stylistics, far from diluting its potential is perhaps its greatest strength as we move further into

45

this new millennium. Kavka writes: "Given that feminism lacks a single origin as much as a single definition, it can also have no single moment of ending" (2001: xi). Likewise, as the trends in feminist stylistics may come, go, and co-exist, so they also point to future points of intersection, fresh questions debates and synergy.

References

Bennison, N. 1993. Discourse analysis, pragmatics and the dramatic "character": Tom Stoppard's *Professional Foul*, *Language and Literature* 2 (2): 79-99.

Brontë, C. 1996 [1847]. *Jane Eyre*. London: Penguin Books.

Brown, P. & Levinson, S. 1987. *Politeness*. Cambridge: CUP.

Bucholz, M. 2003. Theories of discourse as theories of gender. In *The Handbook of Language and Gender*, ed. by J. Holmes & M. Meyerhoff, 43-68. Blackwell: Oxford.

Burton, D. 1996. Through glass darkly: Through dark glasses. In *The Stylistics Reader: From Roman Jakobson to the Present*, ed. by J. J. Weber, 224-240. London: Edward Arnold.

Cameron, D. 1992. *Feminism and Linguistic Theory*, 2nd edition. London: Macmillan.

Cameron, D. 1995. *Verbal Hygiene*. London: Routledge.

Cameron, D. 1998a. Performing gender identity: young men's talk and the construction of heterosexual masculinity. In *Language and Gender: A Reader*, ed. by J. Coates, 270-284. Oxford: Blackwell.

Cameron, D. 1998b. *The Feminist Critique of Language*, 2nd edition. London: Routledge.

Carter, R. & Simpson, P. 1989. *Language, Discourse and Literature: An Introductory Reader in Discourse Stylistics*. London: Routledge.

Case, A. 2001. Authenticity, convention, and *Bridget Jones's Diary*, *Narrative* 9 (2): 176-181.

Fielding, H. 1996. *Bridget Jones's Diary*. London: Picador.

Freeman, J. 1984. Speech and silence in *Jane Eyre*, *Studies in English Literature* 24: 683-700.

Furman, N. 1980. Textual feminism. In *Women and Language in Literature and*

Society, ed. by S. McConnell-Ginet, R. Borker & N. Furman, 45-57. New York: Praeger.

Hess, N. 1996. Codeswitching and style shifting as markers of liminality in literature, *Language and Literature* 5 (1): 15-18.

Kavka, M. 2001. Introduction. In *Feminist Consequences: Theory for the New Century*, ed. by E. Bronfen & M. Kavka, ix-xxvi. New York: Columbia University Press.

Livia, A. 2003. One man in two is a woman: linguistic approaches to gender in literary texts. In *The Handbook of Language and Gender*, ed. by J. Holmes & M. Meyerhoff, 142-158. Blackwell: Oxford.

Mezei, K. (ed.) 1996a. *Ambiguous Voices: Feminist Narratology and British Women Writers*. Chapel Hill: University of North Carolina Press.

Mezei, K. 1996b. Who is speaking here? Free indirect discourse, gender and authority in *Emma*, *Howards End*, and *Mrs Dalloway*. In *Ambiguous Voices: Feminist Narratology and British Women Writers*, ed. by Kathy Mezei, 66-92. Chapel Hill: University of North Carolina Press.

Mills, S. 1995. *Feminist Stylistics*. London: Routledge.

Mills, S. 1998. Post-feminist text analysis, *Language and Literature* 7 (3): 235-253.

Mills, S. 2006. Feminist stylistics. In *Encyclopedia of Language and Linguistics*, ed. by K. Brown, 2nd edition, vol. 12: 221-223. London and NY: Elsevier.

Poovey, M. 1989. *Uneven Developments: The Ideological Work of Gender in Mid-Victorian England*. London: Virago.

Showalter, E. 1989. Women writing: *Jane Eyre*, *Shirley*, *Vilette*, *Aurora Leigh*. In *Modern Literary Theory*, ed. by P. Rice & P. Waugh, 102-108. London: Edward Arnold.

Richardson, B. 2002. Linearity and its discontents: rethinking narrative form and ideological valence, *College English* 62 (6): 685-695.

Toolan, M. 1989. Analysing conversation in fiction: an example from Joyce's *Portrait*. In *Language, Discourse and Literature: An Introductory Reader in Discourse Stylistics*, ed. by R. Carter & P. Simpson, 195-212. London: Routledge

Woolf, V. 1964 [1927]. *To the Lighthouse*. London: Penguin Books.

Woolf, V. 1966. Women and fiction. In *Collected Essays*, vol. 2: 141-148. London: The Hogarth Press.

The Limits of Blending: Extended Metaphor, Simile and Allegory

Peter Crisp
The Chinese University of Hong Kong

This paper does not question the significance and importance of blending theory. It does however want to guard against overgeneralisations of the theory which can only weaken it. If the theory is over generalised it becomes too vague and loose, losing its richness and insights. Allegory in particular will be looked at in the light of blending theory. Allegory is not as such, it will be argued, a blending phenomenon, but blending does provide a series of powerful, striking inputs to allegory.

Before looking at allegory in particular, some general issues raised by blending theory need to be dealt with. Ray Gibbs, while valuing blending theory as a source of potential insight, points out that it has yet to be operationalized in terms of the canons of experimental, cognitive psychology (Gibbs: 2000, 2001). Gibbs emphasizes the difference between linguistic products and linguistic processes. It is one thing to analyze the achieved meaning of a metaphorical utterance; it is another thing to discover what goes on in the largely unconscious processes, measured in milliseconds, that lead up to the production and understanding of that utterance and its achieved meaning. Blending analyses are generally of the previous kind, analysing the achieved products of linguistic processing. Such analyses can be powerful and compelling when applied to phenomena, such as those associated with new, de-automatised, metaphor, where we have explicit, conscious contents in mind that we can analyze, often together with elaborate linguistic expression of the metaphor. Blending theory however usually treats such "spectacular" indisputable examples of blending as merely the tip of the iceberg of a whole range of all pervasive processes of unconscious blending. This is where the issue of testability and falsifiability becomes crucial. We have no direct access to unconscious mental processes and must rely on the testable hypotheses of cognitive psychology for this. But, as Gibbs points out, blending theory has not as yet been experimentally operationalized.

A related point that Gibbs (2001) makes is the possible or probable variety in the forms of metaphorical processing. We cannot assume that all the varied forms of metaphor are processed in the same way. Just as metaphorical products are varied so may the underlying processes of metaphorical cognition be equally varied. This is a rather different perspective from that normally found with blending theorists. There it is generally assumed that the same basic processes of blending underlie all forms of metaphor, as well of course as very much else. The distinction is made between new blends and entrenched blends. With a new metaphor you create a new blend, with a conventional one you re-activate an entrenched blend. The analyses for new metaphors, which involve explicit conscious mental contents, have a great deal of force. The analysis for conventional metaphors, where metaphoricity is often not noticed by either producers or receivers, remains as yet however an untested hypothesis since what is involved are largely unconscious processes to which we have no direct access. There is in fact a considerable amount of psychological and neuropsychological evidence indicating that there could well be considerable differences between the processing of new and conventional metaphors.

Giora (1997), in testing the Graded Salience Hypothesis, has shown that salient meanings are processed more rapidly than non-salient meanings. A salient meaning is one that is conventionally established, frequently used, generally familiar, or primed by the immediately prior linguistic context. This means that conventional metaphorical expressions are generally processed faster than new ones. This by itself of course is perfectly consistent with an "across the board" blending account, for one would naturally expect the creation of a new blend to take longer than the re-activation of an already entrenched one. Dedre Gentner has developed a Career of Metaphor hypothesis that is largely consistent with Giora's Graded Salience Hypothesis but which however emphasizes even more the potential differences between the processing of conventional and new metaphors. Gentner argues that while new metaphors are processed by constructing cross domain mappings, conventional metaphors are processed by constructing single, abstracted, metaphorical categories in the manner hypothesized by Glucksberg & Keysar (1993). This would involve a very considerable difference indeed between the conceptual nature of new and conventional metaphors and so in the nature of their processing. Gentner & Wolff (1997) have experimental evidence indicating that, while the processing of new metaphors involves constructing cross-domain mappings, some conventional metaphors at least are processed simply as metaphorical categories without the construction of any cross domain mapping. One of Gentner's most striking findings involves an asymmetry between the relative processing times of new metaphors and similes and conventional metaphors and similes. New metaphors and similes as a whole take longer to process than conventional metaphors and similes, in line with Giora's findings, but, while new metaphors take longer to process than new similes, conventional metaphors take less time to process than conventional similes (Gentner & Bowdle, 2001). This striking finding will be discussed later in this paper in relation to allegory, but at this point we will simply note that it does seem to indicate some very significant differences between new and conventional metaphorical processing. While a simile is a simile, new or conventional, it seems that new and conventional metaphors contrast with similes in radically different ways.

The studies cited in the previous paragraph were all purely psychological. Neuropsychological evidence is also of course highly relevant to the issue of assessing the possible differences between various kinds of metaphorical processing and, particularly, between the processing of new and conventional metaphors. Giora, Zaidel, Soroker, Batori & Kasher (2000) have shown that while the processing of conventional figurative language is especially associated with the left cerebral hemisphere, that of unconventional figurative language is particularly associated with the right. This study involved left and right brain damaged individuals, together with undamaged controls. All subjects were presented with examples of conventional metaphor and unconventional sarcasm. The LBD subjects performed less well than the RBD ones with conventional metaphor and better than the RBD ones with unconventional sarcasm. That is to say, the left rather than the right hemisphere seemed to be being drawn upon for conventional figurative language processing and the right for unconventional figurative language processing. This is line with numerous findings that the left hemisphere is particularly associated with the processing of conventional language generally, and the right with that of unconventional and innovative language. Ahrens, Liu, Lee, Gong, Fang & Hsu (forthcoming), using functional MRI techniques, have shown that while conventional metaphor processing is mainly supported by the left hemisphere, new metaphor processing is associated with both the left and the right hemispheres. That is to say, the major neural difference between the processing of conventional and new metaphors is the massively greater activation of areas in the right hemisphere in the latter condition. This is consistent with the findings of Giora *et al.* (2000) while bearing specifically on the contrast between the processing of conventional and new metaphors while using the most accurate techniques developed to date for locating neural activation. The neuropsychological evidence thus points towards significant differences in the nature of the processing of new and conventional metaphors. While neither the psychological nor neuropsychological evidence cited here can be said to refute the claim that the same fundamental processes of blending underlie all forms of metaphor, it certainly shows that we cannot assume that there are any such underlying uniform processes and indicates that they may well not exist. Blending may only be an, important, part of the story of metaphor.

Having looked at some relevant general issues in relation to blending, some of which will be further dealt with later, we now turn to allegory. The term *allegory* will be used in this paper in the sense that has been more or less dominant in literary criticism and aesthetics for the last two hundred years or so. This essentially defines allegory as a kind of super-extended metaphor in which all overt reference to the metaphorical target is eliminated. The language of allegory, both literal and figurative, relates directly only to the metaphorical source (Crisp, 2001, 2005a). Prototypical examples of allegory in this sense are Bunyan's *The Pilgrim's Progress*, *Everyman*, and Spenser's *The Faerie Queene*. A work does not however have to be a large scale narrative or drama to qualify as an allegory in this sense. A lyric poem such as Vaughan's *Regeneration* and a brief essay such as Addison's *The Spectator*, *No.3* also undoubtedly qualify as allegories. In all cases the crucial thing is that all the language of the text relates directly to the allegorical source, which thereby becomes a fictional situation like any other fictional situation, but one itself functioning as a metaphorical source. In the older rhetorical tradition, going back to before Aristotle, the term *allegory* was used in a much wider fashion (Crisp, 2001, 2005a). Sometimes it simply meant figurative language as such and it would virtually always include what we now term extended metaphor. The term *allegory* is still subject to a fairly wide range of construals. This paper however follows the tradition of construal, dominant in literary contexts for the last two hundred years or so, that draws a distinction between allegory proper and extended metaphor or, if you like, between super-extended metaphor and mere extended metaphor. It does this because it allows us to draw an important and significant distinction.

An extended metaphor is a conceptual metaphor whose linguistic expression extends over more than one clause. The crucial difference between extended metaphor and allegory proper is that an extended metaphor, like linguistically expressed metaphor generally, contains language that relates to both the metaphorical source and target. This contrasts with allegory proper where there is no overt target reference at all. An analysis of a particular example, from *A Ballad for Katherine of Aragon* by Charles Causley, which, despite its title, is mainly about the Second World War, will help to make this distinction clear:

O war is a **casual mistress**
And the world is **her double bed**
She has a few **charms in her** mechanised **arms**
But you **wake up** and **find** yourself dead.

The metaphor here extends over four clauses and four metrical lines. The metaphorically used words are all marked in bold. The metaphorical source is that of the mistress and her context of activity, the target is that of war. If this extended metaphor were super extended to the point of becoming an allegory proper there would be no overt reference to war. It is the mixture of source and target language that prompts the conceptual mixing of metaphorical source and target.

To talk of conceptual mixing here is to evoke blending theory. The mere fact of their being both source and target related language is by itself though no evidence for the presence of blending. A simple, source-to-target mapping alone, without any blend, could account for the presence of source and target related language. This new, highly foregrounded, extended metaphor is however an indisputable case of blending. This can be established first of all due to its elaborate linguistic expression which, for example, includes the mixing of source and target language in a single noun phrase, *her mechanised arms*, acting as a direct prompt to the fusion of source and target concepts in a blended space. Yet the elaborate linguistic expression is far from being the only evidence here for the presence of blending. The extended foregrounding of this metaphor creates explicit, conscious, mental contents that can be characterized in a fairly direct fashion. In my own case a particular mental content that is created is an image, the image of a mistress on a bed rearing up with extended *mechanical* arms. Such images, with their direct mixture of source and target elements, constitute direct evidence for blending. Yet to note such imagistic mixing is only to begin to do justice to the conscious experience of blending here. A blended space has been set up with inputs from both the source and target spaces. Crucially, war and the mistress in the two different input spaces have been fused into a strange war/mistress entity in the blend. We have to recognize a separate blended space containing this strange, fused war/mistress. In some strange impossible sense war actually *is* that bizarre mistress with mechanical arms. No mere mapping from a source to a target, no mere correlation of two quite separate concepts, could do justice to the sense of fused identity here.

Yet of course it is impossible for war to be identical with a mistress, absolutely impossible, because it is logically impossible. War is an abstract entity, though of course one with concrete manifestations, and, by broadly logical necessity, an abstract entity cannot be identical with a concrete entity such as a mistress. This however creates a major puzzle. We cannot imagine a logically impossible situation, we cannot for example imagine being literally completely in a room while not being completely in that same room at the same time. Yet we seem to imagine that war *is* a mistress when we read Causley's lines. To understand what is going in this strange seemingly paradoxal situation is to understand something very important about blending. The blended space is imaginable because it is internally coherent. There is nothing logically impossible about a woman with mechanized arms. It is the counterpart connections to the input spaces of war and the mistress that create the sense or illusion of the logically impossible being imagined. Barnden's concept of a "pretence cocoon" helps to explain what is going on. Barnden proposes that we provisionally take metaphorical statements as being literally true and derive a range of perfectly literal inferences from them (Barnden, 2001; Barnden & Lee, 1999). Only after these inferences have been derived do we then recognize their metaphoricity and project those that "fit" back to the inputs. In other words we pretend to believe in a literal truth that allows us to generate inferences some of which can then be projected back to what we are truly, literally, interested in. In the case of the war/mistress what is projected back to the target space is that although war is attractive and exciting, it is also fatal. Yet can the notion of pretence do full justice to the sense of fusion created by the war/mistress image? The notion of a full conceptual integration network, as developed by blending theory, is needed to explain the psychological power of the pretence here. It is the simulataneous, linked, co-activation of the input spaces together with the blended space in the whole network that creates the sense of an, in fact impossible, fusion. The scenario in the blended space is internally coherent. It seems to be an imagining of the logically impossible because of its co-activation with the input spaces containing the war/mistress's different counterparts. The blended space itself thus has no definable metaphysical or ontological status. It does not define a possible world or situation but exists in a strange, conceptual, no man's land that exists solely to project inferences back to the other spaces and, in the case of poetic metaphor at least, for the sake of is own intrinsic aesthetic excitement. A blended space is thus a very different kind of thing from a possible world or situation which does have a definable metaphysical status.

Not all blends are metaphorical blends. What Fauconnier & Turner (2002) refer to as Mirror Blends, such as the Buddhist Monk and Regatta blends, are not metaphorical because their input spaces are conceptually too close together. The situations of a monk going up a hill and then down a hill, or of a ship traversing a route in the 19th century and a catamaran traversing the same route in the late 20th century are clearly very alike. They are literally rather than metaphorically similar. Yet the blends themselves are still figurative. To talk of a monk passing himself or of two sea vessels, whose existences are separated by more than a century, racing simultaneously against each other, is to talk figuratively. The blended spaces in which the monk passes himself or the ships from different times race against each other are clearly, like the space of the war/mistress, "pretence cocoons", that is, internally consistent scenarios with no ultimate, definable, metaphysical status allowing the derivation of inferences and having their own strange, anomalous, fascination. Not all blends are metaphorical, but are they all figurative? If the analysis given here is correct then they are indeed all figurative. Since a blended space has no definable ontological status, it cannot function directly as a reality model, as a model of any actual or possible reality. This means that blending always necessarily involves an element of semantic indirection. Semantic indirection is what defines figurative meaning in conceptual terms. To say that all blending is figurative is to disagree with Fauconnier & Turner (2002), who argue that phrases such as *red pencil* and *safe beach*, or *Paul's daughter* and *Sally's father*, all involve blending, that a great deal of blending in fact results in perfectly literal thought and language. It does not seem helpful to classify such phrases and sentences as blends. (Fauconnier & Turner [2002] refer to them as "simplex blends".) To do so is to interpret blending as involving nothing more than the integration of diverse concepts, such as those of RED and PENCIL to form new concepts such as that of RED PENCIL. On this interpretation blending theory would not need to be empirically operationalized since it would be a mere truism. Who would doubt that the bringing together of diverse concepts to form new concepts is all pervasive in both conscious and unconscious cognition? In this paper blending is construed as an exclusively figurative phenomenon. The paper is moreover interested exclusively in the metaphorical forms of blending.

New foregrounded metaphors frequently at least involve blending, and the analysis of such metaphors and of the explicit conscious mental contents they produce can give deep insight into the nature of blending. Let us now look at allegory proper rather than extended metaphor. In contrast to extended metaphor allegory we saw does not mix source and target related language. Let us start by looking at the opening of *The Pilgrim's Progress*. The very beginning clauses of the work occupy a kind of liminal position in relation to the allegorical narrative proper. The issues they raise are of deep interest in their own right but the analysis here begins with the allegorical narrative proper:

... and behold I saw a Man clothed with Raggs, standing in a certain place, with his face from his own House, a Book in his hand, and a great burden upon his back. I looked, and saw him open the Book, and Read therein; and as he Read, he wept and trembled: and not being able longer to contain, he brake out with a lamentable cry; saying, what shall I do?

This seems like a perfectly straightforward fictional situation, and this is what it is in and of itself. All of the language is source related. In fact the underlying metaphor, LIFE IS A JOURNEY, has been super-extended to the point where the language itself is no longer as such metaphorical language. When there is no longer a contrast between source and target related language, linguistic metaphoricity ceases. The language is used directly to characterize a fictional situation. The underlying metaphorical mapping of the allegory proceeds from the fictional situation itself, which has already been characterized by the language of the allegorical narrative. Such language of course, like virtually all human discourse, will contain metaphorical language, but the target of this language will be the fictional situation which itself then functions in turn as the allegorical source. For of course although this opening scene of *The Pilgrim's Progress* is in and of itself simply a fictional situation it is not just that, because this situation is mapped onto the allegorical target of the Christian life. Thus the rags in which the man is clothed map onto sin, the burden on his back maps onto the guilt for sin, the book maps onto the Bible, and his physical isolation maps onto the highly individual nature of Christian conversion as understood by a Calvinist Independent like John Bunyan.

An allegorical scene, for the opening of *The Pilgrim's Progress* displays the fundamental characteristics common to all allegorical scenes, is thus something very different from a blended space. A blended space we have seen has, by its nature, no definable metaphysical status. An allegorical scene however is a fictional situation and as such its metaphysical status is quite clear. It is a possible situation. The whole *feel* of a scene like this is different from that of Causley's war/mistress. It has a vivid sense of actuality; many people have commented on the vivid realism of *The Pilgrim's Progress*. There is of course the extra dimension of excitement coming from the underlying metaphorical mapping that makes the whole scene resonant with further meaning and significance. Nevertheless, there is not the utterly strange sense of anomaly that we have with the war/mistress. This is a graspable, logically possible, situation, though one resonant with extra meaning.

Allegorical scenes are therefore not blended spaces. But might blended spaces have input to the fictional reality spaces of allegorical narratives? Might blending make an important contribution to allegory, even though allegory is not as such directly a form of blending? Mark Turner (1996) has a striking analysis of the closing section of Canto XXVIII of Dante's *Inferno*, in which Dante accompanied by Virgil meets Bertran de Born. De Born had stirred up conflict between Henry II, King of England and his son Prince Henry. He had socially divided father and son. In Hell he appears physically divided. His head has been separated from his body and as it speaks, telling his story, he holds it swinging by its hair. As Turner points out the conceptual metaphor SOCIAL DIVISION IS PHYSICAL DIVISION is at work here. But the crucial point Turner further makes is that there is not just a mapping from source to target; source and target are here mingled in the manner of a blended space because the target element of De Born the stirrer up of strife is mingled with the source element of physical division. Turner argues on the basis of this that the scene with de Born actually is a blended space. But everything that has been said about the opening of *The Pilgrim's Progress* applies to this scene too. It is a vividly concrete fictional situation with a definable metaphysical status as a possible situation; it has none of the strange anomalous status of the war/mistress blend, or indeed of the Buddhist Monk or Regatta blends. It cannot therefore be itself directly a blended space. Rather a blended space has been set up and then fantastic, but logically possible, properties have been projected back from it to the source space that functions as the fictional reality space of Dante's *Inferno* XXVIII. We therefore have a full integration network, including source, target and blended spaces but Dante's allegorical scene itself is the source space of this network, not its blended space, though it receives crucial input from that blended space.

The Pilgrim's Progress and probably most other allegories all contain plenty of scenes in which, as in *Inferno* XXVIII, there is evidence for input to the allegorical fictional situation from a blended space. This is one of the most important sources of the fantastically incredible which, many commentators have noted, is so prominent a feature in allegory. Scenes like this provide clear evidence for blending input. Yet what of those sections of allegorical narratives where there is no such evidence? The allegory in the opening of *The Pilgrim's Progress* we saw can be accounted for by a simple mapping from the fictional situation as source onto the Christian life as target. There is no evidence for any blending input here. Yet might unconscious, underlying, processes of blending still be present? This paper is not written by a psychologist and has no suggestions to make for experiments that could provide evidence bearing directly on this question. However, it will be argued, there is a range of already available psychological evidence which, together with phenomenological evidence drawn from the analysis of conscious experience, suggests a possible answer. To bring this combination of experimental and phenomenological evidence to bear, we need to reformulate our question as to whether or not blending is always present in allegory as an underlying unconscious input to the allegorical, fictional situation in the following manner: is allegory a super-extended metaphor, a super-extended simile, or an alternation of super-extended metaphor and simile? To explain the need for this reformulation, the relation between metaphor and simile needs to be considered.

There is a long tradition, going all the way back to Aristotle, which assumes that there is no fundamental difference between metaphor and simile. For Aristotle, a metaphor was simply an implicit simile or comparison. (The difference between a simile and a literal comparison is that with a literal comparison the compared domains are relatively "close" together conceptually, but with a simile they are conceptually distant; this is what makes similes, like metaphors, figurative.) Whatever its other differences with Aristotle, conceptual metaphor theory too has generally regarded metaphors and similes as being essentially the same kind of thing, as alternative ways of expressing the same underlying cross-domain mapping. The difference between metaphor and simile is generally held to be that a simile overtly signals the presence of such a mapping while a metaphor does not. One can thus sum up this long established tradition by saying that while its members may differ about the conceptual commonality uniting metaphor and simile, they all agree that the difference between metaphor and simile is merely a matter of surface linguistic form and not one of underlying conceptual content. However, in recent decades a range of psychological studies have produced evidence that there are in fact significant conceptual differences between metaphor and simile.

Rather than citing papers individually a summary will be given of the main overall findings of a series of papers on the relation between metaphor and simile (Gibb & Wales, 1990; Aisenman, 1999; Chiappe, 1999; Chiappe & Kennedy, 2001). The most frequent experimental form is one where subjects are asked to choose for a given source and target pair whether the simile or the metaphor form seems the more appropriate for linking source and target. The aim is to find if there is any consistent pattern in the kinds of pairs for which the metaphor form is preferred and the kinds for which the simile form is preferred. There does seem to be a clear pattern. If subjects judge that a source/target pair displays a high degree of perceived similarity or aptness then they generally feel that the metaphor form is more appropriate. If they feel that the degree of perceived similarity or aptness is relatively low, then they feel that the simile form is more appropriate. If a source/target pair comes in the middle of the perceived similarity/aptness range then the metaphor or simile forms are selected in a more or less random fashion. In other words, the stronger the perceived connections between source and target, even though they display a sufficient conceptual distance to qualify as figurative, the greater the preference for the metaphor form, the weaker the perceived connections the greater the preference for the simile form. Another related finding is that source/target pairs in similes tend to be linked by isolated attributes while those in metaphors tend to be linked by common relational structure. Relational structure is of course a much more powerful link between domains than shared attributes. There is thus good psychological evidence showing that source and target are felt to be more closely related in metaphor than in simile.

Israel, Harding & Tobin (2004) have also produced linguistic evidence that points in the same direction as the above cited psychological studies. They cite Grady (1997) to the effect that with metaphor all the details of the source that are explicitly mentioned have to be mapped onto the target, even with an established conceptual metaphor that does not usually map these details. Thus, although THEORIES ARE BUILDINGS usually only maps from the foundations or structure of buildings onto theories, in *This theory has a good foundation but too many gargoyles* you have to map from gargoyles onto the theory in question in order to interpret the metaphor, or else find it uninterpretable. Israel et al point out however that this is not true with simile. It often happens that only parts of the source of a simile are mapped onto its target. Thus, in *The horse ran up the stairs like a boarder late for supper*, only the lateness of the boarder is mapped onto the horse but not his property of being a boarder nor his being late for supper. Likewise, in *When the phone rang, he jumped like a jittery private in a fox hole*, only the private's jumping gets mapped and not his properties of being a private and of being jittery nor his being in a foxhole. This linguistic evidence reinforces the psychological evidence already cited. It seems that with metaphor the relation between source and target is felt to be so close that everything that is explicitly mentioned about the source has to be projected onto the target. With simile however it seems that source and target are felt to be sufficiently separate to allow for only selective projection from source to target. Some elements in the source may remain completely separate from the target. The combination of psychological and linguistic evidence cited indicates that the difference between metaphor and simile involves more than a matter of mere linguistic form, that there is an underlying conceptual difference between the two figures.

None of the psychological studies referred to above make any reference to blending theory. The same is true of the studies by Giora *et al.* , and by Gentner & Wolff and Gentner & Bowdler, referred to earlier. This is presumably because blending theory has not as yet been psychologically operationalized. Israel et al do once briefly mention blending theory, but this single mention seems to presuppose the maximally inclusive and vague interpretation of blending and so to amount to nothing very much. What implications might these independently established findings have for a framework that recognizes blending? A striking suggestion has been made by Cruse that may enable us to answer this question (Croft & Cruse, 2004). He states that while metaphors involve blends, similes do not. Metaphors he says create that sense of fusion that indicates the presence of blending, while similes do not. It is important first of all to note that Cruse seems to have *new* metaphors in mind here. Secondly, that the evidence he appeals to is exclusively phenomenological. This is a little surprising since in his sections of *Cognitive Linguistics*, co-authored with Cruse, he is generally very anxious to cite experimental, psychological evidence for his various assertions. Nevertheless in this case he does not do this but relies solely on the phenomenological appeal to conscious experience. This is presumably because, as we have seen, there are as yet no experimental psychological studies explicitly bearing on this issue. Yet the studies referred to in this paper do provide some support for Cruse's contention. If, as we have seen, source and target are felt to be much more intimately linked with metaphor than with simile, then this should make the production of a blend much more likely with metaphor than with simile. If source and target are felt to be clearly separated then they are likely to be kept separated, but if they are felt to be intimately connected then it is much more likely that elements from both of them will be mingled together in a single blended space.

The earlier cited findings of Gentner & Bowdle also seem to provide further support for Cruse's contention that metaphor involves blending while simile does not, always remembering that Cruse seems talking about *new* metaphor. Gentner & Bowdle show that new metaphors take longer to process than new similes. This would fit in perfectly with the idea that metaphors involve blending while similes do not, for in the case of a metaphor extra processing time would be needed for the setting up of the extra blended space. There is not unfortunately space here to discuss Gentner & Bowdle's own explanation of this difference in processing time, but their explanation could be naturally extended to encompass Cruse's blending hypothesis. Gentner & Bowdle have also shown that conventional metaphors take less time to process than conventional similes. This would indicate that conventional metaphors do not involve blending at all. There is one final striking piece of experimental, psychological evidence indicating that (new) metaphors involve blending while similes do not. Gibb & Wales (1990) cite a finding of Verbrugge (1980), produced long before blending was ever thought of, that when subjects were presented with a source/target pair expressed by a metaphor they produced images that fused source and target elements while with similes they did not do this. This constitutes direct evidence for an association of blending with metaphor but not with simile, and also indicates a possible path, via imaging studies, for operationalizing blending theory.

Having looked at some experimental and linguistic evidence for Cruse's hypothesis, some particular examples of the kind of phenomenological evidence he appeals to will be analysed. Consider the following three examples of poetic simile (selected by the author of this paper):

One of the **low on** whom assurance **sits**

Like a silk hat on a Bradford millionaire

(T. S. Eliot, *The Waste Land*)

... the older men,

With more important **frowns** that seemed to **claim**

Business of state for pretext, **drifting** came

Down the long floor <u>like arctic bergs afloat</u>

(C. S. Lewis, *The Queen of Drum*)

Twice the lightning **blinked**, then a **crash** of thunder.

Three **cliffs** of waves **collapsed** above them, seas

Crushed in his face, he fell down, dazed.

The wind began to **play**, <u>like country fiddlers</u>

<u>In a crowded room, with nailed boots stamping</u>

<u>On the stone cottage floor, raising white ashes.</u>

The sea became a **dance.**

(Richard Murphy, *The Cleggan Disaster*)

The writer of the present paper finds Cruse's contention that (new) metaphor is associated with a sense of fusion, while simile is not, dramatically confirmed by these examples. Each reader will of course have to consult their own phenomenological intuitions. Each of these similes in fact involves a combination of simile and metaphor, something very common with poetic simile. Such combinations can take a number of forms, but in all three of these examples a mapping is first expressed metaphorically and then further extended by simile. (In the third example there is also a return to further metaphorical expression of the mapping after the simile has been completed.) The metaphorically used words in the examples, both those expressing the same mapping as the simile and also any others that are present, are in bold, while the similes are underlined from beginning to end.

Let us look first at the Eliot example. In the first line we are given the image of assurance sitting on a metaphorically low individual. The relevant metaphorically used word forms are *on* and *sits*. This is not an extended metaphor like that of Causley's war/mistress, which was looked at earlier. With such a relative paucity of linguistic expression there is no direct linguistic evidence, like that of Causley's *mechanised arms*, for the fusing of source and target elements in a single blended space. Yet there is still the same sense of fusion. Just as Causley's mistress *is* in some strange, impossible way war, so the abstract property of assurance here actually, impossibly, seems to *sit*, and so by implication to be a person sitting, on this low individual. The same blending analysis given for Causley's war/mistress will account for our ability here to seemingly imagine the logical impossibility of an abstract property performing a physical action. The sense of fusion between the source and target elements, the concrete action of sitting and the abstract property of assurance, disappears however when we move into the simile. First of all, a partial reinterpretation of *sits* is imposed. *sits* is initially interpreted in terms of the first line alone, which, as a single complete noun phrase and an end stopped iambic pentameter, is a relatively separated unit. In this context the most prominent, basic meaning of lexeme **sit** alone, that of a person sitting, is automatically activated which then gives rise to a vivid new metaphor. The element of comparison which does the, implicit, sitting in the simile is a hat. This however, rather than leading to the fused personification of the hat as a sitting person, forces a re-interpretation of *sits*. We can talk quite conventionally of a hat sitting on a person's head. The verb **sit** has a secondary, polysemous, meaning which by metaphorical extension allows objects such as hats to sit. When we move from metaphor to simile we thus move from new to conventional metaphor. The sense of fusion is lost, and never regained. The concept of a silk hat on a Bradford millionaire is mapped onto assurance but there is no sense of fusion whatsoever. The point and purpose of the comparison is evident: ultimately, the vulgarity of the northern English millionaire, associated metonymically with the hat, is being associated with the vulgarity of the first line's low individual. Yet there is no sense whatsoever that the low individual's assurance is a silk hat. The hat and the assurance are clearly separated conceptually. One could talk here of comparison at a distance. One might argue that it is the shift from new to conventional metaphor alone that accounts here for the loss of the sense of fusion. The two following examples however will show the same loss of a sense of fusion without any such shift from new to conventional metaphor. Eliot seems to have combined this shift with that from metaphor to simile because he sensed that simile and conventional metaphor would go together naturally. Gentner & Bowdle's findings, it will be remembered, make it even less likely that conventional metaphors are associated with blending than are similes.

The combination of metaphor and simile in the C. S. Lewis example produces basically the same effect as in the Eliot example. The older frowning men seem to be actually, impossibly, drifting down the long floor. In the simile by contrast their concept is not fused with that of the arctic bergs. The point of the simile is clear. The older men are shown by comparison to be emotionally cold, but this again is comparison "at a distance". There is no sense of fusion between them and the bergs. The Murphy example reveals further aspects of the metaphor/simile contrast. In the first three lines there is a series of metaphors all of which, with the partial exception of *a crash of thunder*, are strikingly new. The mappings here are different from that of the simile that emerges in the following three lines. It is still however worth making the point that the sense of fusion here is very strong: the lightning does seem to strangely, literally, blink and the descending waves do seem incredibly to be collapsing cliffs. In the next line the wind begins to play. This playing could by itself be the kind of playing a child engages in: *play* is followed by a comma and what proceeds the comma can be read initially as a complete, separate, clause that activates only the most prominent basic meaning of lexeme **play** so giving rise to a vivid, new, fused metaphor. (There is an ironic dimension to the metaphor since the playing of the wind is far from being innocent, as play prototypically is.) In the simile that follows a reinterpretation of *play* is imposed. The context of the simile requires that *play* now be understood in terms of musical playing. This "turning" of the verbal sense recalls the Eliot example and again seems to be part of a strategy to emphasize the discontinuity of effect between metaphor and simile.

Murphy's simile is much more extended than those of either Eliot of Lewis. It is an epic simile in the manner of Homer, Virgil or Milton. (This is appropriate since Murphy is describing a disaster in which all the fisherman in the boat were drowned; the associations of the epic simile give stature and dignity to this democratic tragedy.) Epic similes vividly exploit the separation of source and target natural to simile. They develop the source concept in an extended fashion so that is conceived of in its own terms, ones that are clearly separated from those of the target, and are then mapped onto it "at a distance". In the Murphy example, the simile takes us right away from the immediate scene of the sea storm to the vividly detailed scene of an indoor dance with the implied warmth of a fire. There is a mapping from the stamping of the nailed feet onto the striking of the waves against the boat, yet this conveys only a sense of underlying menace, a menace "at a distance". The horror of the fishermen's situation is momentarily distanced by the dancing scene. Note that many of the simile's details, such as that of the raising of the white ashes, do not get mapped onto the sea scene. As Israel *et al* have emphasized, simile mappings are highly partial, giving rise to no sense of fusion. In the following line however the mapping from a dance to the storm is expressed metaphorically and we are then thrust back directly into the scene of the disaster. The sea really does seem to dance, its being fused with the activity of dancing returns us to the full horror of what is happening.

Some might question the appropriateness of combining the essentially phenomenological evidence of the previous three paragraphs with the earlier cited evidence from experimental psychology to make a point about the conceptual differences between metaphor and simile. Can such evidence have any role to play in an analytic approach that places itself within the general context of cognitive science? The answer to this question has been given by Flanagan (1997), who talks of the importance of giving phenomenology its due in any natural approach to the study of consciousness. Phenomenology, neuroscience and psychology all need to be drawn upon as interacting sources of evidence. None can be ignored.

Given the association of metaphor, new metaphor, that is, with blending and the apparent absence of blending with simile, we can now see the sense of the question that was asked earlier: is allegory a super-extended metaphor, a super-extended simile, or an alternation of super-extended metaphor and simile? This is a way asking whether blending is always present as an input to allegory, never present, or only sometimes present. We have already seen that it is not true that it is never present. There are in many, probably most, allegories episodes providing clear evidence for input to the allegorical fictional situation from blended spaces; allegories are thus not generally just super-extended similes. Yet are they just super-extended metaphors? That is, is input from blended spaces to an allegory's fictional situation an occasional phenomenon or is such input continuous throughout the processing of an allegory, whether there is overt evidence for this or not, thus making the allegory a super-extended metaphor? An analysis will now be given of a political allegory by Jonathan Swift that is clearly simile-like in its effects. In fact this is one allegory that does seem to be an uninterrupted, super-extended simile. Its simile-like nature indicates that the most likely account for allegory in general is that it generally functions as a super-extended simile, interspersed at moments of particular intensity with super-extended metaphor, that is, blending when it is present is so only at particularly intense moments. The political nature of the Swift piece is such that he uses the large scale simile form without any blending input at all to gain his effects.

The Story of the Injured Lady: Being a true Picture of Scotch Perfidy, *Irish Poverty and English Partiality* (Swift, 1963) is to be understood in the context of the relations between England, Ireland and Scotland about the time of the Act of Union between England and Scotland in 1707. It takes the form of a letter of complaint written by the injured lady. She describes:

> A Gentleman in the Neighbourhood had two Mistresses, another and myself; and he pretended honourable Love to us both. Our three Houses stood pretty near one another; his was parted from mine by a River, and from my Rival's by an old broken Wall.

The "gentleman" promised marriage to both women and, on the basis of a promise that, in a strictly monogamous society, he knew he could not keep to them both, he debauched them both. He has finally decided to marry the other woman. This of course is absolutely despicable behaviour. The injured lady has been robbed of her "virtue" and left as a "fallen" and "ruined" woman through the deceit of an outrageous rogue. The allegory is clear. The "gentleman" is England; the injured lady is Ireland; the other woman is Scotland; and the marriage of the "gentleman" and the other woman is the Act of Union between England and Scotland. Ireland had been deceived, mistreated and deserted by England. The initial cue for the allegorical interpretation is the subtitle of the piece (see the beginning of this paragraph) and the mapping just outlined is continuously confirmed by details that fit it throughout the text. In the quoted lines above for example the river maps onto the Irish Sea, dividing England and Ireland, and the old broken wall onto Hadrian's wall, dividing England and Scotland.

The satire of *The Story of the Injured Lady* is typical of Swift in being savagely funny. The point of the comparison is clear: England has tricked and mistreated Ireland in a way comparable to the tricking of the injured lady by the "gentleman". The basis of the savage hilarity however is the incongruity of the comparison between the grand actors and themes of national politics, on the one hand, and the common, sordid and despicable domestic dispute described by the injured lady on the other. This hilarious incongruity is brought home in the following lines:

Once, attended with a Crew of Raggamuffins, she broke into his House, turned all things topsy-turvy, and then set it on Fire. At the same Time she told so many Lies among his Servants, that it set them all by the Ears, and his poor Steward was knocked on the Head...

This is an allegorical parallel to the English Civil War in which the Scots intervened on the Parliamentary side, thereby contributing to the execution of Charles I. The knocking on the head of the steward maps onto the execution of Charles I. One way to describe this would be to say that the ridiculous is mapped onto the sublime. Satirically this is very effective. England and Scotland are made to seem despicable by the comparison, and ridiculous by the contrast, between the allegorical source and target. This effect is achieved by the exact opposite of a sense of fusion. It is the distance between source and target that is so striking. The comparison has its satirical effect because it is a comparison "at a distance", at indeed a very great distance. There is nothing remotely like any effect of blending about this.

The Story of the Injured Lady is a continuous super-extended simile. It shows that we cannot assume that there is a continuous input from blended spaces to the fictional situations of an allegory. In a case such as that of Swift's satire there is clearly no such input. This means that we should only assume the presence of such an input when we have clear, explicit evidence for it. Such evidence is provided when an allegorical scene combines elements originating in both the allegorical source and target, elements that must have been mixed in a blended space and then projected back to the allegorical source in the manner described earlier. There are no such scenes in *The Story of the Injured Lady*. The effect of its political satire depends on the lack of any sense of source/target fusion. This may well be typical of political allegory in general. Most allegories, as observed earlier, do however provide evidence for blending input at moments of especial intensity. Allegory generally seems to be a super-extended simile which usually, though not always, is interspersed with moments of super-extended metaphor. Allegorical scenes are never directly blended spaces and receive input from blended spaces only at moments of special intensity.

This paper began by saying that we should be careful about overgeneralizing blending theory, that it is likely to be only a part, although an important part, of any general account of metaphor and by extension of figurative thought and language in general. It has hopefully been shown how such a nuanced approach can in particular give insight into the nature of allegory.

References

Aisenman, R. A. 1999. Structure-mapping and the simile-metaphor preference, *Metaphor and Symbol* 14 (1): 45-51.

Ahrens, K. , Liu, H. O. , Lee, C. Y. , Gong, S. P. , Fang, S. Y & Hsu, Y. Y. (forthcoming) Functional MRI of conventional and anomalous metaphors in Mandarin Chinese, *Brain and Language* 100 (2): 163-171.

Banich, M. T. 1997. *Neuropsychology — The Neural Bases of Mental Function.* Boston & New York: Houghton Mifflin.

Barnden, J. A. 2001. The utility of reversed transfers in metaphor. In *Proceedings of the Twenty Third Annual Meeting of the Cognitive Science Society, Edingburgh*, ed. by Mahwah. NJ: Lawrence Erlbaum.

Barnden, J. A. & Lee, M. G. 1999. An implemented context system that combines belief reasoning, metaphor-based reasoning and uncertainty handling. In *Lecture Notes in Artificial Intelligence*, 1688, ed. by P. Bouquet, P. Brezillon & L. Serafini, 28-41. New York: Springer.

Brandt, P. A. 2005. Mental spaces and cognitive semantics: a critical comment, *Journal of Pragmatics* 37: 1578-1594.

Brandt, L. & Brandt, P. A. 2002. Making sense of a blend, *Apparatur* 4: 1-56.

Chiappe, D. L. 1999. Aptness predicts preference for metaphors and similes, as well as recall bias, *Psychonomic Bulletin & Review* 6 (4): 668-676.

Chiappe, D. L. & Kennedy, J. M. 2001. Literal bases for metaphor and simile, *Metaphor and Symbol* 16 (3 & 4): 249-276.

Coulson, S. & Van Petten, C. 2002. Conceptual integration and metaphor: an event-related potential study, *Memory & Cognition* 30 (6): 958-968.

Coulson, S. & Oakley, T. 2005. Blending and coded meaning: literal and figurative meaning in cognitive semantics, *Journal of Pragmatics* 37: 1510-1536.

Crisp, P. 2001. Allegory: conceptual metaphor in history. *Language and Literature* 10 (1): 5-19.

Crisp, P. 2005a. Allegory and symbol—a fundamental opposition?, *Language and Literature* 14(4): 323-338.

Crisp, P. 2005b. Allegory, blending and possible situations, *Metaphor and Symbol* 20(2): 115-131.

Croft, W. & Cruse, D. A. 2004. *Cognitive Linguistics*. Cambridge: CUP.

Fauconnier, G. & Turner, M. 2002. *The Way We Think—Conceptual Blending and the Mind's Hidden Complexities*. New York: Basic Books.

Flanagan, O. 1997. Prospects for a unified theory of consciousness. In *The Nature of Consciousness—Philosophical Debates*, ed. by N. Block, O. Flanagan & Güzeldere, 97-109. Cambridge, Mass: MIT.

Gentner, D. & Wolff, P. 1997. Alignment in the processing of metaphor, *Journal of Memory and Language* 37: 331-355.

Gentner, D. & Bowdle, B. F. 2001. Convention, form, and figurative language processing, *Metaphor and Symbol* 16(3 & 4): 223-247.

Gibb, H. & Wales, R. 1990. Metaphor or simile: psychological determinants of the differential use of each sentence form, *Metaphor and Symbolic Activity* 5(4): 199-213.

Gibbs, R. 2000. Making good psychology out of blending theory, *Cognitive Linguistics* 11(3/4): 347-358.

Gibbs, R. 2001. Evaluating contemporary models of figurative language understanding, *Metaphor and Symbol* 16(3 & 4): 317-331.

Giora, R. 1997. Understanding figurative and literal language: the graded salience hypothesis, *Cognitive Linguistics* 8(3): 183-206.

Giora, R., Zaidel, E., Soroker, N., Batori, G. & Kasher, A. 2000. Differential effects of Right- and Left-Hemisphere Damage on understanding sarcasm and metaphor, *Metaphor and Symbol* 15(1 & 2): 63-83.

Glucksberg, S & Keysar, B. 1993. How metaphors work. In *Metaphor and Thought*, 2nd ed., ed. by A. Ortony, 401-424. Cambridge: Cambridge University Press.

Glucksberg, S. & McGlone, M. 1999. When love is not a journey: What metaphors mean, *Journal of Pragmatics* 31: 1541-1558.

Grady, J. E. 1997. Theories are buildings (revised), *Cognitive Linguistics* 8(4): 267-290.

Grady, J., Oakley, T. & Coulson, S. 1997. Blending and metaphor. In *Metaphor in Cognitive Linguistics*, ed. by R. W. Gibbs & G. J. Steen, 101-124. Amsterdam, Philadelphia: John Benjamins.

Israel, M. , Harding, J. R. & Tobin, V. 2004. On simile. In *Language*, *Culture and Mind*, ed. by M. Achard & S. Kemmer, 123-135. Stanford: Center for the Study of Language and Information (CSLI).

Lakoff, G. 1986. The meanings of literal, *Metaphor and Symbolic Activity* 1(4): 291-296.

Leech, G. 1967. *A Linguistic Guide to English Poetry*. London: Longmans.

Swift, J. 1963. The story of the Injured Lady: Being a true picture of Scotch perfidy, Irish poverty and English partiality. In *Irish Tracts 1720-1723 and Sermons*, ed. by H. Davis & L. Landa, 1-9. Oxford: Blackwell.

Turner, M. 1996. *The Literary Mind*. New York: Oxford University Press.

Verbrugge, R. R. 1980. Transformations in knowing: a realist view of metaphor. In *Cognition and Figurative Language*, ed. by R. P. Honeck & R. R. Hoffman, 87-125. Hillsdale, N. J. : Lawrence Erlbaum.

The Social Agency of Verbal Art: How Far Can A Systemic Approach Usefully Go in Modelling the Context of Creation?

Abstract

David G. Butt

Macquarie University, Australia

Stylistic argumentation proceeds by systematizing the sampling of texts, by making textual comparisons, and by establishing statistical generalizations. Analyses of style (and of variation more generally) further require that a systematic method becomes increasingly "systemic"—only by mapping out the paradigms of selection available in particular acts of meaning making can we argue for the "value" of a given selection (namely, its degree of markedness; its relation to a pattern of similar choices; or its apparent contrast to a set of choices which may be, paradoxically, of similar value in this particular instance of text). Humans, as cultural "performers" (as social artists), range across many modes of meaning as they enact their social memberships. But we can ask ourselves: what of the social contexts of conventional modes of interaction can be brought to bear in the systemic analysis of verbal art?

In 1921, Jakobson articulated his scornful reaction to the way literary studies had been conducted to that point in academic institutions, namely in ways that have emphasised the historical and social contexts of the work at the cost of what was essential to its status as a literary text:

> The subject of literary science is not literature, but literariness, i. e. that which makes a given work a literary work. Up till now, however, historians of literature have mostly behaved like the police who when they want to arrest someone take in everyone and everything found in the apartment and even chance passers-by. Historians of literature have in the same way felt the need to take in everything—everyday life, psychology, politics, philosophy. Instead of a science of literature we have fetched up with a conglomeration of cottage industries (Jakobson, 1921, in O'Toole and Shukman, 1977: 17).

Jakobson's ideas for a science of literature were most adequately developed by himself and by(in particular) Tynyanov. The crucial breakthrough in theory came with Tynyanov's "systemo-functional" interpretation of text and of crucial textual concepts(viz. the dominant; literary evolution. . .). Yet these concepts and other related concepts in stylistics do not imply that the analysis of a text should be insulated from the social conditions of its construction and of its reception. In fact, quite the opposite:

> Neither Tynyanov, nor Shklovsky, nor Mukarovsky, nor I have declared that art is a closed sphere. On the contrary we have shown that art is part of the social set-up, an element connected with other elements, a variable element, and for this reason we always observe the dialectic in the relationship of art to either parts of the social structure. What we emphasise is not the separatism of art, but the autonomy of the aesthetic function. (Jakobson, 1933, in O'Toole and Shukman, 1977: 19)

Essentially, the earlier Russian Formalist metaphors—text as "machine" or text as "organism"—were translated by Tynyanov into what we could reasonably call "systems thinking" (text as "system": Steiner, 1984). Such a perspective gives greater scope for tracking the "value" of choices across linguistic systems and across text types. This perspective also prefigures many of the scientific ideas concerning dynamic, non linear systems which have gained greater visibility in the last two decades of the 20th century—concepts like "emergent complexity"; ecological modelling; "bootstrapping"; and the notions of "phase space" against which one can establish a multi-dimensional "phase portrait" of the object of study(including a text).

With stylistics renewing its connections to corpus tools, to probabilistic modelling, to the cultural context of artistic expression, and to multi-modal analysis, it is opportune to reconsider Jakobson's two statements and how they might be reconciled. For example, we can ask: how many of the "cottage industries" might now be brought usefully into a science of literature and of the aesthetic function? In particular, can we treat the cultural milieu through parametric and systemic methods, or must the social and personal factors motivating the forms of verbal art be left to the less formal insights of hermeneutics and cultural studies? Naturally, it needs to be made clear what kind of problems might be clarified, what insights forthcoming, from extending our paradigmatic modelling to heuristic contexts of literary construction and out into what the anthropologist Malinowski (1884-1942) insisted on in semantic studies, namely the "context of culture".

My discussion will consider this problem of context in verbal art by setting out from approaches already established in systemic functional linguistics, in particular, methods exemplified in the tradition extending from J. R. Firth (1890-1960) to the work of M. A. K. Halliday and R. Hasan, among others.

Poems to be analysed in this paper include:

XII (from W. H. Auden's "Sonnets from China", 1938)
Here war is harmless like a monument:
A telephone is talking to a man;
Flags on a map declare that troops were sent;
A boy brings milk in bowls. There is a plan
For living men in terror of their lives,
Who thirst at nine who were to thirst at noon,
Who can be lost, and are, who miss their wives
And, unlike an idea, can die too soon.
Yet ideas can be true, although men die:
For we have seen a myriad faces
Ecstatic from one lie,
And maps can really point to places
Where life is evil now.
Nanking. Dachau.
(in Auden & Isherwood, 1973: 253)
Fixed Ideas (Kenneth Slessor, c. 1935)
Ranks of electroplated cubes, dwindling to glitters,
Like the other pasture, the trigonometry of marble,
Death's candy-bed. Stone caked on stone,
Dry pyramids and racks of iron balls.
Life is observed, a precipitate of pellets,
Or grammarians freeze it into spar,
Their rhomboids, as for instance, the finest crystal

Fixing a snowfall under glass. Gods are laid out

In alabaster, with horny cartilage

And zinc ribs; or systems of ecstasy

Baked into bricks. There is a gallery of sculpture,

Bleached bones of heroes, Gorgon masks of bushrangers;

But the quarries are of more use than this,

Filled with the rolling of huge granite dice,

Ideas and judgments: vivisection, the Baptist Church,

Good men and bad men, polygamy, birth-control...

Frail tinkling rush

Water-hair streaming

Prickles and glitters

Cloudy with bristles

River of thought

Swimming the pebbles-

Undo, loosen your bubbles!

(in Heseltine, 1972: 146-147)

References

Auden, W. H. & Isherwood, C. 1973 [1939]. *Journey to a War.* London: Faber and Faber.

Firth, J. R. 1957 [1935]. The technique of Semantics, in *Papers in linguistics 1934-1951.* London: Oxford University Press.

Firth, J. R. , 1957 [1950]. Personality and language in society, in *Papers in linguistics 1934-1951.* London: Oxford University Press.

Hasan, R. 1989 [1985]. *Linguistics, Language and Verbal Art.* Oxford: Oxford University Press.

Heseltine, H. (ed.). 1972. *The Penguin Book of Australian Verse.* Ringwood: Penguin.

O'Toole, L. M. & Shukman, A. 1977. *Formalist Theory.* Russian Poetics in Translation, Volume 4. Oxford, England: Holden Books.

Steiner, P. 1984. *Russian Formalism: A Metapoetics.* Ithaca: Cornell University Press.

Striedter, J. 1989. *Literary Structure, Evolution and Value: Russian Formalism and Czech Structuralism Reconsidered.* Cambridge, Mass: Harvard University Press.

Slessor, K. 1988 [1944]. *Selected Poems.* Nth. Ryde, Aust.: Angus and Robertson.

Self at the Interface of Memory, Experience and Values: The Lexicogrammar and Semantics of Memory in (Auto) biographical Narrative

Abstract

Paul J. Thibault

Agder University College, Norway

This paper presents work I am currently undertaking towards an understanding of narrative discourse and its grounding in prior non-verbal perceptual and semiotic modalities for engaging with and responding to our experiences of the world. I argue that verbal narratives preserve traces of these prior forms, which have been re-contextualised in narrative texts by the semiotic resources of language. I propose that an understanding of how narrative discourse works can be enriched by the exploration of this interface between non-verbal and verbal semiotic modalities. In particular, I shall relate these questions to the question of memory and its recounting in narrative genres. The narration of remembered experience entails the interfacing of various systems on different levels. Cognitive, linguistic, and cultural factors interact and mutually constrain each other in the process of recounting personal experiences and episodes from one's past. Memory of past events and experiences is a long-term cognitive-semiotic process on a different time-scale than the narrative recall of such events and experiences in the here-now scale of their performance in the discursive act of their recall. What is the relation between these different time scales and how do the mental process verbs remember, recall, and so on mediate between these different time scales? What kind of more delicate grammar of remembering can be specified on this basis? These are some of the questions I shall address. At this stage, they are questions that remain without satisfactory answers in current state-of-the-art research.

In discussions of narrative as a discourse genre, the focus has often been on the relations between events and their representation in a narrative sequence. However, narrative is also vitally concerned with the **evaluation** of human experience. Narrative discourse, in this view, explores the motivational relevance of social agents' experiences of the world they live in and, hence, the implications for action of these experiences through the evaluations attributed to them by agents. There is an intimate semantic relationship between remembering and evaluation which will also be investigated and highlighted in my discussion.

I shall explore these questions using the systemic-functional theory of language with specific reference to the lexicogrammatical resources of projection, appraisal, and other interpersonal systems concerned with evaluation as well as the experiential grammar of the mental process verbs *remember*, *recall*, *forget*, and others that are in the same semantic area. I will focus on a few examples such as Helen Keller's autobiographical text *The Story of My Life* and John G. Fuller's *The Interrupted Journey* in order to suggest how narrative interfaces with the development in the individual of an autobiographical self, memory, and the individual's ability to act as an agent in the social world.

Blending and Beyond: Form and Feeling in Poetic Iconicity

Abstract

Margaret H. Freeman

Myrifield Institute for Cognition and the Arts, USA

One of the most important developments in human information processing in recent years has been the emergence of Gilles Fauconnier's and Mark Turner's Conceptual Integration Network theory, or "Blending", as it is more commonly known. Blending is a scientific model that captures and explains many apparently divergent phenomena, from talking donkeys to complex numbers. One of its most significant achievements is its contribution to the question of creativity, in the principled way in which it shows how new meaning can emerge from old information.

Blending, it should be noted, is a theory still in process (as all good theories are), and a great deal of research work is currently taking place to elaborate and extend blending's original formulation. In addition, much interesting work is taking place in applying blending principles to art in general and literary forms in particular. Two specific directions are my concern here: Per Aage Brandt's inclusion of dynamic schemas and situational context into the blending model, and Masako Hiraga's application of blending to explore in detail Charles Sanders Peirce's notion of image, diagram, and metaphor in creating iconicity. To these I would add the role of feeling, following Susanne K. Langer's argument that art is the semblance of felt life, that works of art are images of the forms of feeling.

Applying blending principles to poetry has two complementary results: it illuminates the processes of poetic composition and interpretation at the same time that it suggests ways in which blending may be further developed and refined. For example, one of the still outstanding problems in blending theory is what determines what gets selected for the various mappings across mental spaces to occur. The answer, I believe, lies in the voluminous research over the past century on the role of feeling in formulating thought, in initiating what psychiatrists call "value-driven selection". Form and feeling, or structure and affect, have long been recognized as particular attributes of poetic expression. They mirror the processes of composition and interpretation. That is, the writer experiences the feeling from which form emerges: feeling in sense creates form in sound. The reader experiences the form from which feeling emerges: form in sound creates feeling in sense. The literary scientist, by contrast, attempts to model the relation of form to feeling and feeling to form in the text itself. Poetry thus becomes a natural resource for exploring the relations between form and feeling. When these cohere to assign value to meaning, iconicity results.

The Shudder of the Dying Day in Every Blade of Grass

Abstract

John McRae

University of Nottingham, UK

This paper examines narratorial stance, together with the closely related question of the narrator's self-awareness and self-consciousness, in samples of first-person distanced narrative(i. e. after the event).

It goes beyond the basic point-of-view question of "who chose the adjectives?" It looks at how the reader is given signs that helps in the perception of who the narrator is or might be in terms of age, experience, and attitudes towards the story being narrated.

Moving from Victorian narration of childhood memory to post-colonial expressions of not dissimilar traumatic experiences, it looks at how the narrative voice is concealed or revealed, how memory is handled between narrative past and present, and how the adult voice(author and/or narrator) can be distinguished from the purported younger narrator.

Comparing and contrasting samples of three memory narratives it focuses on language awareness and text awareness as enabling approaches towards deeper reading.

Text-Worlds: The Way We
Think about the Way We Think

Abstract
Joanna Gavins
University of Sheffield, UK

Text World Theory is one of the most dynamic and original approaches to stylistic analysis to have emerged in the field over recent years. It is a cognitive model of human discourse processing which attempts to provide a fully context-sensitive account of our mental representations of language.

This paper tracks the evolution of Text World Theory, from its creation by the late Prof Paul Werth in the early 1990s, to more recent advances made through new applications, to different discourses, and from diverse perspectives. In particular, the paper explores the nature of our experience of literary worlds, investigating the conceptual means by which readers become immersed in a work of fiction.

Part II

Stylistics in China

1. Cognitive Stylistics

A Cognitive Revisit to *The Inheritors*

LIU Shisheng

Tsinghua University

1. William Golding and His Famous Novel, *The Inheritors*

William Golding (1911-1993) was a famous British novelist who won the Nobel Prize in Literature in 1983 "for his novels which, with the perspicuity of realistic narrative art and the diversity and universality of myth, illuminate the human condition in the world of today" (Nobel Foundation, 2006).

Owing to the importance of the author and his novels, there have been many critical writings about him and his works, and in particular about the novel *The Inheritors*, both literary and stylistic. From the stylistic side, two of the analyses are of greatest significance, one by M. A. K. Halliday (1971), a functional understanding, and the other by Elizabeth Black (1993), a rhetorical understanding. The present paper will first summarize these works and based on them, a cognitive understanding will be added to the critical tradition of the novel.

2. Transitivity, Intransitivity and the Linguistic System

M. A. K. Halliday's seminal analysis of the novel (1971) was done in the systemic functional approach and the result and impact of his research were profound. Halliday selected three passages from *The Inheritors*, labeled them A, B, C, and had a detailed analysis of its syntax. His hypothesis was that " In *The Inheritors*, the features that come to our attention are largely syntactic, and we are in the realm of syntactic imagery, where the syntax,... serve a vision of things... " (Halliday, 1971: 345). " [V] ision and subject matter are themselves as closely interwoven as they are in *The Inheritors*" (Halliday, 1971: 346). "The immediate thesis and the underlying theme come together in the syntax; the choice of subject matter is motivated by the deeper meaning, and the transitivity patterns realize both" (Halliday, 1971: 347).

Judging from the transitivity patterns used in the three passages, there are actually two grammars, the grammar of Language A for the Neanderthal man, the primitive people, and the grammar of Language C for the tribe, the new people.

The grammar of Language A features the use of intransitive verbs. Its clauses are mainly clauses of action, location or mental process. Almost all of the action clauses (19) describe simple movements (e. g. *turn*, *rise*, *hold*, *reach*, *throw forward*) and of these the majority (15) are intransitive. The typical pattern can be illustrated by the following two clauses,

The bushes twiched again, and Lok steadied by the tree.

Other examples include,

The man turned sideways in the bushes.

He rushed to the edge of the water.

A stick rose upright.

There were hooks in the bone.

[The bushes] waded out.

The picture is one that in which people act, but they do not act on things; they move but they only move themselves, not other objects (Halliday, 1971: 349). The entire transitivity structure of Language A can be summed up by saying that there is no cause and effect relationship there (Halliday, 1971: 353).

In striking contrast, the grammar of Language C features the use of tansitive verbs. The majority of the clauses in Passage C (48 out of 67) have a human subject; of these, more than half (25) are clauses of action, and most of these (19) are transitive. Judging from this language, the world of the "new people", i. e. the inheritors, is organized as our modern world is (Halliday, 1971: 356). For example,

They cannot follow us, I tell you. They cannot pass water.

Tuami glanced back at the gap through the mountain and saw that it was full of golden light and the sun was sitting in it.

Twal bent over Tanakil and kissed her and murmured to her.

They heard her huge, luxurious yawn and the bear skin was thrown off. She sat up, shook back her loose hair and looked first at Marlan then at Tuami.

Have we water? —but of course we have water! Did the women bring food? Did you bring food, Twal?

Twal lifted her face towards him and it was twisted with grief and hate.

They have given me back a changed Tuami. (Golding, 1955: 228-229)

Here we can see that transitivity is really the cornerstone of the semantic organization of experience, and it is at one level what *The Inheritors* is about. The theme of the entire novel, in a sense, is transitivity: man's interpretation of his experience of the world, his understanding of its processes and of his own participation in them. This is the motivation for Golding's syntactic originality; it is because of this that the syntax is effective as a mode of meaning (Halliday, 1971: 359).

3. Metaphor, Simile and the Thinking Pattern

Elizabeth Black's cognitive approach to the novel (1993) was done according to the experiential view in the cognitive stylistic approach.

For Black, *The Inheritors* is concerned with the activities of a people at the beginning of their linguistic development. Language is only one of the ways in which they communicate and certainly at the beginning of the novel, not the most important. One of the methods Golding exploits most consistently to overcome the difficulties of inadequate language is the use of metaphor and simile (Black, 1993: 37).

Metaphor is free to the extent that it is suggestive and inexplicit; in simile, the comparison is explicit. Research shows that far from being merely a poetic ornament, it is fundamental to the thought. It juxtaposes two entities without necessarily spelling out the connections between them (Black, 1993: 44).

The people are essentially passive and reliant on Oa, i. e. the principle of female production. They perceive parts of their own bodies as independent:

Lok's ears twitched in the moonlight so that the frost that lay along their upper edges shivered. Lok's ears spoke to Lok.

"?"

But Lok was asleep. (Golding, 1955: 43)

They do not distinguish sharply between animate and inanimate; thus

The bush went away and

A puddle of water lay across the trail

will be interpreted differently by the people in the novel and us as readers: they attribute volition to such entities but we do not. They place themselves on the same plane as trees or stones. This is closely linked to their passivity; it does not occur to them that they could make changes in their world. They do not share our sense of causality, and so tend to view events as discrete and unrelated. They are therefore slow to understand the menace of the new people and their weapons (Black, 1993: 38).

Golding uses metaphors to mediate between the people's world view and the reader's. The inanimate are treated as animate to reflect the people's world view. It is notable that this feature, which occurs in direct discourse, is also characteristic of the language of the narrator, so that descriptive passages are mimetic of the thinking patterns of the characters. The result is a discourse in which certain expressions, such as

The river had not gone away either or the mountains

must be interpreted as literally representing the perceptions of the people, whereas for us readers, they would normally have to be interpreted metaphorically. The reading effect for us readers is the juxtaposition of two mind styles. These two mind styles represent two incompatible world views. They are juxtaposed, but must be kept separate; the effect is similar to a bifocal vision. For example,

Lok's feet were clever. They saw. They throw him round the displayed roots of the beeches, leapt when a puddle of water lay across the trail. . . . his feet stabbed, . . . Now they could hear the river that lay parallel but hidden to their left. (Golding, 1955: 11)

We understand the real situation very well but we would not see and express ourselves in this way. For Lok, however, this was the truth. This bifocal vision can be illustrated with a very familiar picture by the Austrian philosopher Ludwig Wittgenstein(1889-1951).

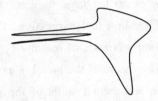

In this picture, some people may see it as a bird's head; others may see it as that of a rabbit. But both images reside in the same picture.

That is the linguistic feature or norm in the first part of *The Inheritors*. In the second part, there is a blend of our present day standard language and the linguistic norm established in the text.

The use of metaphor and simile in *The Inheritors* suggests that the people are not yet capable of developing complicated ideas because of their lack of sound logic and limited analytic abilities. When they make distinctions, a powerful tool for reasoning becomes available to them, i. e. metaphor and simile. Metaphor and simile are used to chart the development of Lok when he is forced by circumstance into leadership. In a crucial explanatory passage the narrator tells us:

> Lok discovered "Like". He had used likeness all his life without being aware of it. Fungi on trees were ears, the word was the same but acquired a distinction by circumstances that could never apply to the sensitive things on the side of his head. Now, in a convulsion of the understanding Lok found himself using likeness as a tool as surely as ever he had used a stone to hack at sticks or meat. (Golding, 1955: 194)

This makes a great step in Lok's intellectual development. The narrator shows the extent to which underlexicalization hampered Lok's thinking. "Like" is a tool which enables Lok to make explicit distinctions. "Like" permits the discrimination between similarity and identity. It is a step towards analysis. When Lok acquires this tool, he goes on to compare the new people to things he is familiar with, noting their menace, power, and sheer attractiveness by comparing them to a famished wolf, the waterfall, honey and Oa (Black, 1993: 45).

In *The Inheritors*, each metaphor possesses an immediate and local value in the creation and maintenance of the people's world view, enriching the texture of the novel. Golding's handling of his language suggests that compared to metaphor, simile has greater clarity of thought and expression. Therefore in *The Inheritors* simile is linked to more explicit processes of reasoning, and metaphor is associated with a less analytical state. The theme of the novel is expounded partly through the development of the linguistic and mental skills of the people. Underlexicalization and metaphor are shown to be inadequate from the development of analytical reasoning skills. With the acquisition of "like" as a tool, the people's capacity for thinking is enhanced (Black, 1993: 46-47).

4. Language, thought and Social Change

According to the theories of cognitive science, humankind recognizes things in terms of three major principles: prototypicality, figure and ground, and conceptual metaphor. Such linguistic terms as syntactical iconicity and word onomatopoeia are related to prototypicality; linguistic methods of comparison and contrast are related to figure and ground. Metaphor is associated with the rhetorical figure or trope in literary studies, grammatical metaphor in linguistics, and conceptual metaphor in cognitive studies. There are also three levels of representations for the recognition: the symbolic level, the conceptual level and the sub-conceptual level (Ungerer & Schmid, 2001). Let us take some linguistic examples to show the differences of these three representation levels.

Example 1 "stylistics" and its cognitive levels

The SUB-CONCEPTUAL Level: "stylistics" is a middle area of research between language and literature in terms of its subjects of study and between linguistics and criticism in terms of its theories and methods:

language   literature
                 stylistics
linguistics   criticism

The CONCEPTUAL Level: Stylistics is the study of "language and literature".

The SYMBOLIC Level: stylistics.

Example 2 "French kiss" and its cognitive levels

The SUB-CONCEPTUAL Level: put one's tongue into the other's mouth and keep maneuvering

The CONCEPTUAL Level: deep kiss/soul kiss

The SYMBOLIC Level: French kiss

The two languages in *The Inheritors* can be also analyzed as the above. Let us see Language A first.

Example 3 Language A and its cognitive level

The bushes twitched again. Lok steadied by the tree and gazed. A head and a chest faced him, half-hidden. There were white bone things behind the leaves and hair. The man had white bone things above his eyes and under the mouth so that his face was longer than a face should be. The man turned sideways in the bushes and looked at Lok along his shoulder. A stick rose upright and there was a lump of bone in the middle. Lok peered at the stick and the lump of bone and the small eyes in the bone things over the face. Suddenly Lok understood that the man was holding the stick out to him but neither he nor Lok could reach across the river. He would have laughed if it were not for the echo of the screaming in his head. The stick began to grow shorter at both ends. Then it shot out to full length again.

The dead tree by Lok's ear acquired a voice.

"Clop!"

His ears twitched and he turned to the tree. By his face there had grown a twig: a twig that smelt of other, and of goose, and of the bitter berries that Lok's stomach told him he must not eat. (Halliday, 1971: 360)

This is Language A and it is obvious that Lok uses metaphor to recognize the action of the new people's shooting at him and represents it at the SUB-CONCEPTUAL level of cognition. It is from the point of view of the primitive people.

Now let us see Language C in the following example.

Example 4 Language C and its cognitive level

The sail glowed red-brown. Tuami glanced back at the gap through the mountain and saw that it was full of golden light and the sun was sitting in it. As if they were obeying some signal the people began to stir, to sit up and look across the water at the green hills. Twal bent over Tanakil and kissed her and murmured to her. Tanakil's lips parted. Her voice was harsh and came from far away in the night.

"Liku!"

Tuami heard Marlan whisper to him from the mast.

"That is the devil's name. Only she may speak it. "

Now Vivany was really waking. They heard her huge, luxurious yawn and the bear skin was thrown off. She sat up, shook back her loose hair and looked first at Marlan then at Tuami. (Halliday, 1971: 362)

This language is obviously at the CONCEPTUAL level of cognition. It is from the point of view of the new people.

At the SYMBOLIC level, from the point of view of the author, William Golding was using the two stages of human cognition to indicate the importance of social change. All people in the novel adapt themselves to the new change of environment and society, either willingly or forced to, except Lok who always stick to his own way of doing and thinking. And the result is his final isolation and substitution by the new people.

To my understanding, *The Inheritors* does not only mean the physical substitution of the primitive people by the new people; it is also a symbolic account of the two intellectual stages of human cognition. This symbolic meaning has permanent values: those who are not willing to adapt themselves to the new changes of environment and society, will sooner or later die out.

Let us see similar examples from the some real estate advertisement.

Example 5 Room to sit in and have a rest(*Beijing Youth Daily* , April 12 , 2006)

This example and the following two, Examples 6 and 7, were respectively taken from *Beijing Youth Daily*, April 12, April 25 and June 8, 2006. To my understanding, these real estate advertisements indicate the changes of ideology in architecture. The world is always changing and people's requirements for room building are also following the suit.

Example 5 indicates that the original purpose of building a room was to let people sit in and have a rest.

Examples 6 Room for bargain in business(*Beijing Youth Daily*, April 25, 2006)

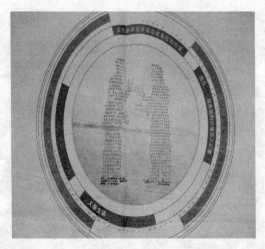

Example 6 indicates that gradually, the purpose of building the room is to let people stand in and argue and bargain in business and trade.

In Example 7, we can see that the room is open and the walls are filled with English letters. With the development of globalization, English is becoming an international language and the room becomes the place for international exchange and cultural communication.

Example 7 Room for international exchange and cultural communication (*Beijing Youth Daily*, June 8, 2006)

At the fierce competition market of room building, building companies and the real estate agencies representing them must follow this change as well. Otherwise, their business will not do well. Here we can see the application of Golding's symbolic meaning in *The Inheritors*: those who are not willing to adapt themselves to the new changes of environment and society, will sooner or later die out.

References

Black, E. 1993. Metaphor, simile and cognition in Golding's *The Inheritors*, *Language and Literature*, 2(1).

Chatman, S. (ed.) 1971. *Literary Style: A Symposium*. New York: Oxford University Press.

Golding, W. 1955. *The Inheritors*. London: Faber and Faber Ltd.

Halliday, M. A. K. 1971. Linguistic function and literary style: An inquiry into the language of William Golding's *The Inheritors*. In *Literary Style: A Symposium*, ed. by S. Chatman. New York: Oxford University Press.

Lan, C. 2005. *Studies of Cognitive Linguistics and Metaphor*. Beijing: Foreign Language Teaching and Research Press.

Liu, S. S. & Zhu, R. Q. 2006. *An Introduction to Stylistics*. Beijing: Peking University Press.

Ungerer, E. & Schmid, H. J. 2001. *An Introduction to Cognitive Linguistics*. Beijing: Foreign Language Teaching and Research Press.

A Cognitive Approach to the Mind Style of Forrest Gump

CAO Jinmei

Shijiazhuang College

1. Introduction

Forrest Gump by Winston Groom is a bildungsroman. In this remarkable comic odyssey, Gump is fashioned into a lovable, Herculean, and surprisingly savvy hero. His IQ is only about 70 and he is repeatedly ridiculed as an idiot. He is put into awkward situations again and again, but he goes to success step by step. After accidentally becoming the star of University of Alabama's football team, Gump goes on to become a Vietnam War hero, a world-class Ping-Pong player, a villainous wrestler, and a business tycoon. The intellectual defect, abominable living conditions and weird experiences help form his unusual viewpoint and way of thinking, that is to say, his particular mind style which is projected on his language. The metaphors, similes, analogies and some other expressions are typically Gump's and they help form the rollicking, bawdy, madcap and sarcastic way of thinking and narrative.

Mind style is a very important concept in stylistics. It refers to the cognitive status reflected in linguistic form. The concept is first put forward by Fowler and is further developed and perfected by such scholars as Leech & Short (2001), Semino & Swindlehurst (1996), and Semino (2002). In the early studies, Fowler and Leech & Short have set up a linguistic-based model and isolated a range of linguistic phenomena that can contribute to the projection of mind style, including choice of vocabulary, grammar, and transitivity. To arrive at conclusions about the minds of characters and narrators, the more recent analyses relate linguistic patterns to cognitive theories, because the ultimate aim of cognitive sciences is to probe into the mind and cognition of human beings. Compared with the linguistic way, the cognitive stylistic approach, in a sense, is more suitable for analyzing mind style, because mind style itself is cognitive and it pays more attention to the interior relation of a text. So it will certainly play a role in grasping the psychology of the characters and help understand the work and characters. In the following article I will try to explore the mind style of Forrest Gump by using the cognitive theories such as schema theory, metaphor theory and blending theory.

2. Schema Theory and the Mind Style of Forrest Gump

All human beings possess categorical rules or scripts that they use to interpret the world. In cognitive linguistics these rules and scripts are called schema or schemata. Schema is the structured portion of background knowledge relating to a particular aspect of reality (Bartlett, 1995; Schank & Abelson, 1977; Schank, 1982; Eysenck & Keane, 2000). Each individual has his unique schema because the schema depends on his or her experiences and cognitive processes. Gump is born as an idiot and treated as an idiot, so the script of idiot has become an indispensable part of his cognition. Gump is a conscious idiot and he never tries to conceal his thought about his idiocy and the life of being an idiot. The sentences relating to this topic can be found everywhere. At the beginning of the novel, there are several paragraphs dealing with the topic of idiot including the summing-up of being an idiot and the reconsideration of his position in the domain of idiots. Gump is honest about his idiocy but he considers that he is "probly a lot brighter than folks think". He ascribes this to "what goes on in my mind is a sight different than what folks see" (p. 9). Once a schema is activated, it drives further processing. And along with the processing, Gump's unique mind style is revealed.

In the process of perception, Gump's schema of idiot has formed and in return it greatly influences his further perception of the world. It is very evident that Gump narrates his adventure from the standpoint of an idiot and during the narration he makes a lot of blunt and caustic comments on the things he encounters. These characteristic comments afford clear clues to Gump's particular way of thinking, in another word, his mind style. At the very beginning, Gump wantonly blazons forth his ignorance and naivety and builds up his image of an idiot and the idiot's angle of view. He alleges that the only thing he does know is about idiots and to him the idiots in literary works are "always smarter than people give em credit for" (p. 10). The intentional simper "Hee, hee" he utters at the end of the comment helps consolidate his idiocy. The idiot schema is thus activated and then it generates a lot of expectations and inferences. Gump makes some judgments on the things he experiences based on this schema. Through these seemingly nonsensical discussions we can clearly sense his strong discontentment and sharp satire.

The first thing he touches is his primary education in the nut school. The purpose of the school is only to prevent them from running around loose. They are only shown "how to read street signs an thing like the difference between the Men's an the Ladies' rooms" (p. 12-13). Even an idiot like him knows that education means teaching some knowledge and the education they get is not education at all. How about the so-called normal people? "Even I could understand that" seemingly is the admission of his slowness but in fact it is a solemn and just condemnation of the hypocritical education system. Gump's discussion about his football career is also very meaningful. He knows nothing about football and the reason for his being chosen is only his stature and weight. The coach is utterly excited at his running speed when being chased. Gump cannot understand his spoffish reaction to that because he thinks it is only the instinct of people. His scorn is clearly shown in the sentence "What idiot wouldn't?" (p. 18) After he enters college, Gump hasn't made any advancement in understanding the matter. What he can understand about the deployment of Coach Bryant is only that "this man mean bidness" (p. 29).

The college life is no less preposterous than that in the nut school. The first representative thing is the confrontation between Gump and Curtis. Gump is excluded from the beginning and he cannot understand Curtis because "everything he say got so many cusswords" (p. 33). Their collision culminates in the "car" affair. Gump who is taken as an idiot offers a suggestion when Curtis cannot find a way out. Curtis is hurt by Gump's cleverness and queries how he can figure that out. Gump retorts with "Maybe I am an idiot, but at least I ain't stupid" (p. 33). Compared with the former ones, this self-identification, being triggered by the adverb "maybe", is less firm. But the power of irony is greatly enhanced by the negation of stupidity. This is an overt attack against the alleged clever people and their self-righteousness and insipience are incisively ridiculed.

Thereafter Gump is put into amazing situations again and again. In these historic but farcical events, his idiocy has not become a barrier to his success but helps a lot. After he becomes a Vietnam War hero, Gump is chosen to participate in the Ping-Pong diplomacy with China. The significance of the event is pre-emphasized and he is told that it might make the future of the human race at stake.

The lack of diplomacy schema leads to Gump's misconception so he takes the information literally, "I am jus a po ole idiot, an now I have got the whole human race to look after" (p. 86). Gump uses the idiot schema once again to expose his thinking. But the establishment of new relationships between the input elements makes Gump recognize himself. He injects great self-sympathy and self-pity in the utterance, which protrudes the sharp contrast between his negligibility and the signality of the task. The satire on the absurdity of the policy is intensified by the bitterness and poignancy in tone.

The idiot schema is the product of Gump's experience and in turn it helps him to perceive the new experience. In another word, the schema has become a standard for him to make judgments and a tool for him to express his opinions. Vietnam War is one of Gump's most painful remembrances because in it he suffers a lot and even losses his best friend Bubba. His hatred for the war can be found in many parts of the narration. When he goes to find Jenny with his Army Uniform, he immediately becomes the target of people's chiacking. "I am beginning to feel like a idiot again" (p. 96). Gump never feels shameful for being an idiot but this time he really senses the humiliation of being an army man. The uniform and the title of War Hero become a stigma rather than honor. Another more direct expression is in his talk with Bubba's father. When he is asked about the aim and function of the war, Gump says, "Look, I'm jus a idiot, see" (p. 213). The idiocy becomes an excuse for him to evade the question, but this fake concession greatly stresses the following transition. The opinion that the war is only "a bunch of shit" becomes clear and powerful. Another most scathing criticism is on the election system. The reason for him to be chosen to run for the Senate is just his idiocy and he is regarded as "salt of the earth" for that. The speech written for Gump's candidacy isn't very long and "don't make much sense". Here Gump straightforwardly points his criticism at the blindness and absurdity of the election. After that he once again activates his idiot schema to accentuate the satire. "… but what do I know? I am jus a idiot" (p. 224). His ignorance serves as a foil to the so-called knowledgeability of the normal people, and in reverse the self-mockery makes the exposure of the emptiness and meaninglessness of the election more profound.

Up to now I have analyzed how Gump uses the idiot schema to interpret his experiences and express his opinions. We have known that schema is the structured portion of background knowledge and it can be reflected in text structures(Halliday & Hassan, 1989). The typical examples are overlexicalization and underlexicalization. Overlexicalization is the result of the solidification of a schema and a person's specific attention while underlexicalization is the product of lack of schema. Besides the function of interpreting the world I have mentioned, schema can also be used to predict situations. When facing a novel experience, a person will start his existed schema to make some inferences and prediction. The processing of new information depends on how it fits into the schema. The more fit, the easier to predict. But the lack of the schema or schemata that are most relevant to the processing of a particular stimulus can lead to failures or errors in comprehension. Sometimes "schema refreshment" (Cook, 1994; Semino, 1995, 1997)occurs, that is to say, the new experience triggers the process of constructing a new schema.

In the novel there is a scene about the appointment between Gump and Jenny in a cinema. Gump is excited at the killing and shooting in the film and bursts laughter now and then. Jenny feels so humiliated at his fuss and stupidity that she tries to hide herself by scrunching down in the seat. The lack of embarrassment schema hinders Gump from correctly understanding the situation, so he makes a wrong prediction that she "felled out of her seat". Once the falling-down schema has been triggered, it begins to play a role in Gump's reaction and behavior. Gump tries to lift her up from the ground, but unfortunately he tears her dress open. This time the humiliation schema malfunctions once again. He wants to cover her up with his hand, but the avoidance of one embarrassment causes a greater humiliation. Jenny starts making noises and flails about wild-like. The new schema continues to function and it leaves little room for the humiliation schema. Till a fellow is attracted by the commotion, Gump still does not forget to hold onto her "so's she don't fall down again or come undone". The lack of schema and the schema refreshment in this case more directly reveal Gump's personality and mind style. On the one hand, Gump is ignorant and stupid, but on the other hand, he is naive, pure, lovely and warm-hearted. But he is far from immaculate because there are still many nasty things in his schema. In the narration, Gump reveals his shabbiness over and over again. The woman teacher who teaches them how to read is the first target for him to show the other side of himself, "She was real nice and pretty and more'n once or twice I had nasty thoughts about her" (p. 16). The low

IQ hasn't influenced Gump's EQ (emotion quotient). His first love is early awakened and the things between woman and man have indistinctly come into his schema. Thereafter he uses the script here and there either frankly or vaguely, which makes the narration bawdy and absurd. But at the same time, the figure of Gump becomes true to life and full.

Besides the ones I have mentioned, some other schemata can also provide clues for the peculiarity of Gump's mind style. Among them, the army schema is a very striking one. To understand this new group, Gump fully mobilizes his existed knowledge. On the basis of comparison with the men he meets before, Gump forms his own understanding of the army. "them people in the Army yell longer an louder an nastier than anybody else. They is never happy. An furthermore, they do not complain that you is dumb or stupid like coaches do—they is more interested in your private parts or bowel movements, an so always precede they yellin with something like "dickhead" or "asshole" (p. 49). The loud yelling, the nasty words, the rude attitude, and the special interest constitute Gump's army schema, which is totally different from the accepted orderly and disciplined army image. In this particular inference Gump expresses his extreme contempt for the US army. He directly points at its shabbiness, dirtiness, coarseness and rudeness. The war experience in Vietnam enriches Gump's army schema. From the beginning to the end, the army acts with great blindness and all the things are desultory and chaotic. Now let us have a look at how Gump comments on the situation of Charlie Company. "It is getting to be dusk an we is tole to go up a ridge an relieve Charlie Company which is either pinned down by the gooks or has got the hooks pinned down, depending on whether you get your news from the Stars and Strips or just looking around at what the hell is goin on" (p. 58). Here Gump saw some other elements of the army—hypocrisy and effrontery. To boast its achievement and to dust people's eyes, the army does not hesitate to tell lies and call white black. As an important part of the army, those officials have not left good impressions on Gump either, "Most of the lieutenants I knowed was bout as simple-minded as me" (p. 69). Along with the self-deprecation, Gump shows no mercy to the army officials. In his eyes, they are at the same intellectual level with himself, in another word, they are no cleverer than an idiot. Here Gump relentlessly sneers at the shallowness and stupidity of the army officials.

The research institutions and government offices in the common people's mind should have the precise style and good attainment, but to Gump they present another view and in his schema there are more traces of facetiosity and frivolousness. Now let us have a look at the American NASA. From the very start, everything related to it seems weird and rough-and-tumble. First, Gump is escorted to the NASA as an experimental sample from a loony bin. Then this idiot, a woman and an ape form the troop for such a serious task. Another ludicrous thing is that the only experienced member is the ape. Even more derisible is that in confusion the officials wrongly put another ape rather than Sue in the spaceship. The random selection, the odd combination, and the chaotic procedure help form Gump's research institution schema which is frivolous and irresponsible. Besides these features, NASA is also hypocritical and deceptive which can be seen from their attitude toward mistakes. When Fritch and Gump point out their mistakes, they react indifferently and refuse to make a correction. Instead, they order the crew to keep the secret. The officials' selfishness and inhumanity are clearly shown. In addition, the work efficiency of NASA is rather low and it takes them nearly four years to search out the endangered crew. The meeting with the rescuer is as much dramatic and burlesque. The guy goes right up to old Sue and calls him Mister Gump. He is so dippy that he cannot distinguish a man from an ape! Up to now, another element—insobriety, is added to Gump's institute schema.

3. Cognitive Metaphor Theory and the Mind Style of Forrest Gump

To the cognitive linguists and contemporary metaphor theorists, the metaphor is not just fancy rhetoric as has been regarded by the traditional theorists, but it is primarily cognitive. As an important tool for thought, reasoning and action, metaphor is a mapping from an experiential domain (source domain) to a target domain (see Figure 3. 1). Metaphor is realised through linguistic instantiations (Lakoff & Johnson, 1980; Lakoff & Turner, 1989; Lakoff, 1993). So it is safe to say that metaphor involves both conceptual mappings and individual linguistic expressions. To make the definitions clearer, the theorists usually use *metaphor* to refer to *a cross-domain mapping in the conceptual system and metaphorical expression refers to a linguistic expression that is the surface realization of such a cross-domain mapping*. In the following analysis, I will also follow this distinction.

SOURCE ———————➤	TARGET
superordinate category based on basic level categories general classes image schemas/gestalts (basic bodily experiences)	

Figure 3.1

Many researchers' studies have shown that the cognitive metaphor theory can account for the role of linguistic metaphorical expressions in the creation of mind style (Semino & Swindlhurst, 1996; Semino, 2002). Generally speaking, the conventional uses of metaphor reflect the worldview that is shared by the members of the same linguistic community. While the creative uses of metaphor provide novel perspectives on reality, either by means of original linguistic realizations of conventional metaphors, or by means of entirely novel conceptual mappings (Semino, 2002: 108). Because of the personal conditions and special experiences, Forrest Gump forms his particular mind style, which also can be seen from the metaphorical expressions he uses in the narration.

Many of the metaphorical expressions discussed in literature on conventional metaphor are idioms. Within cognitive linguistics, idioms arise automatically and they fit one or more patterns present in the conceptual system. When idioms have associated conventional images, it is common for an independently motivated conceptual metaphor to map that knowledge from the source to the target domain. Idioms, as fixed metaphors, show the cognitive state of a linguistic community, but if they are originally or systematically used by an individual, they can be said to reflect an idiosyncratic cognitive habit or a particular mind style. In relating his stories, Gump uses a large number of idioms that have lively images. As shown in Figure 3.2 and Figure 3.3, they are either concerning body and life or concerning animals and objects. When a person's mind is restricted for one reason or another, he or she usually shows more interest in the things he or she is most familiar with. To an idiot like Gump, the things closely connected with him easily become the focus of his attention and further influence the construction of his conceptual system. The basic image schema of "body" becomes the starting point for Gump to interpret the things he encounters. And in his narration, there are many creatively

103

used conventional metaphors drawn from the source domain of body. For instance, he thinks the purpose of the nut school is only to "keep us out of everbody else's hair" which is the opposite linguistic realization of the conventional metaphor "get in sb's hair". The conventional metaphor "get in sb's hair" means "be a burden or annoy sb". The existence of the conventional image helps bridge the source domain and the target domain and make the criticism on the deceptious education have a definite object in view. Except this example, most of the other metaphors concerning body are the mechanical application of the existed idioms such as "armed to the teeth" and "get fed up" and so on. But this doesn't influence their originality because Gump goes rather deep into the source domain of body and has unconsciously made it form a system. The parts concerning the substantial body go from the whole body as shown in "pull oneself together" and "an so hot" to the separate parts like hair, tooth, head, stomach, face, foot, toes, and fingers. In addition, Gump slightly touches upon the intellectual part in "out of one's wits". And there is also the extension to the abstract life and the clothing in "for dear life" and "with sb's pants down" (See Figure 3.2).

Parts concerned	Idioms used by Gump	Meanings of the idioms
body	pull oneself together	regain one's composure
	not so hot	not as expected
hair	keep out of sb's hair	avoid making others annoyed
	hide nor hair	trace or trail
tooth	armed to the teeth	having many weapons
head	lose one's head	become confused
	get the big head	be vainglorious
stomach	get fed up	be bored
	stomach turns flip-flops	be on wings
face	get all red in face	turn red
foot	take a load off one's feet	have a rest
	get off on the right foot	be favoring at the beginning
toes	keep one's toes	be scary or watchful
finger	give sb. the finger	insult sb.
wits	out of one's wits	at a loss
pants	with sb's pants down	be in an embarrassed situation
life	for dear life	desperately, urgently

Figure 3.2

Through their analysis, Semino and Swindlehurst have proved that at an individual level, the systematic use of a particular metaphor or metaphors reflects a personal way of perceiving the world (Semino & Swindlehurst, 1996: 147). Gump is a man with some intellectual problem and most of the time his observations on the surrounding world are proceeding from his instincts. The systematic use of body metaphor is just the reflection of the primitivity of his mind style. But according to my understanding, such idioms still have another important function, that is, they form a series of concrete images which greatly enhance the expressive power of language and the transmission of thought. For example, in the rescue of the Charlie Company, a bullet hits Bone in the head. Gump describes him in this way, "He lyin on the ground, han still holdin to the gun for dear life" (p. 62). Bone has been dead and life has become an impossible thing. The use of an idiom with "life" stands out the contrast between life and death. Afterward, Gump intentionally takes the word "life" literally and adds a non-finite attributive clause "which he does not have any more of now", which constructs a humorous atmosphere. But in this seemingly light-hearted tone Gump's abhorrence of war is expressed.

As idioms, most of metaphorical expressions concerning animals and objects are popularly used such as "count one's chicken before they are hatched", "rain cats and dogs", "take off" and etc (See Figure 3. 3). But the large number of them has formed a system in Gump's narration which further promote the characterization of him. Because of the improper treatment he gets from the childhood on, Gump has formed a deep-rooted idea that the human world is no better than the animal world and material world. At the same time, he feels much more intimate with these two non-human worlds which can be better illustrated by his friendship with the ape Sue. So it is not surprising that he likes to use idioms with the images of animals and objects to present his opinions about himself and the things he experiences. For example, when he talks about his awkward situation, he usually uses "be in the doghouse". This kind of assimilations to animals or objects is very meaningful. On the one hand, it shows Gump's particular way of thinking; on the other hand, it gives prominence to Gump's emotional inclination and strengthens the exposure of the social absurdity.

	Idioms used by Gump	Meanings of the idioms
animals	in the doghouse	in great dishonor or trouble
	count one's chicken before they are hatched	be happy too early
	turn tail	escape
	rain cats and dogs	rain heavily
objects	take off	leave
	up the creek	in a difficult position
	smell ripe	be foul
	vanish into the thin air	disappear
	in the cards	certain to happen
	in the dumps	in dismay
	out of frying pan and into the fire	go from bad to worse
	get weenies to roast	have things to do
	get a day to kill	have a day's time
	rain buckets	rain heavily

Figure 3. 3

Other than the conventional uses of metaphor, there are still a striking number of novel metaphors. Gump's metaphorical expressions to do with food are the realization of an idiosyncratic conceptual metaphor. Gump starts to construct the FOOD metaphor from the very beginning of the novel. Most people are very familiar with the metaphor "life is a box of chocolates" appearing in the movie. But in the novel it is a totally different metaphor: "Let me say this: bein a idiot is no box of chocolates" (p. 9). This is the generalization of Gump's understanding of his life, and also a commanding metaphor in the whole narrative. We all know that chocolates are fragrant and sweet and are the symbols of romance, tenderness and love. But the life unfolds another view for Gump. There are only bitterness, indifference and maltreatment. In the mismatching between the source domain and the target domain, the essence of life is revealed. Food is the most fundamental image schema of all animals including human beings. Gump, because of his idiocy, has much deeper feelings and receptivity for food so that food and the things relating to food have become a solid base for him to make sense of the world. He uses "it still ain't no piece of cake" (p. 24) to comment on the difficulty of the Army test. He uses "two tons of Nebraska corn jackoff beef" (p. 45) to refer to the rival football players who fall on him. The jumbled expression of his thought is "jello" (p. 9). His father is squashed into "a pancake" (p. 11). The football players jam into the bus like "flapjacks" (p. 29). Curtis and himself have the "eggplant" (p. 30) brain. Curtis has a "yeller squash" nose (p. 30) and an "icebox" build (p. 31). Figuring out the equations is easy as "pie" (p. 34). The wounded soldier is carried like a "flour sack" (p. 62). The black markers for landing zone are like "cooking pots" (p. 127). When shocked, people's eyes turn to "biscuits" (p. 67) or "saucers" (p. 129). When angry or excited, their faces are red as "beet" (p. 199) or "tomato" (p. 206). Gump is looking at the world from the viewpoint of an idiot and the FOOD metaphor is the inevitable outcome of this particular mind style. At the same time, the vivid images in the metaphorical expressions make the narration humorous and comic.

4. Blending Theory and the Mind Style of Forrest Gump

In the former two sections, I have explored the mind style of Forrest Gump by using schema theory and metaphor theory. In this part I will continue to penetrate into this matter from the point of view of blending theory. Conceptual blending, also called conceptual integration, is a general cognitive process proposed recently by Fauconnier and Turner. The blending processes mainly proceed via the establishment and exploitation of mappings and the activation of background knowledge (Fauconnier, 1997; Fauconnier & Turner, 1996; Turner & Fauconnier, 2000). In the operations, four mental spaces are involved. "Mental spaces are small conceptual packets constructed as we think and talk, for purposes of local understanding and action. They are interconnected, and can be modified as thought and discourse unfold" (Fauconnier & Turner, 1996: 113). "These spaces include two "input' spaces (which, in a metaphorical case, are associated with the source and target of CMT [conceptual metaphor theory]), plus a "generic' space, representing conceptual structure that is shared by both inputs, and the "blend' space, where material from the inputs combine and interacts" (Grady et al. , 1999: 103) (See Figure 4. 1).

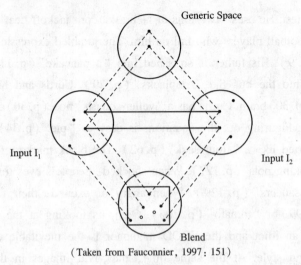

(Taken from Fauconnier, 1997: 151)

Figure 4.1

Conceptual blending, as a theoretical framework for exploring information integration, aims to account for the online construction of meaning (Fauconnier & Turner, 1998, 2002). In this model, the understanding of meaning involves the construction of blended cognitive models that include some structure from multiple input models, as well as emergent structure that arises through the processes of blending. Up to now, the theory has been argued to be involved in a broad range of cognitive and linguistic phenomena, including metaphor, analogy, counterfactuals, nominal compounds, and even the comprehension of grammatical constructions (Coulson & Oakley, 2000; Fauconnier & Turner, 1998).

Analogy and metaphor both crucially depends on the cross-mapping between two inputs, which makes them prime candidates for the construction of blends. In Gump's narration, the analogical and metaphorical expressions are very abundant, which in a sense shows his particular way of thinking. In this portion, I will focus on these kinds of expressions. First, let us have a look at the expressions concerning with other kind of life-forms. His mother talks to him in a way of talking to "a dog or cat" (p. 11). Coach Feller is irritated and flails his arms like "hornets is upon him" (p. 31). People watch him like he is "a bug" when he played the harmonica in a medical class (p. 41). His thirst makes him drink like a "dog" (p. 42). Snake's eyes are wild as a "tigers" (p. 45). Coach Bryant pats him on the head like patting a "dog" (p. 45). Scared by the explosions, soldiers all press on the ground like "worms" (p. 56) and they lead an "animal" (p. 64) life in the jungle. The situation of encountering gooks is similar to stepping on an "anthill" (p. 65). Gump has "rhinoceros" (p. 70) skin in the doctor's eyes. Gump flags his arms like "ducks' wings" (p. 88) to indicate "Peking Duck". The Club girls' hair looks like "a bird gonna fly out of it" (p. 95). Gump and Fritch were hung like "bats" (p. 143) by pygmies and then were carried off like "pigs" (p. 144). The audience of the rassle grunt and strain like "a dog tryin to shit a peach seed" (p. 160). The Turd escapes from Gump's hands like an "eel" (p. 169). Raquel Welch is angry and looks like "a hornet" (p. 194). As said before, blending operates on two input mental spaces. The domain of animals or insects and the domain of persons are the two input mental spaces in the above expressions. Partial structure of the input spaces is inherited and the blend space is yielded. Gump blends the features of animals or insects with himself and persons surrounding him and in the process he creates the new images of people which is the combination of the two species. On the one hand, this blending is an inevitable reflection of his simple-mindedness, but on the other hand, Gump pours ridicule on the people he encounters. His sensitive and caustic character is clearly shown.

Besides the blending of animals and insects with people, Gump also blends people's behavior or appearance with the states of objects. He blends an idiot's shaking with the electric chair (p. 12), the hanging of his tongue with a necktie (p. 31), Bryant's looking in the distance with looking to the moon (p. 32), his body with harmonica (p. 38), his happiness with heaven (p. 40), their military training with robots (p. 54), the soldiers with a cotton baler (p. 56), people's face with death (p. 67), Kranz with a canon (p. 68), his fart with a buzz saw (p. 93), Jenny with a telephone switchboard (p. 96), Rudolph's hair with a dustmop (p. 98), his playing the harmonica with heaven (p. 99), his costume with a diaper (p. 105), Gump, Sue and Fritch with corks (p. 125), his spinning with a top (p. 125), the Professor's bounding off the ropes with a slingshot ball (p. 180), his wrapping with a mummy (p. 181), the heart beating with a drum (p. 206). Gump also blends different objects in the source domain and target domain together. He blends the ball with a goldbrick (p. 22), the taste of drinking with hot socks (p. 42), the jungle with bonfire brush (p. 61), the hospital with a torture chamber (p. 69), the river with sewer water (p. 90), the heath with a march or a filed (p.

104), Sue's jaws with wind-up teeth (p. 123), chair with a throne(p. 131), room with a tomb (p. 206). There are also large amount of blending of the past experiences with the present situations. He blends the escort with the police in the movies (p. 14), the principal with the nut school(p. 14), Jenny's screaming and flailing with the picture show(p. 43), the burden on himself with the bananas on his father (p. 45), the sergeant's frightened look with an automobile wreck (p. 52), people's friendliness with a touchdown (p. 63), the officer's questioning with Johnny Carson show(p. 116), the coon's hair with the Shakespeare play(p. 129). To express his ideas much clearer, Gump also uses the blending of different types of persons. He blends himself with a maniac(p. 24), a Marsman(p. 27), a holdup man(p. 42), spaceman(p. 130) and a lawyer(p. 223). He blends Coach Bryant with the Great Gawd Bud(p. 31), the dishwasher guy with a Rocket Man (p. 52), the kids in the club with geeks at a sideshow (p. 95), Rudolph with a guru and the Pope(p. 98), Ape with a baby(p. 123), the coon with an Arab(p. 129), the new president with Pinocchio(p. 148), the Professor with a magician (p. 181), Mister Felder with a wildman(p. 196), Honest Ivan with Muhammad Ali (p. 204). In the process of the above blending, Gump successfully matches the basic image schemata or bodily experiences with the target domain. The analogical or metaphorical expressions engendered in the blending make clear Gump's profuse imagination and keen discernment. These unique mappings add vulgarity to Gump's language and at the same time make his expressions more humorous and penetrating.

Expressions Concerning "Ass"	Meaning of the Expressions
ass around	enjoy
get/haul/move ass(out of)	leave, escape
turn the ass loose	run as much as one likes
shut the ass(up)	shut up
kick/whip one's ass	triumph over
make an ass(out)of	behave stupidly
you bet your ass	you bet
wash one's hands of sb's ass	turn one's back upon
put one's ass in a fix	be concerned
get one's ass in hot water	be in trouble
have one's ass	give sb. a lesson
stop one's ass cold	block up
work one's ass off	work hard
bite someone on the ass	make love with

Figure 4. 2

Because of the idiocy and poor education, Gump is not an urbane person, which can be seen from his coarse wording in the narration. Such indelicate words as "shit", "damn", "pee", "bastard", "crap", "butt", "fuck", "hell" and so on are so pervasive that they help form a rollicking and bawdy style. Take "shit" as an example, besides the basic meaning of "excrement", Gump either uses it as a noun referring to the disgusting, unacceptable or foolish things, persons or words, or uses it as a verb referring to empting wastes from the bowels, or uses it as an interjection showing annoyance, or blends it with some affix or another word to form a new word such as "shitty", "bullshit", "shithouse", and etc., or blends it with another expression to form a new expression such as "shit on", "and shit", "give a shit", "when the shit hits the fan", "be worth a shit", "get the shit beat of" and so on.

Another more typical example is the use of "ass". Ass is a private part of human body, besides the basic meaning Gump uses it metonymically again and again to refer to a person. The most interesting example is the blend of "ass" with "mouth", in which a new meaning "ask" is coined. Other than these, there are quite a lot of creative expressions rooted in the source domain "ass" such as "ass around", "get/haul/move ass(out of)", "turn the ass loose", "shut the ass", "kick/whip one's ass", "make an ass(out of)", "you bet your ass", "wash one's hands of sb's ass", "put one's ass in a fix", "get one's ass in hot water", "have one's ass", "stop one's ass cold", "work one's ass off", "bite sb. on the ass" and so on (See Figure 4. 2). The expressions with "hell" are also very striking. Gump either uses it as an intensive to show emphasis, or uses it as an interjection to express anger, impatience or disgust, or blends it with other domains to form new expressions such as "to/the hell with", "one/a hell of a", "what the hell", "all hell broke/was let loose", "get the hell out of", "like hell" and the like. Besides the words and expressions mentioned above, Gump also uses many ungenteel words relating to private parts or excreta such as "crap", "butt", "pee", and "turd". Gump either uses them literally to add absurdity or uses them figuratively to show strong emotions. Moreover, many execratory words are used such as "bastid"(bastard), "damn", "damned", "Goddamn", "fuck", "sumbitch"(son of a bitch) and so forth. Gump is a sensitive and acid-tongued idiot. The coarse and slangy language on the one hand is the reflection of his social status and degree of education, but on the other hand it is the certain outcome of his sharp mind. To him, the world is full of absurdity, so he tries every means to poke fun at the things and persons he meets. Here the rollicking, bawdy and absurd language becomes a powerful weapon for him to mock and taunt the ridiculous society.

5. Conclusion

Generally speaking, the ultimate aim of linguistics is to probe into the mind and cognition of human beings through the observation and analysis of language. The occurrence and development of the cognitive sciences especially cognitive linguistics turn to be helpful and efficient in such explorations. Schema is the structured knowledge of a person formed in the process of perception and also the gauge for a new conceptualization. Gump has formed many schemata with his own traits. Among them, the idiot schema is the most prominent one which permeates the whole narration. Gump does not only use it to talk about himself but also uses it as a standard to judge the things and persons he meets. In addition, the army schema and the institution schema also offer clues for us to see what is going on in Gump's mind. According to cognitive linguists, the conceptual networks of human beings are intricately structured by analogical and metaphorical mappings. Gump has formed his unique metaphors, similes and analogies because of the mental conditions and personal experiences. And most of them are concerning life, body, animals, and food which indicates the primitivity of his mind. Apart from these, Gump also coined quite a lot of expressions by blending different structures. He has made a series of expressions concerning animals, insects and objects to talk about people. There are also many of them concerning his past experiences. The expressions consisting of ungenteel words such as "ass", "butt", "shit" and "damn" are also abundant. It is safe to say that these schemata, metaphors, analogies and expressions reflect Gump's mind style. In the process of analysis, the simple-mindedness, naivety, and loveliness of Gump stand out. At the same time, his thinking is brought near to us. The understanding of Gump's comic language, on-target humor, and biting satire becomes easier and the theme of revealing the absurd society becomes evident.

References

Bartlett, F. C. 1995. *Remembering: A Study in Experimental and Social Psychology(reissued)*. Cambridge, MA: Cambridge University Press.

Black, E. 1993. Metaphor, simile and cognition in Golding's *The Inheritor*, *Language and Literature* 2: 37-48.

Boase-Beier, J. 2003. Mind style translated, *Style* 3: 253-265.

Bocking, I. 1994. Mind style as an interdisciplinary approach to characterization, *Language and Literature* 3: 157-174.

Bockting, I. 1995. *Character and Personality in the Novels of William Faulkner: A Study in Psychostylistics*. Lanham/New York/ London: University Press of America Inc.

Cook, G. 1994. *Discourse and Literature*. Oxford: Oxford University Press.

Coulson, S. & Oakley, T. 2000. Blending basics, *Cognitive Linguistics* 11(3/4): 175-195.

Culpeper, J. 2001. *Language and Characterisation: People in Plays and Other Texts*. London: Longman.

Eysenck, M. W. & Keane, M. T. 2000. *Cognitive Psychology: A Student's Handbook*, 4th ed. London: Psychology Press

Fauconnier, G. & Turner, M. 1996. Blending as a central process of grammar. In *Conceptual Structure, Discourse, and Language*, ed. by A. Goldberg, 113-130. Stanford/CA: Center for the Study of Language and Information.

Fauconnier, G. 1997. *Mappings in Thought and Language*. Cambridge: Cambridge University Press.

Fauconnier, G. & Turner, M. 1998. Principles of conceptual integration. In *Discourse and Cognition*, ed. by J. Koenig, 269-283. Stanford: Center for the Study of Language and Information(CSLI).

Fauconnier, G. & Turner, M. 1999. Metonymy and conceptual integration. In *Metonymy in Language and Thought*, ed. by K. Panther, & G. Radder, 77-90. Amsterdam: John Benjamins.

Fowler, R. 1977. *Linguistics and the Novel*. London: Meuthuen.

Fowler, R. 1996. *Linguistic Criticism*. Oxford: Oxford University Press.

Goatly, A. 1997. *The Language of Metaphors*. London: Routledge.

Grady, J. , Oakley, T. & Coulson, S. 1999. *Blending and Metaphor*. In *Metaphor*

113

in Cognitive Linguistics, ed. by R. W. Jr. Gibbs & G. J. Steen. Amsterdam: John Benjamins.

Groom, W. 1994. *Forrest Gump.* London: Black Swan.

Halliday, M. A. K. & Hasan, R. 1989. *Language, Context and Text: Aspects of Language in a Social-Semiotic Perspective.* Oxford: OUP.

Johnson, M. 1987. *The Body in the Mind: The Bodily Basis of Meaning, Imagination and Reason.* Chicago: University of Chicago Press.

Lakoff, G. & Johnson, M. 1980. *Metaphors We Live By.* Chicago/London: University of Chicago Press.

Lakoff, G. 1987. *Women, Fire, and Dangerous Things.* Chicago/London: University of Chicago Press.

Lakoff, G. & Turner, M. 1989. *More than Cool Reason: A Field Guide to Poetic Metaphor.* Chicago/London: University of Chicago Press.

Lakoff, G. 1993. The contemporary theory of metaphor. In *Metaphor and Thought*, ed. by A. Ortony. Cambridge: Cambridge University Press.

Leech, G. & Short, M. 2001. *Style in Fiction: A Linguistic Introduction to English Fictional Prose.* Beijing: Foreign Language Teaching and Research Press.

Schank, R. C. & Aberlson, R. P. 1977. *Scripts, Plans, Goals, and Understanding: An Inquiry into Human Knowledge Structures.* Hillsdale/NJ: Lawrence Erlbaum Associates.

Schank, R. 1982. *Dynamic Memory: A Theory of Learning in Computers and People.* New York: Cambridge University Press.

Semino, E. & Swindlehurst, K. 1996. Metaphor and mind style in Ken Kesey's *One Flew over the Cuckoo's Nest*, *Style* 1: 143-166.

Semino, E. 1995. Schema theory and the analysis of text worlds in poetry, *Language and Literature* 2: 79-109.

Semino, E. 1997. *Language and World Creation in Poetry and Other Texts.* London: Longman.

Semino, E. A. 2002. Cognitive stylistic approach to mind style in narrative fiction. In *Cognitive Stylistics: Language and Cognition in Text Analysis.* ed. by E. Semino, & J. Culpeper. Amsterdam/ Philadelphia: John Benjamins Publishing Company.

Short, M. 1994. Mind style. In *Encyclopedia of Language and Linguistics.* ed. by R. E. Asher. Oxford: Pergamon.

Short, M. 1996. *Exploring the Language of Poems*, *Plays and Prose*. London and New York：Longman.

Steen, G. 1994. *Understanding Metaphor in Literature*. London：Longman.

Turner, M. & Fauconnier, G. 2000. Metaphor, metonymy, and binding. In *Metaphor and Metonymy at the Crossroads：A Cognitive Perspective*. ed. by A. Barcelona, 133-145. Berlin/New York：Mouton de Gruyter.

陈汝东(Chen, N.),2001,《认知修辞学》。广州：广东教育出版社。

冯晓虎(Feng, X.),2004,《隐喻——思维的基础　篇章的框架》。北京：对外经济贸易大学出版社。

葛鲁姆(Ge, L.),2002,《阿甘正传》。北京：人民文学出版社。

胡壮麟(Hu, Z.),2004,《认知隐喻学》。北京：北京大学出版社。

胡壮麟、刘世生(主编)(Hu, Z. & Liu, S.),2004,《西方文体学辞典》。北京：清华大学出版社。

钱建成(Qian, J.),2002,如何分析文体学中的 Mind Style.《信阳农业高等专科学校学报》2：48-50.

束定芳(Shu, D.),2000,《隐喻学研究》。上海：上海外语教育出版社。

赵艳芳(Zhao, Y.),2000,《认知语言学概论》。上海：上海外语教育出版社。

Realization of Subjectivity: An Analysis of the Referential Devices in Narrative Discourse

WANG Yina

Beijing University of Aeronautics and Astronautics

1. Introduction

Subjectivity is an important factor in narrative production and comprehension. In the humanistic sense, it concerns "the involvement of a locutionary agent in a discourse, and the effect of that involvement on the formal shape of discourse" (Finegan, 1995: 1). From the cognitive view, it refers to how one conceptualizes a scene that includes the speaker him/herself. Within the framework of Cognitive Grammar, Langacker (1985, 1990, *etc.*) analyses subjectivity by equating meaning with conceptualization. He outlines a parallelism between perception and conception and claims that the subjective/objective distinction can be seen as the difference between the viewer(or subject of conception) and the viewee(or object of conception) in terms of the stage metaphor[①]. A conception is subjective to the extent that it functions as part of background conceptual structure (normally including the conceptualizer and the attendant circumstances of the speech situation); whereas a conception is objective to the extent that the viewer focuses attention on it and makes it the center of his/her conscious awareness (i. e. a conceptualizer views a given element of conception as distinct from him-/herself).

Any referential situation may be characterized in more than one way, or profiled from different viewpoint. "An expression's meaning cannot be reduced to an objective characterization of the situation described: equally important for linguistic semantics is how the conceptualizer chooses to construe the situation and portray it for expressive purposes" (Langacker, 1990: 6). This cognitive view of subjectivity is largely consistent with its humanistic sense: Language is an expression or an incarnation of perceiving, feeling, speaking subject. While communication does not always take place within a shared situational context, referential expressions

---

① Langacker(1985, 1990, *etc.*) also describes the notion of subjectivity/objectivity as the distinction between the offstage region and onstage region in terms of the theatre metaphor.

vary subtly in their portrayal of a referent, and can activate different realization of subjectivity. Based on this observation, this paper attempts to construct a subjectivity continuum in narrative discourse, by exploring the viewpoint mobility in different mental spaces or conceptual ground. The focus is to investigate whose viewpoint is represented or involved when a referential device is chosen, and by doing so, to demonstrate how the referential device is correlated to subjectivity to different degrees.

2. Subjectivity, Viewpoint and the Referential Form in Discourse

2.1 Three viewpoint cases in narrative discourse

Cognitive linguists seek to show how linguistic expressions evoke conceptual structures as natural reflections of cognitive abilities, such as the cognitive ability of "grounding" or "reference point". At schematic level, the reference point notion describes the conceptual configurations involved with adopting a point of view. It is a conceptualization used as a way of accessing other conceptualizations in relation to it. In this sense, subjectivity/objectivity and viewpoint are similar terms related to aspects of presentation that cannot be sufficiently analyzed in terms of properties of the object of conceptualization.

Viewpoint refers to the conception of an animate entity, typically a person, from whose perspective a conception is construed. Viewing a conception from a particular point of view means setting up a mental space, which represents the imagined viewer's awareness or perceptions (Wang, 2005, 2006). According to Fauconnier(1994), mental spaces are the cognitive domains set up by a viewpoint. The production and comprehension of discourse involves the construction of hierarchical organized and interconnected mental spaces. The starting point of any discourse is the "base" space. Canonically, the base is identified with discourse reality, but as a discourse unfolds, alternate base spaces may be set up (e. g. the reality of the narrator or a character's). Within any mental space configuration, there is always a "viewpoint" space, the space from which other spaces can be accessed. The initial viewpoint coincides with the base space, but it can and often does shift to other spaces within the overall hierarchy.

Based on Langacker and Fauconnier, this paper distinguishes three viewpoint

117

cases in narrative discourse: the addressee viewpoint, the speaker viewpoint, and the character viewpoint, as shown in Table 1 below. The most natural or default viewpoint is that of the speaker or writer from the perspective of the discourse ground, including both the speaker and addressee. It is on this shared addressee viewpoint that most Accessibility[①] analyses are based on. That is, in addressing a referent X, the speaker is obliged to consider the addressee's knowledge of X in both his/her own mental reality and the mental space of the addressee. In this case ground is necessarily implicit despite its pivotal role as a reference point. Nonetheless, the referential device is not always constructed from the addressee's perspective, some uses principally serve to convey the speaker's subjective attitude with regard to the referent, when shared knowledge is not required. Rather than addressee-oriented, the referent can be portrayed from the sole viewpoint of the speaker. Thirdly, the construed material in discourse can be viewed from the perspective of the "surrogate ground"[②], i. e. the viewpoint of a story character, rather than the discourse producer or narrator. In these cases, the choice reflects the viewpoint of a third person referent(e. g. a discourse protagonist). In other words, viewpoint is shifted from the discourse reality(or speaker reality)to the story reality (often an onstage character), which is now the viewpoint space. In such cases, it is also not a necessary condition for speaker and addressee to share knowledge of the referent. The addressee is encouraged to empathize with, or adopt the referent's point of view. Such choice may serve either a referential or expressive function of the implied viewpoint.

Table 1. Viewpoint orientation

Viewpoint	Orientation	Ground	Function
Addressee	Addressee-oriented	Discourse ground	Referential
Speaker	Ego-oriented	Ideological ground	Expressive
Character	Character-oriented	Story ground	Referential/Expressive

① Accessibility is widely discussed in Ariel(1990), mainly based on the degree of mental accessibility of entities attributed to the addressee. That is, a speaker always signals to her addressee how easy or automatic the referent retrieval is. Despite its apparent advantages, this cannot fully explain the referential uses in discourse. See Wang(2006a)for details.

② "A surrogate ground", is used in Langacker(1985: 127-30)as a "perspective from which a situation is viewed", to be distinct from the actual discourse ground of the speaker or narrator. It is a conception of the context of the reported speech event including the vantage point of the speaker and addressee.

For instance: *The idiot was standing next to her*. This utterance may have different acceptable readings in different contexts: If narrated in written discourse, *the idiot* expresses the speaker's subjective stance. But if it is a subjective representation, *the idiot* reflects the subjective feeling of the onstage character, potentially the referent of the referred marker *her* or seeing through the eyes of other subjective character whom the narrator empathizes with.

All language represents conceptual content from some point of view, but events and situations are not necessarily represented from the same viewpoint in the same ground all the time. Viewpoints may be shifted, even intermingled, between the speaker, the addressee, and third persons (onstage character) from different background contexts. This is largely consistent with Werth (1999) 's distinction between discourse world and text world, or Short's claim of three discourse levels[1].

What seems distinct in this study is the explicit demonstration of the expressive layer of the ego-oriented viewpoint, be it the writer's, the narrator's, or a certain character's in discourse. Viewpoint, as a natural reference point, is a central part of the background context within which the viewed conception is construed. It is the center of conceptualization and the consciousness of the self to whom the utterance is attributed. This means that point of view becomes subjective if a speaker connects it explicitly to him-/herself or to another subject in the discourse. Thus, use of language in discourse can be characterized as more or less subjective according to the degree to which the experience itself is foregrounded as an iconic representation that diminishes the presence of the actual speaker and addressee. In other words, what is important is the role played by the conceptualizer within the conceptualization that constitutes an expression's semantic value. This, I argue, is the essential cognitive-functional motivation underlying the referential choices in linguistic communication.

2.2 Subjectivity and referential form correlation

Generally speaking, the referential facts arise from the interaction of semantic and pragmatic considerations. Different kinds of referential makers are integrated

---

① Short(1999: 174) distinguishes three main levels in novel analysis, i. e. the Novelis/Reader; the Narrator/ Narratee; Character A/Character B. The point of view and the deictic centre can be tied to the discourse roles both within the text-external and the text-internal layers.

into different conceptual structures. As proposed by Ariel (1990), among many others, there is an inverse relation between referent accessibility and its linguistic coding information. Different nominal forms, ranging from null pronouns to full noun phrases (NPs), are arrayed on a continuum reflecting the relative accessibility of a referent within a given context. A particular NP form is selected for reference in a given context to reflect the degree of accessibility of the referent in that context.

As discussed above, in constructing mental contact with a referent in discourse, accessibility is just part of the account underlying literary interpretation. In the line of Cognitive Grammar, this paper claims that the subjective meaning is conceptualized and construed together with their referential meaning. The major claim is that distinct nominal markers differ with respect to the degree of subjectivity of the referent in the immediate context. That is, lexical noun phrases tend to indicate a relatively less subjective portrayal of the referent, while pronominal or zero NPs tend to indicate a relatively more subjective portrayal of the referent. That is, the stronger the sense of subjectivity, the more likely the use of a reduced referential form, and vice versa. This is shown in Table 2 below:

Table 2. Subjectivity-form correlation

Maximal subjectivity ← - → Minimal subjectivity
Reduced form ← - → Elaborated form
Zero NP > Pronominal NP > lexical NP

That is, the realization of subjectivity is taken as a two-stage process: The primary stage is to decide the viewpoint center from whose subjectivity the conception is construed; Then the degree of subjectivity, which is largely dependent on the conceptual connectivity between the viewer and the referent, will be reflected in the encoding form of the referent (Wang, 2005: 83-84, 2006a: 84-87). In other words, the distinction between the adoption of a point of view and the construal of a conception more or less subjectively is a question of which mental space is taken as the primary context within which the conception is to be understood. The choice of a relatively reduced or elaborated marker indicates different degree of conceptual or empathetic distance from a certain viewpoint: The more the referent is empathized with, the more likely it is to be coded by a more reduced NP, and vice versa. Next, I will focus on the referential devices through which subjectivity is realized by analyses of text fragments from the collection of 90 Chinese short stories titled *Well-known Chinese Short Stories Over a Century* (《中国短篇小说百年精华》).

3. Realization of Subjectivity: Referential Form Illustrations

Language is used to interpret the world and to operate on it. A referential marker, according to Werth (1999: 156), is being used in order to refer, i. e. to single out some particular object already represented in the mind of the addressee, or to instruct the addressee mentally to set up such an object. In a text of some length, there are two main stages in the process of reference: the establishment stage and the maintenance stage. The establishment of entities is one of the basic acts of text world building. Reference maintenance is the process of keeping entities in the active register of the discourse. When different reference chains cross, a certain reference will be re-established or restored. Now I will come to the use of the referential devices at the opening and referent-retrieval environments in narrative discourse, and discuss the existence of different patterns in terms of subjectivity.

3.1 Initial reference in narrative discourse

In theory, one might expect a discourse to begin with a lexical NP, distinct in lexical length and explicitness, as the referents in the story all remain to be introduced. But that is not always the case. In literary texts, writers also prefer to introduce a character with a pronominal or zero NP, with a sum of characteristics attached. Among the 90 stories I have checked so far, there are about 43.4% (39 tokens) of non-lexical subjects in the discourse-initial positions. Table 3 shows the distribution of different forms at discourse-initial positions, followed by some opening passages.

Table 3. Referential forms at discourse-initial positions

Reference forms	Lexical NP	Pronoun	Zero	Total
Story numbers	51	31	8	90
Percentage	56.6%	34.4%	8.9%	100%

(1) 转弯抹角——他算是我的一个亲戚。我叫他"华威先生"。他觉

121

得这种称呼不大好。(张天翼《华威先生》)

（2）在十二月里，这真是个好天气。…(7 clauses)… 他为高个子修好了伸缩管，瘪起嘴将喇叭朝着地下试吹了三个音，于是抬起来……(陈映真《将军族》)

From the perspective of literary analysis, initial mentions of a reduced form are chosen for suspense, rather than anaphoric resolution. It leaves the readers to keep guessing until further detail is provided and the identity is disclosed. It may possibly explicate some of the cases, but only superficially.

In terms of subjectivity, distinct form selection involves a choice of viewpoint, and the representation of subjectivity. Lexical NPs at initial-mentions are only those chosen to portray a more objective construal of the referents from the common addressee-oriented perspective. The use of reduced forms as initial-mentions, however, has little consideration of the referents' accessibility in the addressee's mental space. Instead, these referents are intended to be prominent or accessible in the narrator's or a character's mental space, rather than the actual discourse space of the speaker and addressee. In the two examples above, the conceptions are more subjectively portrayed from the viewpoint space of the onstage character (or narrator-character) rather than offstage speaker in the discourse space (the speaker-addressee world). This is a common strategy used to initiate a protagonist (a topic referent) in the story, helping create an immediate effect by encouraging the readers to empathize with, or adopt the point of view of a narrator. The use of the proximal demonstrative *this* or *here* ［这］ is another verbal evidence of conceptual proximity.

Even when the pronominal referent is initiated in a non-subject position such as(3) and(4) below, the initial pronominal device still signals their plot saliency in the story, with their social inferiority reflected from their grammatical position.

（3）她底丈夫是一个皮贩，就是……有一天，他向他的妻说……(柔石《为奴隶的母亲》)

（4）她父母小小地发了点财，将她坟上加工修葺了一下……(张爱玲《花凋》)

In discourse-initial conditions, the least-specified reference (pronoun in English, zero in Chinese) is also the marked choice that represents the first mention of the discourse entity in the text. Rather than suspenseful use or high addressee-accessibility, these initial zeroes tend to convey maximal subjectivity and negligibility instead. In other words, they reflect the grounding or subordinate status of the referent(Wang, 2006a: 261-6).

Grounding or subordination is a powerful device of discourse organization. It plays an important role in the combination of clauses into larger units. Superficially it does not seem relevant to the reference area. From my observations, however, subordination, as a general device for marking background, contributes to the choice of under-specified reference, which, in a sense, also verifies its grounding status. This may happen in the author's own narration of the story, showing the author's degrading attitude towards the referred entity, or to convey self-effacement. For example:

(5)1. 上海……沪西……林肯路。Ø① 拎着饭篮，Ø 独自个儿在那儿走着，Ø 一只手放在裤袋里，Ø（看着自家儿嘴里出来的热气慢慢的飘到蔚蓝的夜色里去。…(5 paragraphs)…

6. Ø 一扔饭篮，Ø 一手抓住那人的枪，Ø 就是一拳过去。（穆时英《上海的狐步舞》）

In this example, the zero is chosen to indicate the minor importance of the referent to the story. It is a description of a normal street picture of Shanghai, to set up some background knowledge for the development of the story. What concerns the author is the event rather than the identity of the participant, as he/she is not mentioned later on. This is completely different from the pronoun-initial openings in setting up some thematically important figures for later construal. Compare the zero and pronoun used in the same excerpt below:

(6)"嗨?" Ø(X)问他(Y)。"嗨,"他(Y)说,"马上就好。"（池莉《静物》）

Depending on the speaker's assessment or intentions, one referent or another might be more important to the discourse. In (6), the pronominal referent is the protagonist in the story, while the zero referent might just be some passer-by（a driver maybe)in the discourse background with no name or identity. In these cases,

---

① Ø is a marker for zero reference, while 1 and 6 in the example refer to the paragraph number.

it is not necessary to introduce the exact identity of those referents, nor is it necessary to keep track of the identity of the reference in discourse. The zero-referenced conceptions tend to be negligible because of their grounding status in the discourse context.

In our data, most of zero referents without prior mentions tend to be socially inferior or thematically unimportant in the discourse context. The least-specified encoding is a justified reflection of the psychological weight of the referent in the discourse, in conformity with the competing principles of economy and efficiency in verbal communications. Within the limited capacities of the short-term memory encoding and decoding devices of the interlocutors, more attention is directed to the more noteworthy information when the less important information receives encoding no heavier than necessary(Chen, 1986).

From the perspective of viewing relationship, the viewer-viewed relationship and their positional interchangeability are the conceptual motivation underlying the particular choice in discourse. High vs. low referent-noteworthiness are the two extreme ends of viewpoint effect. Backgrounding or foregrounding the referent in initial reference makes the use of different forms possible in narrative discourse.

3.2 Subsequent reference in narrative discourse

Any linguistic usage event involves two conceptualizers (speaker and addressee)as part of its discourse ground. In common cases, the referent tends to receive reduced forms in subsequent mentions but full forms when accessibility is decreased. However, the referent may also be over-specified or under-specified in these contexts. A common analysis provided in the relevant studies is that such forms of reference are commonly used for reasons of style, emphasis, variation, or to manipulate the structure of the discourse. In this paper I claim that the crucial point is the shift in viewpoint in possible ground, which opens the possibility of an over- or under-specified NP appearing where it would otherwise not be expected.

To understand the intricacies of the viewpoint effect on referential choice, I would like to exhibit a simple data analysis of the first episode(5 pages)of the story *Spirit and Body* [《灵与肉》]. This story is mainly presented from the protagonist *Xu's* viewpoint, as a recollection of his past memories. The statistics in Table 4 may provide some support for the correlation between subjectivity and NP encoding:

Table 4 Correlation between NP forms and viewer

Form / Referent	Lexical NP	Pronoun	Zero	Anaphoricity[①]
Viewer X [许灵均]	1	57	14	72 (71/72: 98.6%)
Viewee Y [父亲]	33	3	21	57 (24/57: 42.1%)
Viewee Z [秀芝]	5	4	2	11 (6/11: 54.5%)

An easily noticed fact of the table is that the protagonist *X* receives a high percentage of pronouns while the co-protagonists *Y* and *Z* receive far more lexical NPs. For instance:

(7)1. 许灵均(X)没有想到还会见着父亲(Y)。(The opening paragraph)

2. 这是一间陈设考究的客厅……他(X)到了这里，就像忽然升到云端一样……

3. "过去的一切就让它过去吧!"父亲(Y)把手一挥。……

4. 房里的陈设和父亲的衣着使他(X)感到莫名的压抑。他(X)想，过去的是已经过去了，但又怎能忘记呢? (张贤亮《灵与肉》)

In the above passage, the protagonist *X* is musing over what happened in the past interposed with his observation of his father *Y*. The passage mainly recounts his thought as a representation of his consciousness. That is, *X*, as a narrator-viewer, views his father as well as himself. This viewing relation explicates why, in the fourth paragraph, the co-protagonist referent *Y* receives full NP (though recently mentioned) but *X* receives pronoun (over a long gap of nearly two paragraphs). These facts have a lot to do with whether or not a referent is the viewpoint center. The character whose subjectivity is being represented will be invoked with a reduced referential form significantly more often than other characters.

This analysis once more demonstrates that the topical referent is typically the character from whose point of view the narrative is construed. As argued by Wiebe (1995: 276), there may be a level of discourse structure at which a discourse segment can include more than one context; as each context (subjective or objective) has its own local "history list", an entity could remain in focus across

---

① Anaphorictity refers to the percentage of reduced encodings (pronouns and zeroes) in relation to the fully specified evocations (by name or description).

context boundaries. The following modified version offers a more convincing illustration:

> (8)1. **Dwayne** wasn't sure what John was scared of. What in the arcade could scare a boy like that? **He** rubbed **his** head under **his** baseball cap. **He** could see tears in John's eyes. **He** could tell they were tears because his eyes were too shiny. Too round. Well, it was all right to cry. **He**'d cried when they took **him** to that place a few years back. Now John was in a new place too. Maybe that was why he was crying.
>
> 2. "I want to leave," **he** said.

In the above passage, two male characters *Dwayne* and *John* are cross-referenced. Contrary to expectation, a pronoun *he* appears at the next paragraph, coreferring with a more distant reference *Dwayne*, when there is a more recent antecedent *John* in the context. Here the extent of subjectivity is the crucial factor: Although *John* is the last-mentioned male entity, the referent of *he* in the last sentence is taken to be *Dwayne*, because *Dwayne* is the subjective character of the discourse from whose point of view this story is construed, and *John* is only a parasitic entity embedded in Dwayne's thought space. Their difference in prominence is also reflected in their difference in anaphoricity: *Dwayne* [8/9: 90%] and *John* [2/6: 33%]. Suppose the relevant conception is about John, surely, the full NP should be taken.

This has implications that "different types of text [context] seem to require different types of cognitive integration" (Emmott, 1999: 7). In narrative, the link between a character and salient entities needs to be set up as the narrative progresses and may be drawn on to interpret particular referential forms.

> (9)……于是，过去的自己和现在的自己在脑海中形成了一个非常鲜明的对比。终于，他(X)发现了他们父子之间隔膜的真正所在：他这个钟鸣鼎食之家的长房长孙，曾经裹在锦缎的襁褓中，在红灯绿酒之间被京沪一带工商界大亨和他们的太太啧啧称赞的人(X)，已经变成了一个名副其实的劳动者了。(张贤亮《灵与肉》)

The whole excerpt is encoded from the perspective of the viewer *X*, the protagonist of the story. The appearance of the over-specified NP to refer to himself signals a somewhat switch from the referent's view to an external perspective, as if the conception represents other people' evaluation of him. By so doing, the character *X* detaches connection from his past and brings his past self onstage to be focus of attention, to express unfavorable feelings. However, from the use of *this* [这个] rather than *that* [那个], we can also see that the conception cannot be wholly distinct from his own mental space. This intermingled conception of two mental spaces collaborates in a certain sense Fauconnier's (1997) theory of "space blending"①, as shown in the figure below.

Space or viewpoint blending is prominent in narrative. Here is another descriptive case of self-reference:

(10)"我知道你不会再爱<u>一个曾经做过妓女的女孩子</u>,<u>我</u>为什么要拖住你呢……"<u>徐文霞</u>说不下去了,又伏倒在床上哭起来。

In this fragment, the speaker-referent does not refer to herself as *me* in the second mention. An over-specified indefinite description is used instead. Such a heavy form is justified as she tends to detach her connectivity with her past self to create a less subjective portrayal. That is, there is a shift of viewpoint from the speaker herself to the addressee *you*. Imagine if the pronoun were chosen, it would convey little attitudinal evaluation. In this case, the element might be more subjective as part of her background conceptual structure, as shown in the subjectivity scale: *indefinite NP* [一个曾经做过妓女的女孩子] < *definite NP* [我这个曾经做过妓女的女孩子] < *Pronoun* [我].

All these indicate that speakers may adopt different or even opposing or intermingled viewpoint to highlight different aspects of a category. The pronominal conceptions in (7) and (8) are more referentially chosen to encode relative subjectivity and prominence of the referents; whereas the descriptive NPs in (9) and (10) are more expressively used, intending to profile a special conception of the referent as an object of viewing, and convey some personal evaluation. That is what I term as the referential and expressive functions of reference, which I intend to argue for. The speaker, in making an utterance, simultaneously comments upon that utterance and expresses his attitude to what he is saying (Lyons, 1977: 739).

---

① "Conceptual blending" refers to a general cognitive process that operates over mental spaces as inputs. In blending, the "blend" space inherits partial structure from the input spaces, and has emergent structure of its own. See Fauconnier 1997 for details.

Although there is no distinct boundary, the expressive use of reference encodes viewpoint differently from the referential function. Whereas the latter is addressee-oriented or character-oriented, the former conveys the speaker's subjective stance towards a referent(This referent might even be the viewer him-/herself sometimes.). It is from this sense, I argue that the viewer and the viewed are interrelated and can be interchangeable in discourse.

4. Conclusion

To conclude, the uses of referential devices in discourse are guided by and convey certain viewpoint. Subjectivity, as a multi-layered concept, shapes reference on different levels, and it is also well manifested in the referential choice in discourse. This is not only true of narrative texts, but also applicable to other types of discourse as demonstrated in Wang (2006a), though there might be subtle stylistic differences in referential options.

The grounding of language in discourse is central to the functional or cognitive account of language. Previous accounts have largely confined the linguistic options in discourse to the realm of topicality and accessibility (Chen, 1986; Ariel, 1990, etc.), or style and aesthetic significance (Shen, 1998; Short, 1999, *etc.*). This paper directs more attention to the interaction between the subject of conception and the object of conception. Discourse is fundamentally subjective in nature. The relationship between a conceived viewer and the material construed from his/her viewpoint is a topic in both stylistics and Cognitive Grammar. It is expected that this discussion, with a focus on the cognitive processing underlying the linguistic choice in narrative, be complementary to the study of subjectivity in both the grammatical and textual account of reference.

References

Ariel, M. 1990. *Accessing Noun-phrase Antecedents*. London: Routledge.

Chen, P. 1986. Referent introducing and tracking in Chinese narrative. In *Unpublished UCLA Ph. D. dissertation*.

Emmott, C. 1999. Embodied in a constructed world: narrative processing, knowledge representation, and indirect anaphora. In *Discourse Analysis in*

Cognitive Linguistics, ed. by K. van Hoek *et al.*, 5-28. Amsterdam: John Benjamins.

Fauconnier, G. 1994[1985]. *Mental Spaces: Aspects of Meaning Construction in Natural Language*. Cambridge: Cambridge University Press.

Fauconnier, G. 1997. *Mappings in Thought and Language*. Cambridge: Cambridge University Press.

Finegan, E. 1995. Subjectivity and subjectivisation: An introduction. In *Subjectivity and Subjectivisation*, ed. by D. Stein *et al.* Cambridge: Cambridge University Press,

Langacker, R. W. 1985. Observations and speculations on subjectivity. In *Iconicity in Syntax*, ed. by J. Haiman, 109-150. Amsterdam: John Benjamins.

Langacker, R. W. 1990. *Concept, Image, and Symbol*. Berlin: Mouton de Gruyter.

Langacker, R. W. 1993. Reference-point constructions, *Cognitive Linguistics* 4: 1-38.

Lyons, J. 1977. *Semantics*(vol. 2). Cambridge: Cambridge University Press.

Short, M. 1999. Understanding texts: Point of view. In *Language and Understanding*, ed. by G. Brown et al. Shanghai: Shanghai Foreign Language Education Press.

Werth, P. 1999. *Text Worlds: Representing Conceptual Space in Discourse*. London: Longman.

Wiebe, J. 1995. References in narrative text. In *Deixis in Narrative*, ed. by J. Duchan *et al.*, 263-286. Hillsdale: Lawrence Erlbaum Associates, Inc.

申丹(Shen, D.), 1998,《文学文体学与小说翻译》。北京：北大出版社。

申丹(Shen, D.), 2005,《叙述学与小说文体学研究》。北京：北大出版社。

沈家煊(Shen, J.), 2001, 语言的主观性与主观化,《外语教学与研究》4: 268-275。

王义娜(Wang, Y.), 2005, 概念参照视点：语篇指称解释的认知思路,《外语学刊》5: 81-85。

王义娜(Wang, Y.), 2006a,《指称的概念参照视点：认知语篇学的探索》。北京：外文出版社。

王义娜(Wang, Y.), 2006b, 由可及性到主观性：语篇指称模式比较,《外语与外语教学》7: 1-4。

中国社会科学院文学研究室选编, 2003,《中国短篇小说百年精华》（上，下）。北京：人民文学出版社。

A Distorted World in a Distorted Mind—The Mind Style of Rosa in Cynthia Ozick's "The Shawl"

LIANG Xiaohui

University of International Relations

1. Introduction

In the short story "The Shawl" Cynthia Ozick, a Jewish American writer, presents to us the pitiful experience of three Jews during the Second World War. A woman, Rosa by name, together with her baby daughter Magda and a 14-year-old girl Stella, is forced into a concentration camp and has gone through various inhuman treatments. Toward the end of the story, the mother even has to watch with her own eyes her little daughter being hurled at an electrified fence.

The story is narrated with third-person pronouns, suggesting the possibility of the authorial omniscient mode, which can be detected from many instances, eg. :

> But Magda lived to walk. She lived that long, but she did not walk very well, partly because she was only fifteen months old, and partly because the spindles of her legs could not hold up her belly.

This calm and logical reasoning belongs to no other than the narrator, as shown from the balanced arrangement of a shorter and a longer sentences, both grammatically complete, with the latter sentence employing all possible connectives needed in its context, "but", "partly because", "and". The narrator knows everything, including the reasons for the daily reality, and is ready to relate what she knows in an objective way.

However, this smooth and eloquent delivery is frequently abandoned in the text, being spiced with broken, less logical sentences. One example may show clearly the contrast between these two different ways of delivery,

> The neat grip of the tiny gums. One mite of a tooth tip sticking up in the bottom gum, how shining, an elfin tombstone of white marble gleaming there.

This example, though, like the first one, also focusing on Magda's new development as a baby, goes very differently from the previous example. It is made up by two sentences, but neither the first sentence nor the three clauses in the second contain any verb to function as a predicate. At the same time, between sentences and clauses, no single connective exists to show the logical relations of different occasions. Besides, the second clause in the second sentence "how shining" is an exclamation in a colloquial form, leaving an impression that all these short and broken sentences and clauses are free indirect speech, from Rosa apparently. Moreover, the comprehensive way of observing and narrating as shown in the former example is replaced with a manner of narrow observation and subjective tone in this latter passage.

This different presentation exhibits a different focalization, limited instead of omniscient, from one character (Rosa) instead of the narrator. Many other similar instances of the text prove that the narrator, from time to time, will retreat to the background and leave us, the readers, observing the world through Rosa's eyes. So, very often, the story is not TOLD by the narrator, instead, it is SHOWN through Rosa. This third-person limited focalization successfully builds up Rosa's mind style, a mind striking in its failure to recognize in a normal way the surrounding world.

The notion of mind style is first introduced by Roger Fowler. He explains.
Cumulatively, consistent structural options, agreeing in cutting the presented world to one pattern or another, give rise to an impression of a world-view, what I shall call a "mind style". (Fowler, 1977: 76)

He later elaborates this world-view as ideational point of view (Fowler, 1986: 130-4). But Semino holds a different opinion. The younger scholar proposes that "mind style is to do with how language reflects the particular conceptual structures and cognitive habits that characterize an individual's world view", and "contrary to Fowler's view, the notion of "mind style' can be seen as complementary rather than synonymous with the notion of "ideological point of view'". The former is "most apt to capture those aspects of world views that are primarily personal and cognitive in origin" while the latter for "those aspects of world views that are social, cultural, religious or political in origin. "(Semino & Culpeper, 2002: 95-7)

In this essay the author will adopt Semino's definition of mind style and will show what linguistic techniques are employed in the construction of the idiosyncratic features in Rosa's mind style and how this mind style is related to the outside world.

2. Rosa's Mind Style and Tense

A peculiar point about the text is that, in Rosa's train of thinking, a ubiquitous simple past tense is employed. Tense of verbs is expected to convert when the time of events changes. "The Shawl" begins with the physical torture of the three females. Having undergone all the harshness, Rosa is so hungry and malnourished that she does not menstruate. So is Stella. And the one-and-half-year-old Magda is so under-nourished as to fall far behind her peers in learning to speak and walk. What is worse, Rosa's milk has dried up. In this desperate state Rosa falls into retrospection and reflection. The story is then mostly involved in Rosa's retrospection of several episodes before they come to the camp, interwoven with the happenings occurring around her right at the moment she is thinking. The story, if arranged chronologically, should go like this: Rosa had planned to give Magda away to the local villagers for the sake of the girl's safety on her way to the camp together with Stella, but had discarded the idea for fear that Magda would be found when being put in others' hands. After she had finally been driven into this concentration camp, she had concealed Magda in a shawl inside the barrack when she had had to go out for the call by the German soldiers. Her milk had stopped for three days out of starvation and now, a little dazed, she was considering what had happened in the past and the problems arising right now. At this moment, Magda's shawl was snatched away by Stella, who felt extremely cold in starvation. Then the baby staggered out of the barrack in searching for the shawl and, found by a German soldier, was hurled at the electrified fence and killed.

However, in this story, the simple past tense is used both for the events right now and the episodes in Rosa's retrospection. The beginning paragraph is followed, with explanation in parentheses from the author of the present essay to distinguish the episodes before Rosa had come to the camp, and her feelings or the events that occurred at the moment of her thinking:

STELLA, cold, cold, the coldness of hell. (*STELLA, the capitalized word is*

Rosa's exclamation, *followed by Rosa's feelings while she was thinking.*) How they walked on the roads together, Rosa with Magda curled up between sore breasts, Magda wound up in the shawl. (*episode before*) Sometimes Stella carried Magda. (*episode before*) But she was jealous of Magda. A thin girl of fourteen, too small, with thin breasts of her own, Stella wanted to be wrapped in a shawl, hidden away, asleep, rocked by the march, a baby, a round infant in arms. (*Rosa's thinking at the moment*) Magda took Rosa's nipple, and Rosa never stopped walking, a walking cradle. (*events while she was thinking*) There was not enough milk; sometimes Magda sucked air; then she screamed. (*episode before*, *since Magda had already stopped uttering any noise*) Stella was ravenous. Her knees were tumors on sticks, her elbows chicken bones. (*Rosa's observation while she was thinking.*)

This extract creates an impression that Rosa has lost a clear sense of time and becomes unable to distinguish what has happened from what is happening, so that in this passage all predicate verbs are arranged in the simple past tense, without any distinction between occasions before or after her coming to the camp. At this time, she has fallen into a state of extreme starvation, a state in which one doesn't feel hungry any more. "She felt light, not like someone walking but like someone in a faint, in trance. . . " On the verge of fainting, she has lost the basic sense. Through Rosa's unclear sense of time, the physical sufferings of the woman and the two girls are intensified. This arrangement neatly conveys the distorted mind style of Rosa and how far the Jewish people are driven by the cruel treatment of the Nazis.

3. Rosa's Mind Style and Speech Presentation

Rosa has not only lost a clear sense of time, but also the ability to judge who is uttering and who is not. In this story, mainly narrated through Rosa's limited focalization, the presentation of speech also has its peculiarities. Throughout the text, direct speech is mostly abandoned. Even when a few direct speeches emerge, they can hardly be counted as any utterance. In the whole text, quotation marks appear only on seven occasions:

1) "Aryan," Stella said, in a voice grown as thin as a string. . .
2) And the time that Stella said "Aryan,". . .

3）... it sounded to Rosa as if Stella had really said "Let us devour her. "

4）Afterward Stella said: "I was cold. "

5）"Maaaa—"

It was the first noise Magda had ever sent out from her throat since the drying up of Rosa's nipples.

6）"Maaaa... aaa"

7）The electric voices began to chatter wildly. "Maamaa, maaamaaa," they all hummed together.

The first quotation from Stella is put in single quotation marks rather than in double like in the fourth to seventh quotations, either because Stella utters it in a very low voice or because it is totally out of Rosa's imagination instead of being actually uttered. Considering Rosa's fainting state, the second reason is not improbable. The second quotation is Rosa's referring back to Stella's word in the first quotation, and the third is Rosa's interpretation of the first, neither being direct speech. So both of them can be left out of the discussion. The fourth one appears in double quotation marks, being direct speech, from Stella this time. However, though without any help of tense changes, it is pointed out in the sentence as being uttered "Afterward" —years later, perhaps even after Rosa and Stella are released from the concentration camp, at least not at the time when Rosa is thinking in the barrack. The seventh comes from Rosa's illusionary hearing of the electricity in the fence.

Therefore, only the fifth and sixth statements are direct speech in its real sense. But both are a one-syllable speech, and furthermore they are produced by Magda, a baby who is still learning to speak. Even this shortest utterance "Maaaa... aaa" is mingled with, and therefore oppressed by, the sound of electricity "Maamaa, maaamaaa. "

As Short points out, in direct speech, all the linguistic features used must be related to the speaker's viewpoint (Short, 1996: 299). In this form, people's voice will be most readily heard and their opinion will be best expressed. The limited use of direct speech in this story echoes the few chances the Jews obtain to utter any voice or express any opinion and therefore indicates a world with all sounds or opinions from the Jews forbidden. With a distorted mind, Rosa fails to recognize what is really happening, rather, she believes that she and her people have lost the ability to speak. For her, they are turning dumb. It enlightens us as to the situation of Rosa or the Jewish people as a whole that in imprisonment no human voice can be heard. If any human voice does occur, this person will be silenced, as in the case of Magda.

Rosa's limited ability in judging the presence of sound can be shown through another instance. Rosa believes "the electricity inside the fence would seem to hum" and she "heard real sounds in the wire", which according to Stella was only an imagining. What matters here is not whether the humming sound is real or imagined, what matters is that the hearers themselves have been tortured to such a degree as to lose their judgment of the presence of any sound. They are turning deaf.

Dumb and deaf, the Jewish people suffer not only physical persecution, but also spiritual control, overwhelmingly exerted by the Nazis.

4. Rosa's Mind Style and Metaphor

In this world of deadly silence, Rosa's distorted mind comes to blur the distinctions between opposite things. This can be shown through the tension between the V-terms and T-terms in the metaphors of this story. According to the metaphor theory, metaphor occurs when the conventional referent, the Vehicle, is used to refer to an unconventional referent, the Topic, on the basis of similarity, so that the comprehension of the Topic will be easier or, if not, the Topic will be more impressive. The expressions used to express them are Vehicle-term(V-term) and Topic-term(T-term)(Lacoff & Johnson, 1980; Goatly, 1997). However, in many metaphors of this text, the similarity does not exist between V-term and T-term in the conventional way, instead, their implications contradict each other.

For example, Rosa's walking as rocking her baby(the T-term)is referred to as a "march"(the V-term). In this metaphor, the V-term and the T-term do not share much in common. The walk of a woman, shaking and tugging her baby, sweet in its own sense, is by no means like a march with a stern nature, apart from the fact that both involve body movement, the only possible ground between them. But to Rosa and Stella, the marching of German soldiers must be so overwhelming that any movement connected with walking comes to be projected by this military act. Therefore, in Rosa's distorted mind, the two originally conflicting concepts are

135

stretched and mingled together.

Similarly, for Rosa, Magda's tooth tip, the most vital image in the gloomy scene, is compared to "an elfin tombstone of white marble." In this metaphor, the V-term "an elfin tombstone of white marble" represents death, while the T-term "Magda's tooth tip" embodies life and vitality. When these two opposite images—sprouting tooth and tombstone—are brought together, based upon the ground that both are white in color, we can detect that in Rosa's mind life and death go side by side. Rosa's distorted inner mind is always charged with the fear of death. Therefore, with a tendency to confuse things with their opposites, she frequently associates life-denoting objects with death.

While the growth of Magda is linked to the image of death, in the mind of Rosa and her companions, the ugliest things like human waste are branded as the most beautiful images.

> ... In the barracks they spoke of "flowers," of "rain": excrement, thick turdbraids, and the slow stinking maroon waterfall that slunk down from the upper bunks, the stink mixed with a bitter fatty floating smoke that greased Rosa's skin.

Here, "flowers," "rain" are used as V-terms to refer to the T-terms "excrement, thick turdbraids". The clashing meanings between the V-terms and T-terms demonstrate that in a world without beauty, people cannot tell the ugly from the beautiful.

Rosa's tendency to blur the distinction between opposite things is very often realized by one linguistic feature—the frequent occurrence of "of" phrases, e. g. , "the little house of the shawl's windpings", "the spindles of her legs", "milk of linen", "the rods of her arms". This is what Goatly would label Genitive Metaphor (Goatly, 1997: 215-20), with the V-term precedes the T-term. Among them, the most significant case is the phrase "the little house of the shawl's windpings". "The shawl's windpings" is compared to "the little house" in the sense that the shawl, by which the story is entitled, firstly rescues Magda by supplying a protection and consolation to the baby, a ground for the metaphor to Rosa. It seems that here no tension exists between the V-term and the T-term. But, tragically and ironically, toward the end of the story, just by fetching it, Magda is found by

German soldiers and finally loses her life. The shawl, therefore, taken as a refuge by Rosa, actually leads her daughter to hell. Therefore, in the metaphor "the little house of the shawl's windpings", the fiercest clash occurs between the references of the V-term and the T-term, implying that Rosa has made the most pitiable wrong judgment about the function of the shawl.

A most striking example with the tension between V-term and T-term comes at the concluding part of the story, when a German soldier finally finds Magda and snatches her and hurls her at the electrified fence. The whole process is hinted at rather than directly portrayed:

> Far off, very far, Magda leaned across her air-fed belly, reaching out with the rods of her arms. She was high up, elevated, riding someone's shoulder. But the shoulder that carried Magda was not coming toward Rosa and the shawl, it was drifting away, the speck of Magda was moving more and more into the smoky distance. Above the shoulder a helmet glinted. The light tapped the helmet and sparked it into a goblet. Below the helmet a black body like a domino and a pair of black boots hurled themselves in the direction of the electrified fence.

This whole extract forms an extended metaphor, supplying a V-term to the T-term "the killing scene", which does not explicitly occur in the text. In this extract, the soldier's act is disintegrated as in a slow movie picture, every part of his body moving step by step, even not without beauty. This is a manner of description suitable for athletic movements, instead of a murdering process. The V-term with its healthy trait and the T-term with its smothering nature clash with each other in meanings. For readers, the divided movements slow down the perception process of Rosa and convey the mounting horror of the hurling act. The pain, felt bit by bit, is even more inundating. And the readers may even realize, it is not the soldier's movement that can be divided into several parts, it is rather—take the reverse side of Rosa's illusion again—Rosa's own heart that is being wrung little by little, until it can't be twisted any more.

In a sense, the whole text forms a metaphor—a distorted world through Rosa's distorted mind is portrayed, functioning as a V-term for the horrible real world in one concentration camp of World War II as the Topic. Though the atmosphere in the camp, the horrible treatment by the German, or even the exact act of the baby-hurling, the T-term, are not described directly, but all the effects of the Nazis' cruelty are brought to light by the exposure of Rosa's peculiar mind style. Through her eyes, we are presented with a dreadful world with more truthfulness. This unique way of narration achieves an effect a normal description would fail.

References

Fowler, R. 1977. *Linguistics and the Novel*. London: Menthuen.

Fowler, R. 1986. *Linguistic Criticism*. Oxford: Oxford University Press.

Goatly, A. 1997. *The Language of Metaphors: An Introduction*. London: Routledge.

Lacoff, G. & Johnson, M. 1980. *Metaphors We Live By*. Chicago: University of Chicago Press.

Semino, E. & Culpeper, J. 2002. *Cognitive Stylistics*. Amsterdam: Benjamins.

Short, M. 1996. *Exploring the Language of Poems, Plays and Prose*. London: Longman.

刘世生(Liu, S.), 1998,《西方文体学论纲》。济南：山东教育出版社。

申丹(Shen, D.), 1998,《叙述学与小说文体学研究》。北京：北京大学出版社。

张德禄(Zhang, D.), 1998,《功能文体学》。济南：山东教育出版社。

2. Functional Stylistics

Internal Contrast and Double Decoding: A Functional-Cognitive Approach to Transitivity in "On the Road"

SHEN Dan

Peking University

1. Introduction

The system of transitivity as first proposed by Halliday (1971) has been widely applied in stylistic analysis (see, for instance, Toolan, 1998; Stockwell, 2002; Simpson, 2004; Ji & Shen, 2004, 2005). Since the transitivity model is concerned with the classification of different ways of organizing the experiential aspect of meaning, it's not surprising that the applications of the model have, without exception, focused on the contrast among different process types. But if we examine literary texts carefully, we may find that in some cases, the writer creates a thematically-motivated contrast within the same type (or sub-type) of process. Such an "internal contrast" may lead, through the readers' double decoding, to a change in the nature of some processes involved. My talk today will focus on this neglected stylistic feature and the text chosen for analysis is Langston Hughes's "On the Road" (1952). A functional-cognitive approach to the thematic interaction in such a text of the "internal contrast" and "double decoding" may help demonstrate how stylistic analysis can uncover hidden literary meaning.

2. Internal Contrast and Double-decoding in "On the Road"[1]

Hughe's "On the Road" very much centers on racial relations.[2] The protagonist of the story, Sargeant, a black hobo, tries to seek refuge in a bitter snowstorm during the Great Depression but is rebuffed by a white Reverend. Then he tries to break into a locked "white folks' church" and is beaten unconscious by white policemen. In his hallucination, the church falls down and the stone Christ, having gained freedom, walks side by side with him in the snow. The pain from the beating of a policeman awakens him from the dream and he finds himself in prison, shaking the cell door and threatening to break it down. However, my concern is not political, but stylistic. I chose "On the Road" not because of the racial issue, but because it well demonstrates the internal contrast and the resultant double decoding.

The opening paragraph of the text goes:

(1) He was not interested in the snow. (2) When he got off the freight, one early evening during the depression, Sargeant never even noticed the snow. (3) But he must have felt it seeping down his neck, cold, wet, sopping in his shoes. (4) But if you had asked him, he wouldn't have known it was snowing. (5) Sargeant didn't see the snow, not even under the bright lights of the main street, falling white and flaky against the night. (6) He was too hungry, too sleepy, too tired.[3]

Out of the six sentences in this paragraph, "snow" is prominent in five: occupying the end-focus position of sentences 1, 2, 4 and 5, and forming the detailed and dynamic Phenomenon in sentences 3 and 5. In cognitive terms, "snow" becomes a salient "figure", foregrounded in the reader's interpretive process. The story begins in *medias res*, and the first curt sentence depicting Sargeant's relation to the snow immediately catches the reader's attention. This relational process "He was not interested in the snow", which appears normal on the surface, in effect deviates from a situational script: when one is extremely cold and hungry, the issue of "being interested in the snow" is out of the question. By focusing, at the very beginning of the text, on what usually falls outside the scope of concern thereby contradicting the reader's relevant situational script, the first relational process brings the protagonist's relation to the snow into the spotlight and signals that this relation is unusual and significant. In this short paragraph, there are four mental processes with the same Phenomenon "snow":

(1) Sargeant never even noticed the snow

(2) he must have felt it seeping down his neck, cold, wet, sopping in

his shoes

(3) he wouldn't have known it was snowing

(4) Sargeant didn't see the snow, not even under the bright lights of the main street, falling white and flaky against the night

In (1), (3) and (4), the realization of the mental processes (notice, know, see) is negated, but (2) affirms in the subjunctive mood the realization of the mental process involved (feel). Halliday (2004: 208-210) distinguishes four different sub-types of mental process: cognitive, desiderative, perceptive, and emotive. The former two types—cognitive and desiderative are of a "higher" level, and the latter two—perceptive and emotive—are of a "lower" level. In Halliday's (2004: 210) classification of the verbs, "notice", "feel" and "see" all belong to the lower-level type of "perception". Compare:

He was so hungry, sleepy and tired that he didn't see, didn't feel and didn't notice the snow. This description would tally with the reader's situational script: when extremely hungry, sleepy and tired, one's senses all tend to go numb. But what actually appears in the original text contradicts this situational script, since there is created an opposition within the same sub-type of "perception" — "seeing" and "noticing" are set in direct contrast with "feeling". While the negation of "seeing" and "noticing" is curt and absolute ("never even"; "not even"), the affirmation of "feeling" is more subtle and complicated. Although an expression of subjective epistemic modality is employed ("must have felt"), the Phenomenon in the perception process is dynamic, involving two embedded material processes ("it seeping down his neck, cold, wet, sopping in his shoes"), which points to the possibility of the protagonist's keen feeling and invites readers to share that feeling. Since the protagonist may keenly feel the movement of the snow, how can he be so blind to it ("Sargeant didn't see the snow, not even under the bright lights of the main street")? In the fifth paragraph, a description with a similar contrast appears:

The big black man turned away. And even yet he didn't see the snow, walking right into it. Maybe he sensed it, cold, wet, sticking to his jaws, wet on his black hands, sopping in his shoes. Again, a contrast is deliberately created within the same sub-type of perception process, contradicting the reader's situational script, that is, one's senses all tend to go numb in such a state. And

141

again, the protagonist is depicted as probably keenly feeling the movement and effect of the snow: "cold, wet, sticking to his jaws, wet on his black hands, sopping in his shoes". Apparently, a person who is probably keenly aware of the existence of the snow **should** be able to "notice" and "see" it. This conventional assumption or interpretive frame is consistently violated by the deviant transitivity patterning.

Significantly, the perceptive "see" and "notice" in this context are put on a par with the cognitive "know". It is true that, apart from referring to awareness through the senses (visual, auditory, tactile, etc.), the term "perception" can also refer to "a way of regarding, understanding or interpreting something" or "intuitive understanding and insight" (*The New Oxford Dictionary of English*, 1998: 1377). But in Halliday's system, since "perception (perceptive) process" is set in contrast with "cognitive process" and classified as a lower-level type of mental process, these cognitive meanings of the term usually do not come into play. However, perception processes in Halliday's system still have both a mental (involving consciousness) and a physical aspect (involving bodily organs). Significantly, the *tactile* "feeling something *external*" (as distinct from *psychological* feeling—a sense of "feel" that does not come into play here) is more directly associated with the body, while "noticing" is more directly associated with the mind. By subtly creating a contrast between "feel"/"sense" on the one hand and "notice"/"know"/"see" on the other, the difference between the more physical and the more mental is highlighted. More specifically, as regards "feel" and "sense" (the latter used in this context only as a synonym of the *tactile* "feel"), the physical aspect is foregrounded and the mental aspect suppressed because of the contrast with "notice", "see" and "know". On the other hand, as regards "notice" and "see", the negation and intensity ("never even", "didn't... not even") seem to suggest that what is involved is not a physical matter (the protagonist cannot "see" and "notice" the snow *even* under such circumstances though his eyesight is fine), but a cognitive matter—not only because of the opposition to the bodily "feel"/"sense", but also because of the association with the cognitive "know".

Here we have a telling case which shows how the conventional nature of processes can be changed by semantic and cognitive reorganization in a literary text. When "see" is put on a par with "feel"/"sense" in relation to "snow", only its visual aspect comes into play in the interpretive process. But when "see" is put on a par with the cognitive "know" and set in direct contrast with the perceptive "feel"/"sense", the reader is led to take "see", on a deeper level, out of the "perceptive" domain into the "cognitive". Similarly, in this context, the deliberately wrought opposition (mental versus physical within "perception") and equation ("notice" is equated with "know" across the sub-types involved) also function to lead the reader to shift "notice" from the "perceptive" domain to the "cognitive". But this change in the nature of the transitivity processes only occurs on a deeper level, which interacts with the surface level where "see" and "notice" remain "perceptive" processes. Indeed, the authorial narrator seems to play deliberately with the contrast between the deeper level and the surface level. On the one hand, the narrator consistently describes "seeing"/"noticing" together with "feeling"/"sensing", which naturally reinforces the perceptive nature of these processes on the surface level. But on the other hand, since the narrator consistently contrasts "see"/"notice" with "feel"/"sense" and puts them on a par with the cognitive "know", the reader may decode these processes on a deeper level as going beyond the perceptive domain into the cognitive.

This "doubling" of the significance of the Process of "seeing" (which depends on the reader's double decoding) is accompanied by the doubling of the significance of the Phenomenon "snow" (which also depends on the reader's double decoding). More specifically, in the interpretive process, the reader may realize that "the snow" not only refers on the surface to the natural phenomenon, but also symbolizes on a deeper level the object of cognition of the protagonist's racially rebellious consciousness. In terms of the latter, the protagonist at first "felt" and "sensed" the existence of "the snow" ("the color line"), but he was psychologically indifferent ("not interested in the snow") and cognitively insensitive towards it (unable to "see" it).

The protagonist's inability to "see" the snow in the first paragraph forms a striking contrast with the reaction of the white Reverend in what immediately follows.

The Reverend Mr. Dorset, however, **saw the snow** when he switched on his porch light, opened the front door of his parsonage, and found standing

there before him a big black man **with snow on his face**, a human piece of
night **with snow on his face**—obviously unemployed.

Said the Reverend Mr. Dorset before Sargeant even realized he'd opened
his mouth: "I'm sorry. No! Go right on down this street four blocks and turn
to your left, walk up seven and you'll see the Relief Shelter. I'm sorry. No!"
He shut the door.

Sargeant wanted to tell the holy man that he had already been to the
Relief Shelter, been to hundreds of relief shelters during the depression years,
the beds were always gone and super was over, the place was full, and they
drew the color line anyhow. But the minister said, "No," and shut the door.
Evidently he didn't want to hear about it. And he *had* a door to shut.

The big black man turned away. And even yet **he didn't see the snow**,
walking right into it. Maybe **he sensed it**, cold, wet, sticking to his jaws,
wet on his black hands, sopping in his shoes. (p. 272, original italics, my
boldface)

While the first paragraph centers on the protagonist's not being able to see the
snow, the second paragraph begins by asserting that the Reverend, by contrast,
readily sees "the snow", a Phenomenon that remains a foregrounded figure in this
passage. In the preceding part, the story is narrated from the point of view of the
omniscient narrator, who refers to the protagonist as "Sergeant", but at the
beginning of this passage, the focalization is shifted to the white Reverend, who
perceives "a big black man", metaphorized into "a human piece of night". This is
the first time the text reveals the racial identity of the protagonist. Usually, "a
piece of" is used to modify a non-human and inanimate entity, and identifying the
black man with "night" as against "daylight" both highlights the black color and
reinforces the dehumanization. The black color is set in repeated contrast with the
white snow ("a big black man with snow on his face, a human piece of night with
snow on his face"). What is implicitly emphasized in the juxtaposition is
apparently "the color line". Here a reader may also perceive two layers of
significance in the white Reverend's immediately seeing the snow and his consistent
attention to the snow: on the surface, snow is just a natural phenomenon and his
seeing the snow is a normal visual activity under comfortable circumstances; but on
a deeper level, snow stands for the white side in the color line and the Reverend's

seeing the snow is a cognitive activity, which both conveys and heightens his racial prejudice. In this passage, there appears the first italicized word "he *had* a door to shut". The question arises: why does the authorial narrator puts emphasis on this relational process? In this narrative, "door" has explicit symbolic meaning, primarily standing for racial discrimination and rejection. The protagonist's rebellion against racial discrimination is symbolized by his trying to break down the doors of "the white folks' church"[4], as well as that of the prison cell. Moreover, the place free from discrimination that the protagonist wants to go to is a place that "ain't got no doors". The emphatic relational process that the white Reverend "*had* a door to shut" implicitly stresses the point that it is his responsibility to maintain racial (and class) discrimination.

In this passage, the expression "And even yet he didn't see the snow, walking right into it" contradicts the reader's expectations, since the reader has seen the protagonist walking "right in (to)" the snow from the very beginning. What the protagonist has walked "right into" at this stage is a situation of racial (and class) discrimination: the white Reverend's rebuffing him primarily because he is black. This is the first time the first-line narrative presents the racial discrimination the protagonist encounters. Compare:

(i) The big black man turned away. And even yet he didn't see the snow, walking right into it.

(ii) The big black man turned away and walked into the street. And even yet he didn't see the snow, walking right into it.

In case (ii), "walking right into it" can only refer to the protagonist's walking into the snow on the street, but since the protagonist has been walking in the snow from the very beginning, the adjunct "right into it" sounds odd and illogical. In case (i), "walking right into it" could refer back to what happened before the protagonist turned away, that is, his being rebuffed by the white Reverend. Indeed, in the original, the narrator's not mentioning the protagonist's re-entering the snowfall as well as his using the adjuncts "even yet", "right into it", seems to be a deliberate attempt to associate "snow" with the racial discrimination the protagonist has encountered for the first time in the first-line narrative. Significantly, this passage, through re-presenting the contrast between "sense/feel" and "see" within the sub-type of perception process, seems to be

145

subtly reinforcing the symbolic meaning of "snow" in relation to the protagonist's consciousness: the protagonist has walked in the first-line narrative "right into" a situation of racial discrimination (snow), which he can sense/feel, but he is still cognitively numb and his racially rebellious consciousness is not yet awakened. But of course, the symbolic meaning only functions on a deeper level, which interacts with the surface level where "snow" is merely a natural entity.

Interestingly, although at the end of the above passage, the perspective is shifted back to the omniscient narrator, the referring expression remains "the big black man" instead of changing back to "Sargeant" (compare the more natural "Sargeant" turned away). This operates not only to highlight the protagonist's racial identity, but also to lend to the symbolic meaning of the referring expression: the protagonist is a representative of the whole black race.

As the story develops, the protagonist's sense of "feeling" remains very keen and his state of being extremely hungry, sleepy and tired remains unchanged, but there is a significant change in terms of "seeing":

Sargeant blinked. When he looked up, the snow fell into his eyes. For the first time that night he *saw* the snow. He shook his head. He shook the snow from his coat sleeves, felt hungry, felt lost, felt not lost, felt cold. He walked up the steps of the church. He knocked at the door. No answer. He tried the handle. Locked. He put his shoulder against the door and his long black body slanted like a ramrod. He pushed. With loud rhythmic grunts, like the grunts in a chain-gang song, he pushed against the door. [...] He pushed against the door. Suddenly, with an undue cracking and screaking the door began to give way to the tall black Negro who pushed ferociously against the door. [...] "Un-huh," answered the big tall Negro, "I know it's a white folks' church, but I got to sleep somewhere." He gave another lunge at the door. "Hug!" And the door broke open. But just when the door gave way, two white cops arrived in a car, ran up the steps with their clubs and grabbed Sargeant. But Sargeant for once had no intention of being pulled or pushed away from the door. [...] The cops began to beat Sargeant over the head, and nobody protested. But he held on. (p. 272-273, original italics; to save space, paragraph division is not indicated)

As soon as the protagonist "sees" the snow, he starts to react against it: "He shook the snow from his coat sleeves". In the preceding context, the protagonist keenly felt the snow "seeping down his neck, cold, wet, sopping in his shoes.... sticking to his jaws, wet on his black hands, sopping in his shoes", but he did absolutely nothing about it. An opposition is created between "feeling" the snow without reacting, but "seeing" the snow with immediate action. This opposition lends itself to the symbolic meaning both of "seeing" (the awakening of the protagonist's racially rebellious consciousness) and of "snow" (the object of cognition of that consciousness). Viewed from this angle, the protagonist's shaking "the snow from his coat sleeves" may be taken as symbolizing his rebellion against racial discrimination. What immediately follows is the description that the protagonist "felt hungry, felt lost, felt not lost, felt cold". The physical condition of the protagonist's being hungry and cold remains the same, but there is a notable mental change: "felt lost, felt not lost". The two parts of this expression can be taken either as antithetic or as progressive. If taken as progressive, it seems to mime the processes of the awakening of the protagonist's racially rebellious consciousness. Even if it is taken as antithetic, it still indicates a change from the protagonist's being completely cognitively numb to a state where he is at least partially "not lost". Following this description, there comes the protagonist's rebellious action against discrimination and rejection: "He put his shoulder against the door and his long black body slanted like a ramrod". Interestingly, although the protagonist is in heavy clothes and his black body cannot be perceived, the narrator directs attention to "his long black body". The narrator, that is to say, is inviting the reader to see what is hidden from view, which is apparently an attempt to highlight the protagonist's racial identity and racial representativity. The use of the redundant epithet "black" in "black Negro" and "black unemployed Negro" lends force to this highlighting. In contrast, the "white folks' church" is depicted as marked by white color: "Broad white steps in the night all snowy white" (p. 272), and the cops and people that come to oppress the black protagonist are described as "white cops" and "white people" (p. 273).

In the preceding part of the text, the protagonist was presented as an extremely passive figure with merely mental, unrealized verbal, relational processes and material processes that do not work on anything external. As quoted above, the text even omitted the protagonist's action of knocking at the Reverend's door. What appears is only the Reverend's activity: "The Reverend Mr. Dorset, however, saw the snow when he switched on his porch light, opened the front door of his parsonage, and found standing there before him a big black man...." . Although due to the relevant situational script, readers can infer that the protagonist must have knocked at the Reverend's door, the narrator's omitting the action and presenting the protagonist merely as the Phenomenon of the Reverend's perception process makes the protagonist appear extremely passive and helpless. But as soon as the protagonist *sees* the snow, he starts to rise up against racial discrimination. At this stage, the transitivity patterning is drastically different: the protagonist is described with a series of goal-directed action processes and realized verbal processes. His rebellious action is persistent and effective, and his rebellious voice loud and forceful.

Interestingly and significantly, a cause-and-effect relationship is established between the following two processes:

(i) **For the first time that night** he *saw* the snow.

(ii) But Sargeant **for once** had no intention of being pulled or pushed away from the door. (boldface added)

The adjunct "for once" in case (ii) makes it clear that the protagonist's resistance against racial discrimination is something that has never happened in his life before. Since case (ii) is a result of case (i), the mental process "he *saw* the snow" is directly linked up with the awakening of the protagonist's racially rebellious consciousness, and its symbolic meaning hence made more apparent. Here a sensitive reader will also have a double decoding. On the surface level, the reader will take case (i) as describing the protagonist's perceiving the natural phenomenon for the first time that night. But on a deeper level, the reader may take case (i) as describing the awakening of the protagonist's racially rebellious consciousness for the first time in his life. Compare:

(i) For the first time that night he *saw* the snow.... And for the first time that night he had no intention of....

(ii) For the first time in his life he *saw* the snow... And for once he had no intention....

The adjuncts in both cases are more compatible than those in Hughes's text.

Logically speaking, since it is the protagonist's "seeing the snow" that has led to his resistance for the first time in his life, his "seeing the snow" on the symbolic plane should also be for the first time in his life. While reading Hughes's text, the need to gain coherence may somewhat suppress the incompatibility between the two adjuncts in the original and extend the first adjunct on the symbolic plane to "for the first time in his life": the protagonist may have *visually* seen snow (natural phenomenon) before, but this is the first time he is *cognitively* seeing the snow (symbolic object). Here, again, we see how semantic and cognitive reorganization in context operates to shape meaning on a deeper level, which interacts with the conventional surface meaning.

One point that may be inferred from the deviant transitivity patterning is that racial discrimination has been mystified and "naturalized" (see Belsey, [1980] 2002; Barthes, 1973) and the protagonist as a representative of the black race at first took it to be natural and physical—to be a result of the difference in physical color rather than as a result of social injustice. So even though at first he "felt" the existence of "the color line", he accepted it and remained very passive and submissive until his racial consciousness against social injustice is awakened.

3. Stylistic Sensibility versus Circularity

In processing Hughes's "On the Road," there may appear three different types of reader with three different kinds of interpretation of the protagonist's (not) seeing the snow. The first type is confined to the literal meaning and just takes "the snow" as a natural phenomenon and the protagonist's (not) seeing it as a matter of visual perception. The second type of reader may see "snow" as a symbolic image, but overlook the subtle and complex symbolic relationship between the snow and the protagonist's cognitive advancement. Relevant existing criticisms usually fall into this type, whose reading of the symbolic meaning of "snow" may be further classified into two different kinds. The first kind sees the depiction of snow as a device in helping create an environmental atmosphere. Janes A. Emanuel (1967: 95-96) says,

All the images of the story comprise a remarkable pattern of sensations that support the action. The technique, which is like the heaping of sensory words

149

in Hawthorne's "The Minister's Black Veil," can be glimpsed in this partial breakdown of the two hundred and ten patterned images in the six-page story, conveyed in fifty-four repeated words, listed by frequency of use: "door" (28 [times]); "snow" (21); "stone" (12); "black" (9); "pull" (8); "cold" (7); "white" (6); "sleepy" (6); "grab" (6); "fall" (6); "wet" (5); "hungry" (5); "tired" (5); "shut" (5); "push" (5); "cross" (5); "break" (5); "wham" (4); "cell" (4) and "jail" (4). Thus running the scale of images—visual, auditory, tactile, kinesthetic—Hughes mounts a total environment that is repellant, binding, crushing, wintry. Sargean's world is closing doors, wet snow, cold stone.

The other kind of reading associates "snow" with the "white" side in the racial opposition. Robert Bone (1988: 267), for instance, observes, "On the micro-level (language), the imagery imparts a rich texture to the prose. Images of white-on-black (snowfall at night, or white flakes on a dark skin) sustain the story's racial overtones." Both kinds of reading are valid and valuable, but both have neglected the complex and dynamic relationship the protagonist bears to the snow, especially in terms of his cognition on the deeper level.

The third kind of reading is stylistically sensitive. It is marked by a sensitive response to the linguistic patterning in the text and pays close attention to the contrast consistently created within the sub-type of perception process. This kind of reading undergoes, through a double decoding, a semantic and cognitive reorganization as directed by the textual clues, thereby succeeding in revealing previously neglected symbolic relationships and meanings. In other words, this kind of reading "offers a raised awareness of certain patterns that might have been subconscious or not even noticed at all" (Stockwell, 2002: 7).

Such stylistic analyses, which offer new interpretations, can effectively counter the charge of " circularity " from many literary critics, who characteristically try to produce new interpretations and who shut the door to stylistics because in their view "a stylistic "discovery' is really only a supplement to what the critic already knows" (Simpson, 1997: 4; see also Fish, 1981). While this "common and perennial misunderstanding" (Simpson, 1997: 4) does not apply to many stylistic analyses which investigate previously-neglected effects as generated by the author's manipulation of language, it can, however, gain support from numerous stylistic analyses whose aim is to make explicit how literary critics' intuitions are arrived at. In the foreword of *Cognitive Stylistics*, Semino and Culpeper (2002:x) make it clear that "a recurrent goal in most of the chapters is that of explaining how interpretations are arrived at, rather than proposing new interpretations of texts". Such "explaining" cognitive stylistic investigations, including those concerned with how the same text has given rise to different interpretations (see, for instance, Hamilton, 2002, Freeman, 2002), are very significant and indispensable, able to reveal systematically various facets of previously-neglected interaction between linguistic choices and cognitive phenomena. While such "explaining" investigations should be further developed, another kind of stylistic analysis should also be much promoted, a kind that aims at offering new interpretations based on the analysis of preciously neglected (responses to) patterns of language. The latter kind of stylistic investigation can demonstrate the power of stylistics in advancing literary understanding, thereby knocking open the door shut by literary critics.

4. Implied Author versus Real Author

Interestingly, the third kind of reading as classified above, which is marked by stylistic sensitivity, may often fail to gain support from the flesh-and-blood authors' overt claims. Langston Hughes once made the following comments on the genesis of the text,

> "On the Road" was not carefully planned as to plot or character. As nearly as I can remember, it was written completely at one sitting, like a poem.... All I had in mind was cold, hunger, a strange town at night whose permanent residents were not so cold and hungry, and a black vagabond named Sargeant against white snow, cold people, hard doors, trying to get somewhere, but too tired and hungry to make it—hemmed in on the ground by the same people who hemmed Christ in by rigid rituals surrounding a man-made cross. (quoted in Emanuel, 1967: 93-94; see also Berry, 1983: 224; Emanuel, 1967: 92; McLaren, 2003: 282; Ostrom, 1993: 75-76; Meltzer, 1968: 188-189)

Hughes's own comments on the genesis of "On the Road" have been widely quoted and have exerted great influence on existing criticism. But a rigorous and sensitive stylistic analysis can reveal that the text is elaborately wrought, carefully patterned, and highly symbolic. Hughes's claim that the text "was not carefully planned as to plot or character" and all he "had in mind was cold, hunger, a strange town at night. . . " is not in accord with the textual reality.

What we have here may be seen as a gap between the author in real life and the "implied" author as based on the text. The concept of "the implied author" was first proposed by Wayne Booth in *Rhetoric of Fiction* ([1961] 1983). The "implied" author is the author's "second self", the "norms" of the work, or the "picture" of the author the reader infers from the text. This concept has attracted a lot of critical attention (for most recent surveys and discussions, see Phelan, 2005: 38-49; Booth, 2005; Nünning, 2005; Shaw, 2005). It goes beyond the scope of the present study to probe into the nuances of the concept and the relevant controversies, suffice it to say that "the implied author" is based on the text itself and, as the "textual author", is usually distinguishable from the flesh-and-blood author.

In terms of "On the Road", the above stylistic analysis, coupled with a careful examination of other parts of the text, reveals a very different "textual author" from the "real author" who made the overt claims as such. The "textual author" carefully plans plot and character, elaborately manipulates language, and purposefully deviates from conventional representation to create symbolic meanings. To see more clearly the "textual" author's careful planning, let's take a look at the following three short paragraphs:

(i) It [the church] had two doors.

(ii) He [the protagonist] pushed against the door.

(iii) And the door broke open. (272-273)

These three short paragraphs are each placed between longer paragraphs, hence made psychologically prominent. They neatly form a three-stage skeleton of this part of the plot, a skeleton that is elaborately enriched and complicated with carefully-chosen details. In terms of the middle stage, the central part of the enrichment goes:

(i) He put his shoulder against the door and his long black body slanted like a ramrod

(ii) He pushed [against the door].

(iii) With..., he pushed against the door.

(iv) He pushed against the door.

(v) ...[he] pushed ferociously against it.

(vi) He gave another lunge at the door.

This is a progressive patterning of transitivity. Case (i) describes the preparatory stage, metaphorizing the protagonist's body into a gun ready to fire. Then there come three parallel processes (ii to iv) depicting the protagonist's "fighting", which echo and interact with each other to foreground the persistent rebellion. Case (v) puts emphasis on the increased intensity of the action, and case (vi) places stress on the sudden charge of the action, which finally succeeds in breaking down the door. This gives us a glimpse of how the "textual author" carefully arranges the plot.

Not only the plot is elaborately wrought, but also the characters are carefully planned. As analyzed above, the protagonist is foregrounded, through an ingenious choice of referring expressions, as a representative of the black race, and the white Reverend well depicted as a representative of the forces enforcing racial discrimination by way of highlighting his prejudiced perspective and rebuff.

But of course, the most subtle and ingenious planning of the text is found in the creation of the persistent internal contrast within the sub-type of transitivity process as analyzed above. This "internal contrast", coupled with "the cross-type equation" as such, leads to a semantic and cognitive reorganization that changes the conventional nature of certain transitivity processes involved. As we have seen, this stylistic device is part of a global symbolic patterning centering on the thematic figure "snow", which begins with the first abrupt sentence "He was not interested in the snow", developed in the depiction of the protagonist's changing relation with snow, and in the contrast between the protagonist's and the white Reverend's relation to snow. This symbolic patterning, which involves the violation of conventional semantic/cognitive organization, calls for stylistic sensitivity in order to have a double decoding with conventional meaning decoded on the surface level and the non-conventional symbolic significance decoded on the deeper level.

Interestingly, if we examine the overt claims made by the real author more carefully, we may detect certain clues to the elaborate textual planning. Although

153

the flesh-and-blood Hughes denied careful planning and claimed to have had in mind only crude facts, he did compare the writing of "On the Road" to the writing of "a poem" which is typically carefully wrought. Like many other literary writers, Hughes seemed to be deliberately challenging the readers' ability in deciphering the "hidden" meaning of the text. On the one hand, he detracted the reader's attention and made the readers' task more difficult by denying careful planning, but on the other, he seemed to be implicitly inviting the reader to read the short story in the way as reading "a poem", which demands close attention to textual planning and patterning.

Now, to get to know "the real author" of a literary text, we need go into the historical context and try to find out information from various sources about that flesh-and-blood being. By contrast, to get to know "the implied author", we need examine every detail of the text to construct the "textual" image of the author's "second self". And one way to help understand the complex relation between the real author and the implied author is to examine the gaps and links between the flesh-and-blood author's claims about his creation and the created literary text in itself.

5. Conclusion

The transitivity model as pioneered by Halliday more than 30 years ago (including its various later modifications) is concerned with how human beings organize "the endless variation and flow of events" into different process types (and sub-types). But as we have seen in Hughes's "On the Road", in literary discourse, the writer may deviate from the conventional classification of process types, create a contrast between processes within the same (sub-)type of process, and put certain processes of one (sub-)type on a par with the processes of another (sub-)type. Such non-conventional contrast and equation, as the present study shows, may lead to semantic and cognitive reorganization that changes the conventional nature of certain processes involved on a deeper level, which interacts with the surface conventional meaning. Such ingeniously-wrought stylistic features point to the careful planning of the text. If the real author makes certain claims that are not in accord with the "textual reality", stylistic analysis may shed light on the gap between the flesh-and-blood "real" author and the textually-based "implied" author. Moreover, the present study shows that the double-decoding of the two contrastive levels of meaning as such demands close attention to language patterning and may involve much stylistic sensitivity. Because of these characteristics, both the stylistic features and the effects involved may have been hidden from the view of literary critics. Stylistic analyses that reveal such hidden meanings may effectively counter the charge of "circularity" and help demonstrate stylistics as a useful and indispensable approach in advancing literary interpretation.

Notes

1. A revised and more technical version of this paper has appeared in "Internal Contrast and Double Decoding: Transitivity in Hughes' ' On the Road ' " published in *JLS: Journal of Literary Semantics* 2007, 36 (1): 53-70. I'm grateful for permission from Mouton de Gruyter to reprint the relevant materials. That *JLS* essay has replaced the third and fourth sections of this paper with a different discussion of "Stylistic analysis in comparison with literary criticism. "

2. The story, which was first written as "Two on the Road" (the protagonist and the freed stone Christ walking together with him on the road in his hallucination), also forms a satire against the institutional church. The latter part of the text very much centers on the protagonist's Christ dream. Due to the constraints of space as well as the focus on the internal contrast in transitivity, the present study refrains from going into that aspect.

3. Langston Hughes, "On the Road" in R. Baxter Miller (ed.) (2002) *The Collected Works of Langston Hughes* Vol. 15, Columbia: University of Missouri Press, p. 272, my numbering of the sentences. All subsequent references to Hughes's "On the Road" are to this edition (p. 272-276) and are cited parenthetically in the text.

4. The church is described as having "*two* doors". The numeral "*two*" is the second italicized word in the text. It may symbolize: (1) both racial and class discrimination, corresponding to the protagonist's double identity as a "black" and "unemployed" person; (2) the heaviness and profoundness of the discrimination and rejection—the protagonist only succeeds in breaking down the first door and is immediately arrested, failing to break down the second.

155

References

Barthes, R. 1973. *Mythologies*. A. Lavers (trans.). London: Paladin.

Belsey, C. 2002 [1980]. *Critical Practice*. London: Routledge.

Berry, F. 1983. *Langston Hughes: Before and Beyond Harlem*. Westport, Connecticut: Lawrence Hill.

Bone, R. 1988. *Down Home: Origins of the Afro-American Short Story*. New York: Columbia University Press.

Booth, W. C. 1983 [1961]. *The Rhetoric of Fiction*. Harmondsworth: Penguin Books.

Booth, W. C. 2005. Resurrection of the implied author: Why bother? In *A Companion to Narrative Theory*, ed. by J. Phelan and P. J. Rabinowitz, 75-88. Oxford: Blackwell.

Emanuel, J. A. 1967. *Langston Hughes*. Boston: Twayne Publishers.

Fish, S. 1981. What is stylistics and why are they saying such terrible things about it? In *Essays in Modern Stylistics*, ed. by D. C. Freeman, 53-78. London: Methuen.

Freeman, M. 2002. The body in the word: a cognitive approach to the shape of a poetic text. In *Cognitive Stylistics*, ed. by E. Semino and J. Culpeper, 23-47. Amsterdam: John Benjamins.

Halliday, M. A. K. 1971. Linguistic function and literary style: Aninquiry into William Golding's *The Inheritors*. In *Literary Style: A Symposium*, ed. by S. Chatman, 330-368. Oxford: Oxford University Press.

Halliday, M. A. K. 2004. *An Introduction to Functional Grammar* (3rd ed. , revised by C. M. I. M. Matthiessen). London: Arnold.

Hamilton, C. 2002. Conceptual integration in Christine de Pizan's *City of Ladies*. In *Cognitive Stylistics*, ed. by E. Semino and J. Culpeper, 1-22. Amsterdam: John Benjamins.

Hughes, L. 2002. On the road. In *The Collected Works of Langston Hughes* Vol. 15, ed. by R. B. Miller, 272-276. Columbia: University of Missouri Press.

Ji, Y. L & Shen, D. 2004. Transitivity and mental transformation: Sheila Watson's *The Double Hook*, *Language and Literature* 13 (4): 335-348.

Ji, Y. L & Shen, D. 2005. Transitivity, indirection, and redemption: Sheila Watson's *The Double Hook*, *Style* 39 (3): 348-362.

Langacker, R. 1991. *Foundations of Cognitive Grammar*, *Vol. II: Descriptive Application*. Stanford: Stanford University Press.

McLaren, J (ed.). 2003. *The Collected Works of Langston Hughes* Vol. 14. Columbia: University of Missouri Press.

Meltzer, M. 1968. *Langston Hughes*. New York: Thomas Y. Crowell Company.

Miller, R. B. 2002. Introduction. In *The Collected Works of Langston Hughes* (Vol. 15), ed. by R. B. Miller, 1-8. Columbia: University of Missouri Press.

Nünning, A. 2005. Reconceptualizing unreliable narration: Synthesizing cognitive and rhetorical approaches. In *A Companion to Narrative Theory*, ed. by J. Phelan and P. J. Rabinowitz, 89-107. Oxford: Blackwell.

Ostrom, H. 1993. *Langston Hughes: A Study of the Short Fiction*. New York: Twayne Publishers.

Phelan, J. 2005. *Living to Tell about It*. Ithaca: Cornell University Press.

Ryan, Marie-Laure. 1991. *Possible Worlds*, *Artificial Intelligence*, *and Narrative Theory*. Bloomington & Indianapolis: Indiana University Press.

Semino, E. & Culpeper. J. 2002. Foreword. In *Cognitive Stylistics*, ed. by E. Semino and J. Culpeper, ix-xvi. Amsterdam: John Benjamins.

Shaw, H. E. 2005. Why won't our terms stay put? The narrative communication diagram scrutinized and historicized. In *A Companion to Narrative Theory*, ed. by J. Phelan and P. J. Rabinowitz, 299-311. Oxford: Blackwell.

Simpson, P. 1997. *Language through Literature*. London: Routledge.

Simpson, P. 2004. *Stylistics*. London: Routledge.

Stockwell, P. 2002. *Cognitive Poetics*. London: Routledge.

Toolan, M. J. 1998. *Language in Literature*. London: Arnold.

Comparativity and Functional Inter-lingual Stylistics[①]

ZHANG Delu

Ocean University of China

1. Intralingual Comarative Stylistics

Halliday says, "Stylistic analysis is comparative in nature" (Halliday, 1973). In intralingual studies, a writer's stylistic choices are always implicitly compared with potential alternatives or the general norm of the language, or a norm of a register or genre, etc. Moreover, the stylistic choices of one text are often compared with those of another in the same genre or register, or those of a text in another genre or register.

In systemic functional stylistics, based on the seminal work done by M. A. K. Halliday, there has been developed a relatively comprehensive framework for analysis. The style of the text is considered to be formed by prominent features motivated by context: the context of situation and the context of culture. In a decoding process, the text is analyzed in terms of its lexical, grammatical and phonological aspects to find out what are the prominent, highlighted linguistic patterns or features. These features consist of two types: incongruity, features departing from the accepted norms in language, and deflection, features departing from the expected frequency of occurrence. Then these features are related to the context of situation and the context of culture, or in the case of literary works, the writer's total meaning to find out their functions in social communication or in achieving the writer's moral, education and aesthetic purposes. This can be shown in Figure 1.

If comparative stylistic investigation is carried out intralingually, a text is usually compared with the norm of the language in general (commoncore), or the norm of a genre or register; or the text with another text of the same author, or of

① The author wishes to express his gratitude to Professor Shen Dan for her valuable suggestions in the design of the paper.

the same period, or of the same genre or register, or that of a different author, or of a different period, genre or register.

The comparison can be made at different levels related to the meaning and function of the text, such as the context of situation, the generic structure, and the lexical, grammatical and phonological features.

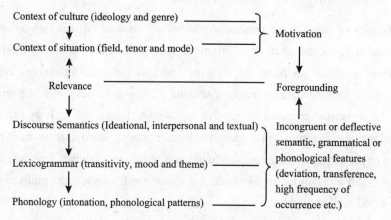

Figure 1: A Functional stylistic framework

The main aim of the comparison is to find out the unique prominent features of the text which characterize the style of the text through the discovery of the similarities and differences in the aspects compared between those in the present text and those in another.

In this case, the procedure of intralingual stylistic comparison involves three main stages: analysis, interpretation and evaluation.

2. Interlingual Comparative Stylistics

While intralingual stylistics has been developing very fast over the past half a century, interlingual stylistics is still waiting to be developed. There have been some pioneering attempts at carrying out interlingual stylistic investigations. For example, Shen (1991, 1992, 1998, 2002) has carried out a series of comparative stylistics investigations, comparing the source text and the target text to reveal the problem of what she calls "deceptive equivalence" in translation, that is, the phenomenon of being equivalent at the lexical and grammatical levels, but not equivalent in terms of stylistic values and literary significance, and find ways to

159

overcome the problem. The present study forms a further attempt in this direction, not in terms of deceptive equivalence in translation, but in terms of general comparison between texts in English and those in Chinese to find their differences and similarities in terms of stylistic values and significance.

2.1 The necessity of interlingual stylistics

The aim of intralingual comparison is mainly to find out the unique stylistic features of a particular text or a group of texts, however, that of interlingual comparison does not focus on the style of one text, but the differences between texts of different languages in terms of stylistic effects or values, so it is significant for all the linguistic practices to involve cross-lingual studies, such as foreign or second language learning, in which the learner has to learn the unique stylistic features in the texts of the target language and avoid interference from the native language, and translation, in which the translator needs to construct equivalence in meaning and stylistic values.

In doing interlingual stylistics, in terms of the data for comparison, we can compare a text in the source language with that translated into the target language without intentional alteration, or a text in the source language with another text in the target language which is of the same register or genre. In the first instance, the focus is on the appropriateness of the linguistic features in the target text as the source text pre-exists and is not necessary to be judged in this aspect, while the quality of the target text is the main object to be evaluated in this respect. In the second instance, the focus is not necessarily on the stylistic features of one text, but on the differences and similarities between the texts of the two languages. However, there can be a shift of emphasis in which one text is taken as the basis of comparison, and the main purpose of the comparison is to find out the stylistic features of the other text. It has great significance not only for translation and second or foreign language learning and teaching, but also for cross-cultural studies.

In an interlingual stylistic investigation, comparison can be made at different levels: we may need to compare the motivations for creating or translating the texts concerned and for the choice of the stylistic features in the texts compared, so we should compare (1) the sociocultural and the ideological aspects as the background features for comparison; and (2) the situational features as the immediate environment for comparison, and (3) the generic and registerial features reflecting differences in language, culture or ideology. Within the text, we can compare both the macro-aspects of the text in terms of generic structure etc., and micro-aspects concerned with the lexical and grammatical features in terms of the prominent semantic and formal features which can realize the style of the text.

2.2 A search for a new theoretical framework

As there has been little study on interlingual comparison, we need to establish a theoretical framework for interlingual stylistic comparison. As the present study is not on the general or comprehensive comparison between the texts of the two languages, but on the stylistic features of the texts, the framework should characterize the styles of the texts. In functional stylistic analysis, three aspects are of special importance. They are the prominent semantic and formal features that are potentially possible to realize the style of the text, the socio-cultural, ideological and situational background as motivation of the selection of these features, and the appropriate relation between the two: the foregrounding. In this sense, roughly, we can present the following framework (Figure 2) to show the relations between the compared texts:

The comparison can be made at different levels because the differences at any level can result in a difference in style.

The framework has one drawback: it does not show how the analysis is conducted so that it does not show what to achieve finally. So, as an addition, we need to develop a procedural framework (see Figure 3).

3. An Example of Analysis

The following is a case study of the comparison of the stylistic features between a Chinese fable and an English one on the basis of the above framework.

3.1 Data-selection

To illustrate, two texts of the same genre in two languages, here an English fable and a Chinese one, are chosen for interlingual comparative stylistic analysis (See appendix 1).

3.2 Data analysis

The text is analysed in a decoding order. As both texts are written, we begin at the lexicogrammatical level.

(1) Grammar and lexis

Transitivity: Text 1: The processes are predominantly (a) mental process of perception, e. g. *listen*; *cognition*, e. g. *believe*; *reaction*, e. g. *surprise*, *shock*; (b) verbal process, introducing quoted speech. Animal participant as medium of process (cognizant, speaker); note that there is a grammatical rule in English that the cognizant in a mental-process clause is always "human", i. e. a thing endowed with the attribute of humanity. (c) Relational process of attribute, e. g. *was spring*, *was young*, *was oblivious*, *was hard*, *sound as lyric*, etc. (d) vocabulary as content (denotative meanings), e. g. *inamoratus* as expression of "mate".

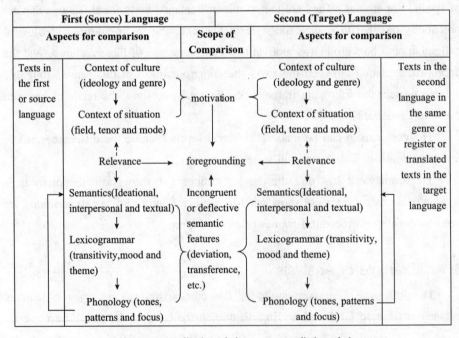

Notions: -→ = realization relation   → = mediating relation

Figure 2: A Framework for functional interlingual stylistics

Select the texts to be compared
(Source (first) —Target (second))

The analysis of the texts in terms of the context of situation and context of culture as motivation, semantic, lexicogrammatical and phonological features as prominent features in a decoding order, or bidirectionally

Determine the unique stylistic features of the second (target) language text as different from those in the first language

Interpret the features to determine the stylistic values of these features and their significance

Figure 3: Procedure of functional inter-lingual stylistic analysis

Text 2: The processes are predominantly (a) material, e. g. such as 做、取、带、藏、打、咬, etc. for introducing fighting actions between husband and wife; (b) mental processes of perception, reaction and cognition, such as 听、看、瞧、见; 爱、戏弄、冲昏、哄骗; 以为、知道、明白、了解, etc., and interestingly, the process of cognition occur predominantly in the end part of the text; (c) relational processes of mainly attribute of negative sense, such as 狭窄、混蛋、坏婆娘、示弱、有个女人、有个男人、没有人影, etc. and verbal, introducing quoted speech, human participant as medium of process (cognizant, speaker), such as 喊起来、骂起来、越骂越气, etc. (d) vocabulary as content of strong attitudinal meaning, e. g. 嫉妒、愤怒、混蛋死鬼. (See Figure 4.)

Process type text	Material	Mental	Relational	Verbal
Text 1	2	8	13	13
Text 2	20	24	12	11

Figure 4: Comparison in process types in transitivity

Mood: Text 1: every clause in narrative portions is declarative (narrative statement), and the vocabulary shows attitude (connotative meanings), e. g. *inamoratus* as expression of mock style, and special mood structure is used for proverbial wisdom, *laugh and the world laughs*. In terms of the dialogue within

163

the text, clauses in dialogue portions switch rapidly among different moods and modulations, e. g. the sequence declarative, modulated interrogative, negative declarative, moodless, declarative (statement, exclamatory question, negative response, exclamation, statement).

Text 2: Mood: in the narrative part, all are declaratives, and lexically, it is full of derogative and cursing words, emotive words: 狭窄, 争吵, 骂, 混蛋, 死鬼, 诬陷, 哄骗, 吩咐, etc. In the projected part, there is interchange of mood: declarative, imperative, interrogative, exclamative.

Modality: Text 1: there are no modals in the narrative part, but in the projected part, there are modals of mainly modulation of inclination and ability, such as can, could, would as soon,

Text 2: there are a few modals of modulations, such as 爱、感. (See Figure 5.)

System / Texts	Projecting	Projected			Modality
	Declarative	Decl	Inter	Imp	Modulation
Text 1	30	6	2	1	4
Text 2	53	9	3	0	2

Figure 5: Comparison in mood and modality

Textual: Text 1: Highly self-sufficient. Cohesion: reference is entirely endophoric (within text itself). Note reference of her as *lass* in title, suggesting highly organized text. There are elliptical clauses in the quoted speech. Lexically, there is higher lexical density per unit grammar (e. g. the first sentence), and grammatically there are less complexity, and more parallelism, of grammatical structure (e. g. there are many simple and hypotactic sentences).

In terms of thematic structure, the thematic variation (marked and nominalized themes), suggests particular information structure because of association between the two systems, "typically of the form" (theme [given]; rheme [new]) i. e. theme within given; rheme within new.

In quoting structures, the thematic form of quoted followed by quoting, with the latter (said + Subject) comprising informational "tail", e. g. "He calls her snooky-ookums," said Mrs Gray, expresses "dialogue in context of original fictional narrative".

164

Text 2: Highly self-sufficient. Cohesion: all references are endophoric. Grammatical structures are quite simple, and it adopts a running way of organization.

Theme: There are few marked themes (2 temporal theme for temporal organization). But there are many elliptical themes (as subject), which reflects the typical way of organization of the text in Chinese, and the unmarked themes are mostly human, here husband or wife or both. In the projected structure, the language is oral, and there are more various grammatical structures, strong emotive words, etc.

System Texts	Quoting		Quoted	
	Unmarked	Marked	Unmarked	Marked
Text 1	11	9	6	0
Text 2	23 +27 (ellip)	2	7 + 5(ellip)	0

Figure 6: Comparison in Thematic Structures

(2) Discourse semantics

Text 1: ideationally, it is mainly concerned with reacting, gossiping and being, that is, when the hippopotamuses are mating, the parrots will react strongly and gossip with each other about them, and when the parrots are mating, the hippopotamuses will react strongly and gossip with each other about the parrots; at the same time, it also describes the characteristics of the setting and characters. Interpersonally, the relationships are two-fold: husband and wife, sharing the same values and attitudes, and hippopotamus pair and parrot pair, showing conflicting views to each other, but sharing the same behavioural patterns. Textually, it is contextually independent, written, the narration and projection are well organized and conjoined in conformity to the generic structure of a fable. This phenomenon is clearly shown in the high frequency of occurrence of mental, relational and verbal processes; the mood and modality patterns and theme and cohesion patterns.

Here, the contrast between the act of mating and that of gossiping, and the parallel pattern are prominent semantic devices for stylistic foregrounding.

Text 2: ideationally, the text is mainly concerned with seeing, reacting and quarrelling. When the wife saw her own image in the water, she reacts irrationally with anger and violence, and the same pattern is repeated in the man's behaviour; interpersonally, there are two relations for the same two participants: husband and wife, and opponents in the conflict, having hostile feelings towards each other. The second manifests their quarrelling, while the first serves as cause of their final reconciliation; it is the same as Text 1. This again is reflected in the transitivity, mood and theme and cohesion patterns.

Here, the irrational reaction and the parallel pattern of behaviour between the wife and husband are highlighted for stylistic effect.

From here, we can see that the two languages employ similar semantic devices although there is the difference between the conflict within the couple in the Chinese fable, and that between the couples in the English one.

(3) Situation: field, tenor and mode

Field: Text 1: the Theme of the fable is human prejudice ("they're different, so hate them!"), projected through the Thesis ("plot"): fictitious interaction of animals: male/female pairs of hippopotamuses, parrots.

Text 2: the Theme of the fable is human jealousy and irrationality ("he takes in others, so hate him!"), projected through the Thesis ("plot"): fictitious interaction of man and wife.

Tenor: The relationship between the participants are twofold: (a) writer and readers; writer adopting role as recounter: specifically as humorist (partly projected through subsidiary role as moralist), and assigning complementary role to audience. (b) Text 1: mate and mate: animal pair as projection of husband and wife; each adopting own (complementary) role as reinforcer of shared attitudes. Text 2: husband and wife: each adopting the role of opponent to the other.

Mode: Text 1 and Text 2: The text is "self-sufficient", as the only form of social action by which "situation" is defined; written medium: to be read silently as private act, and it is a light essay; an original (newly-created) text projected onto the traditional fable genre, structured as narrative—with dialogue, with "moral" as culminative element.

Similarity: The field is the same in the sense of both being concerned with the Theme projected through the Thesis. The Theme in the field is different in the two texts and so is the Thesis, but this difference is irrelevant to culture and language. The tenor is essentially the same in the sense that both are concerned with two level role relations: writer and reader, and that between the characters. The mode is the same.

Difference: The only significant difference lies in the choice of characters. It is rare to find human husband and wife presented as conflicting pairs in the western fables. Even the animal spouses are constructed as being insiders to each other in Text 1.

(4) Culture: Ideology and Genre

As is shown above, the context of culture provide environment for the total choices in a language, and the preferred choices in a language are determined by the ideology of the language community. Martin defines ideology as coding orientations. So the total sets of choices in a culture will be constrained by ideology and actualized by the genre. The habitual, conventional and regular behaviours of the members of the speech community are manifested as generic structures and dynamically as stages of the genre. A fable is one of these genres, defined as "a fanciful, epigrammatic story, illustrating a moral precept or ethical observation. The characters are often animals gifted with speech and possessing the human traits commonly attributed to them, or they may be gods, persons or things. (Longman Modern English Dictionary in English.)

In Chinese, we have a similar genre called Yu Yan (寓言), "a literary work illustrating an argument or lesson by means of a story or personification of things in nature, often satirical or dissuasive" (《现代汉语词典》). In this sense, it is a bit wider in scope than the English fable, as it also includes allegory and parable, etc.

Structurally, the two are very much similar, though the Chinese one exhibits some special characteristics. In the English fable, there are two major obligatory elements: the story and the moral. The story is generally short, but possesses the similar generic structures: setting (initiation)—development (complication)—climax—coda. However, in the Chinese Yu Yan, we have one interesting element which may reflect its general characteristics, that is, there is a general characterization of the characters in the story, so we have the following structures: story + moral, and within the story, we have: general introduction—initiation—complication—climax—coda.

If we compare the morals, we can find that the English one is more behaviour-oriented: what we should do, while the Chinese one is more thought-oriented: what we should think.

4. Comparing the Unique Stylistic Features of the Two Texts

Culturally, both English and Chinese has a fable genre for both educational and aesthetic purposes, however, the Chinese Yu Yan, it seems, is broader in scope than the English fable.

If we compare the morals, we can find that the English one is more behaviour-oriented: what we should do, while the Chinese one is more thought-oriented: what we should think.

In terms of the story part, they are similar in generic structure, but the Chinese one has a general introduction to the basic traits of the characters. This difference is significant because, on the one hand, it shows ideological tendency, or coding orientation, to reason deductively, that is, what follows is out of their own personality or character, and on the other, structurally, it shows a general way of organization of the text.

As far as the content part is concerned, there is also a significant difference in the choice of characters. It is rare to find human husband and wife presented as conflicting pairs in the western cultures, and even the animal spouses are constructed as being insiders to each other as in Text 1.

Grammatically, the reference cohesion and thematic progression show the differences in the choice of characters between the two texts. For the English one, they are predominantly associated with the animal pairs, and in the Chinese one, they are mainly realized by husband and wife, their corresponding pronominal forms and ellipsis.

Semantically, what is highlighted in the English fable is the gossiping and irrational reactions of the animal pairs and their similar behaviour patterns and prejudice against the others, and in the Chinese Yu Yan, it is the lack of careful thought before actions and the irrational reactions, such as scolding each other and fight with each other. This is again realized in grammar as the predominance of verbal processes and mental processes of perception for the English fable, and the predominance of material processes, verbal processes and mental processes of all three subtypes in transitivity structures.

From here, we can see that the two languages employ similar semantic devices but there is the difference between conflict within the couple in the Chinese fable, and that between the couples in the English one, and that between verbal actions without physical actions and those with physical actions.

Interpersonally, the two texts highlight similar aspects: conflicting views and hostile attitudes and prejudice and jealousy towards each other. In accordance with the genre, grammatically this is realized by similar mood patterns, declarative for the projecting narrative part, and various mood types for the projected dialogue part. This is accompanied by strong attitudinal and emotional words and expressions.

The behaviour and thing oriented feature of the English text and the person and thought oriented feature of the Chinese text are also realized in the different thematic progressive patterns: for the English, apart from the animal pairs, we have variety of themes, many marked ones, which denote verbal actions and things, but for the Chinese, almost all the themes are persons. As identical themes run through several clauses in the sentence, they are often elided for cohesive purposes in Chinese.

5. Conclusion

From the above we can see, interlingual stylistics has a different role to play with the intralingual stylistics as the former is mainly to investigate the unique stylistic features of the text under attention, while the latter is mainly to find out the differences and similarities between the texts of the two languages in terms of their stylistic values and effects. In this sense, functional linguistics can serve as a good tool for investigation.

At the same time, it can not only reveal the different stylistic features of the texts of two languages, but also the differences in cultural values, coding orientations, and generic structures and different ways of organization etc. So it will have implications for second and foreign language teaching and learning, for cross-cultural studies and translation studies.

References

Cornor, U. 1996. *Contrastive Rhetoric: Cross-cultural Aspects of Second Language Writing.* Cambridge: CUP.

Halliday, M. A. K. 1973. *Explorations in the Functions of Language*. London: Edward Arnold.

Halliday, M. A. K. 1978. *Language as Social Semiotic: The Social Interpretation of Language and Meaning*. London: Edward Arnold.

Hartmann, R. R. K. 1980. *Contrastive Textology: Comparative Discourse Analysis in Applied Linguistic*. Heidelberg: Julius Groos Verlag.

James, C. 1980. *Contrastive Analysis*. Harlow Essex: Longman.

Martin, J. 1992. *English Text: System and Structure*. Armsterdam: John Benjamins Publishing Co.

Shen, D. 1991. On the transference of modes of speech from Chinese narrative fiction into English, *Comparative Literature Studies* 28(4): 395-415.

Shen, D. 1992. Syntax and literary significance in the translation of realistic fiction, *Babel* 38 (3): 149-167.

Shen, D. 1998. *Literary Stylistics and Fictional Translation*. Beijing: Peking University Press.

申丹(Shen, D.), 2002, 论文学文体学在翻译学科建设中的重要性, 《中国翻译》1: 11-15。

张德禄(Zhang, D.), 1998, 《功能文体学》。济南: 山东教育出版社。

张德禄(Zhang, D.), 2005, 《语言的功能与文体》。北京: 高等教育出版社。

Appendix

Text 1: The lover and his lass

An arrogant gray parrot and his arrogant mate listened, one African afternoon, in disdain and derision, to the lovemaking of a lover and his lass, who happened to be hippopotamuses.

"He calls her snooky-ookums," said Mrs Gray. "Can you believe that?" "No," said Gray. "I don't see how any male in his right mind could entertain affection for a female that has no more charm than a capsized bathtub." "Capsized bathtub, indeed!" exclaimed Mrs Gray. "Both of them have the appeal of a coastwise fruit steamer with a cargo of waterlogged basketballs."

But it was spring, and the lover and his lass were young, and they were oblivious of the scornful comments of their sharp-tongued neighbors, and they continued to bump each other around in the water, happily pushing and pulling, backing and filling, and snorting and snaffling. The tender things they said to each other during the monolithic give-and-take of their courtship sounded as lyric to them as flowers in bud or green things opening. To the Grays, however, the bumbling romp of the lover and his lass was hard to comprehend and even harder to tolerate, and for a time they thought of calling the A. B. I., or African Bureau of Investigation, on the ground that monolithic lovemaking by enormous creatures who should have become decent fossils long ago was probably a threat to the security of the jungle. But they decided instead to phone their friends and neighbors and gossip about the shameless pair, and describe them in mocking and monstrous metaphors involving skidding buses on icy streets and overturned moving vans.

Late the evening, the hippopotamus and the hippopotami were surprised and shocked to hear the Grays exchanging terms of endearment.

"Listen to those squawks," wuffled the male hippopotamus.

"What in the world can they see in each other?" gurbled the female hippopotamus.

"I would as soon live with a pair of unoiled garden shears," said her inamoratus.

They called up their friends and neighbors and discussed the incredible fact that a male gray parrot and a female gray parrot could possibly have any sex appeal. It was long after midnight before the hippopotamuses stopped criticizing the Grays and fell asleep, and the Grays stopped maligning the hippopotamuses and retired to their beds.

MORAL: *Laugh and the world laughs with you, love and you love alone.*

(James Thurber, *Further fables for our time* (London 1956): 369)

Text 2: 夫妻妒影

有一对夫妇，他们的心胸很狭窄，总爱为一点小事争吵不休。有一天，妻子做了几样好菜，想到如果再来点酒助兴就更好了。于是她就拿瓢到酒缸里去取酒。

妻子探头朝缸里一看，瞧见了酒中倒映着的自己的影子。她也没细看，一见缸中有个女人，以为是丈夫对自己不忠，偷着把女人带回家来藏在缸里，嫉妒和愤怒一下子冲昏了她的头脑，她连想都没想就大声喊起来："喂，你这个混蛋死鬼，竟然敢瞒着我偷偷把别人的女人藏在缸里面。你快过来看看，看你还有什么话说？"

丈夫听了糊里糊涂的，不知道发生了什么事情，赶紧跑过来往缸里瞧，看见的是自己的影子。他一见是个男人，也不由分说地骂起来："你这个坏婆娘，明明是你领了别的男人回家，暗地里把他藏在酒缸里面，反而诬陷我，你到底安的是什么心眼！"

"好哇，你还有理了！"妻子又探头往缸里看，见还是先前的那个女人，以为是丈夫故意戏弄她，不由勃然大怒，指着丈夫说："你以为我是什么人，是任凭你哄骗的吗？你，你太对不起我了……"妻子越骂越气，举起手中的水瓢就向丈夫扔过去。

丈夫侧身一闪躲开了，见妻子不仅无理取闹还打自己，也不甘示弱，于是还了妻子一个耳光。这下可不得了，两人打成一团，又扯又咬，简直闹得不可开交。

最后闹到了官府，官老爷听完夫妻二人的话，心里顿时明白了大半，就吩咐手下把缸打破。一个侍卫抡起大锤，一锤下去，葡萄酒从被砸破的大洞汩汩流了出来。不一会儿，葡萄酒流光了，缸里也就没有人影了。

夫妻二人这才明白他们嫉妒的只不过是自己的影子而已，心中很是羞惭，于是就互相道歉，重又和好如初了。

这对夫妻见到自己的影子时，毫不思考分析就被嫉妒冲昏了头脑了，伤了和气。我们遇到怀疑的事，不要过早下结论，要客观、理智地去分析，才能够了解真相。

Transitivity, Indirection, and Redemption in Sheila Watson's *The Double Hook*[①]

JI Yinglin & SHEN Dan

Peking University

1. Introduction

In "What Is Stylistics and Why Are They Saying Such Terrible Things about It?" Stanley Fish makes a most vehement and influential attack on stylistics.[1] A major target of Fish's attack is "circularity", which "makes some people impatient with stylistics and its baggage" (1981: 55). Literary stylisticians investigate the relation between linguistic form and literary significance. But in Fish's view, the literary significance is "preselected" by the analyst and "is, in effect, responsible for its own discovery" (1981: 58). According to Fish, "there is no gain in understanding" in stylistic analysis: "the procedure has been executed, but it hasn't gotten you anywhere" (1981: 55). Fish's view is shared by many literary critics who hold that "a stylistic 'discovery' is really only a supplement to what the critic already knows; a means of offering pseudo-scientific evidence—if such evidence were needed—for an interpretation made entirely through intuition" (Simpson, 1997: 4). While this "common and perennial misunderstanding" (Simpson, 1997: 4) does not apply to many stylistic analyses which shed light on various effects generated by the author's manipulation of language, it could, however, gain support from numerous stylistic analyses which merely aim at substantiating literary critics' intuitions. In *Language and Literature: An Introductory Reader in Stylistics*, Ronald Carter says, "Students of literature frequently say that they are experiencing particular tones, moods of feelings from contact with the text, but often lack the confidence or a method that will give them the confidence, to explore more fully and then explicitly formalise *those same feelings*" (1982, our emphasis). Now, if stylistics only functions to "explicitly formalise *those same feelings*" of literary critics, literary critics could indeed "be forgiven for being

① This essay was published in *Style* 2005, 39(3): 348-362. We are grateful to the managing editor of *Style* for permission to reprint the essay.

reluctant to adopt stylistics as an effective method of literary study" (Simpson, 1997: 3). To show the usefulness of stylistics, it is essential that stylistic analysis sheds new light on the text. The present study forms an attempt to demonstrate the usefulness of stylistics by way of investigating Sheila Watson's *The Double Hook*.

Since its publication in 1959, Sheila Watson's *The Double Hook* has attracted substantial attention from literary critics. Although interpretations of the novella are numerous and diverse, many critics agree upon its theme of redemption. [2] From the very beginning, the novella plunges the reader into a series of violent acts of the protagonist James: he kills his mother as a defiance and rejection of her all-pervasive tyranny that has held him in thrall; he blinds Kip, whose probing insight makes him restless and apprehensive; in a rage he also, before fleeing to the distant town, whips the girl Lenchen, who is pregnant with his baby, and his sister Greta, who subsequently commits fiery suicide. After being duped to a penniless state and disillusioned in town, James finally returns to a new life in his native village, where a spiritual community is formed. Now, although many scholars believe in James's redemption, which is crucial to the holistic pattern of sacrifice and rebirth in the novella, it is challenged by some other critics (Betts, 2000; McKenzie, 1996; Moss, 1985; Nilsson, 1993; Vincent, 2000). Representative of these is George Bowering, who asserts: "Some readers have gone a little too far in their view of James as redeemer and renewer. He did, after all, murder his mother and blinds a young man before returning to the pregnant lass he had abandoned" (1985). Both groups confine their discussion to plot development, hardly paying any attention to Watson's manipulation of language. In the eyes of the former group, although James's actions are violent and destructive in the sense that they result in his mother's death, the blinding of Kip, and the fiery suicide of Greta, these actions are simultaneously productive in that they also lead to the birth of a baby and a fresh land waiting for a new cycle of life (Downton, 1985; Grube, 1966; Morriss, 1985; Moss, 1985). Or in other words, James's redemption is "justified by the overall transformation that occurs in the life of the community" (Jones, 1970; see also Child, 1985, McPherson, 1985, Northey, 1985, Theall, 1985). But given the nature of James's actions, especially that of matricide, this justification based merely on plot development may not sound convincing, thus giving rise to the relevant critical controversy. What has so far been neglected is the hidden yet significant relation between transitivity patterning, indirect presentation, and the theme of redemption. In fact, Watson consciously paves the way for the protagonist's redemption through her ingenious verbal choices rather than through plot arrangement. A transitivity analysis of the verbal choices will shed fresh light on the narrative and help resolve the critical controversy.

As we all know, transitivity analysis is based on M. A. K. Halliday's systemic-functional grammar (1985). Transitivity, an indispensable component of the experiential function of language, refers to the grammatical system by which "the endless variation and flow of events" are sorted out and represented. It construes the world of experience into a manageable set of process types (material, behavioral, mental, verbal, relational, and existential), and a typical process consists of three components: the process itself, participants in the process, and circumstances associated with the process (1973). Following Halliday's influential analysis of the thematic function of transitivity patterns in William Golding's *The Inheritors*, many stylisticians have adopted the transitivity model in investigating Anglo-American literary narratives. To name a few, Michael Short's analysis (1976) of Steinbeck's *Of Mice and Men*; Chris Kennedy's analysis (1982) of Conrad's *The Secret Agent*; Deirdre Burton's analysis (1982) of Sylvia Plath's *The Bell Jar*; Roger Fowler's analysis (1986) of Charles Maturin's *Melmoth the Wanderer*; Marie Hastert and Jean Weber's analysis (1992) of Eliot's *Middlemarch*; Paul Simpson's analysis (1993) of William Golding's *Pincher Martin*; and Peter Stockwell's exploration (2002) of John Donne's "The Extasie".

As regards *The Double Hook*, the transitivity model enables us to make a systematic analysis of the author's way of presenting James's acts of violence, a way marked by such a degree of obliqueness and indirection that it functions greatly to reduce the violence involved, to play down James's role of "victimizer," and to absolve James, to a significant extent, of his responsibility and guilt, thus subtly paving the way for his redemption.

2. The Scene of Matricide: Multiple Indirection

The novella opens with an ordinary scene of one summer morning in a family of a tiny village: "Greta was at the stove. Turning hotcakes. Reaching for the

175

coffee beans. Grinding away James's voice" (Watson, 1989: 1). The scene appears to be quite peaceful, but actually "James's voice" is what he utters while killing his mother. Although the unconventional and metaphorical expression of "Grinding away James's voice" may make the reader feel puzzled to some extent, it surely will not lead to any association with violence or ferocity. And following this peaceful scene comes the depiction of James's matricide, which is unconventionally presented in a highly indirect way:

James was at the top of the stairs. His hand (was) half-raised. His voice
Attribute (cir.)   Carrier Rel.   Attribute Carrier Rel.

(was) Carrier Rel. [3] in the rafters.
             Attribute (cir.)

James walking away.   The old lady falling. There under the jaw of
Actor Mat. Cir. (Extent)   Actor   Mat.   Cir.

the roof.   In the vault of the bed loft. Into the shadow of death. Pushed by
(Location)   Cir. (Location)   Cir. (Accompaniment)

James's will. By James's hand. By James's words: This is my day. You'll not
Cir. (Cause) Cir (Cause)   Cir. (Cause)

fish today. (Watson, 1989: 1)

The first paragraph contains three relational processes, indicating the location of James, the state of his "hand," and the "position" of his "voice" respectively. The absence of action process and the omission of the victim in depicting the matricide result in an unconventionally static scene concerned with James's own location, rather than the usual dynamic one concerned with the victimizer's killing the victim. By this is meant that James's matricide is covered up in a dramatic way (compare: James *half-raised his hand* and *pushed his mother* down to the ground from the top of the stairs). Further, after the paragraph division, we have "James walking away", so the first paragraph is supposed to present the whole event of matricide, but the presentation, through choosing only relational processes with only James himself involved, blurs the picture and totally covers up the killing itself.

The second paragraph, containing eight minor sentences, is marked by disjunctive syntax, but if, for the convenience of discussion, we overlook the unconventional use of full stops, the paragraph can be identified as being composed of two action processes (a. James walking away, b. The old lady falling), with the latter process embracing complex circumstantial elements indicative of location, accompaniment, and causes respectively. The two processes are both intransitive and do not seem to have any connection with each other.

At first sight, the old lady seems to be responsible for her own falling. This view is strengthened by the following three minor or incomplete "sentences," all indicating the location and destination of the falling. The other important participant of the process, that is, the real agent of the act "falling" is made to appear in the process only in the form of circumstantial elements (see below). Furthermore, four elements of location and accompaniment ("There under the jaw of the roof. In the vault of the bed loft. Into the shadow of death. Pushed by James's will") are sandwiched between "The old lady falling" (the effect of the process) and "Pushed by James's hand" (the cause of the process). This, coupled with the separating force inherent in the full stops, operates to dissociate the cause of the process from its effect. Apparently, the unconventionally high frequency of full stops is deliberately employed here to weaken the intrinsic cause-and-effect relation between "The old lady falling" and "Pushed by James's hand." Seen in this light, James's role as the killer is ingeniously veiled and the whole picture of matricide is successfully blurred, keeping to a minimal degree the essential part James plays in this process.

The processes under discussion are also characterized by the progressive aspect (i. e., "walking," "falling") without tense. Such treatment encourages "a reading of the events as simultaneous, rather than sequential" (Marta, 1985). And since "walking away" is presented prior to "falling," if the two acts are taken to be sequential, "walking away" would be taken, at least temporarily, as the first act, thus somewhat dissociating James from the death of the old lady, as if the "falling" had occurred after James had walked away. So understood, this deliberate sequencing also functions to undermine the causal relation between James's pushing and his mother's death.

The paragraph in question is notably marked by an abundance of circumstantial elements. James's volition, words, and action involved in the matricide are lumped together into a circumstantial whole ("Pushed by James's will. By James's hand.

177

By James's words"). It is worth mentioning that the disjunctive syntax resulting from the unconventional employment of full stops here functions to foreground the discrete components involved in the matricide. To quote Geoffrey Leech, the full stop is "the heaviest punctuation mark... the effect of it is to emphasize the autonomy of each piece of information, which is thereby asserted with the maximum force" (1981). Seen in this light, each component involved in the matricide, "will," "hand," and "words" respectively, is highlighted by being endowed with syntactic autonomy and thus becomes the sole focus of their respective minor sentences. Since "will" and "words" have no real power of killing, the "hand," sandwiched in between "will" and "words," seems to have somewhat lost its potency for the physical action of killing.

At this point, the introduction of primacy-effect theory will shed further light on the picture. The central claim of primacy effect can be summarized as follows: the information situated at the beginning of a message has the crucial effect in determining the overall impression of the event, and once a first impression has been formed, it will be taken on trust on the part of the reader, thus making it rather difficult to impose further modification or clarification (see Perry, 1979; also Rimmon-Kenan, 2002). Seen in this light, it is not surprising that "The old lady falling," which temporarily appears to be a spontaneous and discrete incident within the sentence boundary and which is situated at the initial position of the second process, plays a key role in determining the reader's overall impression of the event. Once the old lady's falling has been accepted by the reader as a discrete event without external cause, the retrospective elaboration on it as being "Pushed by James's will. By James's hand. By James's words" may somewhat lose its force. Of course, given that a literary reader would expect the sequel to enrich or modify the first impression she has obtained (Perry, 1979: 57), one may contend that it goes too far in claiming that the impression of "The old lady falling... into the shadow of death" will not be revised by the ensuing phrases. However, the point holds true at least to the extent that readers are unlikely to override or destroy completely their first impression already established in the preceding reading not only because both the old lady's death as a spontaneous occurrence and James's absence from the scene of crime have been rendered psychologically prominent but also because the impression of James's innocence is very much strengthened by the subsequent passages. The paragraph closes with a direct presentation of "James's voice": "This is my day. You'll not fish today." Though it occupies the end-focus position, the words soon lose their potency since they are contradicted and negated by the immediately following narration: "Still the old lady fished". Indeed, the old lady still seems to be living with her fishing beheld by everyone in the village. She is seen by Ara: "Ara saw her fishing along the creek" (Watson, 1989: 12); by Felix: "Felix saw the old lady. She was fishing in his pool... Fishing far from her own place" (Watson, 1989: 15); by Widow Wagner and her boy: "The old lady from the above is fishing down in our pool, he said" (Watson, 1989: 16); by kip: "Your old lady's down to Wagners' he said" (Watson, 1989: 25) and even by Greta on the eve of her fiery suicide: "She turned quickly. Her mother was standing in the stairs" (Watson, 1989: 74). It is true that the reader may take the old lady's appearance as a specter or ghostly presence, but such a supposition is blurred since the presentation of the old lady's emergence apparently contradicts the prototype of a ghost rooted in the reader's mind, something like a slim shadow with a fuzzy face and a hollow voice, wandering around in the inkiness of night. In stark contrast, what we have here is a living figure perceived by everyone in the broad daylight, and most importantly, she is closely associated with concrete actions (e. g. , "draw a line with the barb"; "fishing shamelessly with bait"; "throwing her line into the best pool"), definite images (e. g. , "fishing without glance towards her daughter-in-law"; "So old, So wicked"; "the branches wrapped like weeds above her head"), and meaningful words ("Don't play with those, Greta, she said. They're hard to get. A person has to know how to play with fire"). The reader is therefore given the impression that the old lady is still there, not as an illegible specter but as a living person.

As a result, the reader's interpretation of the old lady's being *killed* by James is constantly challenged and naturally seesaws between affirmation and denial. In chapter 12, there comes the following description:

> And higher up on the far side she [Ara] saw the old lady, the branches wrapped like weeds above her head, dropping her line into the stream.
>
> She saw and motioned with her hand.
>
> Kip's eyes looked steadily before him.

Your old lady's down to Wagners, he said to James.

She's there, Ara said.

James turned his heel. But when he turned, he saw nothing but the water-hole and the creek and the tangle of branches which grew along it.

Ara went down the path, stepping over the dried hoof-marks down to the creek's edge. She, too, saw nothing now except a dark ripple..... (Watson, 1989: 26-27).

What is most notable here is the lack of emotional responses of James when he is guided to look at his mother, the person he has killed. Since the matricide is not directly presented (i. e., "The old lady falling.... You'll not fish today") and since the mother is constantly depicted as living afterwards, James's appearance as a detached onlooker here functions to make the matricide even more opaque. Questions may arise in the reader's mind: Is James the real murderer? Or is the old lady's falling into death just something of James's illusion, an image he has been anticipating for years? Later in the text, there comes the revelation that "The old lady had disappeared" (Watson, 1989: 14), which is repeated more than once, "the old lady had gone" (Watson, 1989: 15); "Now Ma's lying dead in her bed" (Watson, 1989: 37). Though the death of the old lady is somehow affirmed, the repeated resort to the intransitive verb (i. e., "disappeared," "gone," and "lying dead"), which implies a conscious evasion from the use of transitive process (e. g., the old lady had been *killed* by James), functions again to veil James's role as the victimizer responsible for the old lady's death. It should have become clear that Watson purposefully uses various means, especially transitivity patterns, to blur the whole picture of James's matricide, undercutting drastically the violence and brutality associated with the crime.

3. The Scene of Blinding Kip: Whose Responsibility?

As the novella develops, it becomes apparent that indirect presentation as a way to absolve James of his responsibility and guilt is a sustained stylistic strategy. Here is the depiction of James's blinding Kip, where the violent acts of James are purposefully metamorphosed into phenomena of the sensing activities of onlookers:

Then they heard James's voice rising in the barn. They heard a cry.
Cir.   Senser Men.   Phe.   Senser Men. Phe.

They heard Kip's voice: You bastard, James. They heard James's voice.
 Senser Men.   Phe.   Senser Men.   Phe.

They heard his words: If you were God Almighty, if you'd as many eyes as
 Senser Men.   Phe.

a spider I'd get them all.

They heard a bucket overturn and animals move in their stalls.

                  Actor   Mat.   Actor Mat.   Cir.
 Senser Men.   Phe.

 Then they heard James's voice again: Miserable shrew, smell me out if
Cir. Senser Men.   Phe.

you can.
(Watson, 1989: 55)

The passage occurs when James and Kip are engaged in a fierce fight in the barn nearby the house where Greta and Lenchen are standing by the doorway in silence. The literary effect here is primarily ascribable to the deliberate yet ingenious adoption of mental process, and perception process in particular (i. e., "They heard...") as the mode of presentation, a mode that is rendered natural through adopting "the angle of vision" of Greta and Lenchen. Given that the fighting scene under depiction is a highly dramatic one where immediacy and impact usually deserve priority, an alternative mode seems to be particularly called for: the material process to describe concrete physical actions. In that case, it will invite a scenic presentation by an omniscient narrator and will consequently make the potency and impact inherent in James's blow keenly felt by the reader. By way of adopting the focalization of two characters who cannot see but only hear what has happened, the author successfully yet naturally suppresses any direct reference to the act of fighting, restricting the presentation to the focalizing characters' sensing of the "voice" and "noise" involved in the fight, making it appear very much like a quarrel. It is true that the phenomenon of the penultimate process of sensing contains two action processes in it: (a) "a bucket overturn" and (b) "animals move in their stalls." But the first can be the result of someone's or even some animal's accidental movement, not necessarily the result of a fierce fighting; and the second, which is marked by neutrality, does not seem to convey the sense of fierceness and violence. Being subjected to the spatial constraints of the mode of focalization adopted, precise details of the fighting disappear. This makes it impossible to pin down the respective part the two youngsters play in their wrangling. It therefore seems unreasonable to put all the blame on James for Kip's blinding especially when the tangled nature of the fighting is taken into account. In other words, it becomes difficult to accord the role of "victimizer" solely to James and "victimized" to Kip. In short, a highly dramatic scene of wrangling is transformed into a documentary of the witnesses' auditory experience of "voice" and the movement of "a bucket" and "some animals;" thus it drastically undercuts the ferocity and intensity involved. Seen in this light, the mental process as a presentational mode functions as a disguise or cover to veil the brutality of the fighting. The focus of the reader's attention is thus directed to the fighting as a whole rather than to the crucial role James plays in it. And such an impression is further reinforced in the closing part of the novella where Kip himself defends James's violence and readily accepts responsibility for bringing it about: "It's my eyes... but I had it coming... I kept at him like a dog till he beat around the way a porcupine beats with his tail" (Watson, 1989: 102, 117).

Furthermore, the passage is characterized by a remarkable absence of circumstantial elements expressive of the possible feelings and reactions of the witnesses, such as anxiety or apprehension. There thus emerge two uninvolved witnesses, detached from the whole matter and with no intention to interfere. Significantly, the report of the fighting takes on a somewhat neutral tone. This potential suppression of reader's aversion and elicitation of their emotional detachment, coupled with the oblique way the fighting is reported, helps to reduce to a great extent James's barbarity and allows meanwhile sufficient room for the author to redeem her protagonist in the end.

4. The Scene of Lacerating: James's Role Backgrounded

The deliberate yet artful attempt of the author to absolve James from sin or violence also finds its expression in the following several lines describing James's whipping of Greta and Lenchen. Here James's role as a whipper is played down primarily through the adoption of an impersonalized actor:

He lifted his whip. It reached out towards her [Greta], tearing through
                                                                  Material

Actor Mat. Goal Actor   Mat.   Cir. (Extent)

the flowers of her housecoat, leaving a line on her flesh. Then as the thong
   Goal   Mat. Goal Cir.

Cir. (Accompaniment)   Cir. (Accompaniment)   Cir.   Actor

unloosed its sweep, it coiled with a jerk about Lenchen's knees.

  Mat.   Range   Actor Mat. Cir. (Accompaniment)

(Watson, 1989: 56)

This passage is notably marked by the following features in terms of transitivity:

1. There is a preference on the part of the author for nonhuman or inanimate actor—"it" or "the thong"—rather than the conventional personalized one of "he."

2. In the material processes involved, there is a striking absence of goal; that is, most processes are predominantly nondirected.

3. There is an abundance of circumstantial elements. Rather than being static and indicative of extent, location, and the like, these elements are unusually dynamic.

Significantly, the role of the thong is emphasized and magnified to such an extent that the role of its hidden manipulator is completely submerged. That is, this impersonalized actor ("it" or "the thong") functions to make implicit and obscure the key role James plays in the act of lacerating. It seems that what James is responsible for is just "lifting" the whip while the other actions such as "reached out," "tearing through," and "unloose its sweep" are attributable to the thong itself. The reader is thus given the impression that James has no significant bearing on the act of whipping and should not be blamed too much for the ensuing disasters, namely, Greta's fiery suicide in desperation and Lenchen's unexpected birth-giving in nervousness.

What is equally interesting is that Greta and Lenchen, as the targets of whipping, remain absent in the position of goal despite the fact that they are the objects at which the act of "tear" or "sweep" are directed. Their being whipped is presented only circumstantially. This unconventional treatment leads to the impression that lacerating Greta and Lenchen is the unavoidable accompanying circumstances resulting from the thong's own motion.

5. The Revelation of James's "True" Character

It is clear that Watson deliberately and consistently exploits transitivity choices to tone down the violence of James's actions. In so doing, she paves the way for the revelation of James's "true" character in chapter 11, part 4, of the novella:

He climbed the bank. Through Felicia's window he saw Traff sitting at
Act. Mat. Rank   Cir. (manner)   Sen. Men. (perceptive)
Felicia's table counting a handful of bills: ten, twenty, thirty, forty, fifty,
Phe.

sixty, two, four, six. Lilly was sitting on the edge of the table resting back
Act.   Mat.   Cir. (location)

on her hands. In one of them she held a wallet. He put his hand up to his pocket.
Cir. (manner) Cir. (location) Act. Mat. Goal Act. Mat.   Cir. (extent)

His wallet   was   gone.
Carrier Rel. (attributive) Attribute

Traff's head shone yellow in the lamplight. James had no desire to move.
       Act.   Mat.   Cir.   Cir. (location) Possr. Rel. (poss) Possd.
He watched Traff curiously. Traff put the bills in his pocket. Got up. Took
Sen. Men. Phe. Cir. (manner) Act. Mat. Goal   Cir. (location) Mat. Mat.
the lid off the Stove and, reaching for the wallet, tossed it into the fire-box.
Goal Cir. (extent)   Mat.   Goal   Mat. Goal Cir. (location)
James saw him put the lid back. He wondered where Christine, Felicia and
      Senser Men.   Phe.   Sen. Men. (cog.) Phe.
the other man were. Traff had gone over to Lilly. As he bent over her she
                    Act. Mat.   Cir. (extent) Cir. (accompaniment) Act.
curled her legs behind the bend of his knees. They were both laughing.
Mat.   Goal   Cir. (location)   Sen.   Cir. Men.

Alone outside the glass of the cabin window James laughed too. Laughed
       Cir. (location)   Sen.   Men. Cir. Men.
looking in at someone else. The price of his escape lay snug in one of Traff's
Cir. (manner)   Act.   Mat. Cir. (location)

trouser pockets. Traff was bending closer. The girl's hands were on his shoulders.

              Act. Mat.   Cir. Carrier   Rel. Attribute

James turned away from the cabin... (Watson, 1989: 56)

 Act.   Mat.   Cir. (extent)

Here, James stands outside the cabin where Traff, the scoundrel who has duped him, and Lily, the whore who has stolen his wallet, are sharing the booty. In this passage, the majority of the subjects of the clauses (13, 52%) are "Traff," "Lily," or parts of their bodies such as "Traff's head" or "The girl's hands." Among these clauses, 11 (85%) contain action processes[4] and most of them are transitive (e. g., "counting the bill," "took the lid off," "tossed it"). The verbs involved refer to a series of simple movements or gestures (e.g., "put," "got up," "took... off," "reaching for," "tossed"), which are prompt in nature. By contrast, among the 10 clauses with James as the subject, as many as 6 processes[5] belong to the mental type while there are only 3 processes in which James is acting or moving. Of these 3, though there is a case in which James acts actively ("He climbed the bank"), the other two are of a rather passive kind: one indicates unequivocally the departure from the scene ("James turned away from the cabin") and the other ("James put his hand up to the pocket") undermines the reader's expectation that James will take immediate actions to seek revenge on the two scoundrels. Indeed, James's action does not extend beyond himself. Therefore, there is a stark contrast set up between verbs of swift movement in their most active and dynamic shapes (e. g., "put," "took," "reached," "tossed") on the part of the victimizer (Traff and Lily) and the inert perceptive or cognitive verbs (i. e., "saw," "watched," "wondered") on the part of the victimized (James). What is presented is no longer a young man swaying his fist or whip in a rage but instead a rather passive observer with childlike curiosity.

As regards the mental processes, it is particularly important to note that almost all clauses of action ascribable to Traff and Lily can be taken as the "phenomena" of the perceptive activities of James, who is perceiving all the happenings through the glass of the cabin window. And this significantly bears on the covert or implicit shift in focalization. "Traff's head" and "The girl's hand" appear in the thematic position of their respective clauses simply because they are the only things perceivable from James's perspective. Viewed in this way, superficial action clauses such as "Traff's head shone yellow in the lamplight" or "She curled her legs behind the bend of his knees" lose their meaning in autonomy, and it seems more natural and reasonable to view them as the "phenomena" James perceives rather than events presented through a narrator's perspective. It needs to be stressed that there is no immediate justification for the predominance of James's mental process or the lack of his action process, for it is in conflict with what the reader expects: James, upon finding his being coaxed, will fly into a rage, break into the cabin, beat those scoundrels, and take back his money. The unexpected inertia of James perhaps should not be taken as his ineffectual manipulation of the environment but rather as his ready resignation of resorting to violent means for the settling of business. Then what factors underlie this relinquishment? One point that cannot be neglected is that James has fled from the tiny village where, as Margaret Atwood has said, his family (with the eccentric mother and hysterical sister) "huddles together like sheep in a storm or chickens in a coop: miserable and crowded" (1972: 132). That is a rigorously defined world, "so well-defined in fact that it may threaten to overwhelm the individual" (1972: 17). And most probably it is the longing for breaking away from the suffocating environment that motivates James's violence and subsequent escape. Such an awareness may even lead to the reader's assumption that James is probably not brutal by nature, that his violence can be justifiably accounted for by the distortion of character due to the stifling atmosphere of the village. James himself, that is to say, can be regarded as a victim of his environment. The bitter experience in town makes him eventually realize that his escape from the village "resembles those of the three blind men trying to describe the elephant" (1972: 9), and a true identification can only be obtained from the land to which he, as well as other members of the community, is closely attached. Therefore, the only way out is to retreat his steps and embark on a returning journey, by means of which he finally gains redemption and rebirth.

The progression from actor to senser, victimizer to victimized, violence to inertia, and escape to return is by no means abrupt in Watson's text, since, as analyzed above, her subtle choices of transitivity processes, coupled with other devices of "indirect presentation," make James appear to be somewhat "nonviolent" and "guilt-free" from the very beginning.

Many critics share the view that the protagonist James comes to "represent suffering humanity as well as its deliverer" (Grube, 1966: 78). Indeed, James's progression from sin to redemption may be seen as symbolizing a quest myth, related to what Northrop Frye has identified in "The Theory of Myths" as "the "Genesis-apocalypse myth' of the Bible" (1957). And Watson has "displaced" the myth "to a real world so successfully that setting, characters, and events, while not limited to the 20th century interior dry-belt of B. C. [British Columbia], nevertheless are believable in that context" (Mitchell, 1985). Indeed, James's redemption is crucial and indispensable for the accomplishment of a regeneration process where "each member of the settlement comes to grips with the problem of fear and isolation... growing into the new community that is forming" (Grube, 1966: 76). And this "problem of fear and isolation," coupled with the transcendental image of a finally integrated community, is of particular significance to Canada, "a country with disparate regions, an adventurous Western frontier in the recent past, and a large number of ethic groups who have been only partially assimilated" (Grube, 1966: 73). Different readers in different sociohistorical contexts may respond to the theme of redemption in different ways based on their particular experiences and contexts of reading. Stylistic analysis in itself may not be able to add much to such contextual interpretations, but it certainly can help to bring to light the author's thematically motivated verbal choices in the text. It should have become clear that it is the ingenious transitivity patterning in *The Double Hook* that subtly paves the way for the protagonist's redemption in the end.

6. Conclusion

As we know, a narrative is often classified into two levels: story and discourse (see Chatman, 1978; Shen, 2002; Shen, 2001). The level of discourse mainly consists of two aspects: narrative strategies and verbal choices, the former being the focus of attention of narratologists and the latter that of stylisticians (Shen, 2005). Interestingly, while stylistics in various forms has been flourishing in Britain, its development has been rather limited in America, where, however, narratology has enjoyed much greater development. Now, since the writer's verbal choices are very much neglected not only by literary critics, but also by narratologists (Rimmon-Kenan, 1989; Shen, 2005), stylistics has an indispensable role to play, a role that has become more important since the "death" of close reading, an approach which is also concerned with verbal choices and which is now showing signs of return. But of course, we should be aware of the limitations of earlier formalist verbal analyses. In order to gain a fuller picture, we should look into the contexts of production and interpretation. However, the power of stylistics primarily lies in revealing, through systematic linguistic analysis, varied ingenious verbal patterning in texts. As indicated by the present study, stylistic analysis can not only shed fresh light on the narrative but also help resolve relevant critical controversy. Moreover, it is shown that the transitivity model, like many other linguistic models employed in stylistics, can greatly facilitate a systematic analysis of the writer's verbal choices, especially when such choices constitute a sustained stylistic strategy. It is our hope that the present essay, which brings to light the hidden relation between transitivity patterning, indirect presentation, and the theme of redemption in Watson's *The Double Hook*, will help attract more interest in stylistics so that its potential in literary study may be brought into fuller play in the days to come.

Notes

1. This attack is followed by "What Is Stylistics and Why Are They Saying Such Terrible Things about It? Part II", a chapter in Fish's *Is There a Text in this Class?*, which centers on the point that "formal patterns are themselves the products of interpretation" (1980; for a response to this attack, see Shen, 1988).

2. Another much-discussed theme is the theme of forming a mental community. For an investigation of the relation between this theme and transitivity patterning, see Ji and Shen's 2004 essay.

3. The classification of process types is based on Halliday (1985), and the abbreviations of the terms used are as follows:
   Rel. = Relational Process; Cir. = Circumstantial Elements; Inte. = Intensive. Mat. = Material Process; Men. = Mental Process; Phe. = Phenomenon; Act. = Actor; Sen. = Senser; Possr. = Possessor; Poss. = possessive; Possd. = Possessed; Cog. = Cognitive

4. The other two clauses respectively contain a Behavorial Process ("They were

both laughing") and an Existential Process ("The girl's hands were on his shoulders") respectively.

5. "James laughed too" and "Laughed looking into someone else" are identified here also as mental process instead of behaviorial process because the boundary of the latter is indeterminate and what we have here is actually physiological process (*laugh*) manifesting James's state of consciousness.

References

Atwood, M. 1972. *Survival: A Thematic Guide to Canadian Literature*. Toronto: Anansi.

Betts, G. B. 2000. *Severed from Roots: Settling Culture in Sheila Watson's Novels*. Ann Arbor: Univ. of Victoria.

Bowering, G. 1981. Sheila Watson, trickster. *The Canadian Novel* 3: 187-199.

Bowering, G. 1985. *Sheila Watson and* The Double Hook. Ottawa: Golden Dog.

Burton, D. 1982. Through glass darkly: Through dark glasses. In *Language and Literature: An Introductory Reader in Stylistics*, ed. by R. Carter, 194-214. London: Allen.

Carter, R. 1982. Introduction. In *Language and Literature: An Introductory Reader in Stylistics*, ed. by R. Carter, 1-17. London: Allen.

Chatman, S. 1978. *Story and Discourse*. Ithaca: Cornell University Press.

Child, P. A. 1985. Canadian prose-poem. In *Sheila Watson and* The Double Hook, ed. by G. Bowering, 31-34. Ottawa: Golden Dog.

Downton, D. R. 1985. Message and messengers in *The Double Hook*. In *Sheila Watson and* The Double Hook, ed. by G. Bowering, 177-184. Ottawa: Golden Dog.

Fish, S. 1980. *Is There a Text in this Class*? Cambridge, MA: Harvard Univ. Press.

Fish, S. 1981. What is stylistics and why are they saying such terrible things about it? In *Essays in Modern Stylistics*, ed. by C. F. Donald, 53-78. London: Methuen.

Frye, N. 1957. The theory of myths. In *Anatomy of Criticism: Four Essays*, ed. by N. Frye, 131-239. Princeton: Princeton Univ. Press.

Grube, J. 1966. Introduction. In *Sheila Watson and* The Double Hook. Toronto:

New Canadian Library.

Halliday, M. A. K. 1971. Linguistic function and literary style: An inquiry into William Golding's *The Inheritors*. In *Literary Style: A Symposium*, ed. by C. Seymour, 330-368. Oxford: Oxford Univ. Press.

Halliday, M. A. K. 1973. *Explorations in the Functions of Language.* Victoria: Arnold.

Halliday, M. A. K. 1985. *An Introduction to Functional Grammar.* Victoria: Arnold.

Hastert, M. P. & Jean, J. W. 1992. Power and mutuality in middle March. In *Language, Text, and Context: Essays in Stylistics*, ed. by T. Michael, 161-178. London: Routledge.

Ji, Y. & Shen, D. 2004. Transitivity and mental transformation: Sheila Wartson's *The Double Hook, Language and Literature*, 13: 335-348.

Jones, D. G. 1970. *Butterfly on Rock: A Study of Themes and Images in Canadian Literature.* Toronto: Univ. of Toronto Press.

Kennedy, C. 1982. Systemic grammar and its use in literary analysis. In *Language and Literature*, ed. by C. Ronald, 82-99. London: George Allen and Unwin.

Leech, G. & Michael, S. 1981. *Style in Fiction.* London: Longman.

Marta, J. 1985. Poetic structures in the prose fiction of Sheila Watson. In *Sheila Watson and* The Double Hook, ed. by G. Bowering, 149-158. Ottawa: Golden Dog.

Mckenzie, K. 1996. *Positive Values: The Figures of the Trickster as a Catalyst for Community in Selected Works by Sheila Watson and Tomson Highway.* Ann Arbor: Acadia Univ.

Mcpherson, H. 1985. An important new voice. In *Sheila Watson and* The Double Hook, ed. by G. Bowering, 23-25. Ottawa: Golden Dog.

Mitchell, B. 1985. Association and allusion in *The Double Hook*. In *Sheila Watson and* The Double Hook, ed. by G. Bowering, 99-113. Ottawa: Golden Dog.

Morriss, M. 1985. The elements transcended. In *Sheila Watson and* The Double Hook, ed. by G. Bowering, 83-97. Ottawa: Golden Dog.

Morriss, M. 2002. No short cuts: The evolution of *The Double Hook, Canadian Literature* 173: 54-70.

Moss, J. 1985. *The Double Hook* and the channel shore. In *Sheila Watson and The Double Hook*, ed. by G. Bowering, 123-142. Ottawa: Golden Dog.

Nilsson, J. A. 1993. *Mediating Rituals: Meta-myth, Counter-myth, and the Narrative Structure of* The Double Hook. Ann Arbor: Simon Fraser Univ.

Northey, M. 1985. Symbolic grotesque. In *Sheila Watson and* The Double Hook, ed. by G. Bowering, 55-61. Ottawa: Golden Dog.

Perry, M. 1979. Literary dynamics: How the order of a text creates its meanings, *Poetics Today* 1: 35-64, 311-361.

Rimmon-Kenan, S. 1989. How the model neglects the medium: Linguistics, language, and the crisis of narratology, *The Journal of Narrative Technique* 19: 157-166.

Rimmon-Kenan, S. 2002. *Narrative Fiction: Contemporary Poetics*. London: Routledge.

Shen, D. 1988. Stylistics, objectivity, and convention, *Poetics* 17: 221-238.

Shen, D. 2001. Narrative, reality, and narrator as construct: Reflections on Genette's "Narrating", *Narrative* 9: 123-129.

Shen, D. 2002. Defense and challenge: Reflections on the relation between story and discourse, *Narrative* 10: 422-443.

Shen, D. 2005. What narratology and stylistics can do for each other. In *A Companion to Narrative Theory*, ed. by P. James, & R. Peter, 136-149. Oxford: Blackwell.

Short, M. H. 1976. Why we sympathize with Lennie, *MALS Journal* 1: 1-9.

Simpson, P. 1997. *Language through Literature*. London: Routledge.

Thelld, F. 1985. A Canadian novella. In *Sheila Watson and* The Double Hook, ed. by G. Bowering, 35-38. Ottawa: Golden Dog.

Vincent, D. G. A. 2000. Playing with cultures: The role of coyote. In Sheila Watson's *The Double Hook* and Thomas King's *Green Grass, Running Water*. Ann Arbor: Queen's Univ.

Watson, S. 1989. *The Double Hook*. Toronto: McCelland.

3. Drama Stylistics

Politeness Strategies, Characterization Theory, and Drama Stylistics: A Synthetic Case Study with Theoretical Modifications

GAO Jianwu & SHEN Dan

Peking University

1. Introduction

Among the many politeness theories and models, Brown and Levinson (1987) (the B-L model) is generally acknowledged as the most systematic and instinctively appealing. In recent years, there have been a number of applications of the model to the analysis of drama text, such as Simpson (1989), and Abdesslem (2001), to name but a few. However, these applications, with the exception of Abdesslem (2001), are more or less sporadic analyses of short dialogues that fail to reveal the dramatic characterization process as a whole. On the other hand, Culpeper's revision of the flat/round-character dichotomy and of the attribution models takes account of the reader's cognitive process and offers an integrated framework for the analysis of dramatic characterization. This paper, therefore, forms an attempt to combine the B-L model with Culpeper's theory of dramatic characterization in stylistic analysis, and the text chosen for examination is the first act of Christopher Hampton's *The Philanthropist*[①]. The purpose of the investigation, however, is not only to demonstrate the advantages of the synthetic framework, but also to modify both theories on the basis of the textual analysis.

[①] We align ourselves here with Short(1998: 6-18) in prioritizing texts over performances in drama analysis. The justifications that Short lists out include: (1) the director and actors must first read a play before putting it on the stage; (2) textual ambiguities may be forced one way or the other by the production; (3) theatre performances are variable from one to another, thus seriously restricting the common ground for discussion; (4) many productions are merely variations on the same interpretation; (5) the pressure to do something different on the director and actors is likely to result in outrageous treatments of the play text, etc.

2. B-L Model

The core concept of the B-L model is the Model Person (MP). According to Brown and Levinson (1987), an MP is a willful, fluent user of a natural language, endowed with two special properties—face and rationality. Meanwhile, the B-L model presumes that some speech acts are intrinsically face-threatening (FTAs). In order to minimize the face threat of the FTAs, any rational agent will choose various politeness strategies according to different communicative goals, situations, and social relations with the addressee(s), etc. Brown and Levinson (68-9) list 5 suprastrategies arranged according to the increasing degree of situational risk: bald on record, on record with positive redress, on record with negative redress, off record, and refraining from doing the FTA.

According to the B-L model, politeness strategies have their own *a priori* advantages and disadvantages and are fit for coping with FTAs with different degrees of face threat. On the other hand, MPs can infer the weightiness of an act x (W_x) by assessing three sociological variables: (1) the relative power (P), (2) the sociological distance (D) between the Speaker (S) and the Hearer (H), and (3) the absolute ranking of imposition (R) of the FTA in the particular culture. Therefore it can be concluded that the higher W_x is, the safer a politeness strategy will be used.

3. Culpeper's Theory of Dramatic Characterization

Culpeper (2001) puts forward a synthetic model of dramatic characterization on the basis of Foster ([1927] 1987)'s characterization theory, attribution theory, schema theory, and categorization theory. Two aspects of Culpeper's model are particularly noteworthy. One is his revision of Foster's round/flat-character dichotomy, and the other his integration of correspondent inference theory with Kelley's ANOVA model (also known as the covariation model).

Foster ([1927] 1987) categorizes characters into "flat" and "round" ones according to the following three criteria: whether the character is simple or complex, whether the character is static or undergoes changes, and whether the character "surprises" the reader or not. Culpeper (2001), however, seeks a new way of accounting for the three criteria on the basis of van Dijk and Kintsch's (1983) social cognition theory and Fiske and Neuberg's (1990) impression formation theory. According to the two theories, the impression formation process that a reader undergoes when confronted with a character consists of four steps, namely, initial categorization, categorization reinforcement, re-categorization and piecemeal categorization. Viewed from this perspective, the flat-round dichotomy can be redefined as follows: the attributes and features of a flat character are organized according to a preformed category or schema to form a category-based impression; the attributes and features of a round character combine to form a person-based impression. A categorized character implies no change, while the piecemeal integration of a personalized character implies change. The confirmatory categorization of a character means being satisfied that a current schema adequately accounts for the information the reader has about that character, whereas piecemeal integration means that a character will not fit any existing schema and is thus "surprising" (2001: 93-94).

However, this new conception of Foster's classification is not enough. One has to address the issue of how readers interpret the clues into the attributes or features of dramatic characters. Culpeper (2001: 113) agrees with Jones's causal schema theory that people tend to attribute others' behaviors to the latter's dispositions. However, there still exist two problems, namely, the cognitive salience of certain behaviors over others, and the influence of context on the attribution. Culpeper (2001: 128-9) combines Jones's (1990) correspondence inference theory with Kelley's (1967) ANOVA model and claims that a behavior corresponds to an attribute as far as it is:

1. Free from external pressure;

2. Low in ambiguity, i. e. yielding noncommon effects which are few in number;

3. Unusual, i.e. departing from the perceiver's expectations (normative, category-based, or target-based);

4. Part of the following behavioral pattern: low distinctiveness, high consistency, and low consensus.

This revised attribution model, together with the reinterpretation of the traditional flat/round-character dichotomy, forms the basis of Culpeper's theory of dramatic characterization and offers a systematic explanation of how social perceivers draw textual clues to form an impression of a character.

4. Dramatic Characterization in the First Act of *The Philanthropist*

In order to illustrate the advantages of combining the B-L model with Culpeper's theory of dramatic characterization an analysis will be carried out on the first act of Hampton's *The Philanthropist*. At the beginning of this act, John, a young and inexperienced playwright, visits Philip's house, reads his newly-written play (referred to as Play II hereafter to distinguish it from *The Philanthropist*, which is referred to as Play I hereafter), and seeks for Philip's and Don's criticism. Play I begins with the final words of the protagonist in Play II (played by John).

Excerpt 1

John: You needn't think I'm not serious. Because I am. I assure you I am. Can't you see that? I've come here this evening because I think both of you are responsible for this and I think you deserve it as much as I do. If you hate me for doing it, that's your problem. It won't concern me. I just want you to have one vivid image of me, that's all, one memory to last all your life and never vanish, to remind you that if you won, I lost, and that nobody can win without somebody losing. Good-bye. (He puts the revolver to his head.) Bang. (He smiles uneasily at them). Curtain.
(silence)

Abdesslem (2001: 121-2) correctly points out that the revolver that John holds at the beginning cannot really affect his power relationship with Philip and Don. Instead, it increases the discursive power of the protagonist of Play II so that the protagonist can finish the long turn without being interrupted. However, later on Abdesslem seems to have overlooked the different impact of the gun on the power statuses of John in Play I and the protagonist (John plays) of Play II and repeatedly and indiscriminately refers to the two characters as "they":

Their rhetorical question ("Can't you see that?") and *their* anti-climactic proverb ("nobody can win without somebody losing") do not make *them* sound convinced or convincing. *Their* elaborate justification (I've come here this evening...) sounds as though *they* were pleading with *their* interlocutors to consider *their* threat to take *their* own lives more seriously. *Their* argument ("I think you deserve it as much as I do") is an act that is on-record, but sounds as though *the speakers* were showing knowledge of and sensitivity to *their* hearers' wants, and can hardly be considered as a threat to them (122, italics added).

But when we consider the function of the revolver in light of the conversation content and the fact that "it" in excerpt 1 refers to "committing suicide" or "death", we can hardly agree with Abdesslem that the protagonist's words "you deserve it (death) as much as I do" show "knowledge of and sensitivity" to his hearers' wants. In fact, what the reader/audience sees in Play II is a desperate threatening man, with almost all of his utterances forming bald on-record FTAs. "You needn't think I'm not serious. Because I am" and "Can't you see that?" damage the hearers' positive face, as they presume that the hearers have made a mistake; "I think both of you are responsible for this and I think you deserve it as much as I do" poses further threat to the hearers' life; "If you hate me for doing it, that's your problem. It won't concern me" seems to be the sub-strategy "dissociation" under the "negative politeness" category, but such a strategy is more often thought of as an on-record face threat in actual usage (Baxter, 1984: 450). While "I just want you to have one vivid image of me [...]" reduces committing suicide to an effort to impress others, which may be viewed as a negative politeness strategy, the ensuing "reminding" act poses another threat to the hearers' positive face. In a word, the finale of Play II is predominantly composed of the protagonist's on-record threats to the unseen hearers, and almost all of the FTAs are uttered without any politeness redress. Abdesslem unjustifiably minimizes the face threat of the protagonist's utterances as he wrongly puts John in Play I on a par with the protagonist John plays in Play II. To put things in perspective, let's take a look at the following table which shows the differences between the two characters in terms of master, situational and discursive identities (see West & Zimmerman, 1985: 103-24), as well as in other relevant aspects:

Table 1   Comparison between the Protagonist in Play II and John in Play I

	Protagonist in Play II	John in Play I
Master Identity (Static)	Male	Male
Situational Identity (Static/Dynamic)	Unknown	Young Playwright
Discursive Identity (Dynamic)	Someone that Threatens to Commit Suicide	A Playwright who Reads His Work for Comments at One of the Hearers' Home
Relative Power Status in relation with the Hearers	More Powerful than the Hearers (Determined by S's Discursive Identity)	Less Powerful than the Hearers (Determined by S's Discursive and Situational Identities)
Distance between Speaker and Hearers	Distant (Determined by S's Discursive Identity)	Uncertain
Absolute Ranking of Impositions in the Specific Culture (on Hearers)	High Imposition on Both Positive and Negative Faces	Possible Imposition on Hearers' Negative Face as the Latter May Be Forced to Criticize or Praise the Work
Absolute Ranking of Imposition in the Specific Culture (on Speaker)	Low (Except the Admission of S's Losing)	Uncertain (May Court Criticism and Damage S's Own Positive Face or Result in Praises that will Lift S's Positive Face)
Impact of Situational Factors on the Configuration of the Sociological Variables (e. g. the revolver)	Heavy	Light

It can be seen from the table that John in Play I and the protagonist in Play II differ a lot from each other in their identities, speech acts, configurations of sociological variables, as well as in terms of the impact of the situational factors on their respective configurations. Given such differences, the two characters should have taken up different politeness strategies for their respective purposes. However, due to the special structure of "play inside play" the two entirely different purposes (threatening to commit suicide versus reading one's work for comments) are necessarily realized by the same utterances, which gives rise to Abdesslem's misinterpretation.

After performing the suicide scene, John immediately pops out of the deictic level of the protagonist of Play II by smiling uneasily at Don and Philip.

197

Abdesslem (122) thinks that John's smile "is a reminder of the power (P) the latter have on him, the high level of imposition (R) their anticipated criticism would have upon him, and the rather wide distance (D) that separates the young playwright from his critics". We would like to add that here John's smile is not only a reflection of the configuration of the sociological variables, but also a positive politeness strategy that presumes his friendly, "in-group" relationship with Don and Philip and can be seen as his first attempt to change his hearers' assessment of the situation, mainly the distance variable, by using politeness strategies. However, this gesture also has an unexpected side effect, as John seems to confirm to Don and Philip that even the author of Play II feels ill at ease when playing the protagonist and cannot wait to escape his role. This behavior, therefore, indirectly damages John's positive face as the author of Play II.

Despite John's effort to shorten the distance between himself and his hearers, a most unnatural "silence" follows the end of his reading. This indicates Don and Philip's rejection of John as a member of their group. While silence is categorized as the safest "do not do FTA" strategy in the B-L model, here it rather expresses Don and Philip's dissatisfaction and poses even greater damage to John's positive face than outspoken criticism.

In the exchange that follows, John asks, "Do you like it?", which again poses a serious threat to Don and Philip's negative face. Furthermore, given the unpleasantly long silence before his inquiry, John runs an even greater risk of inviting criticism and consequently damaging his own positive face as well. John's uneasy smile and inquisition are high in consistency and low in distinctiveness (as he addresses both Don and Philip), which leaves the reader with an impression of "a diffident, self-conscious greenhorn writer". Philip responds to John's on-record question, with the following words "Very good. Would you like another drink?", which breaks the maxim of quantity and is potentially an off-record strategy to cover up his negative opinion on John's work. The face threat of Philip's offering John a drink, therefore, does not only lie in Philip's pressuring John to accept the favor itself, as Abdesslem (123) expounds in his analysis, but also lie in the fact that it interrupts the coherence in politeness strategy (responding to an on-record strategy with a potentially off-record strategy), making the relationship between the two even more unequal.

When Philip leaves for ice, John asks Don, "He doesn't like it, does he?" By presuming Philip to have a negative opinion on the play, John betrays his diffidence and damages his positive face. This act also strengthens the reader's impression of John as a nervous, diffident author. Don's answer, however, is "Oh, I don't know". As Abdesslem (123-4) correctly points out, here the pressure on Don is double-fold: if he disagrees with John, he would be forced to damage his own negative face by telling a lie; if he agrees, he would damage both John's and Philip's positive face, as that would mean John is a dumb writ and Philip is a false friend. However, Don neither submits to John's pressure nor revolts against it, but addresses it with deliberate ambiguity. According to Culpeper's revised attribution model, Don's behavior is neither free from external pressure nor low in ambiguity and is therefore not significant in the attribution process. However, this speech act betrays Don's interpersonal skills and leads the reader to the categorization of Don as a sophisticated man. Under such circumstances, John has to give up his inquisition and damage his own positive face again. Below is the following dialogue.

Excerpt 2

John: He doesn't. I can tell.

Don: I'm sure he does like it.

John: Do you?

(Philip returns with the ice)

Don: Well. Yes and no. I mean there are some enormously promising things in the play. Obviously it's basically a conversation piece, but you do try to give the customers a bit of everything—a touch of melodrama, the odd *coup de théâtre*, humor, tragedy, monologues and pastoral interludes, yes, yes, I like that, generous. But on the other hand I think there are certain... lapses, which you know, detract from the play as a satisfactory whole.

John: You mean it's stylistically heterogeneous?

Philip: I think Don prefers to see it as an unsatisfying whole. (He laughs merrily and alone.) Sorry. Would you like a chocolate?

John: No thanks.

Philip: Don? I think I'll have one.

200

(He helps himself to one, as he is to throughout this scene.)

John: Tell me what you don't like about it?

Don: Well, one thing is that character who appears every so often with a ladder. What's his name?

John: Man.

Don: Yes. Well, I take it he has some kind of allegorical significance outside the framework of the play. I mean I don't know if this is right but I rather took him to signify England.

John: No, no, erm, in point of fact he signifies man.

Don: Ah.

John: Yes.

Don: Hence the name.

John: Yes.

Don: I see.

John: Although now you come to mention it, I suppose he could be taken to represent England.

Philip: Is that two ns?

John: What?

Philip: In man.

John: No, one.

Philip: Ah, well, you see, I thought it was two ns. As in Thomas.

John: Thomas?

Philip: Thomas Mann.

John: Oh.

Philip: So I thought he was just meant to represent a window-cleaner.

John: Well...

Philip: Under the circumstances, I think you've integrated him into the plot very well.

John: Thank you. (He seems displeased.)

John's self-deprecating statement "He doesn't. I can tell" reconfirms the reader's impression of him as a sensitive, diffident man. In response, Don is forced to tell a white lie to rescue John's face ("I'm sure he does like it"). This positive politeness strategy enhances John's face, shortens the distance between Don and John, and paves the way for John's following inquiry "Do you?".

As it is no longer possible to remain ambiguous about his attitude, Don answers the inquiry with an on-record FTA with abundant positive politeness redress, which forms a contrast with Philip's disguised off-record FTA. Readers can refer to Abdesslem (2001: 125) for an excellent detailed analysis of the politeness strategies in Don's answer, and we would like to point out here in addition to Abdesslem's analysis that Don's answer is viewed as "sincere criticism" partly because he presumes equality between himself and John by using the same "on-record" strategy as John has been using. From John's follow-up question ("You mean it's stylistically heterogeneous"), we can see that John changes his discursive style from casual talk to formal criticism and uses the same positive politeness strategy of "jargons" that Don employs in the previous turn, marking again the dominant status that Don occupies in the conversation.

When John invites Don to make explicit his criticism, Philip returns and intrudes into the talk. While John selects Don as the next speaker, Philip interposes by selecting himself and answering the question in Don's place ("I think Don prefers to see it as an unsatisfying whole"). His answer not only intrudes into the normal turn-taking order of John and Don's conversation, but also breaks the coherence in Don's pattern of politeness strategies and contradicts Don's previous redressive efforts to reduce the weightiness of his criticism. Furthermore, the positive politeness strategy that Philip uses (to presume common ground with Don) tends to create the impression that Don is expressing off-record FTA under the disguise of on-record FRA just as Philip himself does. This speech act, therefore, damages both John's and Don's positive faces, which in turn results in their silence to Philip's laughter. Philip's interruption is highly consistent with his previous unpleasant behavior. As these actions are low in social desirability, the reader is likely to attribute them again to Philip's disposition and confirm the categorization that Philip is "unpleasant by nature" and "indifferent to others' feelings". Meanwhile, Don and John's silence shows their dissatisfaction with Philip's behavior and is again an on-record FTA *per se* instead of "not doing FTA", as classified in the B-L model.

John's silence here, however, has another fold of meaning. It marks a turning point where John starts to apply different politeness strategies in dealing with Don and Philip. He no longer tries to shorten his distance with Philip, but deliberately keeps a distance from the latter. This differentiation in John's treatment of Don and Philip indicates that John's earlier "self-deprecation" may not be due to his own will or disposition, and prepares the reader for John's later confrontation with Don and Philip to protect his own face.

So far politeness strategies have been the major textual clues dictating characters' changes in the reader's impression formation process. At the beginning, John's awkward usage of the same politeness strategies despite his double situational identities (playwright in Play I and actor of the protagonist in Play II) endows him with cognitive salience and complexity. As Play I proceeds, this character somewhat flattens away with his repeated and indistinctive usage of the on-record self-effacing strategy, which forms a structural contrast with the barely off-record, sarcastic Philip that is equally flat. When the reader begins to settle down and take John's humility for granted, however, the characterization becomes complicated again as John starts to apply different politeness strategies to different recipients. The reader is hence forced to slow down the speed of textbase extraction so as to re-categorize the character. John's humble image is under challenge for the first time, and the reader's impression of John is likely to shift from a category-based one to a person-based one.

When Philip finds himself somewhat isolated in the conversation, he adopts the negative politeness strategy of apology ("Sorry"). According to Lim and Bowers (1991), positive face and negative face belong to different wants of people and shall be addressed respectively. That is to say, negative politeness strategies cannot amend positive face loss and neither can positive politeness strategies reduce negative face loss. As Philip seriously damages John's positive face (and Don's positive face as well, as it may lead John to assume that Don is a hypocrite) in the previous turn, the negative politeness strategy of "apology" cannot possibly redress John's positive face loss. The damage that Philip causes in turn results in John's and Don's cold reaction to Philip's conversion of the topic, as both of them (verbally or non-verbally) turn down Philip's offer of drinks. Furthermore, John continues to select Don as the next speaker ("Tell me what you don't like about it"), which precludes the possibility of Philip's intrusion. John's on-record rejection of Philip's offer and exclusion of Philip from the conversation once again leads the reader to revise the first impression of John as a humble, timid character. Although John's invitation for Don to specify the latter's criticism on his work is another example of the self-deprecation strategy that he repeatedly used at the beginning, his selection of Don instead of Philip as the recipient of his politeness strategy further cancels the correspondence of the strategy *per se* with his disposition and paves the way for his desperate suicidal move to protect his own work at the end of the play.

In the dialogue that follows, Don openly challenges the characterization of John's work (Play II). Interestingly, as the author of Play II, John should have more authority in explaining the intended symbolic meanings of characters, but what the reader sees is still a diffident figure whose mind easily sways under Don's influence. After expressing his disagreement with Don's interpretation with negative politeness strategies ("erm" is a hedge that shows his hesitance and "in point of fact" is an attempt to minimize the imposition of the FTA), he then adopts positive politeness strategy to agree with Don's interpretation ("Although now you come to mention it, I suppose he could be taken to represent England"). However, by agreeing with Don John also concedes John's criticism that his character has a symbolic meaning outside the framework of the entire play. This is another example that John deliberately attempts to shorten the distance between himself and Don at the expense of his own positive face.

At this point, Philip selects himself as the next speaker and intrudes again into the talk between Don and John by, introducing the trivia of the spelling of the character's name, thus further confirming in the reader's mind his image as the "unwelcome intruder into conversation". Faced with Philip's FTA, John does not adopt the positive politeness strategy that he uses to Don, but uses the negative strategy of hesitation ("Well...") , so as to widen the distance between himself and Philip while minimizing Philip's face loss. However, he is interrupted by Philip again before he can finish his turn ("Under the circumstances, I think you've integrated him into the plot very well"). The latter half of the utterance seems to be a Face Raising Act; however, its precondition is the utter denial of the symbolic meaning of the character in John's work, which takes place after John's confirmation of it. John's positive face, therefore, is not saved but damaged again, and Philip's "sarcastic, unfeeling" image is once again confirmed in the reader's mind. By contrast, John preserves Philip's positive face by grudgingly saying "thanks" in the next turn, though the ensuing stage direction tells the reader that he seems "displeased". John's self-restraint from retaliating has double meanings: on the one hand, John's behavior proves that he is more sensitive to others' face wants and confirms the reader's impression of him as a sensitive, conflict-avoiding character; on the other hand, however, this is also the first time John adopts the "not doing FTA" strategy instead of the on-record one. John's inconsistent behavior indicates that his role in the conversation has become further marginalized under Philip's attack. The following is the dialogue at the end of the first act:

Excerpt 3

Don: I always think the beginning and the end are the most difficult parts of a play to handle, and I'm not sure you've been entirely successful with either.

John: Aren't you?

Don: I can't really say I like that Pirandello-style beginning. It's been done so often, you know. I mean I'm not saying that your use of it isn't resourceful. It is. But the device itself is a bit rusty.

John: Yes, perhaps you're right. I'm not very happy about the beginning myself.

John: (to Philip) What do you think?

Philip: I liked it.

John: Why?

Philip: No special reason, I just liked it. You shouldn't take any notice of me, though, I am not really qualified to comment.

Don: It just doesn't convince me. It seems artificial. Do you really think he'd commit suicide in front of them like that?

John: Yes. Why not?

Don: It doesn't seem to tie in with his character as we've seen it in the rest of the play.

Philip: I don't know. I liked it.

John: You don't have to say that, you know. I'd much prefer to have honest criticism than your, if you don't mind me saying so, rather negative remarks.

Philip: Please take no notice of what I say. I always like things. I get pleasure from the words that are used, whatever the subject is. I've enjoyed every book I've ever read for one reason or another. That's why I can't teach literature. I have no critical faculties. I think there's always something good to be found in the product of another's mind. Even if the man is, by all objective standards, a complete fool. So you see I'd like a play however terrible it was.

John: So you think my play is terrible.

Philip: I didn't say that, I...

John: I'm not an idiot, you know, I can take a hint.

John (to Don): Now, what were you saying?

Don: I was just wondering whether the suicide is altogether justified.

John: Oh, I think so. Given the kind of man he is, I think it could be quite powerful. (To illustrate, John puts the revolver into his mouth and presses the trigger. Loud explosion...)

At the beginning of this excerpt, Don for the first time imposes on John without the latter's invitation an on-record FTA with positive redress ("I always think [...] I'm not sure you've been entirely successful with either"). When John encourages Don to proceed, the latter tones down the imposition by comprehensively using positive and negative politeness redresses, including minimizing face threat ("I can't really say I like that Pirandello-style beginning", "a bit"), presuming common ground ("you know"), using jargons ("Pirandello-style beginning"), and exaggerating interest in the hearer ("I'm not saying that your use of it isn't resourceful. It is"). One noteworthy point is that although the "Pirandello-style" beginning of John's Play II is kept from the reader's view, we can see another Pirandello-style beginning in Play I, in which drama *per se* becomes the object of dramatic presentation, and the criticism of one play (Play II) largely constitutes the plot of another play (Play I). Don's criticism draws the reader back to the "play inside play" framework, which suggests the parallel between Play I and Play II, and again paves the way for the final confluence of the fate of John in Play I and that of the protagonist in Play II.

As Abdesslem (2001: 131) analyzes, John concedes again in his answer to

Don and this concession is made at the expense of his own positive face ("Yes, perhaps you're right. I'm not very happy about the beginning myself"). However, what Abdesslem does not notice is that despite this concession, John does not inquire further about Don's opinion on the ending. Although Don's previous space-making strategy indicates that he would like to regain the floor after John's reaction, John selects Philip, who has been excluded from the conversation so far, as the next speaker and asks him a vague question: "What do you think?". John's unexpected inquiry not only poses a threat to Don's negative face, as it precludes Don from resuming his criticism, but also deviates from John's previous strategy of distancing himself from Philip while affiliating himself with Don. John's deviation from the reader's expectations in this respect is low in social desirability, which may lead the reader to attribute it to John's own will. We would suggest, furthermore, that John's question here is not intended to provide Philip with another opportunity to damage John's positive face, but to avoid Don's attack on the ending of Play II. John's exclusion of Don from the conversation is salient because of its unexpectedness and is therefore significant in revealing John's true character. It leads the reader to the impression that John actually has high self-esteem and is defensive by nature. The reader, therefore, has to modify his/her categorization of John for the second time due to the change in John's use of politeness strategies.

To John's disappointment, Philip not only falls back on fake FRA again, but also breaks the maxims of manner and quantity, which causes further damage to John's positive face. To make things worse, Don selects himself as the next speaker and criticizes the ending of John's work that John has been trying to protect. Here John's positive face receives a fatal blow. In desperation, John for the first time openly challenges Don ("Yes, why not?") without any redress. While such an act deviates from the previous self-effacing strategy that John adopted with Don, it is a rather convincing development of the plot on the basis of our analysis so far. Therefore, instead of loosening the rein to absurdity, Hampton provides us with a perfect example of a convincingly surprising character towards the end of the first act.

In his reply, Don adopts a negative politeness strategy (minimizing face threat by "seems"), but his criticism is much more direct compared with his previous utterances. Before John can retaliate, Philip interposes again and his barely-disguised off-record sarcasm ("I don't know. I liked it") reconfirms his image in the reader's mind as an acrimonious character. Philip's repeated use of the fake FRA gives rise to John's repulsion and he breaks out an open criticism. Despite the positive and negative politeness strategies that John uses (e. g. showing interest in the addressee: ("if you don't mind me saying so") and minimizing the imposition: ("rather"), the weightiness of this act is still high, especially compared with that of John's previous behavior. The fact that John stops effacing himself and resorts to aggressive means to defend himself further confirms our latest categorization of John as an essentially "defensive" character.

While Philip uses in the next turn such negative politeness strategies as self-minimizing ("I have no critical faculties") and apology ("Please take no notice of what I say"), he fails to redress his imposition on John's positive face. Contrarily, his turn carries presumptions that severely damage John's positive face ("Even if the man is, by all objective standards, a complete fool"; "I'd like a play however terrible it was") and further fuels John's rage. John now has every reason to believe that Philip means to insult him and for the first time he spells out Philip's negative attitude despite the latter's weak protest. The escalation of John's aggressiveness is accompanied by a change of his discursive identity from a meek recipient of criticism to a vengeful criticizer. After retaliating on Philip, he turns to Don and makes his last justification of his play with his suicide. It turns out that John invests in the ending of Play II so much of himself that any criticism of it virtually means a fatal stab on him. By putting the gun into his mouth and ending his life as his protagonist does in Play II, John justifies the validity of his dramatic creation and seems to show Don and Philip that the boundary between absurdity and reality is not as clear cut as it looks.

We can see from the above analysis that the textual clues about Philip confirm his "insensitive, hypocritical, egocentric" image all along. Philip, therefore, is a flat character. Although Don towards the end uses less redress than he did earlier in the play, he has never undergone any significant change and remains the most frequent user of positive politeness strategies and the most sophisticated in interpersonal skills among the three characters. John's characterization, by contrast, undergoes continuous changes and the reader has to constantly readjust his/her categorization process as the play proceeds. At the beginning, John's image is cognitively salient due to the complication of his double situational identities; in the immediate following part, however, the character flattens away with the repeated, indiscriminate usage of self-effacing strategies. This "diffident, conflict-avoiding" image of John changes in its turn when John starts to use different politeness strategies to Don and Philip. Then in the end, John totally abandons the "self-effacing" strategy and directly confronts Don and Philip, culminating in his last resort-suicide-to justify his play. As Abdesslem (2001: 133) focuses only on Don and Philip's politeness strategies, he regrettably overlooks John's changes in politeness strategy usage and attributes the tragic ending solely to Don and Philip's deliberate usage of pragmatic ambiguities. Furthermore, as Abdesslem's analysis is based solely on the B-L model, he inevitably fails to account for the interaction between the dramatic characterization process as a whole and the reader's cognitive integration of new textual clues. His neglect of the changes in John's politeness strategies, especially his neglect of the important role of such non-verbal behaviors as silence and refusing to give the floor, also leads to his simplistic categorization of John as a static character whose only invariant trait is his desperate need of others' outspoken comments.

5. Theoretical Modifications

The analysis above points to the necessity of making some modifications of the B-L model and Culpeper's characterization theory. While the B-L model considers in the discussion of the types of FTAs both the acts that threaten the hearer's face and those that threaten the speaker's face, it only considers the material and service costs of the hearer and the pain the FTA causes the hearer to suffer in the specific calculation of R_x (2001: 77). The value of R_x, therefore, is solely based on the imposition on the hearer's face, which runs contrary to its own previous claim that some acts do impose on the speaker's face. In fact, conversationalists often have to take into consideration the imposition of the FTA on the speaker's face and pay attention to both the imposition on the hearer's face and the protection of the speaker's face. We can see from the above analysis that not only Don and Philip's silence after hearing John's play but also Philip's choice of off-record strategy to answer John's on-record inquiry are aimed at the protection of the speaker's face.

While avoiding direct conflict with John, their strategic choices express their dissatisfaction with John and are even more devastating to John's positive face than direct criticism. Regrettably, the protection of the speaker's face has not received adequate attention from the researchers of the politeness phenomenon. On one hand, the B-L model holds that as the off-record strategy threatens the hearer's face in an indirect and negotiable way, it is the most polite strategy that can reduce the face threat of the act. The Irony Principle that Leech (1983) puts forward also does not consider the protection of the speaker's face. As Leech claims, "if you must cause offence, at least do so in a way that doesn't overtly conflict with the Politeness Principle, but allows the bearer to arrive at the offensive point of your remark indirectly, by way of implicature" (82). On the other hand, many scholars think that the damage irony causes to the hearer may even exceed that done by on-record criticism. Wang (1998), for instance, expounds the necessity to differentiate "false politeness" from "genuine politeness" and points out that excessively covert criticism sometimes equals malignant attack and shall be categorized as fake politeness. Abdesslem also makes a distinction between surface and underlying politeness strategies and claims that on-record FRA can be used as a disguise of the off-record FTA. All the researchers, however, only consider the damage to the hearer's face, whereas in many cases we should also consider the protection of the speaker's face. The purpose of irony, for instance, does not only lie in the damage to the hearer's face, but also in the protection of the speaker's face. Even in terms of the irony that is targeted for deliberate damage, its ideal effect is to insult the hearer while prevent the latter from fighting back directly.

Second, as the B-L model is based on speech act theory, it is confined to verbal acts while neglecting non-verbal ones. In the B-L model, all the FTAs are verbal, whereas "not doing FTA" is defined as "S avoids offending H at all with this particular FTA" (2001: 72). However, we can see from the above analysis that both Don's silence to Philip's offer of a drink and John's selection of Don as the next speaker immediately after Philip's turn cause damage to Philip's face and are in effect FTAs. Therefore, both verbal and non-verbal behavior (silence and exclusion of someone from conversation) may become FTAs in specific contexts, and the scope of FTA should be extended and the definition of the "not doing FTA" strategy in the B-L model be modified.

Besides, the B-L model only pays attention to the static values of the sociological variables while neglecting the dynamic process of value assignment in communication. As can be seen from the above analysis, John, Don, and Philip's politeness strategies serve as important indicators of their respective discursive identities, and the changes in their politeness strategy usage gives rise to changes in their respective discursive identities and the corresponding configurations of such sociological variables as P and D. John's distancing from Philip and affiliation with Don, for instance, cause changes in the values of the relevant sociological variables. It shows that the calculation of Wx should consider both the static and dynamic identities. It is out of this consideration that we differentiate in Table 1 and the ensuing analysis the "master identities", "situational identities" and "discursive identities" in line with West & Zimmerman (1985).

Culpeper's model claims that correspondent behaviors have to be free from external pressure. However, our analysis shows that although external pressure has "discounting effect" (e. g. John is forced to thank Philip for his offer of a drink), it can still indicate certain features of the character (e. g. we can form the impression of John as a conciliatory, sensitive character). More importantly, in a conversation with more than two participants, external pressure may not be unidirectional, but multidirectional. That is to say, submitting to the pressure from one participant may mean defiance to that from another, and participants with more interpersonal skills can often deal with multidirectional external pressure properly. For instance, when John asks Don about Philip's opinion on his play, Don is faced with pressure from both John and Philip. His ambiguous answer "I don't know" neither damages Philip's positive face nor forces himself to compliment John as Philip does. Contrary to Culpeper's claim, this behavior shows Don in a better light as a worldly, sophisticated character. We have reasons, therefore, to believe that characters' reaction under external pressure may provide important indication of their features, and that external pressure should not be excluded from the consideration of attribution.

6. Conclusion

In the stylistic analysis of the first act of *The Philanthropist*, we have adopted a synthetic model, which combines the B-L model and Culpeper's theory of dramatic characterization, as well as drawing on the related ideas of Grice, West and Zimmerman, Lim and Bowers, etc. The result shows that such a synthetic model can redress the one-sidedness of the analysis based on the B-L model alone, reveal the interaction between dramatic characterization and the reader's extraction and integration of textual clues, and come up with a more integrated interpretation of the play. Meanwhile, we have also suggested some modifications of the two major theoretical models on the basis of the analysis. Dramatic characterization is a complicated process, which calls for synthetic stylistic analysis. We hope that more synthetic analyses of drama stylistics will be carried out in the future so as to give dramatic characterization a fuller account, and more efforts will be made, when necessary, to modify the relevant theoretical models in order to achieve more descriptive and analytical adequacy.

References

Abdesslem, H. 2001. Politeness strategies in the discourse of drama: A case study, *Journal of Literary Semantics* 30(2): 111-138.

Baxter, L. A. 1984. An investigation of compliance-gaining as politeness, *Human Communication Research* 10(3): 427-56.

Brown, P. and Levinson, S. 1987. *Politeness: Some Universals in Language Use*. Cambridge: Cambridge University Press.

Culpeper, J. 2001. *Language and Characterisation: People in Plays and Other Texts*. Harlow, England: Longman.

Fiske, S. T. and Neuberg, S. L. 1990. A continuum of impression formation, from category-based to individuating processes: Influences of information and motivation on attention and interpretation. In *Advances in Experimental Social Psychology*, ed. by M. P. Zanna 1-74. New York: Academic Press.

Forster, E. M. [1927] 1987. *Aspects of the Novel*. Harmondsworth: Penguin.

Grice, P. 1975. Logic and conversation. In *Syntax and Semantics: Speech Act*, ed. by P. Cole and J. Morgan, 41-58. New York: Academic Press.

Hampton, C. 1971. *The Philanthropist: A Bourgeois Comedy*. London: Faber and Faber.

Jones, E. E. 1990. *Interpersonal Perception*. New York: Freeman.

Kelley, H. H. 1967. Attribution theory in social psychology. In *Nebraska Symposium on Motivation*, ed. by D. Levine, 192-238. Loncoln, Nebraska: University of Nebraska Press.

Leech, G. N. 1983. *Principles of Pragmatics*. London: Longman.

Lim, T-S. and Bowers, J. W. 1991. Facework: Solidarity, approbation, and tact, *Human Communication Research* 17(3): 415-50.

Myers, G. A. 1991. Politeness and certainty: The language of collaboration in an AI project, *Social Studies of Science* 21(1): 37-73.

Sacks, H., Schegloff, E. and Jefferson, G. 1974. A simplest systematics for the organization of turn taking for conversation, *Language* 50(4): 696-735.

Simpson, P. 1989. Politeness Phenomena in Ionesco's *The Lesson*. In Carter and Simpson (eds.) 1989. 171-193.

van Dijk, T. A. and Kintsch, W. 1983. *Strategies of Discourse Comprehension*. London: Academic Press.

West, C. and Zimmerman, D. H. 1985. Gender, language and discourse. In *Handbook of Discourse Analysis* 4, ed. by T. A. van Dijk, 103-124. London: Academic Press.

王建华(Wang, J.), 1998, 礼貌的相对性,《外国语》第 3 期。

Discourse Role Switching and Characterization in Drama

YU Dongming

Shanghai International Studies University

HAN Zhongqian

Shaoxing College of Art and Science

1. Introduction: Discourse Role vs. Social Role

Social role refers to the social relationship obtaining between one interactant and another, whereas discourse role refers to the relationship between the interactant and the message (Is she/he producing it, receiving it, or transmitting it on behalf of another, etc. ?).

2. Discourse Roles (I)

2.1 Producers of talk

On the basis of differing degrees of responsibility for the message being transmitted, Thomas (1991) has distinguished five different categories of producer of talk. **Speaker**: The default term for the person who is currently speaking, and who, unless indications are given to the contrary, is assumed to be speaking on her/his own behalf and on her/his own authority. **Author**: The non-speaking originator behind a message. **Reporter**: A person who self-selects to relay a message. **Spokesperson**: An individual speaking on behalf of another/others, representing what s/he believes to be their views, without necessarily relaying a message verbally. **Mouthpiece**: The person who relays usually verbalizes the author's message.

Speaker is the unmarked term denoting the person who is currently talking. Unless otherwise indicated, the speaker is assumed to speaking on his/her own authority (i.e. speaker combines in one person the discourse roles of author and mouthpiece).

The discourse role of **author** is different in several respects from the other

213

producer roles. The first and most obvious difference is that there is no direct channel link between the author and the receiver, although the author, like the speaker, is both the originator of and the authority behind the illocutionary act being transmitted. The second difference is that, unlike all the other discourse roles, there is no obvious default linguistic term for the role. Authors in naturally occurring language and some dramatic dialogues, tend to be referred to by their social or institutional role (For example, *Dad says*, *The University regulations state*). The term "author" is used to distinguish the originator or authority behind a speech act from the person who actually utters it the "mouthpiece" or "spokesperson". For example, when Moses came down from the mountain and delivered the Ten Commandments, he was only the mouthpiece, while God was the author. Often people will indicate in some way whether or not they are speaking on their own authority or on someone else's by stating explicitly the authority behind the message:

> "But I tell you, you're to come down. Miss, this minute: your mother says so. "

> > (*The Mill on the Floss*, Ch. VII)

More frequently, the fact that a message is being transmitted on behalf of another is signaled by the use of modality alone: I have to inform you. Similarly, in official letters or notices, the fact that the signatory is not the author may be signaled by passivisation or by agent-deletion. For example: *Trespassers will be prosecuted*; *Infringing the rules of the library may lead to the suspension of borrowing rights*. On occasions, social or institutional norms or existential truths may be invoked as authors. For example:

> The regulations clearly state that all course work has to be submitted by the deadline.
> Someone's got to tell you.
> Brian, you can't go around insulting people!

This has the effect of distancing the utterer from what is being said; the utterer is merely the passive transmitter of something with which s/he may or may not agree but which is "universally" held to be true.

The distinction between **spokesperson** and **mouthpiece** is less marked than the distinction between, say, speaker and mouthpiece. The prototypical discourse role of spokesperson could be roughly characterized in the following way: A spokesperson is a representative of an individual, or a member or representative of a group, whose illocutionary intent s/he represents. A mouthpiece is a representative of a group or individual (but not part of it), representing their rather than his own illocutionary intent. Whereas a spokesperson may be identified closely with the source of the illocutionary act (and therefore bear some responsibility for that act), the mouthpiece is not (and does not).

The discourse role of reporter differs from the other two "relayers of illocutionary acts" in that she/he has no mandate of any kind from the author and does not represent the author, but instead has self-selected to report an illocutionary act. Reporting is different from being a surrogate in that, although a reporter is by definition not the originator of the illocutionary act she/he transmits, there is no direct, ratified link from the source to the receiver. In consequence, the reporter is not, as a rule, held responsible for the illocutionary act, nor, typically, identified with the source. Nevertheless, as she/he has chosen, rather than been required, to transmit the illocutionary act, she/he may at times be held to some degree responsible.

2.2 The switching of producer role

The most common switching of producer role is role switching from "mouthpiece" or "spokesperson" to "speaker". For example:

Laird: Our senior shop stewards called together our members just a few weeks ago and asked them would they be prepared to work in a defense project and the answer was er 2500 "yes" and 35 "no". I don't know who Bruce Kent speaks for but I speak for our members...

Generally speaking, the switching of producer role can be regarded as a kind of pragmatic strategy whereby the speaker involved is able to assess how much responsibility he would like to bear for a particular illocutionary act in interaction with others (cf. Yu Dongming, 1996).

3. Discourse Roles (II): Receivers of Talk

It should be noted that the categories suggested should not be seen as hard-

and-fast. Clearly there are areas of overlap, or you may feel that it is necessary to add additional categories. The following chart indicates the criteria we will use for establishing categories for the discourse roles-receivers of talk:

	Addressee	Audience	Bystander	Eavesdropper
Target of I. A. ?	Y	N	N	N
Able to speak?	Y	Y/N	Y/N	N
Allowed to speak?	Y	N(?)	N	N
Affects form of I. A. ?	Y	Y	Y	N
Sanctioned member of speech event?	Y	Y	N	N

Figure 1

Target of Illoc. -act: Is the illoc. -act designed to produce a particular perlocutionary effect on this participant?

Channel-limitation: It is taken for granted that all receivers can hear. "Limitation" here refers to the speaking channel.

(Adapted from Thomas, 1991)

From the above figure, we can see that receivers of talk can roughly be divided into four categories: Addressee (the "default" term); Audience (also auditor); Bystander/over-hearer and Eavesdropper. More specifically, the **addressee** is the person to whom an utterance is directed, whereas an **auditor** is a sanctioned member (legitimately present at a speech event), but not the one currently being addressed. An auditor may be considered to have rather less right to reply than the addressee, but may nevertheless self-select and take a speaking turn. For example:

Woman: Go away, smelly!
Man: Thanks!
Woman: The dog, you idiot!

In this example, the "man" is the auditor, while the "dog" is the real addressee directed at by the "woman". On many occasions, we may also distinguish between "Real" and "Ostensible" addressee. In the following two examples, the mother and the man smoking a pipe are the "real" addressee, whereas the infant and the young man's companion are the "ostensible" addressee:

"Doesn't your mommy change your diapers?" (Old woman to an infant crying in its pram and whose mother was present)

"Some people have no consideration at all!" (On a long-distance coach, on which a man was smoking a particularly malodorous pipe, a young man says to his companion.)

Alternatively, it could be the case that the person to whom the speaker wished to convey a message is perfectly addressable (a fellow student, perhaps) but the message itself is too face-threatening to be directed, however obliquely, at the person concerned. For example, in college kitchens in UK food has a way of going missing from the communal refrigerators. A friend of mine reports saying pointedly to another Chinese student in the presence of the prime suspect: I'm sure I put a yogurt and some milk in here at lunchtime! The concept of "real" versus "ostensible" addressees can also explain apparent violations of the Maxim of Quantity, which frequently occur in radio or television broadcasts and in dramatic discourse.

The distinction between addressee(s) and audience is rather slight. The main difference is that audiences at best have reduced speaking rights (studio audiences may sometimes ask questions, heckle, etc.), but more frequently have no speaking rights at all. Nevertheless, both audience and addressees are active participants in the speech event—it is for the benefit of theatre audiences that plays are staged, and their reaction has a direct effect on the livelihood of the actors. It is not unknown for performers to be booed off the stage or for plays to be taken off in the face of adverse audience reaction. Perhaps the concept of audience would be better replaced by a category of addressee with reduced speaking rights. This would be helpful in explaining incidents in dramatic discourse where a different message is conveyed by the actor-speaker to the actor-addressee from that conveyed by the actor-speaker to the audience. It often happens in drama that a different speech act or implicature is conveyed by the addresser (the script-writer) to the audience (real addressees) from that conveyed by the speaker (actor) to the (ostensible) addressee. For example, in an episode of the soap opera in 1990 in UK. The Archers, Tony Archer is talking to Phil Archer, who has recently grown a beard which he is very proud of but which everyone else thinks looks awful:

Phil: Is something wrong with my face?

Tony: Sorry I was miles away. I wasn't thinking about your beard at all.

Clearly, Tony wishes to imply to Phil that he was not thinking about his beard (even though Phil may infer otherwise), whilst the writer wishes to imply exactly the opposite to the audience, viz. that Phil's beard was uppermost in Tony's mind.

A bystander/over-hearer is someone who is known by the speaker to be within earshot, but who is not, unlike an auditor, a sanctioned member of a speech event with a right to take a speaking turn. Auditors, even when not directly being addressed, are acknowledged as legitimately present (e.g. students in a seminar group, members of a family) and are entitled to listen in to what is said. Bystanders are not the targets of the speaker's message, but they may nevertheless affect the way she/he speaks.

An eavesdropper, like a bystander, is not a sanctioned member of a speech event. Indeed, as a rule, the speaker does not even realize the eavesdropper is there, and certainly does not make allowance for the fact that the eavesdropper is within earshot Eavesdroppers, like bystanders/over-hearers, do not normally assume speaking rights. It may, of course, happen that a bystander/an over-hearer believes an utterance to have been directed at her or him (i. e. that she/he is the intended addressee) and interpret the utterance accordingly, as in the following example:

[Speaker A (female) and Speaker B (male) were at a party. They were standing with their backs to the rest of the company, and A was berating B for eating too much. Unfortunately, B's response (but not A's initial comment) was overhead by their hostess, who interpreted it as a criticism of her hospitality]:

A: You're putting it away, you gutsy swine!

B: I'm absolutely famished!

C: There's loads more food in the kitchen. I'm bringing it through as fast as I can!

B: Oh, I didn't mean...

It should be noted that all the categories for receivers of talk have been described with a single participant occupying each role. It is worth noting that in every category more than one person could fulfill the function Just as an audience can be made up of one or more people, so one can have several speakers (e. g. speaking in chorus) multiple addressers, addressees, etc.

4. Discourse Roles and Their Switching in the Dramatic Text

As we will see in this section, the category of discourse roles and their switching is also widely and fruitfully exploited by the playwright Cao Yu in his play *The Thunderstorm* to help to depict the personality traits of the dramatic personae, to propel the plot development and dramatize the conflicts and clashes between the characters in the play.

In 2.1, we have distinguished five different kinds of producers of talk on the basis of differing degrees of responsibility for the message being transmitted: Speaker, Author, Reporter, Spokesperson and Mouthpiece. As we will find in the following examples, the above five different discourse roles and their switching are widely and fruitfully utilized for dramatic purposes.

a 鲁四凤：太太，您脸上像是发烧，还是到楼上歇着吧。

b 周繁漪：不，楼上太热。

c 鲁四凤：**老爷**说太太有病，嘱咐过请您好好地在楼上躺着。

In this speech event, Lu Sifeng in **turn a** is obviously playing the discourse role of the speaker on her own behalf and on her own authority, persuading Zhou Fanyi to go upstairs to take a good rest. It is because she fails to perform the speech act that she resorts to revealing to Zhou Fanyi the author of the message——老爷 and switches to the discourse role of a mouthpiece in **turn c.** Lu Sifeng's switching of discourse roles can be regarded as a kind of pragmatic strategy via which she is actually shirking responsibility to perform a negative face-threatening speech act.

In the following example, the discourse role of spokesperson is also fully exploited by the playwright for similar dramatic purposes:

鲁大海：可是你完全错了。**我们**这次罢工是有团结的，有组织的。**我们代表**这次来，并不是来求你们。你听清楚，不求你们。你们答应就答应；不答应，**我们**一直罢工到底，我们知道你们不到两个月整个地就要关门的。

Lu Dahai is obviously playing the discourse role of a spokesperson on behalf of the miners, representing what he believes to be their views, without necessarily relaying the message verbatim. Interestingly enough, as the confrontation between Lu Dahai and Zhou Puyuan intensifies, Lu Dahai automatically switches his discourse role from a spokesperson to a speaker, which indicates that the clash develops into a face-to-face confrontation and portrays Lu Dahai as a hot-tempered and courageous young miner who is prepared to shoulder the responsibility for the ill-starred consequences of his illocutionary acts in interaction with Zhou Puyuan:

鲁大海:**我**就是要问问懂事长，对于我们工人的条件，究竟是答应不答应?

·······

鲁大海:···——**我**问你，你的意思，忽儿冷，忽儿热，究竟是怎么回事?

Similarly, the five different discourse roles for receivers of talk described in 2.1, i.e. addressee, auditor/audience, bystander and eavesdropper can also be easily identified and discerned in the play and their frequent switching is the rule rather than the exception. In the following example, the switching of discourse roles traverses the boundary of receivers of talk, with the three dramatic characters switching from the discourse role of speaker to addressee and then to bystander:

a 周　冲:哥哥，母亲说好久不见你。你不愿意一齐坐一坐，谈谈么?

b 周繁漪:你看，你让哥哥歇一歇，他愿意一个人呆着的。

c 周　萍:那也不见得，我总怕父亲回来，您很忙，所以——

d 周　冲:你不知道母亲病了么?

e 周繁漪:你哥哥怎么会把我的病放在心上?

f 周　冲:妈!

g 周　萍:您好一点了么?

·······

周繁漪:你在矿上作什么呢?

周　冲:妈，你忘了，哥哥是专门学矿科的。

周繁漪:这是理由么，萍?

周　萍:说不出来，像是家里住得太久了，烦得很。

In **turn a**, Zhou Chong switches his role from a reporter to the speaker, addressing Zhou Ping, while Zhou Fanyi plays the discourse roles of both the author and bystander. Then from **turn b** to **turn g** the three characters switch their respective discourse roles in succession, as revealed in Figure 2:

Turn	a	b	c	d	e	f	g
说话人	周 冲	周繁漪	周 萍	周 冲	周繁漪	周 冲	周 萍
受话人	周 萍	周 冲	周繁漪	周 萍	周 冲	周繁漪	周繁漪
旁听者	周繁漪	周 萍	周 冲	周繁漪	周 萍	周 萍	周 冲

Figure 2

In the second half of the above conversation, the discourse roles seem to be more fixed, with Zhou Fanyi and Zhou Ping playing the discourse roles of speaker and addressee respectively, and Zhou Chong chiefly playing the discourse role of bystander. More interestingly, in **turns b** and **e** in the first part of the conversation, Zhou Chong is only the "ostensible addressee" and the "real" addressee is Zhou Ping.

A bystander/over-hearer is someone who is known by the speaker to be within earshot, but who is not, unlike an auditor, a sanctioned member of a speech event with a right to take a speaking turn. In the following example, Zhou Ping and Zhou Chong are only a bystander, who is not assumed to have the right to speak in this particular dramatic scene and this fact explains why they are scolded by their father several times:

鲁大海: ……你们这种卑鄙无耻的行为!
周　萍: 你是谁? 敢在这儿胡说?
周朴园: 没有你的话!
……
鲁大海: 你们的钱这次又失灵了。
周　萍: 你混账!
周朴园: 不许多说话!
……
鲁大海: 开除了!?
周　冲: 爸爸, 这是不公平的。
周朴园: 你少多嘴, 出去!

In the play, the discourse role of an eavesdropper is frequently and fruitfully exploited by the character Lu Gui who utilizes it as a kind of pragmatic strategy to realize his personal purposes in several scenes in the play:

周繁漪：你为什么不早点来告诉我。

鲁　贵：我倒是想着，可是我(低声)刚才瞧见太太跟大少爷说话，所以就
　　　　没敢惊动您。

周繁漪：你，你刚才……

鲁　贵：太太，您好。

周繁漪：你来作什么?

鲁　贵：给您请安来了。我在门口等了半天。

周繁漪：哦，你刚才在门口?

鲁　贵：对了。我看见大少爷正和您打架，我，——我就没敢进来。

Obviously, Lu Gui in the above two scenes intentionally reveals the fact that he has played the discourse role of an eavesdropper twice to Zhou Fanyi in order to blackmail her and to realize his own mean purposes. It is worth noting in passing that in the above two scenes, the speaker Zhou Fanyi certainly does not realize that Lu Gui is actually within her earshot when she is quarreling with Zhou Ping. Otherwise, she should have been more careful in wording to cover up her abnormal relationship with her stepson Zhou Ping. Put it differently, if the speaker realizes the existence of an eavesdropper within earshot, she/he will pay more attention to and even change the content and surface linguistic form of their speech acts. The following is a case in point:

鲁四凤：(忽然聆听)您别说话，我听见好像有人在客厅咳嗽似的。

鲁　贵：(听一下)别是太太吧? (走到饭厅的门前，由锁眼窥视，忙回来)
　　　　可不是她，奇怪，她下楼来了。别慌，什么也别提，我走了。

5. Conclusion

From the above brief analysis, we can easily see that the analytical category of discourse roles is fully applicable to the analysis of the dramatic conversations and their frequent switching turns out to be the rule rather than the exception. The majority of the discourse roles actually can be identified in this dramatic text. Almost every character in a particular play may play different discourse roles, switching their discourse role from the producer of the talk to the receiver of the talk and vice versa. Similarly, different characters can play the same discourse role in different contexts of dramatic situations. It should be noted at this point that in this section we have not touched upon another two discourse roles, i. e. the author and audience on account of the assumption that the prototypical discourse role of author normally refers to the playwright of a particular play. So in the present case, the author is certainly the playwright of Cao Yu. Naturally, the prototypical discourse role of audience should refer to the theatergoers for a particular performance of a play who vary from each performance of a particular play. It follows naturally that with these two stereotypical discourse roles included, we actually can identify all the discourse roles described even in this one drama, which proves and verifies the validity and feasibility of this analytical category in the study of dramatic texts.

References

Hou, W. R. 1996. *Literary Stylistics.* Shanghai: SISU.

Leech, G. & Short, M. 1981. *Style in Fiction.* London: Longman.

Short, M. 1996. *Exploring the Language of Poems*, *Plays and Prose.* London, England, New York: Longman.

Thomas, J. 1991. *Pragmatics: Lecture Notes.* Lancaster University Press.

Yu, D. M. 1997. Style and interpretation of MA Feng's *My First Superior*, *Journal of Foreign Languages and Literature* 2.

Yu, D. M. 2000. Towards a functional and pragmatic approach to the study of dramatic texts. Presented at *the 27*[th] *International Systemic Functional Linguistics Congress*, July 9th-14th 2000. Australia: The Univ. of Melbourne.

俞东明(Yü, D.),1993,《戏剧文体学的范围、性质和方法, 英语百人百论(下卷)》。成都: 四川科技出版社。

俞东明(Yü, D.),1996,话语角色类型及其在言语交际中的转换,《外国语》第1期。

The Stylistics of Drama: The State of the Art

LI Huadong

Hangzhou Dianzi University

1. Introduction

After a diachronic review of the stylistics of drama, I will in this paper compare and contrast the different approaches to the study of the dramatic text, advocate the pragmastylistic approach, and consider the necessity for an integration of the different pragmastylistic approaches.

Before the birth of "stylistics" as a separate discipline which applies modern linguistic theories to literary texts, people had been doing studies on dramatic texts[①]. For the convenience of discussion, I will call this period "the pre-stylistic period".

Afterwards, some scholars began to develop a separate field, namely, "literary stylistics", for the analysis of literary texts. Although at this stage they primarily focused on the literary genres of poetry and fiction, they touched a little bit upon the genre of drama, regarding it either as poetry or as fiction. I shall call this period "the early stylistic period" with a subtitle of "the poetic-fictional approach".

The stylistics of drama did not take its current shape until people realized the fundamental difference of drama from poetry or fiction. This difference lies in that the main means of expression is dialogue, and therefore the dramatic text should be analyzed by utilizing the new techniques of "discourse analysis". The early analysis achieved a certain degree of "descriptive adequacy", but failed to explain how the dialogue contributes to the appreciation or interpretation of the drama. Soon scholars began to combine discourse analysis with pragmatics so as to achieve

---

① Shen (2000) gave a brief diachronic survey of Western stylistics. According to Shen, the first monograph in this field, *On Style*, written by Demetrius, appeared in 100 AD. The founder of Western stylistics was Charles Bally (1865-1947), a student of the Swiss Linguist Ferdinand de Saussure. Bally did not pay attention to literary texts though. The founder of Western literary stylistics was the German scholar Leo Spitzer (1887-1960). He analyzed novels by an approach named "the philological circle".

The discussion of style in drama has been very rare in history before the end of the 21st century. Liu (2004: 1-18) did a brief survey of dramatic theories, which indicates that scholars seldom devoted their efforts to dramatic text analysis. An exception was Eliopulos (1975), who used a rhetorical-poetic approach to the analysis of Samuel Beckett's dramatic language.

the "explanatory adequacy". In so doing, they have achieved the goal of stylistics, i. e., to interprete the text. I shall call this period "the pragmastylistic period" with a subtitle of "the study of the dialogue". This approach yielded satisfactory results in analyzing the realistic drama and is still prevalent in the field.

In analyzing the Theatre of the Absurd, some scholars began to take stage directions into account, which is a traditionally neglected object of dramatic stylistic analysis. As these absurd dramatists often degraded the communicative function of language, they often had to turn to stage directions to describe a kind of absurd setting, to indicate silence and to direct actions. They even went to the extreme of producing some plays with no words at all, as Beckett did in his *Act Without Words I* and *II*. Scholars began to be conscious that in doing stylistic studies of such drama, stage directions have to be an important object for analysis. I shall call this period "the pragmastylistic period" with a subtitle of "the study of stage directions".

2. The Pre-stylistic Period

2.1 The traditional literary critical approach

People who adopt the traditional literary critical approach are usually from the circle of literature. The traditional theories of drama started from Aristotle's categorization of drama in his *Poetics* into six elements, namely, plot, character, thought, diction, music and spectacle. He put forward a concept called "*mimesis*" (imitation), and believed that the process of drama production is *mimesis* (Liu, 2004: 1-13; Luo, 2004). Aristotle's theories of drama are the starting point and the cornerstone for later discussions of plays.

After Aristotle, many theories of drama had been formulated, either adherent or opponent to his *mimesis* theories. These drama theories had various labels. The theories adherent to Aristotle's include Neoclassical in the 17th century, Naturalism and Realism in the 19th century and early 20th century. The drama theories opponent to Aristotle's range from Romantics in the 18th century, Symbolism in the 19th century, and such Avant-garde Theories as Futurism, Surrealism, Expressionism, and the Theatre of the Absurd in the 20th century. Drama Critics of the 20th century looked at drama from even more diversified theoretical perspectives, borrowing concepts from different schools of thoughts (Liu, 2004: 14-18).

The traditional literary critical approaches to drama primarily focus on the overall theatrical effect, with the text analysis being considered as a compensational tool. Borrowing from different schools of thought, their techniques are kaleidoscopic, ranging from new criticism, structuralism, Marxism to Daoism, etc. However colorful they are, these analyses are impressionistic. They have produced random results in terms of the stylistic features. During this pre-historical period, the dramatic text has never been the main focus of study.

2.2 The rhetorical-poetic approach

In exploring the features of Samuel Beckett's dramatic language, Eliopulos (1975) began to focus on the dramatic text. He adopted a rhetorical-poetic approach by following the trace of Aristotle. He argued that both rhetoric and poetic share the elements of communicator (author), purpose, audience, occasion (circumstances), method (form), subject matter (ideational content), medium, style, identification and stance. He further argued that the distinctions between rhetorical and poetic elements are not absolute but a matter of degree or emphasis (Eliopulos, 1975: 14-26).

Based on the assumption that dramatic language could be described with greater precision if both rhetoric and poetic elements are employed, Eliopulos identifies eleven characteristics of style in Samuel Beckett's dramatic language, namely repetition, monologue, stichomythia, phatic communion, word groupings, intentional dystax, contradictions, clichés and pitfalls, indelicacies, structural closure, and absence of language (silence) (*ibid.*: 59-101). According to Eliopulos, these "linguistic stylistic features" reveal Beckett's rejection of the traditional form, helping to produce the unique form with direct compact for the audience.

Although Eliopulos had based his criticism mainly on the study of the dramatic text, he did not have a coherent linguistic theory as a basis for analysis. If we consider the definition of stylistics as the interpretation and criticism of literary text by using linguistic theories, we will consider his analysis as "traditional" or "pre-stylistic" in this sense. To support this statement, we may point out that his "eleven stylistic features" are overlapping and that a different analyst, taking his approach, may arrive at a different number, fewer or more than the eleven, of stylistic features in Beckett's dramatic language.

3. The Early Stylistic Period: The Poetic-fictional Approach

Stylistics as an interdisciplinary area of study in British and American literary field began to be given significant attention to at the Conference of Stylistics held in University of Indiana in 1958. At the conference, Roman Jakobson (1960: 377) made his famous claim that "If there are some critics who still doubt the competence of linguistics to embrace the field of poetics, I privately believe that the poetic incompetence of some bigoted linguists has been mistaken for an inadequacy of the linguistic science itself."

What is the accepted definition of stylistics then? Here are two definitions from different sources:

Stylistics: A branch of linguistics which studies the characteristics of situationally-distinctive uses of language, with particular reference to literary language, and tries to establish principles capable of accounting for the particular choices made by individuals and social groups in their use of language (*The Fontana Dictionary of Modern Thought*, 1977, 2nd edition 1988).

Stylistics: The study of style; ... just as style can be viewed in several ways, so there are several different stylistic approaches. This variety in stylistics is due to the main influences of linguistics and literary criticism. ...

By far the most common kind of material studied is literary; and attention is largely text-centered. ... The goal of most stylistics is not simply to describe the formal features of texts for their own sake, but in order to show their functional significance for the interpretation of the text; or in order to relate literary effects to linguistic "causes" where these are felt to be relevant. ... Stylisticians want to avoid vague and impressionistic judgments about the way that formal features are manipulated. As a result, stylistics draws on the model and terminology provided by whatever aspects of linguistics are felt to be relevant.

(Wales, 1989: *A Dictionary of Stylistics*)

From these definitions we can say that some key aspects of stylistics are:

- The use of linguistics to approach literary texts;
- The discussion of texts according to objective criteria rather than purely to subjective and impressionistic values;
- Emphasis on the aesthetic properties of language.

However, the early stylistic studies were mainly concerned with two genres of literary texts, namely, poetry and fiction (see, for example, Leech, 1969; Leech and Short, 1981; Widdowson, 1992). The situation in China was the same, except that relevant publications appeared a little later (see, for example, Liu Shisheng, 1998; Zhang Delu, 1998; Wang Shouyuan, 2000; Hu Zhuanglin, 2000). The reason for neglecting drama as an object of stylistic analysis was commented by Short as follows:

> If we compare them with poems and fictional prose, play-texts have in general received relatively little attention from both twentieth-century literary critics and stylisticians. Part of the problem may lie in the fact that spoken conversation has for many centuries been commonly seen as a debased and unstable form of language, and thus plays, with all their affinities with speech, were liable to be undervalued. (Short, 1998: 3)

A few stylisticians (e. g. Jakobson, 1960; Jakobson and Jones, 1970; Leech, 1969) did some work on plays by Shakespeare and other Elizabethan playwrights. But they did so because of the fact that these plays were treated as "dramatic poems". By denying these plays their status as "spoken conversation to be performed", they were considered stable texts worthy of close analysis.

Some stylisticians (e. g. Thornborrow and Wareing, 1998: 119-120) suggested that one way of analyzing drama is to treat it more or less like fiction as "The two components of plot and character clearly are as significant in dramatic texts as in fiction."

4. The Pragmatic and Discourse Analysis Period: The Study of the Dramatic Dialogue

The development of stylistics of drama entered a fruitful period when scholars began to notice that the main means of expression in this literary genre was dialogue and when pragmatics and discourse analysis were combined to study the dialogue. Some studies focused on the linguistic structure of dramatic dialogue (e. g. Burton, 1980; Herman, 1991). Some used politeness theory to illuminate the social dynamics of character interaction (e.g. Simpson, 1989; Leech, 1992). And others (e. g. Short, 1989, 1996) drew eclectically from pragmatics and discourse analysis in order to shed light on aspects such as characterization and absurdity.

Culpeper, Short & Verdonk (1998) set the landmark in this field because their book was the first one (in fact it is a compilation of papers from many scholars) wholly devoted to stylistics of drama. More recent development in the field was Culpeper (2001) who outlined an interdisciplinary approach to characterization which drew in particular upon theories from social and cognitive psychology in an attempt to explain how characters were constructed in the interaction between readers and play texts.

In China, Yang (1989), Yu (1999) and Wang (2000) promoted stylistic studies of dramatic dialogue. These scholars combined principles and techniques from pragmatics and discourse analysis in their study of dramatic text. Yu (1999) established a framework for the analysis of the dialogue of drama, using categories such as speech acts, cooperative principle, politeness principle, presupposition and deixis, discourse roles and their switching, pragmatic ambivalence and conversational strategies, register analysis, and turn-taking, etc. He tried his framework on the traditional drama, producing systematic, detailed and convincing results. Wang (2006) also tried different models, one at a time, on stylistic analysis of drama. The models that she used include turn-taking analysis, discourse structure, speech act, cooperative principle, politeness principle and sociolinguistics. From this list, we can find that although she claimed she studied dialogue as discourse, she actually borrowed many concepts or categories from pragmatics.

5. The Pragmatylistic Period: The Study of Stage Directions

Successful as the stylistics of dramatic dialogue seemed, such studies neglected a component of the dramatic text, i. e. , stage directions. As a result, these studies were seldom successful in analyzing the non-realistic drama, in which stage directions are usually essential in meaning construction. Take the Theatre of the Absurd as an example. Absurd dramatists often degraded the function of verbal communication. Therefore they had to turn to stage directions rather than dialogue to convey their meaning. Some absurd plays even went to the extreme of excluding dialogue all together, such as Samuel Beckett's *Act without Words* I and II.

It goes without saying that the inability to interpret such non-realistic plays as the absurd drama leads to doubt about the frameworks already constructed in stylistics of drama. Burton (1980: 22-23) realized this in his analysis of the modern drama by pointing out silence as an important feature of Pinter's plays. Feng (2002: 107-110) places even more importance on stage directions by considering them indispensable in many plays. He reasonably asserts:

> Stage directions operate in rather different ways in different plays. Their importance varies, ranging from being optional to being absolutely indispensable. (*ibid*: 108-109)

Stage directions provide information about the character and the mood as well as the usual notations of entrances and exits and places where the action occurs. Of course, one may notice that many traditional plays were written without stage directions since information concerning the entrances, exits and setting could be inferred from dialogue. In fact, Nash (1989) showed, through paraphrasing an episode of Shakespeare's play, *Hamlet*, that stage directions were optional only in the sense of being implicit, and it was only a choice whether the playwright explicitly spelled out stage directions. But Feng (2002: 109) believed that in many modern plays, the use of extensive stage directions is not a matter of choice but one of importance. For example:

> In most plays of the Theatre of the Absurd, stage directions are absolutely indispensable. .... An extreme case is Samuel Beckett's *Act without Words* (1956), where stage directions are the only language of the play, and, without stage directions, there would be no play. (Feng, 2002: 109)

Even in the traditional plays, stage directions deserve a certain degree of attention. Take Bernard Shaw's plays for example.

Although most of Bernard Shaw's stage directions may seem superfluous, when they were experimentally removed, the plays would be quite different: not everything is, or always is, available in and inferable from the dialogue. (Feng, 2002: 109)

Although Feng (2002) saw the importance of stage directions in his formulation of a "multi-level structure of dramatic discourse" (*ibid*: 120)[1], he did not, in theory or practice, specify how stage directions interact with dialogue and how this interaction contributes to the appreciation and interpretation of the play. In this sense, he had not yet served the purpose of "stylistics", namely, the revelation of the aesthetic value.

6. A Comparison and Contrast of the Different Approaches

Although these approaches share the goal of identifying the stylistic features of aesthetic value in drama, they are different in three ways: their primary focus, their techniques, and their final outcome (see Table 1).

Table 1   The differences of the three approaches
to the study of dramatic texts

Approaches		Focus	Techniques	Result
Traditional literary critical		Text as a compensation	Impressionistic	Random, accidental
Rhetorical-poetic		Text as the main focus	Rhetorical (Aristotelian)	A little more systematic and objective
Poetry-fiction approach		Text as the main focus	linguistic (drama as poetry) Literary and linguistic (drama as fiction)	More systematic and objective
Pragma-stylistic	Study of dialogues	Dialogue as the main focus	Pragmatics, discourse analysis	Systematic and objective
	Study of stage directions	Stage directions as an important component	Pragmatics, discourse analysis	Systematic and objective

From Table 1, we can see that stylistics of drama has shifted its focus and varied its techniques, thus produced different results. This is mainly due to the

---

[1] There will be more detailed discussion of Feng's "multi-level structure of dramatic discourse" in 4.1.2 of this dissertation.

development of relevant theories. For a long time, when people had never heard the term of "stylistics", their study of dramatic texts had been influenced by Aristotle's theories of drama. When linguistics became an important discipline and attracted scholars' attention, some of them began to use linguistic theories to approach literary texts of poetry and fiction. During this period, some scholars who studied the usually neglected or even ignored genre of literary texts of drama tended to regard it either as poetry or fiction. One reason might be that linguistics was at that time still focusing on phonology, morphology, syntax and semantics.

However, when pragmatics appeared as a field of linguistic study to account for some phenomena insufficiently dealt with in semantics, and when linguistics began to shift from the sentence level to discourse level, stylisticians began to be more powerfully equipped. They began to examine dramatic texts at the discourse level, while making use of pragmatics as a powerful weapon of interpretation. It is reasonable that they first noticed the more noticeable part of the dramatic text, the dialogue, and that they first applied these theories to the more accepted realistic drama. It is also reasonable that they soon spotted the neglected part of the dramatic texts, the stage directions, when they began to try their techniques on modern drama, where stage directions are used more extensively.

It is worth noting here that stylistics is different from traditional literary critics in that it attempts to find "hard" and more systematic evidence for the appreciation of aesthetic value. This goal is better achieved when such analysis is based on a systematic and objective analytical framework. In this sense, stylistics of drama has been making progress toward this end, if we assume that there is an end. Thus the rhetorical-poetic approach is more systematic and objective than the traditional literary critics, the poetry-fiction approach is even more so, and the pragmastylistics is the most systematic and objective so far.

7. Conclusion

To summarize, the pragmastylistic approach that combines discourse analysis with pragmatics seems to be the most appropriate approach to stylistics of drama because it has covered the main components of dramatic texts: the dialogue and the stage directions, and the meaning generation of dramatic texts in context. It is in this sense that stylistics of drama began to take its current shape and started out a potentially productive journey.

But two fundamental questions still remain of theoretical and practical importance.

Question 1: Why do I, as well as some other scholars (e. g. Feng, 2002) call such analysis "pragmastylistics"? In other words, what kind of contribution does pragmatics make to stylistics of dramatic texts? Does it provide just a number of tools that constitute the stylistic "tool kit", or does it provide a perspective on dramatic texts?

Question 2: What is the discourse structure of dramatic texts? What kind of interaction do dialogue and stage directions have for the realization of aesthetic value?

These two questions are closely related to two concerns of a scientific study: the research methodology and the object for analysis. They should be tackled in further research.

References

Burton, D. 1980. *Dialogue and Discourse: A Sociolinguistic Approach to Modern Drama and Naturally Occurring Conversation*. London: Routledge and Kegan Paul.

Bussmann, H. 1996. *Routledge Dictionary of Language and Linguistics*. London: Routledge/ Beijing: Foreign Language Teaching and Research Press (2000).

Culpeper, J. 2001. *Language and Characterization: People in Plays and Other Texts*. Essex: Pearson Education Ltd.

Culpeper, J., Short, M. & Verdonk, P. 1998. *Exploring the Language of Drama*. London: Routledge.

Eliopulos, J. 1975. *Samuel Beckett's Dramatic Language*. The Hague: Mouton.

Feng, Z. 2002. *Pragmastylistics of Dramatic Texts: The Play off the Stage*. Beijing: Tsinghua University Press.

Hartnoll, P., & Peter, F. 2000. *Oxford Dictionary of Theatre*. Shanghai: Shanghai Foreign Language Education Press.

Herman, V. 1991. Dramatic dialogue and the systematics of turn-taking, *Semiotica* 83: 97-121.

Hu, Z. 2000. *Theoretical Stylistics*. Beijing: Foreign Language Teaching and

Research Press.

Jakobson, R. 1960. Closing statement: Linguistics and poetics. In *Style in Language*, ed. by T. A. Sebeok, 350-377. Cambridge: MIT Press.

Jakobson, R. , & Jones, L. G. 1970. *Shakespeare's Verbal Art in " Th' Expence of Spirit"*. The Hague: Mouton.

Leech, G. N. 1969. *A Linguistic Guide to English Poetry*. London: Longman / Beijing: Foreign Language Teaching and Research Press (2001).

Leech, G. N. 1992. Pragmatic principles in Shaw's *You Never Can Tell.* In *Language, Text and Context: Essays in Stylistics*, ed. by Toolan. London: Longman.

Leech, G. N. , & Short, M. 1981. *Style in Fiction: A Linguistic Introduction to English Fictional Prose.* London: Longman / Beijing: Foreign Language Teaching and Research Press (2001).

Li, H. 2006. *From Page to Stage: A Pragmastylistic Perspective on Stage Directions of Drama.* Shanghai: Shanghai International Studies University.

Liu, H. 2004. Introduction to drama and dramatic theory. In *British and American Drama: Plays and Criticisms*, ed. by Liu, H. Shanghai: Shanghai Foreign Language Education Press.

Liu, S. 1998. *Outlines of Western Stylistics*. Jinan: Shandong Education Press.

Morris, C. W. 1938. Foundations of the theory of signs. In *International Encyclopedia of Unified Science*, ed. by O. Neurath, O. Carnap, & C. Morris, 77-138. Chicago: University of Chicago Press.

Nash, W. 1989. *Rhetoric: The Wit of Persuasion*. Oxford: Basil Blackwell Ltd.

Richards, J. C. , Platt, J. & Platt, H. 1992. *Longman Dictionary of Language Teaching and Applied Linguistics*. London: Longman / Beijing: Foreign Language Teaching and Research Press (2000).

Short, M. 1989. Discourse analysis and the analysis of drama. In *Language, Discourse and Literature*, ed. by R. Carter & P. Simpson. London: Routledge.

Short, M. 1998. Introduction. In *Exploring the Language of Drama*, ed. by J. Culpeper, M. Short & P. Verdonk. London: Routledge.

Short, M. 1996. *Exploring the Language of Poems, Plays and Prose*. Essex: Addison Wesley Longman Ltd.

Simpson, P. 1989. Politeness phenomena in Ionesco's *The Lesson*. In *Language,*

Discourse and Literature, ed. by R. Carter & P. Simpson. London: Routledge.

Thornborrow, J. & Wareing, S. 1998. *Patterns in Language: Stylistics for Students of Language and Literature*. London: Routledge / Beijing: Beijing Foreign Language Teaching and Research Press (2000).

Wales, K. 1989. *A Dictionary of Stylistics*. Longman: World Publishing Corp.

Wang, S. 2000. *Essentials of English Stylistics*. Jinan: Shandong University Press.

Widdowson, H. G. 1992. *Practical Stylistics*. Oxford: Oxford University Press / Shanghai: Shanghai Foreign Language Education Press (1999).

Yu, D. 1999. *Style in Drama: Towards a Pragmatic Approach to the Study of Dramatic Texts*. Shanghai: Shanghai International Studies University.

Zhang, D. 1998. *Functional Stylistics*. Jinan: Shandong Education Press.

罗念生(Luo, N.)(译),2004,《罗念生全集》,第一卷,文论。上海:上海人民出版社。

申丹(Shen, D.),2000,西方现代文体学百年发展历程,《外语教学与研究》第1期。

王虹(Wang, H.),2006,《戏剧文体分析——话语分析的方法》。上海:上海外语教育出版社。

杨雪燕(Yang, X.),1989,试论戏剧在语言文体学中的地位,《外国语》第1期。

4. The Stylistics of Fiction and Poetry

Metalanguage in the Making of Fiction

FENG Zongxin
Tsinghua University

1. Introduction

Although it is nearly five decades since Roman Jakobson discovered the "metalingual function" of language in his well-known closing statement "Linguistics and Poetics" at the Style Conference in Indiana in 1958, published in Jakobson (1960), specialized study on metalingual function or metalanguage in literature has been rare, except for some discussions on literary metalanguage, e. g. in the sense of "a set of conceptual and analytical tools" (Pier, 1985). This paper takes the nature of linguistic metalanguage, in opposition to logical metalanguage, with various features as its basis, discusses important roles that metalanguage plays in the making of fiction.

2. The Nature of Metalanguage

Modern logic and linguistics have made distinctions of object language and metalanguage, e. g. "*London* is situated on the Thames" vs. "London is a proper noun of two syllables" (Bussmann, 1996: 303), echoing the distinction of "use" and "mention" in the philosophy of language (see Searle, 1969). While the above example of metalanguage contains a "metalingual" mentioning of the lexical item "London", the statement as a whole is a "metalinguistic" proposition, i. e. describing language rather than things in the object world.

There are at least two types of metalanguage: logical metalanguage and linguistic metalanguage. The former evolved mainly to solve the "liar's paradox", while the latter is principally the linguist's tool. Since "metalanguage" has two adjectival forms, "metalingual" and "metalinguistic", there should be a distinction

236

between language that is used "metalingually" and language that is used "metalinguistically". When language is used in the Jakobsonian (1960) sense of "glossing", it is "metalingual". However, when language is used as linguistic (phonological, lexicogrammatical, semantic, pragmatic, etc.) description in a technical sense, it is "metalinguistic". Thus, there are two types of linguistic metalanguage: ordinary language referring to language in the "metalingual function" and technical language (linguistic terminology) describing various levels of language system in the "metalinguistic function" (Feng, 2005). This echoes McDonough's (2000) observation that one must distinguish between metalinguistics involving "the language-as-object conception" and metalinguistics "as a second-order reflection on language".

3. Metalanguage in Fiction

Since the major task of a fiction is to "show" by verbal means what happened or is happening in a possible world on the level of "story", attention is more often on the unmarked first-order object-language for narration. Although both stylisticians and narratologists have paid some attention to "telling" on the level of "discourse", studies on aspects related to the second-order language (metalanguage) in fictional discourse still remain scanty.

In her monograph, *The Fictions of Language and the Languages of Fiction*, Fludernik (1993: 35) only mentions a "metalinguistic feature" discovered in Quine's musings on the *de dicto* versions of various sentences, saying that the *de dicto* concept is "apparently meta-linguistic". She writes,

> "the snub-nosed man" (in reference to Socrates) is *de dicto* since *qua* descriptive term, it requires a speaker to enunciate this description with the function of making reference to the individual commonly referred to as Socrates. Such reference reflects the irreducible essentiality of the proper name as the designator of individuality.

It's clear that Fludernik's discussion is largely within the scope of classical logic and modern language philosophy concerning reference. What interests the present author is the second-order language in the making of fiction.

In her *A Dictionary of Stylistics* (1989: 294), Wales notices that language is used metalingually to "frame utterances by drawing attention to them for some reason; to check on a particular pronunciation; to note an ambiguity, etc. specific metalinguistic features of language include adverbials like *frankly* or *bluntly*, and the tags of speech in direct and indirect discourse in the presentation of speech (e. g. "*Go away*", *she ordered*).

Numerous instances can be found in Wales's sense of "metalingual" use of language in fictional discourse, as in,

(1) "I've got a nice place here," he said, his eyes flashing about restlessly.

(F. S. Fitzgerald: *The Great Gatsby*, 1950: 13)

(2) "Why, no," I answered, rather surprised by his tone.

(F. S. Fitzgerald: *The Great Gatsby*, 1950: 18)

(3) "You live in West Egg," she remarked contemptuously. "I know nobody there".

(F. S. Fitzgerald: *The Great Gatsby*, 1950: 16)

While Wales' observations mainly focus on "metalingual" uses of language in fiction, some subtle features may call for our attention when we take a closer look at the "adverbials" in the presentation of speech, for example,

(4) "Well, I married him," said Myrtle, ambiguously. "And that's the difference between your case and mine. "

(F. S. Fitzgerald: *The Great Gatsby*, 1950: 36)

The underlined part in (4) is syntactically similar to that in (3) with an "adverbial" that goes with the reported speech of the character. However, "*ambiguously*" is derived from a metalinguistic term that belongs to the "linguist's jargon". While "*contemptuously*" is used for "description" of a particular manner of a speech act, "*ambiguously*" is used for "evaluative comment" on a reported speech itself, much like an "evaluative clause" (See Labov, 1972: 39).

Narratologists admit two or more levels in narratives. Since there is always a teller in the tale, there is a distinction between "story" and "discourse". In his seminal work *The Rhetoric of Fiction*, Booth (1961) demonstrated with examples that "even the most impersonal narration must employ language which is impregnated with a personal and evaluative burden". Chatman (1978: 248) distinguished the narrator's explicit pronouncements into "interpretation, judgment, generalization" and "discourse comments", only mentioning that those which "undercut the fabric of fiction" are "self-conscious narrations". Since the teller of the tale is never isolated from the narrative discourse, metalinguistic evaluations and comments are in fact an essential part in presenting maximal fictional reality.

Malmgren (1986) distinguished three types of commentary on the plane of the speaker. In addition to "personal comments" and "ideological comments", he has proposed a category of "metalinguistic comments", consisting of explicit comments on, or reference to, the narrative act. He cites an example from Gogol's *The Overcoat*, in which after introducing a minor character, Gogol's speaker adds,

> Of course this tailor I ought not, of course, to say much, but since it is now the rule that the character of every person in a novel must be completely drawn, well, there is no help for it, here is Petrovich too. (Gogol, *The Overcoat*, 1978: 387)

Malmgren wrote that such "metalingual interpolations" help to destroy the fictional illusion, and that each narrative situation tends to establish its identity by emphasizing aspects of the enunciation as its dominant. His discussion is only meta-discursive and meta-fictional because this is typical of the practice in literary studies where metalanguage is taken as a semantically-closed language on the logical level. Thus it is a tool of writing the writing, not an approach for reading the writing.

In his article "Metalinguistics and Science Fiction", Rabkin (1979) studied three types of metalinguistics: (1) self-reflexivity of language; (2) language used being that of the reader, and then the language of the narrator or of characters; (3) the use of language as context. He argued that many examples of metalinguistic function can be found in science fiction, because it "shares the property of making a reality claim for the text that employs it". And narrations encourage explicit consideration of the nature of the narrative worlds themselves.

Rabkin's approach is on the meta-discursive level, i. e. by seeing what H. G. Wells writes as having truth, we (or rather he) recognize in another sense that this "fiction" is no "more stroke of art". By reflecting on the nature of the utterance as fiction, the speaker reveals his common agreement with his hearers and readers about a fact: that the tale is a fiction.

> I cannot expect you to believe it. Take it as a lie—or prophecy. Say I dreamed it in the workshop. Consider I have been speculating upon the destinies of our race until I have hatched this fiction. Treat my assertion of its truth as a mere stroke of art to enhance its interest. And taking it as a story, what do you think of it.
>
> (H. G. Wells, *Time Machine*, Chapter 12)

According to Rabkin, metadiscursive comments serve to direct the interpretation of an utterance to which they refer. They allow speakers to characterize their own discourse in order to make explicit the status they wish to attribute to what they express.

Apart from taking metalanguage as meta-discourse and metalingual comments as part of the meta-fiction in "implied authorial comments", my observation is that in the first place, all these three types of narrative comments can be realized by linguistic metalanguage. In the second, comments of a metalingual and metalinguistic nature actually cover a wider range and may work in more ways than has been realized. For example, in *Gulliver's Travels*:

> (5) When this method fails, they have others more effectual, which the learned among them call acrostics and anagrams. First, they can decipher all initial letters into political meanings. Thus, *N* shall signify a plot; *B* a regiment of horse; *L* a fleet at sea. Or secondly by transposing the letters of the alphabet in any suspected paper, they can discover the deepest designs of a discontented party. So for example if I should say in a letter to a friend, *Our brother* Tom *has just got the piles*, a skillful decipherer would discover that the same letters which compose that sentence may be analyzed into the following words: *Resist, a plot is brought home*: *The tour*. And this is the anagrammatic method. (J. Swift: *Gulliver's Travels*, 1994: 210-211. Chapter 6, Part 3. Italicization original)

> (6) To return from this digression; when I had crept within four yards of the throne, I raised myself gently upon my knees, and then striking my

forehead seven times on the ground, I pronounced the following words, as they had been taught me the night before, *Ickpling gloffthrobb squutserumm blhiop mlashnalt zwin tnodbalkguffh slhiophad gurdubh asht...* It may be rendered into English thus: *May your Celestial Majesty outlive the sun, eleven moons and a half.* To this the King returned some answer, which although I could not understand, yet I replied as I had been directed: *Fluft drin yalerick dwuldon prastrad mispush,* which properly signifies, *My tongue is in the mouth of my friend,* and by this expression was meant that I desired leave to bring my interpreter; whereupon the young man already mentioned was accordingly introduced, by whose intervention I answered as many questions as his Majesty could put in above an hour. I spoke in the Balnibarbian tongue, and my interpreter delivered my meaning in that of Luggnagg. (J. Swift: *Gulliver's Travels*, 1994: 225, Chapter 6, Part 3. Italicization original)

All the underlined parts are metalinguistic expressions. Some are Wales's observation of Jakobsonian "metalingual" use of language, some are Chatman's "discursive comments" and others are Malmgren's "metalingual comments". Such unusual narrative means of a metalinguistic nature actually work on both the level of *story* and the level of *discourse*, combining narrating and commenting in a seamless whole.

More prominent features of metalinguistic features can be found, as I have discussed elsewhere, in George Orwell's *Nineteen Eighty-Four*:

(7) People simply disappeared, always during the night. Your name was removed from the registers, every record of everything you had ever done was wiped out, your one-time existence was denied and then forgotten. You were abolished, annihilated: *vaporized* was the usual word.

(G. Orwell: *Nineteen Eighty-Four*, 1954: 19)

(8) It was almost normal for people to be frightened of their own children. And with good reason, for hardly a week passed in which *The Times* did not carry a paragraph describing how some eavesdropping sneak—"child hero" was the phrase generally used—had heard some compromising remark and denounced his parents to the Thought Police.

(G. Orwell: *Nineteen Eighty-Four*, 1954: 23)

(9) Years ago—how long was it? Seven years it must be—he has dreamed that he was walking through a pitch-dark room. And someone sitting to one side of him had said as he passed: "We shall meet in the place where there is no darkness. " It was said very quietly, almost casually—a statement, not a command.

(G. Orwell: *Nineteen Eighty-Four*, 1954: 23)

The whole excerpts are largely the narrator's commentaries rather than describing specific speech acts of a certain character. We can imagine that Orwell as narrator or the implied author could have chosen the most accurate and strongest lexical item in (7) and the more vivid phrase in (8) as he himself seems to prefer. In (9) the narrator goes out of his way to assign an extra pragmatic interpretation ("statement" rather than "command") to the character's speech, leaving more traces of "artificiality" to "cut the fabric of fiction". All these metalinguistic means serve to enhance a paradoxical reality in the fictional world.

4. Conclusion

Although the most prominent feature of matalanguage in fiction is within Wales's observation, metalanguage manifests itself in different ways. Firstly, some such features and devices can be part of the narration itself on the level of "story" as well as commentary on the level of "discourse". While most metalinguistic statements belong to authorial comments with a personal and evaluative burden, quite a large number of them *tell* as well as *show*, without necessarily going "beyond narrating, describing, or identifying". In this way, they linguistically conglomerate the tale and the teller on the implied authorial level. Secondly, the conventional concept of "metalingual comments" only deals with meta-discourse in the authorial or the implied authorial commentary. Discourse of a metalinguistic nature is largely metalingual on the first level and linguistic-technical on the second level, providing more detailed descriptive and evaluative information on fictional characters' verbal behavior in the fictional world. Thirdly, second-order language constitutes a special register in the narrative code and a distinct narrative voice.

Although metalinguistic comments are explicit "discourse comments", they serve more than "self-conscious narrations", without necessarily undercutting "the fabric of fiction", but enhancing the paradox of reality, with greater exactitude and verisimilitude.

References

Booth, W. 1961. *The Rhetoric of Fiction*. Chicago: University of Chicago Press.

Bussmann, H. 1966. *Routledge Dictionary of Language and Linguistics*. London & New York: Routledge.

Chatman, S. 1978. *Story and Discourse: Narrative Structure in Fiction and Film*. Ithaca: Cornell University Press.

Feng, Z. X. 2005. On linguistic metalanguage and metalinguistic studies. *Foreign Language Teaching and Research* 6: 403-410.

Feng, Z. X. 2007. Metalinguistic devices in fiction: Narrative and commentary. *Foreign Language Education* 2: 7-11.

Fitzgerald, F. S. 1950. *The Great Gatsby*. Harmondsworth: Penguin Books.

Fludernik, M. 1993. *The Fictions of Language and the Languages of Fiction: The Linguistic Representation of Speech and Consciousness*. London: Routledge.

Gogol, N. 1978. *The Overcoat*. New York: Dover Publications, Inc.

Jakobson, R. 1960. Linguistics and poetics. In *Style in Language*, ed. by T. Sebeok, 350-377. Cambridge: MIT Press.

Labov, W. 1972. *Language in the Inner City*. University Park: University of Pennsylvania Press.

Lyons, J. 1981. *Language and Linguistics*. Cambridge & New York: Cambridge University Press.

Malmgren, C. D. 1986. Reading authorial narration: The example of *The Mill on the Floss*, *Poetics Today* 7: 471-494.

McDonough, S. 2000. Reflections on reflexivity. *Language Sciences* 22 (2): 203-222.

Orwell, G. 1954. *Nineteen Eighty-Four*. Harmondsworth: Penguin Books.

Pier, J. 1985. Metalanguage and the study of literature. *Poetics Today* 6 (3): 521-535.

Rabkin, E. S. 1979. Matalinguistics and science fiction. *Critical Inquiry* 6 (1)：79-97.

Searle, J. 1969. *Speech Acts*：*An Essay in the Philosophy of Language*. Cambridge：Cambridge University Press.

Swift, J. 1994. *Gulliver's Travels*. London：Penguin Books.

Toolan, M. 2001. *Narrative*：*A Critical Linguistic Introduction* (2nd edition). London & New York：Routledge.

Wales, K. 1989. *A Dictionary of Stylistics*. Harlow：Longman.

Stylistic Analysis of a Love Story in Network Literature

——The Salty Coffee

LI Yanmei & DONG Qiming

Capital Normal University

1. Introduction

In the twenty-first century, personal computer and internet technology are rapidly developing, and the Internet is playing a more and more important role in people's life. Reading and writing on internet has become popular and fashionable. Thus, a brand-new form of literature—network literature accordingly comes into being, which exists and spreads through the medium of computer and Internet, and rises abruptly with modern digital technology. It has become a significant topic in the 21st century's writing. Theoretically, just like traditional literature, network literature has a wide range of subject matters, and any literature topic in the written literature can be realized in network writing. However, in practical writing of net works, the topics are quite narrow. Most of the works describe personal emotional experiences in city life. The story we excerpt—*The Salty Coffee* is a typical work of such kind of theme. It is chosen from a webpage which centers on the short sad love stories. This story describes the sincere love of a couple: The man drank the salty coffee for the whole life just because at the first time they dated, he asked for some salt into coffee due to nervousness. But to cover up his embarrassment, he told a white lie that he liked salty coffee. So in his later life he had been drinking salty coffee until his passing away. To have a better understanding, we will make a complete stylistic analysis of *The Salty Coffee* by adopting Functional Grammar Theory and analytical pattern of General Stylistics, so that we can know more about this work and enhance our ability to appreciate other network love stories.

2. Stylistic Analysis

Halliday (1976), one of the founders of Functional Stylistics, proposes that language has three metafunctions—the ideational function, the textual function and the interpersonal function. In the following part, we will make a detailed stylistic analysis of *The Salty Coffee* from the three aspects.

2.1 The ideational function of language

"The ideational function is to convey new information to communicate a content that is unknown to the hearer" (Liu & Feng, 2004: 326). To realize this function, the author uses language to conceptualize the story, especially through his creation of symbols.

Literary language often depends on the use of symbols to amplify meaning. "A symbol is something that casts meanings beyond its factual reality" (Xu, 2005: 231). For example, "rose" may be symbolic of "purity", and "dove" may be symbolic of "peace". In the story we excerpt, "the salty coffee" is the symbol of "love". "Salt" is common, and "coffee" is common too, while the "salty coffee" is uncommon, and no one knows its taste. But it is right the salty coffee that makes their beautiful beginning and leads them into happy life. It is the witness of their love, and the symbol of their true love. This network love story seems simple and easy, but it is quite meaningful, so the whole story seems tender but not vulgar.

Here we can see, by using salty coffee as symbol of love, the author views the world as that true love often exists in a common way in life and that true love cannot be defeated.

2.2 Textual function of language

"The textual function refers to the fact that language has mechanisms to make any stretch of spoken or written discourse into a coherent and unified text and make a living message different from a random list of sentences" (Liu & Feng, 2004: 336). Each level of language is interactional and interrelavant. In the following part, we shall explore the author's preference in four aspects of linguistic description: syntax, lexicon, graphology, and semantics.

2.2.1 Syntactical features

An obvious character of network love story is that the structure of the sentence is simple. In this story, there are 57 independent clauses and 578 words. The average sentence length is 10.1, which is easy because it is below the average sentence length of various English styles (17. 6). This feature displays the popularity of network love story, because it is convenient to read and easy to understand, especially for ordinary people. Loose sentences are greatly used, which has the quality of easiness, relaxation, informality. For instance,

> I was so nervous at that time, actually I wanted some sugar, but I said salt. It was hard for me to change so I just went ahead. I never thought that could be the start of our communication!

In this passage, these loose sentences express the linear chain of ideas which follow the linear progress of the text. Employment of loose sentences makes things easy for the readers, and it does not require the readers to hold in mind everything before the end.

Sentences may be long or short. Long sentences are capable of expressing complex ideas with precision, while short sentences are capable of rendering emphasis to a point. For example,

> Suddenly he asked the waiter, "Would you please give me some salt? I'd like to put it in my coffee. " Everybody stared at him, so strange!

The succession of short sentences in this section is life-like, emotional and close to daily-used words. They are the copy of daily words, short and straightforward.

From the analysis above, we can clearly see the syntactic features of network love story: sentences are usually simple and short, easy to understand and easy to organize; the structure is relatively easy; short sentences and loose sentences are frequently used. All of these are different from traditional literature, because network love stories are created and published on the net, with the characteristics of popularity and openness, they should be short and simple so that people could approach and accept it easily.

2.2.2 Lexical features

In the choice of words, the network love story has a typical feature: few big, hard words, no archaic words or technical terms, most are common, colloquial and concrete words.

In this story, there are altogether 578 words, in which there are 25 words with more than 7 letters, 8 hard words (words with three or more than three syllables). The longest word has 13 letters, that is, *communication*. The fog index of the story is 6. 76:

Fog index = 0. 4 (H + L)

L = the average sentence length

H = the percentage of hard words (Qian, 1991)

The fog index of this story = 0. 4 (15. 6 + 1. 3) = 6. 76

Qian Yuan (1991) points out in her *Practical English Stylistics*, the text is easy if the fog index is under 10. So this story is easy and simple.

The choice of verbs is also quite narrow. In the story we excerpt, nearly all the verbs are Anglo-Saxon words, like *meet*, *feel*, *ask*, *have*, *live*, *speak*, etc. This is a necessary choice, because network love story aims at eliminating the nobility of literature and cultivating a civilian literary sense.

The percentage of personal pronouns is high in this story. From the very beginning, the personal pronouns occur frequently, we can take the first paragraph as an example,

He met her at a party. She was so outstanding, many guys chasing after her, while he was so normal, nobody paid attention to him.

In this passage, there are altogether 25 words, of which 6 are pronouns. In the following passages, the author also uses a lot of pronouns to take place of the names of the two characters in the story. This feature shows the directness and compactness of network love story.

So, we can see, network love story shows a preference for concrete, colloquial and common words, with an absence of archaic or professional terms. Using the basic vocabulary can come straight to the point and is convenient for the net readers to have a quick look without careful thinking. In addition, it is also an effective way to attract net readers' eyeball.

2.2.3 Graphological features

Graphological features of network story are obviously different from that of traditional love story. In the story we except, there is no blank in the beginning of every paragraph. What is more, every two lines have single space, while every two paragraphs have double space. This makes each paragraph much clearer.

Another character is that a lot of quotation marks are used. Some quotations are reflection of the inner thought of the major character, some taking the form of dialogue, some taking the form of monologue. The use of quotation marks makes the story more real and natural.

Frequent use of commas is also noticeable. For example, in the second paragraph, "*They sat in a nice coffee shop, he was too nervous to say anything, she felt uncomfortable, and she thought to herself, 'Please, let me go home...'*" Here, 5 commas are continuously used, without even one full stop. Such kind of use of commas caters for the taste of the readers, because they want to finish reading the story in one breath. It is ungrammatical, but it reflects the freedom of computer writing.

Because of computer writing, the setting of the letterform is more flexible. The author can set the letter in any shape, any color and any size depending on his needs. In this story, the title has different colors from the body part, the former uses red color while the latter uses black color. This point is not common in traditional literature.

From the analysis above, we know, network love story has great differences from traditional love story at the graphological level. Network love stories have wider range of choice, with some random and ungrammaticality. Also it is quite unique in the use of punctuation (e. g. comma) and the format of paragraphs and letterform. However, these characters are not rejected by net readers; on the contrary, they are much easier to be accepted because it caters for people's taste and gives people a fresh feeling.

2.2.4 Semantic features

Rhetorical devices are usually a major semantic style marker in traditional literature, while in this network love story, not many rhetorical devices are found. This is a new feature of network love story. Because the internet is a free room, mostly aiming at ordinary people, using life-like and popular language, and displaying the true quality of common life. The author of network love story would express the emotions and feelings in a short, common and fast way rather than indulge in the ornament of language (Ouyang, 2003).

From the analysis above, we know, because of the popularity, openness, freedom and casualness of computer writing, network love story is inclined to use common and basic words, short and loose sentences, few figures of speech and unique graphological style markers. This makes the whole story more natural and real, and reduces the break to the original feeling due to the strong reasonable hand writing.

2.3 Interpersonal function

According to Halliday (1976), in addition to the ideational and textual functions, language has another function—the interpersonal function, which embodies all use of language to express social and personal relationships. Corresponding to this function, we shall examine the author's employment of various points of view, and various ways of presenting speech and thought.

2.3.1 Point of view

Point of view refers to angle of vision—the point from which the people, events and other details in a story are viewed and told in the story (Xu, 2005). There can be many variations in point of view, such as the first person point of view and the third person point of view.

In the story selected, the third person point of view is employed. The two characters are referred as "he" and "she". The narrator has an omniscient point of view, he knows everything about the two characters, and he reveals the inner world of the characters to the readers. For example, the last part of the third passage,

"... Now every time I have the salty coffee, I always think of my childhood, think of my hometown, I miss my hometown so much, I miss my parents who are still living there. " While saying that tears filled his eyes. She was deeply touched. That's his true feeling, from the bottom of his heart. A man who can tell out his homesickness, he must be a man who loves home, cares about home, has responsibility of home... Then she also started to speak, spoke about her faraway hometown, her childhood, her family.

Here the "omniscient narrator" (Qin, 2002) knows the man was making excuse for his embarrassment, and he knows very well that the woman was deeply touched. What is more, the narrator clearly reveals the inner world of the woman. So, to describe a story in the third person point of view is freer than from the first point of view. In this way, the author and the narrator are combined into one, and the information could be directly passed to the readers.

In English network love stories, most of the authors show preference for the third person point of view, because the computer uses Cyberspace to offer people a shared platform in which the popular cultures are shared. In such a space, people could use the third person to behave the "real oneself" (pick off their masks) so as to arouse more emotions. Different points of view will have different effects on the story, so proper point of view can make the story more acceptable and readable.

2.3.2 Ways of presenting speech and thought

To help with plot development and characterization, the authors aim at a truthful presentation of conversation as it happens in real life, thus giving a life-like description of a character's attitude, mood, and thought on an occasion.

There are four ways of presenting speech: Direct Speech (as: I said, "she has come.'), Free Direct Speech (as: She has come, I said.), Indirect Speech (as: I said that she had come.), Free Indirect Speech (as: He had come.) (Xu, 2005).

In the story we excerpt, what is mostly used is Direct Speech, for example,

> e. g. 1. She asked him curiously, "Why you have this hobby?"
> e. g. 2. Someday someone asked her, "What's the taste of the salty coffee?"
> e. g. 3. She replied, "It's sweet. "

Here, the author uses Direct Speech to show its directness and vividness, and the author could well depict the thought and mood of the woman by using Direct Speech.

Parallel to these four ways of speech presentation, there are four ways of presenting thought: Direct thought (as: I thought, "she will come".), Free Direct Thought (as: She will come, I thought.), Indirect thought (as: I thought that she would come.), Free Indirect Thought (as: She would come.) (Xu, 2005).

In this story, Free Indirect Thought has the highest frequency. Take for example,

> e. g. 1. A man who can tell out his homesickness, he must be a man who loves home, cares about home, has responsibility of home...
> e. g. 2. He had tolerance, was kind hearted, warm, careful.

This character is similar with that in traditional love stories in the 20th century. It can represent the original inner world of the character and keep much vividness of Direct Thought without artificiality of the "speaking to oneself" conversation.

Here, we can see, the ways of presenting speech and thought in network love story are similar with that in traditional love story. Both kinds of stories employ various ways of speech and thought, especially Direct Speech and Free Indirect Thought.

3. Conclusion

In the analysis above, by adopting Functional Grammar Theory and the analytical pattern of General Stylistics, we have made a complete stylistic analysis of the network love story (*The Salty Coffee*) from three major aspects: the ideational function, the textual function and the interpersonal function of language. However, network literature is a newly-borne matter, and works of different qualities are intermingled, so there is still a certain time to make perfect analysis in every aspect. Only one analysis of the network love story—*The Salty Coffee* is not enough, but through this analysis, we can catch a glimpse of the general stylistic features of the network love stories and enhance the ability to appreciate more network love stories.

Reference

Halliday, M. A. K. 1976. *System and Function in Language*. Oxford: Oxford University Press.

Dong, Q. 1999. *General Stylistics for Graduate Students*. Beijing: Beijing Normal University.

胡壮麟(Hu, Z.), 2000,《理论文体学》。北京: 外语教学与研究出版社。

刘润清(Liu, R.), 2002,《西方语言学流派》。北京: 外语教学与研究出版社。

刘润清(Liu, R.)、封宗信, 2004,《语言学理论与流派》。南京: 南京师范大学出版社。

欧阳友权(Ouyang, Y.), 2003,《网络文学论纲》。北京: 人民文学出版社。

欧阳友权(Ouyang, Y.), 2004,《网络文学本体论》。北京: 中国文联出版社。

钱瑗(Qian, Y.), 1991,《实用英语文体学(上)》。北京: 北京师范大学出版社。

秦秀白(Qin, X.), 2002,《英语语体和文体要略》。上海: 上海外语教育出版社。

申丹(Shen, D.), 1998,《叙述学与小说文体学研究》。北京：北京大学出版社。

谭德晶(Tan, D.), 2004,《网络文学批评论》。北京：中国文联出版社。

王佐良(Wang, Z.)、丁往道,1987,《英语文体学引论》。北京：外语教学与研究出版社。

徐有志(Xu, Y.), 2005,《英语文体学教程》。北京：高等教育出版社。

杨林(Yang, L.), 2004,《网络文学禅意论》。北京：中国文联出版社。

喻天舒(Yu, T.), 2004,《西方文学概观》。北京：北京大学出版社。

Appendix

The Salty Coffee

He met her at a party. She was so outstanding, many guys chasing after her, while he was so normal, nobody paid attention to him.

At the end of the party, he invited her to have coffee with him, she was surprised but due to being polite, she promised. They sat in a nice coffee shop, he was too nervous to say anything, she felt uncomfortable, and she thought to herself, "Please, let me go home..."

Suddenly he asked the waiter, "Would you please give me some salt? I'd like to put it in my coffee." Everybody stared at him, so strange! His face turned red but still, he put the salt in his coffee and drank it. She asked him curiously, "Why you have this hobby?" He replied, "When I was a little boy, I lived near the sea, I liked playing in the sea, I could feel the taste of the sea, just like the taste of the salty coffee. Now every time I have the salty coffee, I always think of my childhood, think of my hometown, I miss my hometown so much, I miss my parents who are still living there." While saying that tears filled his eyes. She was deeply touched. That's his true feeling, from the bottom of his heart. A man who can tell out his homesickness, he must be a man who loves home, cares about home, has responsibility of home... Then she also started to speak, spoke about her faraway hometown, her childhood, her family.

That was a really nice talk, also a beautiful beginning of their story. They continued to date. She found that actually he was a man who meets all her demands; he had tolerance, was kind hearted, warm, careful. He was such a good person that she almost missed him! Thanks to his salty coffee! Then the story was just like every beautiful love story, the princess married to the prince, and then they were living the happy life... And, every time she made coffee for him, she put some salt in the coffee, as she knew that's the way he liked it.

After 40 years, he passed away, left her a letter which said, "My dearest, please forgive me, forgive my whole life's lie. This was the only lie I said to you—the salty coffee. Remember the first time we dated? I was so nervous at that time, actually I wanted some sugar, but I said salt. It was hard for me to change so I just went ahead. I never thought that could be the start of our communication! I tried to tell you the truth many times in my life, but I was too afraid to do that, as I have promised not to lie to you for anything... Now I'm dying, I'm afraid of nothing so I tell you the truth, I don't like the salty coffee, what a strange bad taste... But I have had the salty coffee for my whole life! Since I knew you, I never feel sorry for anything I do for you. Having you with me is my biggest happiness for my whole life. If I can live for the second time, still want to know you and have you for my whole life, even though I have to drink the salty coffee again."

Her tears made the letter totally wet. Someday, someone asked her, "What's the taste of salty coffee?" She replied, "It's sweet."

Pass this to everyone because love is not to forget but to forgive, not to see but understand, not to hear but to listen, not to let go but HOLD ON!!!!

Two Different Views of London—A Comparative Stylistic Study of "Composed upon Westminster Bridge" and "London" [①]

XUE Shunyan

Capital Normal University

1. Introduction

William Wordsworth, one of the earliest and perhaps the greatest of English romantic poets, did a lot to restore simple diction to English poetry and to establish romanticism as the era's dominant literary movement. William Blake, a visionary English poet and painter who was a precursor of English Romanticism, is often referred to as a social commenter. A large number of Blake's poems focused on similar themes that were relevant to the society in which he was writing. Poems on industrialization, child labor and the more general notions of man versus nature appear frequently in his works.

William Wordsworth's "Composed upon Westminster Bridge" and William Blake's "London" are both poems about London; but the two poets see London with different views. William Wordsworth's "Composed upon Westminster Bridge" presented London as a "touching", "bright", "glittering", "beautiful" city; While William Blake's "London" presents London as a "charter'd", "black'ning", "mind-forg'd" city. Wordsworth tells us the beauty of London; while Blake tells us the darkness and ugliness of London. So as we, readers, read these two poems, we get two quite different impressions of London. We have a sense of greatness and wonder at the beautiful, tranquil morning of London when we read "Composed upon Westminster Bridge"; but we may have a completely different sense of London: darkness, bondage, poverty, and helplessness when we read "London". How do these two poems give us such contradictory impression of the same city of London? In this article, we will appreciate together the different styles

---

① I appreciate Professor Dong Qiming's suggestions and comments on my paper.

of these two poems, and will, from phonological level, lexical level, syntactic level and semantic level, make a comparative study of the two poems.

2. At the Phonological Level

Poetic language is a rhythmic language. Poetry, as the formal and significant part of literature, has its distinctive style, which usually gives people a sense of beauty of music, visualization, imagery and allegory (Zhang, 1998). The first impression we get from poetry is usually its beauty of rhythm and sound patterning. Rhythmic language, not only gives the poem the beauty of music, but also strengthens the thematic meaning of the poem(Wang, 2004).

2.1 Rhythmic characteristics of "Composed upon Westminster Bridge" and "London"

Wordsworth's "Composed upon Westminster Bridge" is a Petrarchan sonnet, where lines are rhymed in a group of eight (an octave) and a group of six (a sestet). A poem rhymed in this way usually looks at an idea from one angle for the first eight lines, and then from another angle for the last six (Thornborrow & Wareing, 2000). By employing such a highly structured form, Wordsworth was able to use a strictly patterned rhyme scheme to link his ideas. The iambic pentameter flow of "Composed upon Westminster Bridge" leads the reader to follow and appreciate the morning sunrise calmly and tranquilly. The metrical pattern and rhythm pretty well reinforce the meaning of the poem: a calm and tranquil morning sunrise and a beautiful wonderland of London. In order to avoid banality, and express his gratefulness and happiness for seeing such majestic scenery, Wordsworth surprises us with "Dear God!" in line 12. Wordsworth suddenly gives out an exclamation of great wonder and thankfulness with the spondee in "Dear God!" from the alternative stresses to the continuous stresses of both "Dear" and "God". Blake's "London" is a song like lyrical work. The general heavy, slow, measured rhyme is quite similar to the drudgery of London. The iambic tetrameter of the first two stanzas leads the readers wander through the streets observing lives of London, but Blake switches his rhyme half way in his poem. He switches to a trochaic tetrameter intensifying his feeling of anger built with stress on the beginning of the first word in every line of the last two stanzas.

Also in the last two stanzas, the abab pattern stresses the desperation and darkness of London. The atmosphere of desperation and death is reinforced by"... harlot's curse"(12) and "marriage hearse"(14).

2.2 Sound patterning of "Composed upon Westminster Bridge" and "London"

The great English neo-classic poet, Alexander Pope, has pointed out that"The sound must seem an echo to the sense." Sound patterning, such as rhyme, alliteration, assonance, reverse rhyme and consonant patterning are features of language which poets and prose writers exploit to create effects such as beauty or emphasis in their writing (ibid). Leech said in his book: Exactly what a person means when he says that a piece of poetry is "musical" eludes analysis. But it is very likely that alliteration, assonance, consonance and other sound echoes play an important part in it (Leech, 2003). So we can know that sound patterning plays an important part in echoing and reinforcing the meaning.

In "Composed upon Westminster Bridge", Wordsworth frequently employs vowels, such as /ai/ as in "by", "sight", "like", "silent", "sky", "lie", "bright"; /eə/ as in "fair", "wear", "bare", "air"; /aː/ as in "pass", "garment", "heart"; /əu/ as in "soul", "domes", "smokeless", "open". These diphthongs and long vowels not only slow down the steps of the reader in order to see the morning scene, but also give readers a sprightly, clear, and warm feeling just like the feeling of the poet himself. The rhyming words "steep, deep and asleep" in "... beautifully steep."(9), "... calm so deep!"(11) and "... houses seem asleep"(13), help to place an emphasis on the serenity of the morning. The rhyming words "hill", "will" and "still" help create an atmosphere of stillness. While in "London", Blake frequently uses the sound /m/ as in "mark", "meet", "mind-forg'd", "manacles", "midnight", "marriage"; /w/ as in "wander", "where", "weakness", "woe", "sweeper"; /n/ as in "man", "ban", "manacles", "sign", "run", "blackning"; and /l/ as in "appalls", "walls". Liquids and nasals: /l/, /m/, /n/ and/r/ belong to the soft sound (Leech, 2003). Here in "London", the frequent appearance of these consonants gives us a sense of heaviness, slowness and bondage, which is precisely what the whole poem wants to present to the readers. Both Wordsworth and Blake skillfully use "sound enacting senses" (Leech, 2003) and pretty well achieve Pope's advocacy of "The sound must seem an echo of the sense."

3. At the Lexical Level

Both Wordsworth and Blake's choosing of words is skillful and is greatly helpful for their thematic expression. We will have a look at Wordsworth's and Blake's choosing of words respectively.

3.1 William Wordsworth's choosing of words

Many of Wordsworth's poems are about tranquil nature. "The principal object, then, which I proposed to myself in these poems was to choose incidents and situations from common life,... in a selection of language really used by men", "... because such men hourly communicate with the best objects from which the best part of language is originally derived" (Wordsworth, 1979b). He successfully practices his poetical theory in his own works, so the language of "Composed upon Westminster Bridge" is very easy to follow. Most of the nouns are parts of nature, that is to say, concrete words, such as "earth", "fields", "sky", "sun", "river". Wordsworth also employs a good number of favorable words as "fair", "touching", "majesty", "silent", "open", "bright", "glittering", "mighty", which clearly express the poet's feeling about the glorious and peaceful sight. Wordsworth appeals to almost all the senses of the readers. The words "steep", "smokeless", "sweet" and "silent" respectively stimulates the reader's sense of touch, smell, taste and hearing, and in the whole, makes the reader steeped in the warm, sweet and peaceful sunrise. Wordsworth not only wants to make the reader take notice of the sunrise, but also wants the reader to be absorbed in the warm rays and the beautiful scenery. Qianyuan (1991), distinguished the meaning of verbs into stative meaning and dynamic meaning. Stative meaning refers to the situation that is conceived as existing, rather than happening, and as being continuous and unchanging throughout its duration. Dynamic meaning refers to a happening or occurrence, which has a definite beginning and end. It may be moment or durative; it may or may not be under the control of a deliberate or self-activating initiator of the action—an agent. When we come to see more carefully about the verbs in "Composed upon Westminster Bridge", the seven verbs (has, steep, saw, felt, glideth, seem, is), we notice that most of the verbs are link verbs or verbs indicating state with only one exception, that is, the word "glideth", which describes the movement of the river as a glide—moving at its own pace and its surface so smooth that one can not be certain if it is moving at all. These verbs successfully create a kind of comfortable and beautiful calmness and tranquility. "Never saw I, never felt, a calm so deep!" With the same object "calm" of both verbs "saw" and "felt" in "Composed upon Westminster Bridge", the speaker and the whole city are united into one, as the sun illuminates the landscape, and the landscape illuminates (or supplies a calm to) the speaker. The two verbs "saw" and "feel" show that the speaker has melded the external and internal; he not only sees the "calm" of the city, but also feels a "calm" within himself. "Lying" and "still" together give both the poet and his readers the sense of calmness and tranquility.

3.2 William Blake's choosing of words

One outstanding feature of Blake's choosing of words in "London" is that many words in "London" contain layered meanings and references. These associative meanings of these well-chosen words give readers a feeling of bondage and darkness. For example, the word "charter'd" means "preempted" as private property, and "rented out", a reference to the aristocracy's ownership and landlording. Blake also employs a series of words that create a series of images and appeal to our vision and hearing. We can visually see the signs of sadness and desperation on the faces of the citizens with "And mark in every face I meet,/ Marks of weakness, marks of woe." (9, 10) The images created by such words as "plagues", "blood", "death", "blights", "tears", "blackning" and "hearse" make readers see more clearly the color of the city. The feeling of sorrow and darkness is greatly strengthened with the word "midnight", because midnight is often viewed as the hour of great darkness which is also a symbol of ignorance, impurity and death. The repetition of "cry" in "In every cry of every Man,/... cry of fear" (5, 6) ; "... Chimney-sweeper's cry" (10) and "And the hapless soldier's sign" (12) make the readers hear the desperate voices of the people in London. The images in poetry, usually by touching people's sense organs, stimulate the sense or feeling of the readers, who will follow the images directly into the deep part of the poem and become absorbed in it(Qin, 2002). It seems to

259

be more specific as the poem progresses, from the repetition of "every" in the second stanza to "the Chimney-sweeper's cry, hapless soldier's sign and Harlot's curse." We may also notice that the capitalization of the first letters in "Man", "Infant", "Chimney-sweeper", "Soldier", "Harlot". The capitalization of these words tells us that these individuals are merely representatives of the oppressed within London at that time. The "Chimney-sweeper" represents the vicious use of child labor in general and the vast injustice and abuse they suffered. The "hapless Soldier" is symbolic of all individuals who have given their life to serve the oppressive system.

4. At the Syntactic Level

"Composed upon Westminster Bridge", as a Petrarchan (Italian) sonnet, is formed in two parts: an octave and a sestet, and looks at an idea from one angle for the first eight lines; and then from another angle for the last six. After a careful reading, we find that the first eight lines are in fact only one sentence, in which Wordsworth describes the beauty of the morning as wearing a garment. In the last six lines, Wordsworth shows the beauty open to the fields and to the sky, and then comes back to the beauty and tranquility of the centre of the city (the mighty heart).

Blake's "London" is a song like, lyrical work. The poem is clearly divided into four quadrants (each stanza composed with 4 lines), which share a heavy, slow, rhythmic scheme. There is also a less obvious divider with line eight ("The mind-forg'd manacles I hear.") being the central point of the poem. The previous seven lines are a lead up or foundation for this statement, while the following eight are a more specific description of this statement. The first two stanzas tell generally the "marks of weakness, marks of woe." When we come to the last two stanzas, we see and hear more specifically the "Chimney-sweeper's cry, hapless soldiers sign, the youthful harlot's curse." And the "I hear" in line eight leads the following two stanzas and make readers hear what the speaker hears. Both Wordsworth and Blake separate their poems into two parts with each part coming to their points from different angles.

5. At the Semantic Level

Both Wordsworth and Blake display their writing skills by employing figures of speech in their poems to create more vivid images. We will appreciate their employing of figures of speech in details.

5.1 Figures of speech in "Composed upon Westminster Bridge"

Wordsworth employs personification to show the beauty of the sunrise and the morning scenery. London takes human traits as alive and beautiful. He personifies the city as wearing a "garment"; he personifies the houses as"... the very houses seem asleep."(13) The sun is personified as "Never did the sun more beautifully steep! / In his first splendor..."(9, 10) He also gives the river a will. "The river glideth at his own sweet will."(12) Although comparing a city to "heart" has become a quite common metaphor, here Wordsworth gives the city a living heart which strengthens the beauty and life of the city with a chain of personifications. Wordsworth also employs repetition of "never" in "Never saw I, never felt, a calm so deep!"(11) to reinforce the beauty of the morning and his wonderment and gratefulness for seeing such a scene that he has never seen. All these use of the figures of speech gives us the feeling that everything is alive. It is really a wonderful thing to live in such a beautiful world in which everything has life.

5.2 Figures of speech in "London"

Except the well-chosen words and their associative meanings that we have mentioned in the lexical level part, Blake also employs some figures of speech to present the picture of the ugliness and darkness of the life of citizens in London. One obvious impression we get from "London" is the repetition: the respective repetition of "charter'd", "mark", "every" and "cry". The function of repetition is almost the same, no matter where the repetition appears. One function is to stress the theme and produce an atmosphere; another is to produce an echoing effect(Wang, 2004). The repetition of "charter'd" in "charter'd street" and "charter'd Thames" emphasizes how everything has been taken over and oppressed by the aristocracy and the rich. "Every" almost appears in every line of the second stanza. This keeps stressing the theme that the unhappiness affects everybody and no one is excused. The repetition of "cry" makes readers hear the cry of the "Infant" and the "Chimney-sweeper" everywhere. This helps to intensify the sadness by the fact that infants and childhood are supposed to be joyful and cherish; yet the misery has blighted any childhood chance of happiness. Metaphor is also an outstanding figure of speech in Blake's "London". "Mind-forg'd manacles" in "The mind-forg'd manacles I hear" (8) is the central metaphor of the poem. "Manacles" are constrains used in prisons to hold back and limit the movement of prisoners. Here it is used metaphorically to indicate that the poor in London are not only being constrained by the wealthy, but also constrained by themselves in mind. This is typical of the negative images used throughout. From "Every blackning church appalls", we may literally understand that the church is becoming black as a result of its filthy surroundings, but it also metaphorically indicates that the church is becoming corrupted and evil. "Marriage hearse" in the last line is an oxymoron. "Marriage" is associated with happiness and laughter; "hearse" is associated with sadness and tears. It shows the conflict within the society. By employing these figures of speech and words' connotation, Blake draws a helpless and desperate picture of the London people.

6. At the Contextual Level

Language cannot be studied outside the wider framework of human activity, and it should be studied in connection with the context in which language is used.

Polish Anthropologist Malinowski first brought up the notion of "context of situation" and then expanded the notion of context with "context of culture". In the 1950s, J. R. Firth, influenced by Malinowski, emphasizes the study of language in relation to context in which it is used. Firth, from Malinowski, takes over the notion of context of situation and ultimately develops the notion of context which covers both linguistic context and non-linguistic context. M. A. K. Halliday, the founder of systemic functional linguistics, has contributed to the context study with the notion of "register". *A register can be defined as the configuration of semantic resources that the member of a culture typically associate with a situation type. It is the meaning potential that is accessible in a given social context*(Halliday, 2001). Halliday divided "register" into three aspects: the field, the tenor and the mode of discourse.

The field of discourse is the social action in which the text is embedded. It largely determines the "content" of what is being said, and it is likely to have the major influence of the selection of vocabulary, and also on the selection of those grammatical patterns which express our experience of the world.... The tenor is the set of role relationships among the relevant participants; and influences the speaker's selection of mood and modality, etc.. The mode, which discovers both the channel of communication, written or spoken, and the particular rhetorical mode selected by the speaker or writer, tends to determine the way language hangs together—the texture (Halliday, 2001).

"Composed upon Westminster Bridge" was written in 1802, and "London" as a song of experience and was published in 1794. Both of the appearance of "Composed upon Westminster Bridge" and "London" have their contexts and the two poets have chosen their language in the influence of the context. The setting of William Wordsworth's "Composed upon Westminster Bridge" is a bright, sunshine morning. At the beginning of a new day, and in such a fogless, clear morning, the poet's feeling was just like the bright and peaceful environment, or we can say, the poet himself was greatly influenced by the beautiful, tranquil morning. The beautiful field, sky, sun, river, valley, etc. made the poet's heart light, peaceful and happy, therefore produced such a light, happy and grateful poem in which the nature and the city were given the human characters. The gratefulness of the poet for seeing such a morning had its context. In the beginning of 19th century, because of the Industrial Revolution, smoke and fog have become the characteristics of London. Even in the morning, people could seldom have the chance of breathing fresh air and appreciating the original beauty of the morning. Everything was covered with smoke and dust. So the poet had an unexpected happiness when catching a moment of a smokeless and bright morning.

Being a song of experience and published in 1794, "London" was the result of the industrialised, oppressive, class based society in which they were written. It maintains the somber, dark moods and images that are typical of both the period and the collection of poems. "London" is a direct commentary on such a society, commenting on the injustices, filth and hypocrisy that was rife at the time. Except the environmental pollution, following the Industrial Revolution appears the lack of labors. The owners of the factories paid no attention to the life of the labors, and only forced the labors to overwork everyday in order to make the greatest benefit. They even hired the children for lack of labors. The chimney sweeper represents the vicious use of child labor in general and the vast injustice and abuse they suffered. As a result of mass capitalism, where money is god, everything was commercialized. The setting of "London" is a dark night. Night has always its dark meaning. It is appropriate to describe the "charter'd street," "charter'd Thames" "Marks of weakness", "marks of woe" and the desperate people in it. The dark night context effectively strengthens the defloration of people living in London; and the rottenness and result of the industrial revolution.

7. Conclusion

William Wordsworth's "Composed upon Westminster Bridge" and William Blake's "London" display quite contrary scenes. Wordsworth sets a scene of calm and glistening beauty, a scene of a kind of fairytale and wonderland, by re-creating a beautiful, awe-inspiring morning sunrise; whereas Blake sets a scene of helpless and oppressed desperation, a scene of a kind of dark hell, by emphasizing the dreary bondage of the London citizens. Wordsworth's language use and imagery place the readers in a calm, tranquil and appreciating situation; Blake's language use and imagery place readers in an angry, intensified and piteous situation. Both authors express their feelings and achieve their purposes admirably by integrating the form and content.

References

Blake, W. 1979. London. In *Norton Anthology of English Literature* (4th ed. Vol. 2) , ed. by M. H. Abrams. London: W. W. Norton & Company Inc.

Firth, J. R. 1957. *Papers in Linguistics 1934-1951*. Oxford: Oxford University Press.

Halliday, M. A. K. 2001. *Language as Social Semiotic: The Social Interpretation of Language and Meaning*. Beijing: Foreign Teaching and Research Press.

Hasan, R. 1985. Meaning, context and text: Fifty years after Malinowski. In *Systemic Perspectives on Discourse, Volume 1: Selected Theoretical Papers from the 9'th International Systemic Workshop*, ed. by J. D. Benson & W. S. Greaves. Norwood, NJ: Ablex Publishing.

Leech, G. N. 2003. *A Linguistic Guide to English Poetry*. Beijing: Foreign Language Teaching and Research Press.

Thornborrow, J., & Wareing. S. 2000. *Patterns in Language: Stylistics for Students of Language and Literature*. Beijing: Foreign Language Teaching and Research Press.

Wordsworth, W. 1979a [1802]. Composed upon Westminster bridge. In *Norton Anthology of English Literature* (4th ed. Vol. 2), ed. by M. H. Abrams. London: W. W. Norton & Company Inc..

Wordsworth, W. 1979b [1802]. Preface to lyrical ballads with pastoral and other poems. In *Norton Anthology of English Literature* (4th ed. Vol. 2), ed. by M. H. Abrams. London: W. W. Norton & Company Inc..

钱瑗(Qian, Y.), 1991,《实用英语文体学》。北京：北京师范大学出版社。

秦秀白(Qin, X.), 2002,《英语语体和文体要略》。上海：上海外语教育出版社。

王佐良、丁往道(Wang, Z. & Ding, W.), 2004,《英语文体学引论》。北京：外语教学与研究出版社。

张德禄(Zhang, D.), 1998,《功能文体学》。济南：山东教育出版社。

Appendix

Composed upon Westminster Bridge

Earth has not anything to show more fair:
Dull would he be of soul who could pass by
A sight so touching in its majesty:
This City now doth, like a garment, wear   5
The beauty of the morning; silent, bare,
Ships, towers, domes, theatres, and temples lie
Open unto the fields, and to the sky;
All bright and glittering in the smokeless air.
Never did sun more beautifully steep
In his first splendour, valley, rock, or hill;

Ne'er saw I, never felt, a calm so deep!   10
The river glideth at his own sweet will;
Dear God! the very houses seem asleep;
And all that mighty heart is lying still!
　　　　　　——William Wordsworth

London

I wander thro' each charter'd street,
Near where the charter'd Thames does flow,
And mark in every face I meet
Marks of weakness, marks of woe.

In every cry of every Man,   5
In every Infant's cry of fear,
In every voice, in every ban,
The mind-forg'd manacles I hear.

How the Chimney-sweeper's cry
Every black'ning Church appalls;   10
And the hapless Soldier's sigh
Runs in blood down Palace walls.

But most thro' midnight streets I hear
How the youthful Harlot's curse
Blasts the new born Infant's tear,   15
And blights with plagues the Marriage hearse.
　　　　　　——William Blake

5. General Stylistics

PowerPoint：Tool，Discourse，Genre and Style

HU Zhuanglin

Peking University

1. PowerPoint 软件的发展过程

PowerPoint（PPT，电子幻灯片）的前身是黑板，白板，可翻转的胶片，投影仪。网络上对 PowerPoint 软件提供的定义有简有繁。简单的可一句话，指"用来制作幻灯片、讲义、摘记和大纲的演示软件"[1]；有的强调其制图功能，如"制作图像的演示软件，声音可有可无"。[2]《Wikipedia 网络百科全书》较为详细，"微软 PowerPoint 是由微软 Windows 和 Mac OS 计算机操作系统发展而来的普及型演示程序。由于商人、教育工作者和受训人员广为应用，它是诱导技术最盛行的形式之一。"[3]

当人们讨论计算机介入性话语分析时，一般都会谈到电子邮件、网络会议、联机谈话、google 等，但从事语言研究的学者很少有人谈及 PowerPoint。事实上，在过去几年中，PowerPoint 早已成为最标准的演示工具。也正因为这个原因，人们对其褒贬不一。如何拨开迷雾，看个明白，这是本文要讨论的重点。

2. 对 PowerPoint 用途的质疑

在美国，对 PowerPoint 首先发难者是耶鲁大学教授 Tuffe(2003a，2003b)。Tuffe 把哥伦比亚航天飞机空难作为典型例子，指出美国宇航局曾采用PowerPoint 演示，没有引用具体数据，掩盖了问题的严重性。以至独立调查委员会根据 Tuffe 的报告作出如下反应："显而易见，一个高级管理人员可以看到这个 PowerPoint 的幻灯片，但没有意识到它谈的是一件生死攸关的事件。"如

---

① www. gslis. utexas. edu/ ~ vlibrary/ glossary/
② drworkshop. org/moodle/mod/glossary/view. php
③ en. wikipedia. org/wiki/PowerPoint

果说 Tuffe 把自己的文章题名为"PowerPoint 是恶魔"的话，美国的一位教育顾问 James McKenzie 措辞更为强烈："我把它叫做病毒，而不是一种叙述形式。""它对文化危害更大"（Schwartz，2003）。

Tuffe 对 PowerPoint 的具体评论是 PowerPoint 把格式看得比内容和受众更重要，暴露了它的商业化意图。它使说话人凌驾于受众之上。其次，就教育来说，PowerPoint 不能让小学生们学会造句、写报告，而是学会像推销员那样唱高调，他们做的幻灯片每张才 10-20 个词，两边有一个剪贴画。如果一个星期做 3-6 张幻灯片，总共才 80 个词，这个量默读下来才 15 秒钟。还不如学校索性在那几天给学生放假，让学生自己找材料看，然后写一篇解释性的文章。第三，在商业背景下的 PowerPoint，每片大约 40 个词，相当于 8 秒种的默读材料。每张幻灯片的信息量很小，以至需要制作大量的幻灯片。受众得忍受这么一张一张地翻页。由于幻灯片不时地变换，学生很难理解语境和评价幻灯片之间的关系。如果相关的信息放在一起，视觉效果会更好一些。一般来说，信息越具体，便越清楚，也越容易理解。对阅读目的是比较统计数据的演示来说，更是如此。演示者一般得依靠内容的确实性，相关性，和完整性。如果他的用词或图像不对路，幻灯片色彩再怎么艳丽也是无济于事的（Tuffe，2003a）。

继 Tuffe 之后，Altman（2004）总结了导致 PowerPoint 有此污名的四大罪状：

罪状 1：动画制作过于华丽。动画的映现有两种：一种是在屏幕上出现后消失；另一种以某种方式进入，但需待在固定空间稽留一段时间后消失。大部分效果差的动画属于前者。总之，采用让事物逐步放大或消失的方式比飞入、跳跃或旋转的方式好。

罪状 2：过分运用色彩的对比。其效果不如过去的黑白分明好。特别是一旦屏幕和投影仪有了变换或损坏，往往弄巧成拙。

罪状 3：幻灯片切入时发出的声音令人感到别扭。例如，当幻灯片引出一个事物时，总是发出 whoosh 那样的声音，或者采用打字机模式引入词语或图像时，发出的声音像机关枪那样的 rat-a-tat-rat-a-tat-tat。事实上，我们打字时发出的声音并非如此。

罪状 4：照片的滥用：在演示中插入照片是可以容许的，但必须是真实反映事物的照片。但现有的 PowerPoint 中出现的照片或与内容无关，或喧宾夺主。

总之，PowerPoint 成了人们使用的目的，而不是手段。PowerPoint 是难以归纳远为复杂的语料的，它只能体现一个想法，一个信息，或一个观点。根据

Altman 的统计，每一个小时的 PowerPoint 演示，有 40 分种只是让受众感受，涉及具体内容的才 20 分种。

更有甚者，美国有人在网上搞恶作剧，把美国已故林肯总统 1863 年的演讲改编成 PowerPoint 演示方式。演示者的口述部分如下：

The Gettysburg PowerPoint Presentation
11/19/1863

And now please welcome President Abraham Lincoln.

Good morning. Just a second while I get this connection to work. Do I press this button here? Function – F7? No, that's not right. Hmmm. Maybe I'll have to reboot. Hold on a minute. Um, my name is Abe Lincoln and I'm your president. While we're waiting, I want to thank Judge David Wills, chairman of the committee supervising the dedication of the Gettysburg Cemetery. It's great to be here, Dave, and you and the committee are doing a great job. Gee, sometimes this new **technology** does have glitches, but **we couldn't live without it, could we**? Oh—is it ready? OK, here we go：

接着，被模拟的林肯开始演示他准备的幻灯片，第一张是准备演讲的内容介绍。

Click here to start

Table of Contents

Gettysburg Cemetery Dedication

Agenda

Not on Agenda！

Review of Key Objectives & Critical Success Factors

Organizational Overview

Summary

Speaker Notes

Author：Abraham Lincoln

Email：president@ whitehouse. gov

Home Page：http://www. whitehouse. gov/

Download presentation：Gettysburg. ppt

This presentation prepared with the help of Microsoft PowerPoint Autocontent Wizard. Where could we go without it?

Peter Norvig—See the making of the presentation and a related essay. —Permission is granted to use this presentation in any course or educational presentation.

显然，改编者的意图是向人们提示，林肯总统的讲话本来是很自然的，很有内容的，很有煽动力的；让他采用 PowerPoint 演示方式，操作时手忙脚乱，讲话方式学究气十足，受众又要听又要看，无所适从。

3. 对 PowerPoint 质疑的回应

就上述用 PowerPoint 演示方式模拟林肯总统的演讲纯属调侃之作，而且当代的克林顿总统或布什总统也没有使用 PowerPoint 发表重要演讲，无可比性。

对 Tuffe 等人的非议立即作出回应的是微软公司的销售部门负责人。根据微软公司负责包括 PowerPoint 在内的 Office 软件产品经销的 Dan Leach 的报道，全世界已有 4 亿个用户。每天使用 PowerPoint 制作的演示件约有 3000 万个。PowerPoint 的早期产品—Hypercard 的研究者 Bill Atkinson 指出，这样的批评纯属误导，PointPoint"只是帮助你表达自己"，"人们能选择的工具越多，我们就越方便"（Schwartz，2003）。由于 PowerPoint 是微软公司自己的产品，没有就对方所谈的实质性问题进行回答，收效不大。正如 Loisel & Galer (2004) 所言，就 PowerPoint 的发展需要说明的问题是作为一种演示方法，PowerPoint 究竟是提高了还是降低了它的教育价值？下面是他们针对 Tuffe 等人的意见所作的反应：

(1) Tuffe 认为 PowerPoint 演示"减少了演示的分析质量"，这种批评是不全面的，因为他只看到幻灯片一面，而没有考虑整个演示过程。事实上，PowerPoint 只对演讲者起辅助作用，不能代替演讲者。即使支持 Tufte 的 Sherry Turkle 也不得不承认"在一个有经验的老师手中，字数少图象多的 PowerPoint 演示可作为一次漂亮演讲的跳板。"一个教师可以就演示的内容进行解释和扩展（Turkle，2004）。

(2) Tuffe 认为 PowerPoint 的分辨率低，使信息稀释，一张幻灯片的信息量很少，或者需要"很多很多幻灯片"。从他们所在学校学生的实践看，通过对文稿的压缩是可以增加信息量的。学生有时使用字数不多的较多幻灯片，是为了便于理解。总之，将一次演讲切分成若干要点，能帮助听众抓住要旨（Loisel & Galer，2004）。

(3) 许多学生不单纯依靠幻灯片，他们自己带来电影、录像或书本，解释自己的要点，并不单纯依靠 PowerPoint。听众应当关注整个演讲的观点，而不是仅仅几个要点（Loisel & Galer，2004）。

(4) Tuffe 所批评的幻灯片翻转"一张接一张，没完没了"，这可以和其他不用 PowerPoint 的演示方式比较，然后评价，例如写一份供大家看的报告，做一次没有直观教具的讲课。前者由于完全没有信息发送者和接受者之间的接触或互动效果不好，因为要点内隐于书面语篇之中不易发现。PowerPoint 演示既提供要点，并可由演讲者提供细节。至于单纯的演讲常使人发困，而作为"原创性的表达工具"，使用音乐和艺术手法可以使 PowerPoint 演示生动活泼（Vienne，2003）。

（5）Tuffe 将一次 PowerPoint 演示的失败归之于 PowerPoint 程序本身是毫无道理的。"PowerPoint 演示得不成功只能说明制作者还没有掌握简单的幻灯片设计原理和基本的信息递送的技巧，而且最为重要的是最基本的修辞技巧"（Communication Partners，2003）[①]。

（6）Tuffe 说 PowerPoint 的点句或项目字符（bullet point）并不总是有效，这没有错，但这样的缺陷是可以避免的。例如人们可以使用这样一个总的原则："对每一张幻灯片，制作者应阐明一个要点：一个单一的离散的范畴，其子项应与范畴始终有关"（Communication Partners，2003）。

（7）Loisel & Galer（2004）的实验也表明，PowerPoint 演示对教师和学生都起到正面的效应。对演示者来说，PowerPoint 作为工具可以在演示时不单纯靠词语，而是多种方法，如每张幻灯片上不同的色彩和背景，各种音响效果，多种图片结合动画技巧，都能抓住受众的注意力，内容比单一的演讲更能记得住。随同这些技术的应用，学生们也能抓住围绕这些演示方法的气氛，学生记住的不仅仅是观点和事实（Loisel & Galer，2004）。

（8）Louise 和 Galer 所做实验的 16 个学生中，有 15 个学生选择 PowerPoint 演示工具，只有一人选用了 Dreamweaver 软件[②]。这说明对演示者和受众来说，PowerPoint 比其他演示方法如讲义，幻灯片，或大纲等更受到欢迎。学生之所以喜欢 PowerPoint，因为它使用简便。只要点一下鼠标或敲一下键盘上的箭头，可以前后变换幻灯片。它特别适用于教室环境（Loisel & Galer，2004）。

由于参加 Loisel 和 Galer 实验的学生，既是 PowerPoint 文稿的制作者，也是观看其他同学 PowerPoint 演示的受众，两位教师让他们把自己的感受从不同演示者和受众两个角色进行表决。结果表明，普遍反映 PowerPoint 是"一种学起来容易又能很好设计的程序。"对演示材料感到容易理解，因为所有信息一方面由学生口述，又有投影仪在屏幕上放映，从而能跟得上演示者的意图。幻

① 我最近参加某校一位博士生论文的答辩。该生准备的 PowerPoint 幻灯片每张上塞满密密麻麻的文字，似在对受众进行快速阅读的训练。
② Dreamweaver 是 Macromedia 公司推出的可视化网页制作工具，它与 Flash、Fireworks 合在一起被称为网页制作三剑客。Dreamweaver 主要用来制作网页文件，制作出来的网页兼容性比较好，制作效率也很高，Flash 用来制作精美的网页动画，而 Fireworks 用来处理网页中的图形。

灯片前后翻转，能重复前面讲过的内容，或进行提问。总的来说，四分之三的受众感到满意。仅少数学生认为可以不用直观教具。PowerPoint 的主要缺点是使一些受众有时光听讲、不看屏幕，有时光看屏幕、不听讲，不能两者兼顾。

4. 工具，语篇和语类

从上面两种有时针锋相对的意见来看，有的分歧来自评论者对争论对象 PowerPoint 的内涵不明确或不一致，也就是说，没有区分作为演示手段的 PowerPoint（工具），作为演示文稿的 PowerPoint（语篇），和作为演示类型的 PowerPoint（语类）（Yates & Orlikowski，待发表）。

PowerPoint 工具（tool）是用来制作表达直观内容的软件；随着技术的发展，可同时表达图像、动画和音响内容。它是由微软公司科学家设计的，是 Office 中的一个软件。PowerPoint 工具使用户能够传递信息，但本身不表达意义。

PowerPoint 语篇（text）狭义地说指用 PowerPoint 工具制作的各种视觉的、图像的、音响的和视听的文稿内容。广义地说，演示者每次使用 PowerPoint 演示的报告、演讲或授课的全过程都是一个 PowerPoint 语篇的组成部分。

PowerPoint 语类（genre）是把 PowerPoint 演示方式及其产品（语篇）作为一个整体，是一个与信件、留言、故事、谈话、小说、演讲、剧本等相对应的概念。在过去几年中，人们把 PowerPoint 演示看作为信息传递的工具，但今天人们倾向于把它看作语类，即"我们把语类看作是信息传递不时重复的类型（House, et al. 2005）"。House 等人还指出："如果我们开始说我们正在做一次'PowerPoint 演示'，而不说，一次'研究报告'，或'进度报告'，这意味着我们开始把'PowerPoint 演示'看作一种语类，它具有一定的人人使用时都要遵循的常规"。

把这三个概念分别清楚了，就不难发现上述的有些争论没有抓住要害，或者说，各吹各的号，各唱各的调。例如，Tuffe 对 PowerPoint 的许多意见是把矛头对准 PowerPoint 工具的，不具说服力。人们如果觉得这个工具不理想，完全可以弃而不用。Tuffe 不如直接告知演示制作者应如何提高制作质量，在每个语篇，以至每张幻灯片上合理地提供更多的信息，但又要清晰易懂。同样，对 PowerPoint 语类的评价要和其他语类比较，不宜轻易一概否定。事实上，也做不到，不然，为什么一面在批，一面有更多人在使用这种语类讲课、做报告、宣读论文呢？反之，PowerPoint 的设计者和开发商应多听取学者们的批评，努力完善这个演示工具，提高其信息递送能力，而不应满足于在销售数量上所取得的业绩。至于 PowerPoint 演示的具体制作者则应充分掌握这个工具，应具体了解需要递送的信息内容，更要分析信息接受者——受众的接受和理解能力。具备一定的语篇衔接和连贯的修辞知识是必要的，一方面表现在语篇本身的内部衔接，即各个幻灯片之间的衔接，另一方面表现在语篇和演示者、受众、语境、社会文化因素等外部因素的衔接，最后实现整个演示的连贯。

5. PowerPoint 语类的常规和变异

5.1 常规

语类既然是重复出现的语篇类型，在目的、内容、形式、参与者、时间和地点包含着可以预期的若干常规(Yates and Orlikowski，待发表)。

——目的：语类总是使人们可以预期社会上公认的意图，就 PowerPoint 演示来说，它总是被典型地用来对受众进行阐述、告知、劝诱或说理。这样，一套 PowerPoint 的演示可实现两个功能，第一个功能是作为一种可视的辅助工具，以支持非正式的口语演示；第二个功能是可以独立存在，自动翻页，报告一个项目的结果和结论。

——内容：语类可以使人们预料信息传递的内容，PowerPoint 演示的典型结构可以帮助人们制作或理解演讲的内容，

——参与者：语类可以对信息传递互动所涉及的参与者以及他们的角色作出预期的估计，如何启用这个语类？对象是谁？有时一个 PowerPoint 演示由若干人协作完成，采用每人负责一部分，再由一人集中完成的方式。

——形式：语类提供对其形式的预期，包括媒体、构建的方法和语言成分。PowerPoint 语类的标准形式表现为一人站在多人之前演讲，同时放映幻灯片。幻灯片的翻页决定于演讲内容的进展。

——时空：语类经常可以预期特定的时间，虽然这些估计不一定有明显的说明，一般是上午、下午和晚上的一段便于集体活动的时间。语类也可预期场所的选择，但这些预期总是明显的。如在一个具有电子投影设别的大房间或大厅内。在实时情况下，演示者讲话，受众听，同时放映和观看幻灯片。

5.2 变异

Yates 和 Orlikowski 的观点可以说明 PowerPoint 之所以被接受为一种语类在于它的常规性，但我认为他们只看到问题的一半。PowerPoint 语类既然是重复出现的语篇类型，这里的"重复出现"不是绝对的等同。具体到每一个语篇还是有这样那样的差异的，上面谈到的各种因素也是造成这些变异的基本原因。再进一步说，这些差异导致 PowerPoint 演示的不同文体风格。

273

就目的来说，有的 PowerPoint 演示件的制作是培养小学生多态识读能力（multiliteracy），要求学生不仅掌握传统的文字识读能力，而且学会运用其他表示意义的手段。这样，Tuffe 对美国小学生做的幻灯片每张才 10-20 个词的批评反映了他对二十一世纪的教育要求并不了解，何况 PowerPoint 演示语类既要求演示文稿的制作，也要求相应的口语表达能力。

PowerPoint 演示的内容有的是课堂讲解、有的是工作汇报，有的是学术报告，有的为商业宣传，有的出于教育需要。应该说，有关工作汇报的 PowerPoint 演示要求层次分明，条理清楚；有关学术报告的演示时有图表和结构剖析；为商业宣传和娱乐编制的演示材料讲究美观、色彩、图像和动画的应用；为课堂讲学编制的演示材料则提纲挈领，深入浅出，便于学生记忆。

PowerPoint 演示的参与者至少带来两个变数，即制作者和演示者本人的水平。前者表现为不是所有的制作者具有同样的技术知识和技能，这导致幻灯片制作质量的不同，后者表现为演示者如何在屏幕和受众之间互动，演示者应具有对具体的受众的兴趣和问题做出灵活反应的能力。受众的不同也会要求不同的制作方式。例如，微软公司的 PowerPoint 为制作者做新幻灯片时，提供了可供选择的 12 种形式，包括标题、项目符号表（a bulleted list）、图像、表格和空白片供插入剪贴艺术画、照片或其他图像。这又要根据目的、内容和参与者的不同进行考虑后选择。

进行 PowerPoint 演示受到时空的限制。以宣读论文或做报告为例，同样一个内容，在学校上课或讲学可以长达 1-1.5 个小时，演示者可以对幻灯片的某些细节做补充或发挥，或与受众进行互动，但在大型学术会议上，演示者往往被要求在 20-60 分种的时间内完成论文的宣讲。这时，不论是演示者的言语或幻灯片的放映时间往往是蜻蜓点水，一带而过。

所有这些都说明，PowerPoint 演示这一语类可体现多种文体和风格。对它提出千篇一律的要求和规定是不切实际的。也只有多种文体和风格的存在，PowerPoint 演示这一新语类才具有无限潜势的生命力。

6. PowerPoint 语类的文体学

基于上述认识，我们可以把 PowerPoint 语类的各种语篇大致归纳为四个基本类型，如下表所示：

- 模态　　　　点句　　　图像　　　图表　　　　色彩/音响
功能
- 提示性　　　　　类型 1

- 直观性　　　　类型2
- 分析性　　　　类型3
- 劝诱性　　　　类型4

类型1的主要功能是提示性，帮助演示者组织思路，层次分明，重点突出，演讲有序，因而这一功能主要采用点句的模态来实现，如图1的主题是谈修辞学。演示着准备谈 Aristotle，Cicero 和 Peter Ramus 三个古代学者的观点。每个学者的观点又分成3-5个方面，便于受众掌握。

图1

类型2的功能是直观性的，凡一人一物，一事一地，采用图像的方法将真实世界展示在受众之前，使受众既增长对世界的了解，也能加深印象。

图2主要介绍英国约克郡的布莱德福城，演示者选用该市的一个街道，使人有亲临其境的感受。

图2

类型3实现分析性的功能，一般见之于学术性的或商务性的演讲，演示者为了分析某事物或项目的运作系统，或内部关系，或发展趋势，便得仰仗于图表。右边的图3是介绍对138家公司雇员构成的分析，如雇员在5人或5人以下的有71.0%，6-17人的为16.4%，20-24人为4.9%，50-499人为5.4%，而500人以上的大公司仅2.3%。

图3

类型4是劝诱型的，演示者通过色彩、动画和音乐等模态的运用，使受众产生美的感受，接受幻灯片的内容，实际上实现了演示者的劝诱意图。这种类型一般在从事宣传、促销、或专题竞赛时使用。图4以一个富有诗意的"一个骑在羊背上的国家"为标题，介绍澳大利亚的养羊业。图中的喇叭提示我们原作品配有音乐。

需要说明的是这四种类型是原型性的。各个演

图4

示者可以因主题、环境、对象和本人技术水平的不同作更精密的选择，若将某些功能和某些模态有机融合，可以产生 n 种文体。由于篇幅的关系，我们这里只能介绍一个例子。譬如说，作文课教学在一般人心目中是枯燥的，以教师为中心的。清华大学杨永林教授采用 PowerPoint 演示的方法，图文并茂，音响与动画相结合，引导学生就如何从事"自由写作"进行讨论，产生很好的教学效果。杨的文稿有若干个主题，每个主题含若干张幻灯片。这里，转录其中两张。图 5 提出 What is free writing？ —You may ask. 对这个问题初步讨论后，进入到图 6 的问题 Does it mean absolute free？鉴于书面模态的限制，这里我们无法显示色彩、动画和音乐等模态。有一点是肯定的，PowerPoint 的演示方式在今后的课堂教学中必将为更多的老师所采用，为更多的学生所接受。

图 5   图 6

最后，既然 PowerPoint 语类可以有多种文体，最好的办法是采用系统的方法进行描写，这就是说，不同的演示者在精密度上可以有不同的选择，从而形成数目众多的文体，如下图所示。

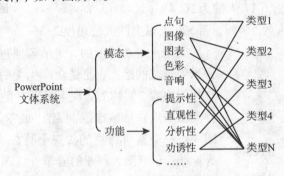

参考文献

Altman, R. 2004. The deadly sin of modern PowerPoint usage. www. Presentersuniversity. com/Visuals_deadly_sins. php.

Communication Partners. 2003. The great man has spoken. Now what do I do? www. communipartners. com/documents/cominsv1. – 000. pdf.

Belleville, C. 2005. A Bit Better t man has spoken. Now what do I do? *Communication Insight*. Vol. 1 Communication Partners.

Edwards, R. T. *The Cognitive Style of PowerPoint.* Graphics Press, 2003.

Herring, S. C. 1996. Computer-mediated discourse analysis. *The Electronic Journal of Communication*, 6(3).

House, R. , Anneliese W. and Julia W. 2005. Work in progress—What is PowerPoint? Educating engineering students in its use and abuse. A paper presented at *35th ASEE/IEEE Frontiers in Education Conference.*

Kennedy, D. 2005. *Bringing Presentation Technology into Your Practice.* November 15, 2005. DennisKennedy. com

Loisel, M. and Galer, R. S. 2004. Uses of PowerPoint in the 314L classroom. *Computer Writing and Research Lab.* 5 May 2004. Online.

Microsoft Corporation, 2006. Microsoft Office PowerPoint 2003 简介. Microsoft Office Online.

Schwartz, J. 2003. The level of discourse continues to slide. The New York Times Company.

Tuffe, E. R. 2003a. PowerPoint is evil. *Wired Magazine.* September, 2003. Online.

Tuffe, E. R. 2003b. The cognitive style of PowerPoint. *The New Yorker* (May 28)L 76-87.

Turkle, S. 2004. How computers change the way we think. *The Chronicle Review.* January 2004. < http://chronicle. com/weekly/v50/i21/21b02601. htm >.

Vienne, V. 2003. David Byrne's alternate PowerPoint universe. The New York Times Company. August 2003. < http://www. princetonol. com/groups/ iad/Files/ PPT. htm >.

Hu, Z. L. and Dong J. Forthcoming. How is meaning construed multimodally? A paper presented at the founding of HKCU's Halliday Research Centre, March 26-29, 2006.

Online Self Introduction Languages on the Internet

LÜ Zhongshe

Tsinghua University

Introduction

In today's world, many communication functions which were previously performed by other means are now channeled through the Internet. As a result, the Internet has become essential, not least in competitive situations involving well known organizations and institutions. For universities throughout the world, the Internet "homepage" is as vital to their identity as a face is to a person. The web homepage reveals to the reader the first key impression of the university and the first opportunity to influence that person's preferences. Frequently, prospective researchers seeking to learn more about a university for purposes of future collaboration can easily locate it on the Internet using a search engine. They can then go to the university's homepage and familiarize themselves with the university through the introduction, which is usually labeled on the homepage "About us". At this point, words play a critical role, particularly to those who have never come to China and who know nothing about Chinese culture.

Good introductions make self-conscious use of rhetoric. They seek to shape a reader's attitudes, beliefs, and emotions. They reach out to grab a reader's attention, persuade the reader, influence his/her opinions and preferences, and, most importantly, prompt the reader to explore further the institution's web site. On the other hand, poorly written introductions quickly lose web surfers to the more refined use of language on competitors' websites.

For Chinese universities, the online English introduction is often the first opportunity to connect to distant foreign teachers, researchers and students or simply to grab the attention of casual web surfers. Due to the inherent differences in linguistic and cultural expressions between Chinese and English speaking peoples, however, a beautifully written self-introduction in the eyes of a Chinese writer may not be perceived as attractive and appropriate to people from other cultures.

This paper compares the online introductions of eight chosen universities, four from China, two from Great Britain, and two American. The paper compares the self-introductions using stylistic analysis techniques in terms of their linguistic aspects and substantive content. The paper, furthermore, attempts to isolate web page aspects that may cause confusion to English speakers. The research questions which the paper addresses are as follows:

a. A comparison of Internet online self introduction home pages reveals striking differences in the use of language and content between selected universities in China and their counterparts in the English speaking world.

b. Chinese and English speakers employ different criteria and value systems in appraising their relative success at projecting an attractive image and promoting themselves to the rest of the world.

The paper is organized into four parts: Section One specifies the theory to be used in the analysis; Section Two introduces the data resources to be analyzed and explains how and why the eight universities are selected; Section Three discusses the findings of the comparative analysis of language and content while isolating the sources of confusion and effectiveness; Section Four draws the paper's conclusion.

1. Theory to Be Used in the Analysis

Constrained by time and space, Internet writing can be distinguished from other types of writing. It has unique features, such as being short, concise, fetching to the eye, and informative.

1.1 Language features of Internet writing

The Internet has its own characteristics: "Any author who has tried to put text from a previously published book on the Web knows that it does not translate onto the screen without fresh thought being given to layout and design" (Crystal, 2002: 199). Online information needs to be highly condensed and well organized. Internet browsers are not as forbearing as book readers. They respond to simplicity and concision. The first sentence or introduction must capture immediately their attention and urge them to continue. This is a challenge to any information provider. It is an even greater challenge to Chinese English writers. Much of what may be considered stylistically good Chinese writing may not appeal to English readers because of the differences in language, in culture, in ideology, and in other respects. The cultural differences extend especially to subjective differences in their respective ideals of design, format, and writing style. China's English writers cannot literally translate everything from Chinese and simply transplant it to the website and expect it to be well received.

1.2 Cultural differences between English and Chinese

Because of the tremendous differences between the English and Chinese languages and cultures, it is a demanding task for Chinese writers to translate an idea into an acceptable equivalent in English. Language translation requires not only a deep understanding of words, grammar, syntax and semantics, but also of linguistic and social appropriateness. It is well known that, until one has a good command of a foreign language, one's speech and writing in the foreign language is bound in some degree to be misguided by one's mother tongue.

The Chinese English writer not only needs to achieve English language proficiency. He/she must also develop an in depth understanding of English speaking cultures and a good sense as well of an English reader's expectations in order to decide what to render and what style to use in English writing. In this respect, Chinese writing is absolutely different from English writing. The two vary both in style and content. Chinese and English are wide apart in that there are many terms, expressions, and ideas in Chinese that are culture-bound concepts which cannot be simply translated into English. These types of culture bound concepts must be adapted to English in order to be culturally acceptable. They cannot go culturally "unchanged", as this will easily confuse English readers and consequently become an obstacle to understanding. What is more, those Chinese online English self introductions are explicitly intended to target readers who are unable to read Chinese.

These hypothetical English readers, understandably enough, are not equipped to understand the nuances of Chinese cultural features and rhetoric masquerading as the Queen's English. Consequently, Chinese English writers are both linguistically and culturally charged here. It is an advantage if they can phrase the target text so that it catches—and holds—the attention of a native speaking English internet browser. The Chinese English writer, furthermore, must find a way to face the challenge of shaping a target text which realises a balance between intended meaning and anticipated reception. The text itself and its individual elements must be carefully construed to deliver the appropriate message in culturally understandable terms.

1.3 Theme choices from Systemic Functional Grammar

Halliday's functional grammar indicates that the English language reflects the metafunctions of the culture behind language itself. Different wordings of texts reflect the cultural and ideological expectations of the producers and their audience (Thompson, 2000). "Halliday's view is that all linguistic choices are meaningful, and all linguistic choices are Stylistic" (Leech & Short, 1981: 33). In a message, theme serves as the point of departure while rheme is the remainder of the message (Halliday, 1994). Theme has two major functions:

a. Serves as a point of orientation by connecting back to previous stretches of discourse and maintaining a coherent point of view

b. Serves as a point of departure by connecting forward and contributing to the development of later stretches

Different theme choices contribute to different meanings and to the development of a clause and communicative effect of the message (Thompson, 2000).

2. The Chosen Eight Universities

In order to illustrate the language differences in online self introductions between Chinese English speakers and native English speakers, four Chinese top universities are chosen, namely: Peking University, Tsinghua University, Nanjing University and Zhejiang University. They are all quite internationalized and famous by Chinese standards. Oxford and Cambridge from Great Britain and Harvard University and Massachusettes Institute of Technology from the United States are selected because they are the best known universities to Chinese students. Their websites are as the following:

Peking University (北京大学 http://www. pku. edu. cn)

Tsinghua University (清华大 http://www. tsinghua. edu. cn)

Nanjing University(南京大学 http://www. nju. edu. cn)

Zhejiang University (浙江大学 http://www. zju. edu. cn)

Oxford University (http://www. ox. ac. uk)

Cambridge University (http://www. cam. ac. uk)

Harvard University (http://www. harvard. edu)

MIT (http://www. mit. edu)

3. Analysis and Interesting Findings

Data extracted from the website self introductions of the eight selected universities identified above will be analyzed from three aspects: layout, linguistic features and content.

3. 1 Layout

All Chinese, American and British universities divide the introductions into sub-categories. For example, Oxford's "Introduction" lists:

- *History of Oxford University*
- *The Structure of the University*
- *The University and the Colleges*
- *Studying at Oxford*
- *Visiting the University*
- *Business and Community Liaison*
- *University Legislation and Policies*

Chinese universities show a preference for general introductions or overviews. The Nanjing University (1789 W) and Tsinghua University (718 W) introductions, by contrast to Oxford, display very long "General information" sections in a single piece of extended text punctuated only by paragraph breaks. To get a complete idea of the university, readers have to scroll down the screen from the beginning to the end. British universities have very brief overviews: Oxford 140 W; Cambridge 248 W. The two American universities have no general introduction, no overview at all but provide convenient links to very detailed items. The Harvard and MIT sites assume an elitist tone. They deliberately couch their images under the veiled assumption that everybody already knows Harvard and MIT. They do not have to waste time introducing them selves. They come directly to the point. They save time and space and guide people directly to the real business of the site.

3.2 Linguistic features

The linguistic features of the university self introductions are mainly found in the use of culturally embedded number abbreviation, word choice, sentence structure, and theme choice.

3.2.1 Culturally embedded abbreviations of numbers

Chinese often use abbreviations of numbers or nouns to refer to movements, concepts or projects, e. g. :

nine eight five program（"985 计划"）

two bombs and one star medal（"两弹一星"勋章）

one two one student movement（"一二·一"学生运动）

May 4th Movement（五四运动）

December 9th Movement of Patriotism and Democracy（"一二·九"学生爱国运动）

the Democratic Party Nine Three Society（民主党派：九三学社）

Project 211（"211 工程"）

Project Hope（希望工程）

The use of abbreviations in this way is obviously culturally embedded. They add perhaps an element of readability to a Chinese university's self introduction. They are short and simple, and arguably known to every Chinese. For Chinese, in fact, they often connote broad and profound meanings, but foreigners may find these expressions odd or weird. The average English speaking reader would have no clue to their meaning unless they possessed a long acquaintance with and deep understanding of Chinese culture.

3.2.2 Choice of words

British universities routinely employ objective, user-friendly words or sentences like, "*Welcome to the University of Oxford...*" and neutral words like "*The Way It Works*"（Cambridge）. The Chinese universities, on the other hand, show a marked propensity to use what in English would be considered subjective, overly self-congratulatory words. The Chinese university introductions, for example, are full of such words as *"prestigious"*, *"outstanding"*, *"glorious"*, *"great"*, *"chief"*, *"lasting"*, *"significant"*, *"modern"*, *"splendid"*, *"breathtaking"*, *"advanced"*, *"famous"*, *"pioneering"*, *"eminent"*, etc. Native English speakers show a marked self consciousness about using such subjective terminology. They implicitly convey the attitude that such self praise is in bad taste. Nobody at least in polite society is supposed to appraise them selves in these terms. Chinese English writers, even with the best of intentions, run the risk of offending western sensibilities with the use of such terminology in such an obviously self-referential context. Such verbal constructs may trigger an adverse connotative turn to the one intended. Therefore, westerners don't use highly positive words like these as frequently as the Chinese do. In Chinese contexts, such words are incorporated into such sentences as the following:

"Endowed with a pleasant climate, picturesque surroundings and a favorable academic atmosphere..." (http://www. zju. edu. cn)

"Situated on several former royal gardens of the Qing Dynasty, surrounded by a few historical sites in Northwest Beijing, is the campus of Tsinghua University. The garden like landscape, with Wangquan River meandering through, has inspired and motivated generations of students" (http://www. tsinghua. edu. cn).

To Western readers, such sentences are boring and meaningless if not pretentious and exaggerated. They would look for and expect something more informative and substantial.

3.2.3 Sentence structures

Chinese tend to use longer sentences compared to native English speakers. The following table shows the differences in length between Chinese and English:

	Text length/number of sentences	Average sentence length	Words of the longest sentence	Words of the shortest sentence
Peking University	431/17	25.59	48	8
Tsinghua University	713/31	23.8	56	7
Nanjing University	1789/166	27.1	84	9
Zhejiang University	463/17	27.24	43	13
Cambridge University	267/15	17.8	45	3
Oxford University	140/9	15.6	40	6

Most long Chinese authored sentences are heavy headed, convoluted, and often difficult to untangle. They are comprised of strings of parallel verbs/nouns which share the same subject/predicate all connected by multiple conjunctions and qualified by heavy prepositional phrasing. The longest sentence consists of 84 words listing 35 celebrities, e. g. :

"Many famous scientists and scholars, such as Li Ruiqing, Wu Youxun, Zhu Kezhen, Mao Yisheng, Liu Yizheng, Hu Xiaoshi, Tao Xingzhi, Guo Bingwen, Chen Heqin, Tang Yongtong, Ma Yinchu, Li Shutong, Xiong Qinglai, Tong Dizhou, Jin Shanbao, Wen Yiduo, Zhang Daqian, Xu Beihong, Fu Baoshi, Yan Jici, Wu Jianxiong, Li Guoding, Luo Jialun, Gu Yuxiu, Li Fangxun, Wu Mi, Zhu Guangya, Zhao Zhongyao, Pearl S. Buck, Yang Xingfo, Lu Shuxiang, Liang Xi, Dai Anbang, Chen Baichen and Kuang Yaming, have studied or worked here". (http://www. nju. edu. cn)

In reading the above sentence, foreign readers would no doubt be deterred by the details because of the heavy head. Most of the names, furthermore, would be meaningless to a foreign reader. It is quite possible they would lose patience with such syntactical constructions because the most important information comes at the very end. This type of phenomenon is a clear example of the native language imposing its conventions on a subsequently learned language. Chinese prefer to start a sentence with a heavy head. This is a carry over from normal practice in Chinese writing:

"从 1994 年以来,南京大学获得的国家自然科学基金项目、国家社会科学基金项目等,在全国高校中也名列前茅。Since 1994, the number of National Natural Sciences Fund programs and National Social Sciences Fund programs undertaken at Nanjing University has been among the highest of all Chinese universities". (http://www. nju. edu. cn)

"校园依山傍水,环境幽雅,花木繁茂,碧草如茵,景色宜人,与西湖美景交相辉映,相得益彰,是读书治学的理想园地。Endowed with a pleasant climate, picturesque surroundings and a favorable academic atmosphere, Zhejiang University is an ideal place for teaching". (http://www. zju. edu. cn)

The following is an example of a sentence which risks confusing a foreign reader by trying to load too much information in one syntactic unit. The sentence overflows with three parallel verbal phrases and three parallel noun phrases followed by a long, tacked on attributive clause. If readers stop before the end, the sentence makes no sense. They must endure a forced long march of sorts to get to the point:

> "They actively resisted the Japanese invasion, participated in the influential 'December 9th Movement of Patriotism and Democracy' and the movement of the 'Struggle Against Starvation, Civil War and Persecution', and devoted themselves to the pursuit and spread of the truth that would give new birth to the nation in the midst of her struggle for independence".
> (http://www.tsinghua.edu.cn)

The variation in sentence structures makes for considerably different impacts in helping readers absorb the information. Different wordings of texts reflect the cultural and ideological expectations of the producers and their audience (Thompson, 2000: 214). As mentioned previously, because of the differences between Chinese and English, a beautifully written piece of Chinese writing may not aesthetically appeal to the typical westerner. It may instead frustrate them, irritate them, and ultimately lose them. Therefore, the above three sentences need to be carefully translated into amore user friendly, conventional or idiomatic English by simply recasting the syntax or breaking them up into simpler syntactic units.

3.2.4 Theme choices

As a matter of fact, sentence structure has a lot to do with theme choices. From the table below we can see that Chinese self introductions incorporate more themes than English, which in part explains why Chinese has more heavy headed sentences.

	Topical themes	Marked themes	Existential themes	Textual themes
Peking University	8	2	0	1
Tsinghua University	19	12	0	1
Nanjing University	27	37	2	3
Zhejiang University	6	10	1	3
Cambridge University	6	4	0	0
Oxford University	7	1	1	0

- Topical theme provides information to people.
- Marked theme functions effectively in conveying a message.
- Textual theme helps create a smooth texture and facilitates communication.
- Existential theme mainly has grammatical function.

Although different theme choices contribute to different meanings and to the development of a clause and the communicative effect of the message (Thompson, 2000) as mentioned above, the use of too many themes in a text can also frustrate and confuse the reader.

3.3 Features in substantive contents

Chinese universities share common features in substantive contents in phases such as directly translated slogans, conventional values based on awards and government confirmation.

3.3.1 Directly translated slogans and sentences carrying political senses

Sentences replete with slogans and carrying political senses are very much culture loaded and often culture bound. If written in translated "culturally unchanged" expressions and phrases, they mean nothing to native English readers. No wonder westerners often complain about getting lost in Chinese English writings. These culturally embedded slogans and sentences, however, are pervasive in the sampled introductions, e. g.

"Anti-Hunger, Anti-Civil War and Anti-Persecution"

"In 1919, the anti-imperialist and anti-feudal May 4th Movement was initiated from the university, which had been the centre of the Chinese New-Culture Movement and the earliest base for the dissemination of Marxism in China."

The table below summarizes the number of directly translated slogans and the number of sentences that carry political senses or implications in the sampled data:

	No. of slogans	No. of sentences carrying political senses	Percentage
Peking University	0	4 out of 17	24%
Tsinghua University	4	2 out of 31	19%
Nanjing University	3	9 out of 66	18%
Zhejiang University	2	0	12%

Apparently, those slogans and sentences raise the readability level of the introductions. Westerners have reasons for not being able to understand them.

3.3.2 Conventional values

Previous studies demonstrate that Chinese, like all peoples, have their own conventional values (Hu, 1999: 19). Linell Davis, for example, categorizes conventional social relationships in China into hierarchy, group and individual. Chinese culture is to an extent hierarchical in its structure, meaning people obey authority and look to authority figures to know what to do (Davis, 2001: 189). This kind of social attitude is embodied in the content focus of Chinese university self introductions.

Nanjing University emphasizes that the university functions directly under the Ministry of Education, and that important people like former US President George Bush, former French President Francois Mitterrand, and former Australian Prime Minister Robert Hawk all visited the university. It also employs four paragraphs to list over 800 national, ministerial, and provincial awards, including awards won by students in English speech contests. Nanjing University also recounts how, "The reforms and development of Nanjing University have received attention from the Chinese Communist Party and China's Government, as well as public support". "As a successful model of Sino-US educational cooperation, the Center for Chinese and American Studies has received attention and acclamation from the leaders of both countries..." Zhejiang University uses sentences like, "Approved by the State Council...", "Under the direct administration of China's Ministry of Education, the new Zhejiang University is a key comprehensive university..." All universities mention their social and political roles in building the society and the nation.

The above writings illustrate how Chinese English writers, sometimes unconsciously, convey a Chinese ideology. Naturally, they think and evaluate things in a very Chinese way. It is not necessarily true, though, that the Chinese government these days still exercises control over all types of writing. Rather, it is more the Chinese English writers who embody and still emphasize those conventional values as they did before. Such content means nothing to western readers. Sometimes it even has the effect of confirming lingering Chinese stereotypes. In any event, it makes their reception of Chinese English writing more difficult. Much worse, it renders the introductions less appealing to them. People from other cultures are not likely to show any interest in or have a sophisticated understanding of Chinese politics. Unless they are specialists, they in no way aspire to understand China's political situation. As a result, the average western reader is unable to comprehend those embedded propaganda slants. According to Zukaluk and Samuels (1988: 121-133), reader interest and text topic familiarity/ prior knowledge are two of the major factors that influence readability.

4. Conclusion

Internet writing comes equipped with its distinguishing linguistic features. Relatively short sentences with simple structures and simple concepts are generally preferred in order to keep the Internet surfers interested, focused and responsive. It is difficult for someone to stare at a computer screen for an extended period of time. The difficulty is doubled or tripled if readers are forced to concentrate on long, verbose writings, especially when the self introductions are written with many directly translated phrases, expressions and sentences that are "Chinese cultural oriented". The analysis of the four chosen universities' online self introductions reveals how those English writings carry too much unwanted Chinese cultural baggage in both linguistic style and substantive content. Many words, phrases and sentences have been expressed from a strictly Chinese point of view. They do not carefully consider language and cultural differences between Chinese people and native English speakers. Format design ignores the special features of Internet writing. Even substantive content is judged according to conventional values which confuse or scare a foreign reader. The ultimate purpose of these online self introductions is to project an image of those universities to the world. The introductions, therefore, are deliberately and exclusively intended for foreign readers. Under these circumstances, there is no point to maintaining in the writing such a culture bound Chinese focus. It is obvious that self introductions with so many Chinese culture-featured phrases, expressions and contents only drive westerners away. A well crafted web site self introduction must be guided and shaped equally by language awareness and cultural awareness. The Chinese English writer needs to produce more culturally accurate and targeted writings. Chinese English writers will have to remember that their responsibility is not just to write grammatically correct sentences. The Chinese English writers of the future need to deliberately adopt English rhetorical strategies crafted to achieve carefully calibrated communication objectives. They need to anticipate the overall effect and reception of their texts.

References

Crystal, D. 2002. *Language and Internet*. Cambridge: Cambridge University Press.

Davis, L. 2001. *Cross-Cultural Communication in Action*. Beijing: Foreign Languages Teaching and Research Press.

Halliday, M. A. K. 1994. *An Introduction to Functional Grammar*. London: Edward Arnold.

Hu, W. 1999. *Culture and Communication*. Beijing: Foreign Language Teaching and Research Press.

Leech, G. N. & Short, M. H. 1981. *Style in Fiction*. New York: Longman.

Thompson, G. 2000. *Introducing Functional Grammar*. Beijing: Foreign Language Teaching and Research Press.

Zukaluk, B. L. & Samuels, S. J. 1988. Toward a new approach to predict text comprehensibility. In *Readability: Its Past, Present and Future*, ed. by B. L. Zukaluk & S. L. Samuels, 121-144. Newark: International Reading Association.

Websites used:

http://www.pku.edu.cn

http://www.tsinghua.edu.cn

http://www.nju.edu.cn

http://www.zju.edu.cn

http://www.cam.ac.uk

http://www.ox.ac.uk

http://www.harvard.edu

http://www.mit.edu

Evaluation in Abstracts: A Contrastive Study of Student Writing and Published Writing

XU Guohui

Beijing Institute of Educations

1. Introduction

As every academic scholar, junior or senior, can see, it has been a long tradition that academic writings should be objective, impersonal, neutral, author-evacuated or fact-centered. That's why we are always asked to hide our presence to report what the world is exactly like by avoiding using first person pronouns such as *I* or *WE* and employ more passive voice sentences to show that we write in a formal and objective way in academic writings.

However, in recent 20 years, a rapidly increasing number of researchers and scholars begin to focus their interest on the interpersonal instead of ideational character in academic discourses (Myers, 1989; Swales, 1990; Hunston, 1993, 1994; Hyland, 1998a, 1998b, 2000; Bhatia, 2004; Hyland and Tse, 2005). They propose that the nature of any successful academic writing is not only objective and impersonal but also subjective and interpersonal, for any academic writing could not be produced without subjective negotiation, arguments and judgments and in our writings we need to negotiate and persuade our potential readers to accept our own ideas or findings to promote our academic products.

The same is true with academic research paper abstracts, for abstracts are more likely to be significant carriers of a discipline's epistemological and social assumptions than to be a factual and informative summary of a longer report, and they are a rich source of interactional features that allow us to see how individuals position themselves within their communities. It means that when writers present their knowledge claims and account for their actions, it will involve not only cognitive factors, but social and affective elements, and to study these necessarily moves us beyond the ideational dimension of the texts to the ways they function at the interpersonal level.

In abstracts, writers have to clearly demonstrate that they have something worthwhile to say to gain the interest of their potential readers and persuade them to read on, which means that interpersonal or evaluative meanings are the key features of these texts. Besides, academic writers have to use some interpersonal linguistic devices to negotiate with their ideal readers to fulfill their aims. Hence, abstracts can be considered to be a potentially rich database of evaluative and persuasive resources (Hyland, 2000; Hyland & Tse, 2005). Although a fair amount of work has been done on the stylistic and generic features of the abstracts (see Swales, 1990; Salager-Meyer, 1992; Bhatia, 1993; Hunston, 1993, 1994; Hyland, 2000; Stotesbury, 2003; Yu, 2003; Lorés, 2004; Samraj, 2002, 2005; Hyland and Tse, 2005) and Zhang and Zu (2006) begins to touch upon the interpersonal function of the academic abstracts, there are still several limitations: 1) too much focus has been given to the impersonal aspect of abstracts while the interpersonal character of abstracts has been ignored to some extent; 2) most studies on abstracts are restricted to the research article rather than theses and dissertations, let alone the status quo of thesis abstract written by the students from the mainland of China; 3) fewer studies have been done on abstracts in the field of humanities and social sciences than the natural sciences.

2. Data Collection

This study is based on two corpora of naturally occurring English abstracts collected from L2 M. A. students' theses and published journal articles in the field of English linguistics.

The Thesis Abstracts Corpus (TAC) comprises of 30 abstracts from theses submitted in 2004 by the MA students majoring in Foreign Languages and *Applied Linguistics* from key universities in the mainland of China. These 30 MA thesis abstracts are sampled systematically out of 625 theses from the CDMD (China Doctoral/Master's Dissertation) Full-text Database in the National Digital Library of China.

The Journal Abstracts Corpus (JAC) consists of 30 article abstracts systematically sampled from three leading journals of linguistics published in 2004: *Applied linguistics* (AL) published by Oxford University Press, *English for Specific Purposes* (ESP) and *Journal of Pragmatics* (JP) published by

Elsevier. These journals are chosen because they include mainly primary research or empirical research articles that are nearly the same genre as MA theses that have been focused on, so that the abstracts in both TAC and JAC can form an efficient contrast. Ten abstracts have been selected respectively in each linguistic journal. These journals are recommended by several specialists from Capital Normal University, Beijing. Then to determine whether the electronic versions of the journals are available, a preliminary survey has been taken.

3. Modeling Evaluation Analysis Framework in Abstracts

Although there are a huge number of interpersonal resources that can be identified in abstracts, inspired by the Genre Analysis theory, Appraisal theory within Systemic Functional grammar, General stylistic theory and some relevant pragmatic theories, I developed an evaluation analysis framework in abstracts of my thesis. Using this model, in this paper I have decided to follow and modify Hyland and Tse's (2005) pattern but only examine three evaluative categories that are likely to be of most interest and challenge to both teachers and researchers and postgraduates: *evaluative event* (what to be evaluated), *evaluative source* (who to evaluate) and *evaluative stance* (how to evaluate). By exploring their occurrences, space occupation and functions, I'd like to look at the similarities and differences between student and expert writers to see whether they can manage the two demands of persuasion and objectivity.

3.1 Categorizing evaluative events

In each abstract, it is necessary for us to know what academic writers have chosen to evaluate in academic abstracts and how much space academic writers have chosen to given them. Evaluative events are examined with the inspiration of Swales (1990), Bhatia's (1993) works on genre analysis or generic moves of several samples of research article abstracts and Hyland's (2000) study on the rhetorical structure of research article abstracts in a large corpus.

Table 1　Proposed model of five evaluative events

Event	Function
Background	Gives the background or motivation of the study or research by highlighting the importance or pointing out the research gap, etc. E. g. ***The role of extensive reading in building vocabulary continues to receive considerable...***　　　　　　　　　　　　　　　　　　　　(Text 1 in JAC)
Topic	Presents the topic or thesis of the study or indicate the purpose. E. g. ***This paper attempts to*** *adapt Relevance Theory to guide the analysis of the subtitles translation...*　　　　　　　　　　　　　　　　　　(Text 3 in TAC)
Method	Includes methods, models, approaches, theories, data, argument for the thesis, and describe the brief organization of the article. E. g. ***Using an analytical framework*** *that combines insights...*
Product	States main findings or results. E. g. ***The discussion reveals*** *that among the...*　　　　　　　　　(Text 28 in TAC)
Conclusion	Interprets or extends results beyond the scope of paper, draws inferences, points to applications or wider implications and suggestions. E. g. ***The conclusion suggests*** *that advance preparation by the teacher, suitability of the course syllabus, students' motivation...*　　　　　　　(Text 13 in JAC)

3.2 Categorizing evaluative sources

　　Taking Hyland and Tse's (2005) work as my prototype and inspired by the valuable ideas mainly drawn from Hunston's (2000) works on statement sources and White's (2001a, 2001b) study on engagement system within the Appraisal framework in Systemic and Functional Linguistics, a renewed pattern below of evaluative sources is proposed to explore the possible evaluative sources to see whether the author employs those strategies equally frequently or just favors some of them.

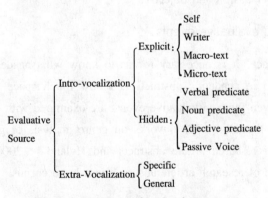

Figure 1.　A survey of evaluative sources

　　Details of the categorization of evaluative sources in abstracts are listed as follows:

3.2.1 Intra-vocalization: it includes evaluative sources that are internal to
   the text.

   3.2.1.1   Explicit: sources can be identified

   a. Self: *I, we, my, our* etc.

   ...I try to demonstrate that expository metaphors... (Text 26 in JAC)

   b. Writer: the *author, writer* of the study or the article

The author thinks *that pragmatic theory is of great use in...* (Text 8 in
TAC)

   c. Macro-text: *paper, study, thesis, dissertation, article* etc.

This paper argues *that "active metaphors"...* (Text 26 in JAC)

This study intends to... (Text 1 in TAC)

   d. Micro-text: *model, theory, result, conclusion* etc.

The conclusion suggests *that advance...* (Text 13 in JAC)

   3.2.1.2   Hidden: sources that can not be identified. The sub-categories
below are classified based on the types of sentence predicates.

   a. Verbal predicate (vt/vi): *News English, as a professional..., **has**...*
(Text 24 in TAC)

   b. Noun predicate: **There is no doubt** *that politeness is a...* (Text 18 in
TAC)

   c. Adjective predicate: *The detection... **is extremely important**...* (Text 4 in
JAC)

   d. Passive voice: *The letters in the corpus **were classified**...* (Text 14 in
JAC)

3.2.2 Extra-vocalization: it includes evaluative sources that are external to
   the text.

   3.2.2.1   Specific: specific single or group sources.

*"Rhythm is one of the most pervasive aspects of the human condition; it
is..."* [*Auer, P. , Couper-Kuhlen, E. , & Muller, F.* (1999). *Language in
time: the rhythm and tempo of spoken interaction. New York: Oxford University
Press*]. (Text 12 in JAC)

   3.2.2.2   General: not specific sources, identified or not.

It is assumed *that cultural differences affect...* (Text 14 in JAC)

It is generally held that the ultimate purpose of foreign. . . (Text 8 in TAC)

3.3 Categorizing evaluative stance

With the support of Hyland and Tse's (2005) model, the attitude system in the appraisal framework (see Hood 2004) and some other researchers' study such as Stotesbury (2003) and Koutsantoni (2004), the *evaluative stance* pattern below (see Figure 2) is formed to conduct a comprehensive study of the evaluative stance sources distributed in JAC and TAC.

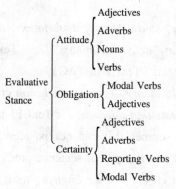

Figure 2. A survey of evaluative stance sources in abstracts

3.3.1 Attitude

3.3.1.1   Adjectives (attributive adjectives, predicative adjectives): *important*, *new*, etc.

3.3.1.2   Adverbs: *importantly*, *significantly* etc.

3.3.1.3   Nouns: *significance*, *novelty*, *pity*, *failure* etc.

3.3.1.4   Verbs: (a process infused with attitudinal meaning) *favor*, *like*, *help* etc.

For example:

This paper is intended to **enrich** [*attitudinal verb*] *the study of. . . advertisements which embody a far* **vivid** [*attitudinal adjective*] *feature of metaphor and plays an* **important**. . . [attitudinal adjective] (Text 6 in TAC)

3.3.2 Obligation:

3.3.2.1   Modal verbs: *should*, *need*, *must* etc.

3.3.2.2   Adjectives: *necessary* etc.

For example:

*Accordingly, to understand ways of speaking which belong to a culture alien to us we **must** learn to "hear" them in their proper cultural context...* (Text 23S in JAC)

To be exact, obligation could be put into the category of attitude, but it is quite different from other attitudinal language, so it will be analyzed as an individual category.

3.3.3 Certainty:

3.3.3.1 Adjectives: 1) HIGH: *obvious, apparent, sure* etc. ; 2) LOW: *possible* etc.

3.3.3.2 Adverbs: 1) HIGH: *obviously, clearly* etc. ; 2) LOW: *possibly* etc.

3.3.3.3 Reporting verbs: 1) HIGH: *show, demonstrate* etc. ; 2) LOW: *indicate; suggest* etc.

3.3.3.4 Modal verbs: 1) HIGH: *will and be going to* etc. ; 2) LOW: *may, could* etc.

4. Evaluation Analysis

Table 2   Frequency of each evaluative event in JAC and TAC

	Background	Topic	Method	Product	Conclusion	Pro. or Con.
JAC	14	30	25	21	18	28
TAC	26	29	25	22	26	27

Table 3   Space occupation of each evaluative event (X%)

	Background	Topic	Method	Product	Conclusion	Total words
JAC	679	925	1434	1422	659	5119
X%	13	18	28	28	13	100
TAC	4767	1221	3752	1942	1097	12779
X%	37	10	29	15	9	100

4.1 In evaluative events: virtually all abstracts in JAC and TAC include the evaluative event *topic* and nearly two thirds of the abstracts include the evaluative event *product*. It seems to us that both writers in JAC and TAC equally know how to persuade their readers in abstracts with the exception that far more student writers prefer to evaluate the background of the study than expert writers. If we investigate these evaluative events in a different perspective—their space occupation in each text, Table 3 will tell us some interesting differences: more student writers prefer to highlight the *background* part, while expert writers spend more time and give more space to the two evaluative events: *topic* and *product* instead (See Table 2 and 3), which can be evidenced by Text 9 in TAC:

1) Each language exists in a number of varieties and in one sense the sum of those varieties. . .

As a variety of language, "dialect" plays an important role in the language research. There are two separate ways of distinguishing "language" and "dialect". . .

The earlier study of the Hakka dialect mainly focused on its etymology. In the first half of the 20th century, some scholars. . . // (**Background: 729 words**)

Through a profound investigation of the social factors contributing to the formation of the characteristics of the Hakka dialect// (**method**), this paper tries to reveal the internal and external factors that lead to the characteristics of the Hakka dialect (**purpose**). // It provides brand-new aspects of studying social dialects that are of significant meaning in probing into the deeper social contents lying behind the language itself. In addition, it provides a new clue to the study of a nation's history and culture (**conclusion**). (**808 words in total**) (Text 9 in TAC)

Table 4 Distribution of evaluative sources in JAC and TAC

Corpus		Intra-v								Extra-v		Total
		Explicit				Hidden				Spe	Gen	
		Self	Writer	Mac	Mic	Vp	Np	Ap	Pv			
JAC	Sen. No.	19	1	49	30	37	15	9	34	2	2	198
TAC	x%	9.6	0.5	24.7	15.2	18.7	7.6	4.5	17.2	1	1	100
Sen. No.	19	18	88	44	136	93	35	168	18	15	634	
	x%	3.0	2.8	13.9	6.9	21.5	14.7	5.5	26.5	2.8	2.4	3.0

4.2 In evaluative sources: few extra-vocalizations sources are found in either TAC or JAC with several exceptions occurring in the background part of students' abstracts; more hidden evaluative sources are found in TAC than JAC in the form of passive voice in particular, whereas expert writers favor attributing the evaluative source to themselves, macro-texts or micro-texts; furthermore, more student writers like to overuse and misuse inclusive *we* while more expert writers (co-authored texts instead of single authored texts) tend to use exclusive *we* to refer to their own work. (See Table 4, 5 and 6)

For instance:

2) ***This paper describes*** *some simple simulation models of vocabulary attrition. The attrition process is modelled using a random autonomous Boolean network model, and some parallels with real attrition data are drawn.* ***The paper argues*** *that applying a complex systems approach to attrition can provide some important insights, which suggest that real attrition data may need to be treated with caution.* ***It concludes*** *that simulation methods...* (Text 3S in JAC)

Table 5   Distribution of evaluative sources in each evaluative event in JAC

				Background	Topic	Method	Product	Conclusion	Total
JAC	In-V	Exp	Self	0	5	8	3	3	19
			Writer	0	0	0	0	1	1
			Mac	0	32	10	2	5	49
			Mic	0	0	5	22	3	30
		Hid	Vp	14	1	8	14	0	37
			Np	4	1	3	4	3	15
			Ap	4	1	2	2	0	9
			Pv	2	5	10	8	9	34
	Ex-V	Specific		1	0	1	0	0	2
		General		1	1	0	0	0	2
Total				26	46	47	55	24	198

Table 6   Distribution of evaluative sources in each evaluative event in TAC

				Background	Topic	Method	Product	Conclusion	Total
TAC	In-V	Exp	Self	5	2	8	2	2	19
			Writer	2	5	6	4	1	18
			Mac	0	43	26	11	8	88
			Mic	0	0	24	9	11	44
		Hid	Vp	85	5	25	12	9	136
			Np	49	10	12	19	3	93
			Ap	24	1	5	2	3	35
			Pv	53	2	55	37	21	168
	Ex-V	Specific		16	0	2	0	0	18
		General		15	0	0	0	0	15
Total				249	68	163	96	58	634

4.3 In evaluative stance: both writers in JAC and TAC favor expressing their attitudes towards the propositions in an implicit way by *appreciation* instead of *affect and judgment* under the attitude system in the appraisal theory; a few student writers overuse the word *should* to emphasize their claims, which seems too authoritative for their potential readers when obligation resources are investigated (see Table 7); low certainty expressions occur more frequently than high certainty expressions and verbs such as reporting verbs and modal verbs play an important role in both low and high certainty expressions. Both JAC and TAC writers try to offer their propositions in a less assured way with the help of some low certainty devices, so that they can make their own claims more negotiable with their potential readers.

Table 7   Occurrences of obligation resources

	must	should	need	have to	it is necessary	it is incumbent	Total	Per 1000 words
JAC	4	1	3	0	0	1	9	1.8
TAC	4	20	3	3	2	0	34	2.5

5. Suggestions for Further Study

5.1 Suggestions for studies on other evaluative resources

There is still another category of evaluative devices needing to be considered, and it is known as *counter-expectancy* that can bring in some external voices for the authors to negotiate with their possible readers. In terms of the evaluative function of language, traditional stylistic features or markers such as sentence tenses and text layout can be also taken into account with the help of engagement system in SFL and the concepts of metaphor and iconicity in cognitive linguistics.

5.2 Suggestions for studies based on large text corpora

Analysis of a large number of real texts, computer processing of texts in particular, can show us quite unsuspected patterns of language. Nevertheless, the technology now is not available to enable us to analyze the evaluative resources at the discourse semantic level. With the development of some more advanced text analysis tools, further studies on the interpersonal devices based on large numbers of naturally occurring texts are expected.

5.3 Suggestions for studies on other genres

This study focuses chiefly on the evaluative resources of abstracts in the linguistic field and further research on the evaluation in other disciplines is needed, contrastive studies between soft and hard sciences in particular.

Moreover, the analysis of evaluation in other academic genres such as acknowledgements, book reviews or other parts of academic papers, or even possibly non-academic genres such as speeches and advertisements is needed too.

Appendix A *Journal Abstracts Corpus*

Applied Linguistics

1. GARDNER, D. Vocabulary input through extensive reading: A comparison of words found in children's narrative and expository reading materials. *Applied Linguistics*, 2004, 25(1): 1-37.

2. CARTER, R. & MCCARTHY, M. Talking, creating: interactional language, creativity, and context. *Applied Linguistics*, 2004, 25(1): 62-88.

3. MEARA, P. Modelling vocabulary loss. *Applied Linguistics*, 2004, 25(2): 137-155.

4. HANEDA, M. The joint construction of meaning in writing conferences. *Applied Linguistics*, 2004, 25(2): 178-219.

5. BASTURKMEN, H., LOEWEN, S. & ELLIS, R. Teachers' stated beliefs about incidental focus on form and their classroom practices. *Applied Linguistics*, 2004, 25(2): 243-272.

6. WALTER, C. Transfer of reading comprehension skills to L2 is linked to mental representations of text and to L2 working memory. *Applied Linguistics*, 2004, 25(3): 315-339.

7. BIBER, D., CONRAD, S. & CORTES, V. If you look at...: Lexical bundles in university teaching and textbooks. *Applied Linguistics*, 2004, 25(3): 371-405.

8. SOLAN, L. M. & TIERSMA, P. M. Author identification in american courts. *Applied Linguistics*, 2004, 25(4): 448-465.

9. EADES, D. Understanding aboriginal English in the legal system: A

Critical Sociolinguistics Approach. *Applied Linguistics*, 2004, 25(4): 491-512.

10. COTTERILL, J. Collocation, connotation, and courtroom semantics: Lawyers' control of witness testimony through lexical negotiation. *Applied Linguistics*, 2004, 25(4): 513-537.

English for Specific Purposes

11. PICKERING, L. The structure and function of intonational paragraphs in native and nonnative speaker instructional discourse. *English for Specific Purposes*, 2004, 23: 19-43.

12. MURPHY, J. Attending to word-stress while learning new vocabulary. *English for Specific Purposes*, 2004, 23: 67-83.

13. ALMAGRO ESTEBAN, A AND PÉREZ CAÑADO, M. L. Making the case method work in teaching Business English: A case study. *English for Specific Purposes*, 2004, 23: 137-161.

14. VERGARO, C. Discourse strategies of Italian and English sales promotion letters. *English for Specific Purposes*, 2004, 23: 181-207.

15. HYON, S. AND CHEN, R. Beyond the research article: University faculty genres and EAP graduate preparation. *English for Specific Purposes*, 2004, 23: 233-263.

16. LORÉS, R. On RA abstracts: From rhetorical structure to thematic organisation. *English for Specific Purposes*, 2004, 23: 280-302.

17. MORELL, T. Interactive lecture discourse for university EFL students. *English for Specific Purposes*, 2004, 23: 325-338.

18. HARWOOD, N. AND HADLEY G. Demystifying institutional practices: Critical pragmatism and the teaching of academic writing. *English for Specific Purposes*, 2004, 23: 355-377.

19. CORTES, V. Lexical bundles in published and student disciplinary writing: Examples from history and biology. *English for Specific Purposes*, 2004, 23: 397-423.

20. FOREY, G. Workplace texts: Do they mean the same for teachers and business people? *English for Specific Purposes*, 2004, 23: 447-469.

Journal of Pragmatics

21. O'CONNELL D. C. , KOWAL, S. & DILL, E. J. Dialogicality in TV news interviews. *Journal of Pragmatics*, 2004, 36(2): 185-205.

22. SHIMOJO, M. Quantifier float and information processing: A case study from Japanese. *Journal of Pragmatics*, 2004, 36(3): 375-405.

23. WIERZBICKA, A. Jewish cultural scripts and the interpretation of the Bible. *Journal of Pragmatics*, 2004, 36(3): 575-599.

24. PAGIN, P. Is assertion social? *Journal of Pragmatics*, 2004, 36(5): 833-859.

25. PORHIEL, S. Linguistic controls that are used to assess a reader's understanding. *Journal of Pragmatics*, 2004, 36(6): 1009-1035.

26. GODDARD, C. The ethnopragmatics and semantics of "active metaphors". *Journal of Pragmatics*, 2004, 36(7): 1211-1230.

27. KOESTER, A. J. Relational sequences in workplace genres. *Journal of Pragmatics*, 2004, 36(8): 1405-1428.

28. TEA, A. J. H. & LEE, B. P. H. Reference and blending in a computer role-playing game. *Journal of Pragmatics*, 2004, 36(9): 1609-1633.

29. AIJMER, K. & SIMON-VANDENBERGEN, A. M. A model and a methodology for the study of pragmatic markers: The semantic field of expectation. *Journal of Pragmatics*, 2004, 36(10): 1781-1806.

30. LADEGAARD, H. J. Politeness in young children's speech: Context, peer group influence and pragmatic competence. *Journal of Pragmatics*, 2004, 36(11): 2003-2022.

Appendix B Thesis Abstracts Corpus

1. AN C. Investigation into the factors affecting small group discussion. Hangzhou: Zhejiang University, 2004.

2. DENG J. Subjectivity of the translator and its effects on literary translation. Guangzhou: Guangdong University of Foreign Studies, 2004.

3. HU J. Relevance theory and film subtitles translation: A case study of Feng Xiaogang's films. Guangzhou: Guangdong University of Foreign Studies, 2004.

4. LI C. A forensic psycholinguistic analysis of deceptive confession discourse. Guangzhou: Guangdong University of Foreign Studies, 2004.

5. YU H. A corpus-based analysis of syntactic performance in Chinese EFL written production. Guangzhou: Guangdong University of Foreign Studies, 2004.

6. GENG Y. A study of advertisement translation—Metaphor translation from the perspective of cognition. Xi'an: Northwestern Polytechnical University, 2004.

7. LI D. Help individual learners build up the model of metacognition in listening comprehension. Xi'an: Northwestern Polytechnic University, 2004.

8. ZHANG Y. Vocabulary and its acquisition in pragmatic awareness. Wuhan: Wuhan University of Technology, 2004.

9. SU J. On social factors contributing to the characteristics of Hakka dialect. Wuhan: Wuhan University of Technology, 2004.

10. SONG Y. A children-adults comparison in second language acquisition and children second language teaching. Xi'an: Xidian University of Technology, 2004.

11. PENG J. The impact of extensive reading on EFL learners' motivation to read—A preliminary study among English learners in senior high school. Beijing: Capital Normal University, 2004.

12. ZHENG L. Ditransitive construction in English: A cognitive approach. Jinhua: Zhejiang Normal University, 2004.

13. WANG X. A quantitative stylistic analysis of Internet homepages. Dalian: Dalian Maritime University, 2004.

14. LI R. The application of cognitive strategies to reading comprehension in CET–4. Dalian: Dalian Maritime University, 2004.

15. ZHAO D. Research on the phenomenon of repair in conversation. Dalian: Dalian Maritime University, 2004.

16. QIU B. Research on decoding and using fuzzy words. Dalian: Dalian Maritime University, 2004.

17. LIU Y. A contrastive study of English and Chinese cohesive devices in legislative texts. Beijing: Beijing Language and Culture University, 2004.

18. HAO W. Contrastive study on Chinese—English compliment response behavior. Changchun: Jinlin University, 2004.

19. ZHANG M. A pragmatic study on verbal humor. changchun: Jinlin University, 2004.

20. PAN X. Speech act of apology in Chinese and American English: A cross-cultural study. Chengdu: Southwest Jiaotong University, 2004.

21. WEN L. Cultural model of values through conceptual metaphor—A study on the American cultural values in the presidential inauguration addresses. Chengdu: Southwest Jiaotong University, 2004.

22. TANG L. Constructing a tag set for Chinese learner's English corpus. Changsha: Hunan University, 2004.

23. LIU X. Intertextual analysis of reported speeches in Chinese & English news texts on "Shenzhou V". Changchun: Northeast Normal University, 2004.

24. XU G. The study of hard news English—An approach of genre analysis. Qingdao: Ocean University of China, 2004.

25. BAI J. Translator assessment: Suggestions for NAETI test designing and translation evaluation. Qingdao: Ocean University of China, 2004.

26. ZHAO H. A 3-map model in translation process. Chongqing: Chongqing University.

27. LI C. The language analysis on the fuzziness in the legal text. Chongqing: Chongqing University, 2004.

28. ZHAO D. Exploring text-type-based translation equivalence. Shanghai: Shanghai International Studies University, 2004.

29. XIONG T. Viewing court interpreting in civil trial proceedings in China and the United States. Chengdu: Sichuan University, 2004.

30. ZHANG Y. A study of the Candidates' test anxiety in the CET-SET context. chongqing: Chongqing University.

References

Bhatia, V. K. 1993. *Analyzing Genre: Language Use in Professional Settings*. London: Longman.

Bhatia, V. K. 2004. *Worlds of Written Discourse*. London: Continuum.

Hood, S. 2004. *Appraising Research: Taking a Stance in Academic Writing*. Sydney: University of Technology.

Hunston, S. 1993. Evaluation and ideology in scientific writing. In *Register Analysis: Theory and Practice*, ed. by M. Ghadessy, 57-73. London: Pinter.

Hunston, S. 1994. Evaluation and organization in a sample of written academic discourse. In *Advances in Written Text Analysis*, ed. by M. Coulthard, 191-218. London: Routledge.

Hunston, S. 2000. Evaluation and the planes of discourse: Status and value in persuasive texts. In *Evaluation in Text: Authorial Stance and the Construction of Discourse*, ed. by S. Hunston, & G. Thompson, 176-207. Oxford: Oxford University Press.

Hyland, K. 1998a. *Hedging in Scientific Research Articles*. Amsterdam: John Benjamins.

Hyland, K. 1998b. Persuasion and context: The pragmatics of academic metadiscourse. *Journal of Pragmatics* 30: 437-455.

Hyland, K. 2000. *Disciplinary Discourses: Social Interactions in Academic Writing*. Harlow: Longman.

Hyland, K. & Tse, P. 2005. Hooking the reader: A corpus study of evaluative that in abstracts. *English for Specific Purposes* 24: 123-139.

Koutsantoni, D. 2004. Attitude, certainty and allusions to common knowledge in scientific research articles. *Journal of English for Academic Purposes* 3: 163-182.

Lorés, R. 2004. On RA abstracts: From rhetorical structure to thematic organization. *English for Specific Purposes* 23: 280-302.

Myers, G. 1989. The pragmatics of politeness in scientific articles. *Applied Linguistics* 10 (1): 1-35.

Salager-Meyer, F. 1992. A text-type and move analysis study of verb tense and modality distribution in medical English abstracts. *English for Specific Purposes* 11: 93-113.

Samraj, B. 2002. Disciplinary variation in abstracts: The case of wildlife behaviour and conservation biology. In *Academic Discourse*, ed. by J. Flowerdew, 40-56. London: Pearson.

Samraj, B. 2005. An exploration of a genre set: Research article abstracts and introductions in two disciplines. *English for Specific Purposes* 24: 141-156.

Stotesbury, H. 2003. Evaluation in research article abstracts in the narrative and hard sciences. *Journal of English for Academic Purposes* 2: 327-341.

Swales, J. M. 1990. *Genre Analysis: English in Academic and Research Settings*. Cambridge: Cambridge University Press.

White, P. R. R. 2001a. An introductory tour through appraisal theory. Retrieved May 14, 2005, from http: //www. grammatics. com/appraisal.

White, P. R. R. 2001b. Appraisal: An overview. Retrieved May 14, 2005, from http://www.grammatics.com/appraisal.

Yu, H. 2003. *Discourse as Genre: Arresting Semiotics in Research Paper Abstracts*. Kaifeng: Henan University Press.

Zhang, Y. & Zu, D. 2006. Evaluation: Growth point of the schematic macrostructure TC in English and Chinese research article abstracts of finance and economy field. *Foreign Language Education* 27(2): 39-43.

Discourse Analysis of 2004
American Presidential Debates

CHEN Jian, GUO Jian & LI Jiehong
Graduate School of Chinese Academy of Sciences

1. Introduction

Discourse refers to a lengthy discussion of a subject, either written or spoken (Matthews, 2000: 100). It is a general social cultural phenomenon. If there is no discourse, there is no culture. Besides, people carry out social activities through discourse. As the linguistic research got deepened, linguists began to put discourse in a certain context to study. Therefore, discourse analysis has become a new and considerably valuable study in modern linguistic field.

Discourse analysis is "the attempt by various linguists to extend the methods of analysis for the description of words and sentences to the study of larger structures in, or involved in the production of, connected discourse" (Matthews, 2000: 100). In 1952, Harris issued *Discourse Analysis*, in which the term "discourse analysis" was first used. Since then, modern discourse analysis has remained an important and independent research in modern linguistics (Hu & Jiang, 2002).

As linguistics has become all the more popular in the field of politics, discourse analysis is widely applied in political research. In fact, "discourse" itself is politicalized, and polity is an important part of discourse. When people are speaking or writing, what they are talking about must show their attitudes and involve the ideas more or less indicating their attitudes (Brown & Yule, 2000). Thus, discourse analysis is a very useful and effective means in linguistic polity.

Chilton and Schäffner take politics as "text and talk" (Fetzer & Weizman, 2006: 143), by which the interface of political discourse and media is closely performed in the political arena. Fetzer & Weizman (2006) put forward two types of political discourses from a communication viewpoint, " monologue-and dialogue-oriented discourses" (146). Faced up with all the changes in printed, audio, audio-visual and electronic media, politics has found its way to make good use of those advanced methods and has become a media endeavor (Fetzer & Weizman, 2006).

Fairclough (1998) also takes a deep look into political discourse in the contemporary mass media. The political media discourse articulates together "the orders of discourse of the political of system, of the media, of science and technology, of grassroots sociopolitical movements, of ordinary private life, and so forth—but in an unstable and shifting configuration" (Fairclough, 1998: 146).

In the year of 2004, one of the most attractive issues on international political stage was 2004 American Presidential Election. As a recent important political event, it was a very successful reflection of discourse in politics. Especially, during its final phase, there were three brilliant live broadcasts of presidential debates between President George W. Bush, the Republican nominee, and Senator John Kerry, the Democratic nominee, moderated respectively by Jim Lehrer of PBS, Charles Gibson of ABC, and Bob Schieffer of CBS. Each of the debates lasted ninety minutes, following detailed rules of engagement worked out by representatives of the candidates (Transcript, 2004a). The umbrella topic of the first debate was foreign policy and homeland security. For each question there could only be a two-minute response, a ninety-second rebuttal and, at the moderator's discretion, a discussion extension of one minute. Different from the first one, the format of the second one was a town-hall meeting, in which the debaters were asked questions by the audience. The topic of the third debate was domestic affairs, but the format was the same as the first one. The three sparkling debates are worth profound linguistic study by means of discourse analysis.

This paper first introduces the discourse topic of the presidential debates. Then it analyzes the great linguistic effects of the debates on the election from the perspective of discourse context and discourse coherence.

2. Topic of the Debates

The notion of "topic" is clearly an intuitively satisfactory way of describing a strict principle that people have been in obedience with for quite a long time. According to this principle, one stretch of discourse talks about something, and the next stretch talks about something else. Hence, it is used very frequently in discourse analysis. However, the basis for the identification of "topic" is rarely made explicit. In fact, "topic" could be described as the most frequently used, but unexplained term in the analysis of discourse (Brown & Yule, 2000: 76).

In the debates, Bush and Kerry were asked questions of many different kinds, either difficult or embarrassing. Though in each debate, the umbrella topic was fixed, the specific subjects were chosen by the moderators or the audience, and the questions were composed by them. The candidates had to respond right after the questions without any delay. Besides, they were not only asked to speak, but speak topically.

Brown & Yule (2000) conclude that there are two topics at different levels: sentential topic and discourse topic, in the analysis of discourse. Each has its own functions in the expression of speech. In addition, if there is a given topic, it means that the speech has been restricted within a topic framework.

2.1 Comparison of sentential topic

Halliday (2000) keeps an eye on theme and rheme in functional grammar, which, from the view of discourse analysis, can be treated as topic and comment. "A distinction can be made between the topic and the comment in a sentence, in which the speaker announces a topic and then says something about it" (Brown & Yule, 2000: 70). Here, the topic is associated with sentence structure, so it's called "sentential topic". In English, sentential topics (theme) usually are subjects, and comments (rheme) are predicates. As a result, sentential topic is a grammatical term, "identifying constituents in the structure of a sentence" (Brown & Yule, 2000: 70).

(1) **Bush**: A president must always be willing to use troops. It must—as a last resort.

(2) **Bush**: I work with Director Mueller of the FBI; comes in my office when I'm in Washington every morning, talking about how to protect us.

(3) **Kerry**: I know the president will join me in welcoming all of Florida to this debate.

(4) **Kerry**: This president has made, I regret to say, a colossal error of judgment. (Transcript, 2004a)

If we analyze these four sentences at the level of sentential topic, we will find some delicate differences between the speech of Bush and Kerry.

Table 1   Analysis of sentential structure

Speaker		Sentential topic (Subject)	Comment (Predicate)
Bush	(1)	a president	must always be willing to use troops. It must—as a last resort
	(2)	Director Mueller	comes in my office when I'm in Washington every morning, talking about how to protect us
Kerry	(3)	the president	will join me in welcoming all of Florida to this debate
	(4)	this president	has made a colossal error of judgment

It is in evidence that Kerry has a more distinct sentential topic than Bush. In sentence (2), the sentential topic is rather vague. It could be "I" or "Director Mueller", but the comment is "comes in my office when I'm in Washington every morning, talking about how to protect us", so the sentential topic is Director Mueller of the FBI. In sentence (1), though the sentential topic is easy to tell, the comment is so confusing that you have to reconstruct it. "It" in "it must—as a last resort" is apparently a wrong use. Thus, sentence (1) becomes "a president must always be willing to use troops as a last resort". In Bush's speech, there are so many sentences like this without a distinct sentential topic, which results in the confusing sentential structure.

In sentences (3) and (4), Kerry's skillful use of English helps him understand with obvious sentential topics and elaborate comments. Of course, everybody understands what they are talking about, yet it is such an important political debate watched by a considerably large audience that the quality of sentential topic is a basic regard. Bush's informal English makes him in an inferior position from the very beginning.

2.2 Comparison of discourse topic

Sentential topic is not the traditional topic we usually mean. Therefore, in an attempt to distinguish the notion of traditional topic from the sentential topic, discourse analysts use the term "discourse topic" to refer to the traditional topic in a common sense, which means whatever a conversation or a text is about. This might be identified explicitly (e.g. I want to talk about ×.) or implicitly because discourse topic is not simply a NP or a sentence. According to Schiffrin (1994), it is the proposition about which the claim is made or elicited. The discourse topic summarizes, reduces, organizes and categorizes the semantic information of discourse.

(5) **Lehrer**: New question, two minutes, Sen. Kerry. If you are elected president, what will you take to that office thinking is the single most serious threat to the national security to the United States?

Kerry: Nuclear proliferation. Nuclear proliferation. There's some 600-plus tons of unsecured material still in the former Soviet Union and Russia. At the rate that the president is currently securing it, it'll take 13 years to get it. I did a lot of work on this...

(6) **Schieffer**: ... Both of you are opposed to gay marriage. But to understand how you have come to that conclusion, I want to ask you a more basic question. Do you believe homosexuality is a choice?

Bush: You know, Bob, I don't know. I just don't know. I do know that we have a choice to make in America and that is to treat people with tolerance and respect and dignity. It's important that we do that. And I also know in a free society people, consenting adults can live the way they want to live. And that's to be honored... (Transcript, 2004a)

There is a given discourse topic chosen by the moderator in each conversation. The discourse topic of conversation (5) is "what is the most serious threat to national security", and that of conversation (6) is "is homosexuality a choice". In conversation (5), Kerry answered the question as soon as Lehrer finished it without a slight hesitation. At first, he directly gave us a highly generalized answer by "nuclear proliferation", and repeated it with emphasis so that the audience would have a deep impression. Then, he stated the existing problem that Bush has secured less nuclear material in the last two years since 9/11 than they did in the two years preceding 9/11. Finally, he proposed what he would do. It is a neat arrangement strictly according to the discourse topic.

In conversation (6), it is hard to say that Bush told us whether "homosexuality is a choice". However, he did organize a decent answer, which satisfied the audience later. Since homosexuality is a sensitive issue, Bush chose a wise way to avoid expressing his attitude but showed his consideration and tenderness. Hence, nobody would care whether he was talking the discourse topic or not. A proper way of expressing the discourse topic will effectively represent a different judgment of what is being talked about in a discourse.

As a result, both Bush and Kerry have done remarkably well in this respect. It is a very even contest. Yet it is known to everyone that Kerry is eloquent, so Bush's marvelous speech surprised those who wanted him to bring shame on himself, and his clumsy image also held him in a modest position.

2.3 Topic framework

The notion that topic is what is being talked about is attractive because "it seems to be the central organizing principle for a lot of discourses. It may enable us to explain why several sentences or utterances should be considered as a set of some kind, separate from another set" (Brown & Yule, 2000: 73-74). It might also provide a means of characterizing the type of feature in contributions to a discourse, that is, the topic framework, which depends on the feature of context activated in a particular piece of discourse.

There are a potentially large number of different ways of expressing the topic of a speech. How do we determine which is the correct expression of the topic for the speech? The answer is that there is no completely correct expression of the topic for any fragment of discourse. However, if there is a topic framework, i. e. the characterization of the topic, by which listeners can incorporate all reasonable judgments of what is being talked about (Brown & Yule, 2000: 74).

(7) **Bush:** September the 11th changed how America must look at the world. And since that day, our nation has been on a multi-prolonged strategy to keep our country safer. We pursued Al Qaeda wherever Al Qaeda tries to hide... We've upheld the doctrine that said if you harbor a terrorist, you're equally as guilty as the terrorist... We continue to pursue our policy of disrupting those who proliferate weapons of mass destruction... And, as well, we're pursuing a strategy of freedom around the world, because I understand free nations will reject terror. Free nations will answer the hopes and aspirations of their people. Free nations will help us achieve the peace we all want. (Transcript, 2004a)

The topic of the above passage is about preventing another 9/11-type terrorist attack on the United States. Bush used sentences of concatenation to state what he had done, what he was doing, and what he was going to do—"we pursued Al Qaeda, we've upheld the doctrine, we continue to pursue our policy and we're pursuing a strategy of freedom", with "we" as the starting of a sentence.

Furthermore, he used "September the 11th changed how America must look at the world" and another group of concatenated sentences with "free nations" as the sentential starting to establish a complete beginning-middle-end speech. In terms of topic framework, it is a correct expression of the topic. As the President of the United States, Bush was speaking to the audience from all over the country. He definitely has the right to say "we", not making anyone feel uncomfortable of his address. Although he ventured into the "blinking red" territory (the time-up warning) a few times, Bush still appeared entirely within the bounds of acceptability. All in all, he chose a proper way of expressing the topic in terms of topic framework.

2.4 Speaking topically

When we have identified the topic framework of a discourse, there is "some basis for making judgments of relevance with regard to conversational contributions" (Brown & Yule, 2000: 83). "Relevance" was proposed by Grice in 1975 in his famous conversational maxims, which put forward the research on pragmatic inference. The four maxims are: quantity (informativeness), the quality (truthfulness), the manner (clearness) and relevance. Grice discusses the first three maxims, but he does not explore relevance (1975: 84).

Thus, Sperber and Wilson (2001) supplement "relevance" by replacing "mutual knowledge" with "mutual manifestness". They think mutual knowledge is unreasonable, because it cannot reflect communicators' cognitive situation in communication. So, mutual manifestness is the way to describe the information all communicators understand in cognitive environment where communicators know everything. As a result, mutual manifestness of cognitive environment is a key factor to the success of communication.

Under the new concept of relevance, speaking topically means making your cognitive contribution relevant in the topic framework. The presidential debate is the type of conversational situation in which the participants are concentrating their talk on one particular issue. They should have mutual manifestness in political cognitive environment.

(8) **Lehrer**: ... Are there also underlying character issues that you believe, that you believe are serious enough to deny Senator Kerry the job as commander in

chief of the United States?

Bush: ... Well, first of all, I admire Senator Kerry's service to our country... My concerns about the senator is that... he changes positions on the war in Iraq. He changes positions on something as fundamental as what you believe in your core, in your heart of hearts, is right in Iraq... And that's my biggest concern about my opponent. I admire his service. But I just know how this world works... Of course, we change tactics when need to, but we never change our beliefs, the strategic beliefs that are necessary to protect this country in the world. (Transcript, 2004a)

We could see that Bush was solid and did little to alienate or offend Kerry. In answering Lehrer's question, he did speak on the topic within the topic framework. First, he complimented Kerry's service to our country. Then, he began to express why Kerry did not fit the job of president. It is a big KO that he pointed out Kerry's changing positions on the issue of Iraq. However, Bush's last sentence was rather irrelevant, which revealed his lack of self-confidence. "We change tactics when need to, but we never change our beliefs" explicitly helped explain why Kerry changed his positions at times, for the positions here belonged to either tactics or beliefs. It weakened his strong attacks on Kerry to some degree, and the audience would probably forget the salient elements in his former eloquence. Therefore, it is not wise enough if the speaker does not speak topically.

3. Context of the Debates

Context is an important pragmatic approach, which refers to any relevant features of setting where a language is used. In discourse analysis, it deals with what people are doing, and takes the linguistic features in the discourse as the means employed in what they are doing (Brown & Yule, 2000). If we pay much attention to contextual description in the presidential debates, we will notice what President Bush and Senator Kerry were doing, the complicated relationships between the contextual features, and how the context exerted a powerful impact on the debates.

3.1 Discourse context

Instead of "context", Brown and Yule (2000) use "discourse context" in discourse analysis to distinguish the one in pragmatics. Discourse context is "more concerned with the relationship between the speaker and the utterance, on the particular occasion of use, than with the potential relationship of one sentence to another, regardless of their use" (2000: 27). Reference, presupposition, implicature and inference are used to describe what speakers and listeners are doing.

3.1.1 Reference and presupposition in the debates

Saeed (2000) points out that some words refer to specific entities in the world, or derive their value from their position within the language system. Thus, reference means the relationship by which language hooks onto the world. Yet discourse analysts appeal to this concept that reference is the speaker who refers. So, it is treated as an action on the part of the speaker (Brown & Yule, 2000). Green (1989) also describes reference as indicating the means by which a speaker utters a linguistic expression in the expectation that it will enable his addressee to infer correctly what entity, property, relation, event, or the like he is talking about.

Reference is closely related to presupposition, which is defined in terms of "propositions whose truth is taken for granted in the utterance of a linguistic expression, propositions without which the utterance cannot be evaluated" (Green, 1989: 71). In other words, it is participants' common ground in the conversation; at least the speaker thinks so.

Since the presidential debates were oral discourses, there were many types of references. If there were no presupposition, nobody would understand what Bush, Kerry and the moderators were talking about, and things would be in a mess. Reference and presupposition are two fundamental elements for the debates.

(9) **Kerry**: ... this president didn't find weapons of mass destruction in Iraq, so he's really turned his campaign into a weapon of mass deception...

Gibson: Mr. President, a minute and a half.

Bush: ... He said that he thought Saddam Hussein was a grave threat, and now he said it was a mistake to remove Saddam Hussein from power. (Transcript, 2004b)

In the above conversational fragment, we shall say that Kerry used the expressions, *this president* and *he*, to refer to one individual. It is enough, because we will not say that *he* refers to Gibson. Bush used the expression *he* twice, and we will not find any other name except *Saddam Hussein* in the whole passage. However, we all know that *he* refers to his opponent Kerry. The reference here is obvious because of the common ground, which is involved in a characterization of presupposition.

Kerry kept using "this president" to address Bush all through the debates, and Bush often used "my opponent". In this sense, Kerry's way of addressing was more aggressive than Bush's. Though his background as a prosecutor seemed to favor him as a rhetorical pugilist, Kerry was not as friendly as Bush. Both ways were right at the level of reference and presupposition, but Bush's was more likely to be accepted by the audience. It is just Bush's modest way of addressing and his Texas farmer image that made him more credible.

3.1.2 Implicature and inference in the debates

Implicature is used to account for "any meaning that a sentence may have that goes beyond an account of its meaning in terms of truth condition" (Matthews, 2000: 172). In discourse analysis, it is what a listener can imply from the speaker's utterance (Brown & Yule, 2000). In order to understand the implicature and arrive at the intended meaning beyond the literal meaning, certain facts about the world should be known. Thus, the listener has to "rely on a process of inference to arrive at an interpretation for utterances or for the connections between utterances" because inferential comprehension is a central thought process (Brown & Yule, 2000: 33).

(10)**Gibson**: The next question... comes from Ann Bronsing.

Bronsing: Senator Kerry, we have been fortunate there have been no further terrorist attacks on American soil since 9/11. Why do you think this is?

Kerry: ... This president chose a tax cut over homeland security. Wrong choice. (Transcript, 2004b)

In America, or almost anywhere around the world, when mentioning 9/11, we know that its implicature refers to an airplane-crashing catastrophe made by terrorists from Al Qaeda, and the date 9/11 has become a synonym of this event. Kerry surely infers that it's a question related to homeland security. Obviously, Kerry demonstrated his superiority in immediate reaction and direct answers.

The presidential debates were full of political and cultural implicatures. On occasion, even the American people did not quite understand what Bush and Kerry talked about, unless they knew about the plays on current political stage. However, it is necessary for them to do so, because it is a political election of the highest level in America. As long as the American people could understand most of the debates, Bush and Kerry did not need to simplify their speech, or their political accomplishments would be doubted. In other words, the speakers cannot pay too much attention to the hearers' inferences in order not to be restricted within a speech frame.

3.2 Situation context

"Since the beginning of the 1970s, linguists have become increasingly aware of the importance of context in the interpretation of sentences" (Brown & Yule, 2000: 35). Firth uses ""context of situation' to cover all the relevant circumstances in which a specific act of speech takes place" (Matthews, 2000). In order to go further research, we need to be able to specify what are the relevant facts of the context of utterance. Then, Hymes thinks that a context can support a range of meanings, and specifies the features of context relevant to the identification of a type of speech event. Therefore, he abstracts eight terms to describe the features of the context of situation, which are "addressor, addressee, topic, setting, channel, code, message-form, and event" (Brown & Yule, 2000: 38).

From the table, we can find almost all general background information of the debates. The addressors were Bush, Kerry, and three famous moderators respectively from PBS, ABC, and CBS. We all know the event was part of 2004 American Presidential Election in form of debate, so they all spoke English. The addressees were also the addressors as well as the present audience or those in front of TV. The three debates were all set at fixed time, at famous universities and with fixed umbrella topics. It is such an important event in America that the moderators must be skilled, experienced and popular among the audience. Therefore, it is rather natural and fair that the moderators were offered by the three largest broadcasting companies in America. Obviously, universities were also perfect places to hold the debates because it provided ideal environment and well-educated audience. In addition, faced up with the outstanding audience, the two debaters were able to bring their best into play, and the quality of the debates could be ensured. Moreover, well-educated audience at present would not ask inferior questions in the second debate. All these contextual features revealed the importance of the debates, and we can imagine how much pressure Bush and Kerry shouldered.

Table 2 Contextual features in the debates

Terms	Explanation (Brown & Yule, 2000: 38)	Presidential debates		
		First	Second	Third
Addresser	the speaker who produces the utterance	Bush, Kerry and three moderators		
Addressee	the hearer who is the recipient of the utterance	Bush, Kerry, three moderators and audience		
Topic	what is being talked about	foreign policy and homeland security	questions asked by audience	domestic affairs
Setting	both where the conversation is situated in place and time, and the physical relations of the interactants with respect to posture and gesture and facial expression	Univ. of Miami Convocation Center in Coral Gables, Florida; Sep. 30, 2004	Field House at Washington Univ. in St. Louis; Oct. 8, 2004	Arizona State Univ. in Tempe, Arizona; Oct. 13, 2004
Channel	how is contact between the participants in the event being maintained	Speech		
Code	what language, or dialect or style of language is being used	English		
Message-form	what form is intended—chat, debate, sermon, sonnet...	Debate		
Event	the nature of communicative event within which a genre may be embedded	2004 American Presidential Election		

4. Coherence of the Debates

Coherence "concerns the ways in which the components of the textual world, i. e. the configuration of concepts and relations which underlie the surface text, are mutually accessible and relevant" (de Beaugrande & Dressler, 1981: 4). In attempt to achieve efficient understanding and communication, one has to shun ambiguous expression to some extent.

4.1 Discourse coherence

Discourse analysis does not mean we concentrate on the syntactic structure and lexical items of utterances, or operates only the literal input to our understanding. When a speaker produces a perfectly grammatical sentence we can derive a literal interpretation from it, but we cannot understood its meaning, simply because we need more information (Brown & Yule, 2000: 223). Discourses make sense because there is a continuity of senses among the knowledge activated by the expressions of the discourses (de Beaugrande & Dressler, 1981: 84). Hence, discourse coherence is also important in communication.

There were not too many complicated sentences in the debates, but even we understand the words and structures, there was still something we could not quite get.

(11) **Bush**: I'll tell you what PAYGO means, when you're a senator from Massachusetts, when you're a colleague of Ted Kennedy, PAYGO means: you pay, and he goes ahead and spends. (Transcript, 2004c)

Bush was obviously talking about *PAYGO* which Kerry had talked about before. This utterance, though literally complete, has only partially described the fact. We could guess that *PAYGO* might be some policy or law. For the sake of understanding, we needed more information otherwise we would be puzzled.

(12)**Schieffer**: ... how can you or any president, whoever is elected next time, keep that pledge without running this country deeper into debt and passing on more of the bills that we're running up to our children?

Kerry: I'll tell you exactly how I can do it: by reinstating what President Bush took away, which is called pay as you go. During the 1990s, we had pay-as-you-go rules. If you were going to pass something in the Congress, you had to show where you are going to pay for it and how... (Transcript, 2004c)

By adding Schieffer's question and Kerry's former utterance, it is easy to get *PAYGO's* background and content. *PAYGO* means pay as you go, which originated in the 1990s. It is a popular tax policy in America, and Bush is the only president in history who has taken it away.

As a result, discourse coherence "depends not on the properties of the text components themselves, either individually or in relation to each other, but on the

320

extent to which effort is required to construct a reasonable plan to attribute to the text producer in producing the text" (Green, 1989: 103).

4.2 Speech act

Speech act refers to "an utterance conceived as an act by which the speaker does something" (Matthews, 2000: 349). Austin (1962) originated Speech Act Theory, and he thinks sentences can often be used to report states of affairs (Brown & Yule, 2000: 231). For instance, "I will get up early tomorrow" is an utterance by which one makes a promise or a prediction: i. e. , one performs an act of promising or predicting.

(13) **Schieffer**: Well, gentlemen, that brings us to the closing statements. Senator Kerry, I believe you're first.

Kerry: ... I think the greatest possibilities of our country, our dreams and our hopes, are out there just waiting for us to grab onto them. And I ask you to embark on that journey with me...

Bush: ... My hope for America is a prosperous America, a hopeful America and a safer world. I want to thank you for listening tonight. I'm asking you for vote. God bless you. (Transcript, 2004c)

Schieffer operated the beat of the debate by saying "that brings us to the closing statements", and he euphemized that "I believe you're first" to tell Kerry to do the closing statement. It is interesting to see two different ways of asking for vote in the two closing statements. Compared with Kerry's tactful utterance of "I ask you to embark on that journey with me", Bush's "I'm asking you for vote" couldn't be duller. However, simplicity does not always mean stupidity. The audience preferred a performative which was easy to understand, and meanwhile, Kerry's smooth tongue was not popular enough.

5. Discussion

Discourse topic, discourse context, and discourse coherence are three essential fundaments in discourse analysis. Throughout the paper, we have insisted on the view which puts the speaker at the centre of the process of communication in that it is people who communicate and people who interpret. Moreover, it is speakers who have topics in topic framework, implicatures, and presuppositions, who

321

assign speech act, and who make reference. It is hearers who interpret and who draw inferences.

In 2004 American Presidential Debates, both President George W. Bush and Senator John Kerry gave us excellent speeches, though politically speaking, neither of them exerted potent attacks on each other. All things considered, the president tended to have stronger stances and a more fitting style. The dramatic pauses and charisma in his speeches naturally beat out Senator Kerry's formal, surgical approach to his speeches, shown in responses to questions like the influence of faith on his leadership. Bush did not answer arguments well, yet was able to maintain his ground with clear, strong speaking. Ultimately, it is difficult to decide who won the presidential debates. However, Bush did not jump out of the linguistic principles in discourse analysis, and he set up a humble and less aggressive image among the audience.

Politics is a complicated subject to study. In the past, no one would consider it could be closely related to linguistics, yet in this present-day world of advanced media technology and great communication, linguistics is playing an important role on politics, and it is used more widely by wise statesmen. Since it is an elementary tool in linguistic polity, discourse analysis will fully realize its powerfully potential impact on the political stage in time.

Acknowledgments

Our sincere gratitude goes to Dr. David Cahill of Beijing Foreign Studies University, for his valuable suggestions, and devoted and unselfish help. We also want to thank the teaching stuff in Department of Foreign Languages of Graduate School of Chinese Academy of Sciences, for their generous support in literature.

References

Austin, J. L. 1962. *How to Do Things With Words*. Oxford: Oxford University Press.

Brown, G. & Yule, G. 2000. *Discourse Analysis*. Beijing: Foreign Language Teaching and Research Press.

Cheng, X. T. 2005. *A Functional Approach to Discourse Analysis*. Beijing:

Foreign Language Teaching and Research Press.

Beaugrande, R. De. & Dressler, W. U. 1981. *Introduction to Text Linguistics*. London & New York: Longman.

Fairclough, N. 1998. Political discourse in the media: Analytical framework. In *Approaches to Media Discourse*, ed. by A. Bell, & P. Garret, 142-162. Oxford & Cambridge: Blackwell.

Fetzer, A. & Weizman, E. 2006. Political discourse as mediated and public discourse. *Journal of Pragmatics* 38 (2): 143-153. Retrieved April 20, 2006, from http: //www. sciencedirect. com/science?_ob = MImg&_imagekey = B6VCW − 4H3Y9R8 − 3 − 1&_cdi = 5965&_user = 1999578&_orig = browse&_coverDate = 02%2F28%2F2006&_sk = 999619997&view = c&wchp = dGLbVlb-zSkzV&md5 = 4788321cf0042e04ffb7698f8dc5be07&ie = /sdarticle. pdf.

Green, G. M. 1989. *Pragmatics and Natural Language Understanding*. New Jersey: Lawrence Erlbaum.

Halliday, M. A. K. 2000. *An Introduction to Functional Grammar*. Beijing: Foreign Language Teaching and Research Press.

Matthews, P. H. 2000. *Oxford Concise Dictionary of Linguistics*. Shanghai: Shanghai Foreign Language Education Press.

Saeed, J. I. 2000. *Semantics*. Beijing: Foreign Language Teaching and Research Press.

Schiffrin, D. 1994. *Approaches to Discourse*. Oxford & Cambridge: Blackwell.

Sperber, D. & Wilson, D. 2001. *Relevance: Communication and Cognition*. Beijing: Foreign Language Teaching and Research Press.

Transcript. 2004a. Retrieved October 25, 2004, from http: //www. cnn. com/2004/ALLPOLITICS/09/30/debate. transcript.

Transcript. 2004b. Retrieved October 25, 2004, from http: //www. cnn. com/2004/ALLPOLITICS/10/08/debate. transcript.

Transcript. 2004c. Retrieved October 25, 2004, from http: //www. cnn. com/2004/ALLPOLITICS/10/13/debate. transcript.

胡壮麟、姜望琪(Hu, Z. & Jiang, W.), 2002,《语言学高级教程》。北京：北京大学出版社。

6. Pedagogical Stylistics

An Integrated Stylistic Approach for English Majors

DONG Qiming

Capital Normal University

1. The Integration of Stylistics and Intensive Reading

1.1 The present situation of Intensive Reading in China

English Reading courses in universities in China can be classified into Intensive Reading and Extensive Reading, and the former has been given special attention for English majors for many years. The time allocated to this course is more than any other courses (4-8 class hours each week), and students also pay much attention to this course. In fact, it is a comprehensive course of listening, speaking, reading, writing, and translating (Dong, 2006). It cannot be denied that this course has made great contribution to foreign language education in China. But as time goes on and as society develops, it can no longer meet the needs of the fast developing society. The main problems are: 1) The teaching focus is not clear—as mentioned above, it covers almost every aspect of language learning, and as a result, no aspect is deeply left in the mind of the students. 2) The reading material is limited. In the whole semester, only a few texts are involved. No quantity, no quality. It is very difficult to develop students' sense of language. 3) Many universities use the same textbook for many years—some for almost 20 years without changing. Therefore, the language is no longer fresh, or even out of date. 4) It is very difficult to use student-centred teaching method. The teacher, in order to fulfil his task, has to do the explanation himself all the time, and the students listen and take notes passively. As a result, in higher grades, students even go backwards as far as their listening and speaking abilities are concerned. 5) this course takes too much time, and leaves no time for new subjects.

1.2 The integration of Stylistics and Intensive Reading

Because of the problems of Intensive Reading, an experiment of this course has been going on in Capital Normal University for 5 years by combining stylistics with Intensive Reading for the third year students of the English majors.

1.2.1 Choose a proper textbook

We chose the textbook *English Book 6* compiled by Professors Huang Yuanshen and Zhu Zhongyi (1990). The other one is *Advanced English* (Book 1 & Book 2) compiled by Zhang Hanxi (2001). . In *English Book 6*, after each lesson, there are some *Notes on Style*, which, fist of all, give some fundamental knowledge of *style* and *stylistics*, and then give a brief stylistic analysis of the text involved, telling the students the striking stylistic features of the text from different levels of language—lexis, graphology, syntax, semantics, as well as some contextual factors, such as field of discourse, tenor of discourse, and mode of discourse.

1.2.2 Have a stylistic analysis of the text

Based on the theories of Stylistics and methods of stylistic analysis, the analysis of the text is usually carried out, at different levels of language—lexis, graphology, syntax, semantics, as well as some contextual factors, such as field of discourse, tenor of discourse, and mode of discourse. In this way, students will get a more comprehensive picture of the text apart from the language alone.

1.2.3 Offer some extra knowledge of stylistics

Apart from this, the teacher offers some extra knowledge of stylistics to the students. As a result, the students have developed their "sense of style", and get to know the different functions of linguistic items, such as capitalization, paragraphing, italics, etc. at the graphological level; NP/VP, archaic/ neologism, favourable/unfavourable, general/specific, etc. at the lexical level; different clause types, different sentence types, word order, active/passive, etc. at the syntactic/grammatical level. Therefore, the students' abilities of understanding, creating and appreciating new materials have been raised.

1.2.4 Find the prevailing stylistic features of the text

After the analysis of the text at different levels, the students will find some prominent stylistic features easily, and can have a better understanding of the text.

For example, there is such a sentence in the text "Pub Talk and the King's English":

When E. M. Forster writes of "the sinister corridor of our age", we sit up at the vivid phrase, the force and even terror in the image. But if E. M. Forster sat in our living room and said, "We are all following each other down the sinister corridor of our age", we would be justified in asking him to leave.

When the teacher asks the students the reason for us to "ask him to leave", the students can analyze it from the point of view of stylistics: different situation requires different style, the home situation requires an informal style, and Forster's formal writing style, which is full of images and metaphors, cannot be used here (in the living room). If so, it is stylistically wrong.

The following table indicates the attitude of the students toward this integrated course:

From this table we can see clearly that for Question 1 (*My opinion on the integration of Stylistics and Intensive Reading*), all the 24 students attending this course are *Satisfied* (62%) or *Very Satisfied* (38%) with this integrated course. No one chose *Dissatisfied* or *Greatly Dissatisfied*. As to Question 2 (*Compared with pure Intensive Reading, this integrated course is...*), all the 24 students considered this integrated course is *Better* (58%), and *Much Better* (42%). No one chose *Worse*, or *Much Worse*. To Question 3 (a multiple choice one) (*After taking this integrated course, I feel...*), 16 students (67%) chose A (*I can better understand the text of Intensive Reading.*); 19 (79%) chose B (*I can better appreciate the text.*); only one student (4.2%) chose C. (*There is not much difference.*); and no one chose D (*No better than before.*) Question 4 (a multiple choice one) concerns the opinion of the students towards the integration of Stylistics with other course: 13 (54%) students considered that Stylistics can be integrated with Translation, 11 (46%) with Composition, 5 (21%) with Extensive Reading, 11 (46%) with Prose Appreciation, 6 (25%) with Poetry, and 9 (38%) with all the above courses, and no one considered that Stylistics cannot be integrated with the above course.

Results of the Questionnaire

(**Integrated Course of Stylistics and Intensive Reading**)

(**24 respondents**)

1. My opinion on the integration of Intensive Reading and Stylistics is							
A. Very Satisfied		B. Satisfied		C. Dissatisfied		D. Greatly dissatisfied	
9	38%	15	62%	0	0	0	0

2. Compared with pure Intensive Reading, this integrated course is							
A. Much better		B. Better		C. Worse		D. Very much Worse	
10	42%	14	58%	0	0	0	0

3. After taking this integrated course, I feel (Multiple choice)							
A. I can better understand the text of Intensive Reading		B. I can better appreciate the text		C. There is not much difference		D. No better than before	
16	67%	19	79%	1	4.2%	0	

4. As far as course integration is concerned, I think Stylistics can also be integrated with (Multiple choice)													
A. Translation		B. Composition		C. Extensive Reading		D. Prose Appreciation		E. Poetry Apprecia-tion		F. All of the above courses		G. None of the above courses	
13	54%	11	46%	5	21%	11	46%	6	25%	9	38%	0	

The response of the students clearly indicates that the integrated course of Stylistics and Intensive Reading is successful, and more integrated courses are expected.

2. The Integration of Stylistics and Rhetoric

Rhetoric is the study of how to express oneself effectively. The three subjects Stylistics, Rhetoric and Grammar concern different things: Stylistics mainly concerns **appropriateness**; Rhetoric mainly concerns **beauty**, while Grammar mainly concerns **correctness**. Of the three subjects, the first two have a closer relationship, since stylistics is derived from ancient rhetoric. The combination of these two courses is natural.

This integrated approach began two years ago in the 3rd year students of the English majors in Capital Normal University.

What we have done in this course is as follows:

a) The explanation of the relationships between Stylistics and Rhetoric;

b) The explanation of Communicative Rhetoric and Aesthetic Rhetoric;

c) The explanation of different figures of speech;

d) The explanation of the theories of Stylistics and methods of Stylistic analysis;

e) Stylistic and rhetoric analysis of sample texts concerning different varieties of English such as conversation, public speech, news reports, advertisements, novels, poems, EST texts, and legal documents.

At the end of this integrated course, there was also a questionnaire concerning this course. And the result is satisfactory.

The following table indicates the attitude of the students towards this integrated course:

Results of the Questionnaire
(Integrated Course of Stylistics & Rhetoric)
(22 respondents)

1. My opinion on the integration of Stylistics and Rhetoric is							
A. Very Satisfied		B. Satisfied		C. Dissatisfied		D. Greatly dissatisfied	
8	36%	14	64%	0	0	0	0

2. Compared with pure Stylistics, this integrated course is							
A. Much better		B. Better		C. Worse		D. Very much Worse	
10	45%	12	55%	0	0	0	0

3. After taking this integrated course, I feel (Multiple choice)							
A. The two subjects can facilitate each other;		B. I know the relationships of the two courses much better than before;		C. There is not much difference than the single course;		D. The single course is better than the integrated course.	
19	86%	14	64%	1	4.5%	0	

4. As far as course integration is concerned, I think Stylistics can also be integrated with (Multiple choice)													
A. Transla-tion		B. Composition		C. Extensive Reading		D. Prose Appreciation		E. Poetry Appreciation		F. All of the above courses		G. None of the above courses	
13	59%	16	73%	7	32%	9	41%	6	27%	5	23%	0	0

From this table we can see clearly that for Question 1 (*My opinion on the integration of Stylistics and Rhetoric is...*), all the 22 respondents had positive answers: 8 (36%) chose A (*Very Satisfied*), 14(64%) chose B (*Satisfied*), and no one chose C (*Dissatisfied*) or D (*Greatly Dissatisfied*). As to Question 2 (*Compared with pure Stylistics, this integrated course is...*), all the 22 respondents gave positive answers: 10 (45%) chose A (*Much Better*), and 12

(55%) chose B (*Better*). To Question 3 (a multiple choice one) (*After taking this integrated course, I feel...*), 19 (86%) chose A (*The two subjects can facilitate each other*), 14 (64%) chose B (*I know the relationships between the two course much better than before*), 1 (4.5%) chose C (*There is not much difference than the single course*), and no one chose D (*The single course is better than the integrated course*). Question 4 (another multiple choice one) concerns the integration of Stylistics with other courses. Again, all the 22 respondents gave positive answers: 13 (59%) chose A (*with Translation*), 16 (73%) chose B (*with Composition*), 7 (32%) chose C (*with Extensive Reading*), 9 (41%) chose D (*with Prose Appreciation*), 6 (27%) chose E (*with Poetry Appreciation*), 5 (23%) chose F (*with all of the above courses*), and no one chose G (*None of the above courses*).

Again, the response of the students clearly indicates that this integrated course is also a success, and more integrated courses are expected.

3. The Integration of Stylistics and English Newspaper Reading

3.1 The present situation of English newspaper reading in China

Many universities have offered English newspaper reading course for English majors since the 1980s. Many corresponding textbooks have been published. The most popular ones are *A Quality Selection of Articles From American British Press*, compiled by Zhou Xueyi; *Reading Course in American& British News Publications*, compiled by Duanmuyiwan. *Journalistic English*, compiled by Li Ziqiang. There are also similar kinds of textbooks. Newspaper Reading course is optional with two class hours per week. Generally speaking, this course has contributed a lot to foreign language teaching. But there are also problems. 1) The news stories in the textbooks become old in a few year's time and no longer fresh; 2) Many teachers pay attention only to the contents of the news reports without analysing the stylistic features of this particular variety of language; 3) Students have learned some journalistic words, but have not developed the ability of creating new text of the same variety, because they do not know the linguistic and textual schema of news reports.

3.2 An experiment of the integration of stylistics and English newspaper reading

In order to solve the above-mentioned problems, an integrated course of stylistics and English newspaper reading was offered in Capital Normal University for the third year English majors.

3.2.1 Compile a textbook of our own

First, a provisional textbook *Journalistic Stylistic Reader* was compiled, which includes three parts: Part One is the theoretical preliminaries of stylistics and the methods for stylistic analysis; Part Two is an introduction to news reports and their textual formats; Part Three is the sample news reports and the stylistic analysis of these reports, which are renewed each year. The course is mainly based on this textbook. But when there is some striking and exciting news events, the teacher would offer them to the students right away the next day, which would arouse the students interest.

3.2.2 Do stylistic analysis of the sample texts

After finishing the first two parts, emphasis is put on the actual stylistic analysis of the sample texts from different levels. At first, students had some difficulties in finding the stylistic features. With the help of the teacher, they can do the analysis easily. At the end of the course, there was also a questionnaire concerning this integrated course.

The following table is the result of a questionnaire:

Results of the Questionnaire (Stylistics and Newspaper Reading)
(41 respondents)

Number	Contents	Results							
1	My opinion on the integrated course of Stylistics & English Newspaper Reading is	Very satisfied		Satisfied		Dissatisfied		Very Dissatisfied	
		7	17%	31	76%	3	7%	0	0
2	Compared with a single course, this Integrated course is	Much Better		Better		No difference		Worse	
		12	29%	22	54%	7	17%	0	0
3	After leaning this course when I read English newspapers, I feel (Multiple)	Easier than before		Know how to read		Like to read English newspapers		No progress at all	
		7	17%	30	73%	7	17%	3	7%

continuous

Number	Contents	Results							
4	When I read the texts of Intensive Reading after learning this course, I feel (Multiple)	My abilities to understand, appreciate the text are improved		I have a more profound understanding of the text		No difference		No progress	
		17	41%	21	51%	6	15%	0	0
5	Stylistic theories to English learners are, in my opinion,	Very important		Important		Not important		Not necessary	
		7	17%	29	70%	4	10%	0	0
6	To carry out stylistic analysis of the texts will (Multiple)	Help understand and appreciate the texts		Helpful to English composition		Helpful to my future teaching work		No benefits at all	
		25	61%	37	90%	14	34%	0	0
7	Compared with Intensive & Extensive Reading, this integrated course is	Very interesting		Interesting		No difference		Not interesting at all	
		7	17%	27	66%	6	15%	0	0
8	Compared with other courses, this integrated course is	Very difficult		Difficult		Moderate		Comparatively easy	
		0	0	12	29%	22	54%	7	17%
9	Intensive Reading course is necessary in the first 2 years, but it can be replaced by other courses in the last 2 years.	Totally agree		Basically agree		Disagree		Not clear	
		22	54%	12	29%	6	15%	1	0.2%
10	Traditional Intensive/ Extensive reading courses in the last 2 years can be replaced by	Stylistics		Stylistics integrated courses, such as with composition, with translation, etc.		No change		Can be discussed	
		5	12%	32	78%	1	0.2%	4	10%

4. Suggestions for Further Integration

Based on the experiments carried in Capital Normal University, and the suggestions and expectations of the students, some other integrated courses are suggested here.

Stylistics and Translation—Translation is re-invention of the original in both content and style. An effective translator should present the stylistic features of the source language in the target language. Therefore, translation has a close relationship with stylistics. The style of the target language must be the same as the style of the source language, and the translator should keep to the same style from beginning to the end. The integration of these two courses is natural. Professor Liu Miqing's book (1998) *Style and Translation* can be used as a very good textbook of this integrated course. And Professor Shen Dan's Book (1995) *Literary Stylistics and Fictional Translation* can be used as a textbook for post-advanced students, or reference book for the teacher.

Stylistics and Composition—English Composition is a very important course in universities. Traditionally, the composition course book mainly concerns with a) types of writing, such as exposition, narration, description, argument, etc; b) different stages of writing, such as sentence writing, paragraph writing... whole composition writing; c) techniques in writing, etc. But these are not enough, since composition also has a close relationship with style. The integration of these two courses will achieve good effects. *Advanced English Composition* compiled by Professor Wang Zhenchang and other three professors (2004), including the writer of this paper, can be used as a good textbook for this integrated course. In this text book we combined composition with style, which can be reflected mainly by the exercises after each text (which include four big kinds of exercises: **Reader and purpose** [tenor of discourse], **Organization** [mode of discourse], **Sentences** [syntactic analysis], and **Diction** [lexical analysis]. This integrated course has been given in many universities in China for several years, and all achieved good results.

Apart from these, Stylistics and Extensive Reading, Stylistics and Prose Appreciation, and Style and Poetry Appreciation, etc. can also be experimented.

References

Carter, R. & N ash, W. 1990. *Seeing Through Language: A Guide to Style of English Writing*. Oxford: Blackwell Publishers Ltd.

Crystal, D. & Davy, D. 1969. *Investigating English Style*. London: Longman.

Dong, Q. M. 2006. Stylistics and course reform in universities. *Foreign Language*

Teaching and Translation 2: 58-60.

Huang, H. S. ,& Zhu, Z. Y. 1990. *English*, *Book* 5 & *Book* 6. Shanghai: East China Normal University Press.

Leech, G. N. & Short, M. H. 1981. *Style in Fiction*. London & New York: Longman.

Liu, M. Q. 1998. *Style and Translation*. Beijing: China Translation Publishing House.

Shen, D. 1995. *Literary Stylistics and Fictional Translation*. Beijing: Peking University Press.

Simpson, P. 2004. *Stylistics: A Resource Book for Students*. London & New York: Routledge.

Wang, Z. C. , *et al.* 2004. *Advanced English Composition*. Beijing: Foreign Language Teaching and Research Press.

Winddowson, H. G. 1975. *Stylistics and the Teaching of Literature*. Hangkang: Longman.

Wright, L. & Hope, J. 2000. *Stylistics: A Practical Coursebook*. Beijing: Foreign Language Teaching and Research Press.

Zhang, H. X. 2001. *Advanced English* (Book 1 & Book 2). Beijing: Foreign Language Teaching and Research Press.

Appendix

Questionnaire (1) (Integrated Course of Intensive Reading and Stylistics)

1. My opinion on the integration of Intensive Reading and Stylistics is
   A. Very satisfied   B. Satisfied
   C. Dissatisfied   D. Greatly dissatisfied
2. Compared with pure Intensive Reading, this integrated course is
   A. Much better   B. Better
   C. Worse   D. Very much worse
3. After taking this integrated course, I feel (multiple choice)
   A. I can better understand the text of Intensive Reading;
   B. I can better appreciate the text;
   C. There is not much difference;
   D. No better than before.

4. As far as course integration is concerned, I think Stylistics can also be integrated with (multiple choice)

    A. Translation   B. Composition

    C. Extensive Reading   D. Prose Appreciation

    E. Poetry Appreciation   F. All of the above courses

    G. None of the above courses

Questionnaire (2) (Stylistics & Rhetoric)

1. My opinion on the integration of Stylistics and Rhetoric is

    A. Very satisfied   B. Satisfied

    C. Dissatisfied   D. Greatly dissatisfied

2. Compared with pure Stylistics, this integrated course is

    A. Much better   B. Better

    C. Worse   D. Very much worse

3. After taking this integrated course, I feel (Multiple choice)

    A. The two subjects can facilitate each other;

    B. I know the relationships of the two courses much better than before;

    C. There is not much difference than the single course;

    D. The single course is better than the integrated course.

4. As far as course integration is concerned, I think Stylistics can also be integrated with (multiple choice)

    A. Translation   B. Composition

    C. Extensive Reading   D. Prose Appreciation

    E. Poetry Appreciation   F. All of the above courses

    G. None of the above courses

7. Views on Stylistics

On the Orientation of Modern Stylistics:
A Reply to Some Remarks about Stylistics

XU Youzhi

Henan University

Ever since the middle of 1980, stylistic teaching and research has been experiencing a fast and steady development in China. This is first shown in the formulation of the Syllabus for English Stylistics in 1985, and the publication of *Introduction to English Stylistics* and other monographs or textbooks. The convening of the four Stylistics Conferences in between 1999 and 2004, respectively in Nanjing, Jinan, Chongqing, Kaifeng, embodies another upsurge of stylistic studies. More and more scholars are joining force, and in 2004, to our great joy, China's Stylistics Association was formally founded (in Kaifeng). When scholars of stylistics both old and young are rejoicing over the prosperous future of stylistic studies, we can hear some scholars complaining that stylistics is limited in its scope, and stylistic studies of texts are shallow as it just concentrates on the superficial phenomena of language. They say that there is not much to be done in the sphere of stylistics and stylistics is dying out. This set us into deep thought. Is there really not much prospect for stylistic studies? How is it that people feel the limitedness and shallowness of stylistics?

It then occurred to us that things may not be so serious as some believed it to be. There is still a vast area where stylisticians can give a full play of themselves. The so-called limitedness and shallowness of stylistics might come from an insufficient understanding of the orientation of stylistics. Hence the necessity of a discussion.

Let's first discuss the question of the "limitedness" of stylistics.

Modern stylistics is a discipline that can be subdivided into general stylistics and literary stylistics. As a discipline, both general stylistics and literary stylistics are concerned with the application of concepts and techniques of linguistics to the study of styles of language use, with the former concentrated on the studies of the sum total of stylistic features characteristic of the different varieties of a language, including the general features of the main literary genres, and the latter focused on the particular language styles of literary texts, relating description of language features to the interpretation of their artistic function. We know all branches of learning have their own scholastic boundaries; and the boundaries between different branches of learning and especially between different courses of study need to be made clear. Stylistics as a branch of learning, especially as a course of study, in claiming its own objects of study and its scope of concern, must define its relationship with its neighbour disciplines: rhetoric, literary criticism, language teaching, etc., so that it can better clarify its various functions. In this way, stylistics seems to be really limited in its objects of study and its scope of concern. Yet this is just what is required of a course of study. It is not limitation but self-restriction.

We know stylistics is the continuation and development of rhetoric; yet, it discards the traditional practices of rhetoric to establish norms for people to model on, and turns to the presentation of the functional features of language. That is to say, it is descriptive, not prescriptive.

Stylistics may also be said, on the other hand, as the continuation and development of the scientific school of literary theorists such as Russian formalism, New Criticism, Structuralism etc. which have all placed language in the central position of their theories. Yet stylistics has brought a whole set of metalanguage renewed by modern linguistics and modern literary theory and pushed the linguistic turn to its extreme, making literary research still more scientific and accurate, and broadening the vision of literary criticism.

Then we are aware of the orientation of stylistics: it is a borderline discipline between linguistics and literary criticism, aimed at the stylistic effects of language use in both literary and non-literary texts. It is this orientation that dictates its objects of study and scope of concern, and naturally its self-restriction (cf. Wang, 1980).

Now we discuss the so-called "shallowness" of stylistic analysis. Is stylistic analysis really shallow?

Modern stylistics as a discipline has made use of various theories and patterns of modern linguistics, and this has got a number of theoretical frameworks with which to deal with whatever kind of varieties and subvarieties of language, both old and newly arisen ones, to explore their sum total of linguistic features and their innate essential properties, to reveal and describe their classification and their different functions. For functional varieties, there can be as many fields as the level of detail we hope our discussion will require. Take the English of science and technology (EST) for example. EST is a cover term. It includes in its category many fields of discourse: the English of mathematics, physics, chemistry, biology, psychology, linguistics, etc. under each of which there are various academic theses, and within each of the academic theses, there are commonly shared layouts or designs, such as abstract, the introduction section, the literature review section etc. So in analyzing a subvariety of language like the introduction section of an academic thesis, we are likely to be struck first by its textual structure—what elements there are and how they are organized. We can find that the introduction consists of, according to Swales model (Swales, 1990), a three-move structure: first, establishing a territory; second, establishing a niche; third, occupying the niche; each move is realized in the form of schema labeled as "step" which operates singly or sequentially. Then we may find that elements of such semantic structure are realized by texture, the property of "being a text", which shows the patterns of semantic connectivity of the Introduction: how it is, as a whole, realized lexically and grammatically (cf. Hasan, 2004).

This example tells us: stylistic analysis is not confined to the description of lexico-grammatical features of a text but also its cognitive structures. The 90 Years of Studies in Modern Stylistics (Xu, 2000) pointed out the necessity of genre analysis of texts, emphasizing the transition from surface description to deep understanding of the macro-structure and communicative function of texts. Maybe by now stylistic analysis does not appear so "shallow" as some thought it to be at first glance.

Secondly, modern stylistics is always ready to make use of and apply all useful and newly arisen linguistic and/or literary/ psychological theories into the analysis of the language art of literary texts, and so, as a result, there have appeared so many different stylistic schools since 1960: formalist, transformational, functionalist, affective, pragmatic/ discoursal, etc., (see Xu, 2003) each of which has a theoretical framework of its own and delves into literary texts from a particular perspective, and each of which deals with the stylistic meaning of either the linguistic form (like the formalist), or the deep structure (like the transformational), or the structural function (like the functional), or the reader response (like the affective), or the discourse (like the pragmatic), or the social significance (like the critical, the feminist), or the cognition (like the cognitive). In those analyses, literary texts are approached from the inside to the outside, and back from the outside to the inside – all centering on a single point: the aesthetic and stylistic meaning of a literary text. See as an example Shen Dan (1998). This then is not at all a "shallow" description but an indepth exploration.

Actually, the styles confronting stylistics workers are many. They include diatypic (variety/genre) styles, which are subdivided into oral style and written style. Oral style is divided into conversational, argumentative, and public speech styles, whereas written style is divided into advertising, newsreporting, religious, business & trade, scientific, legal, and literary genre styles. In parallel to the diatypic styles just mentioned, there are also dialectal styles used in literature; temporal styles, regional styles, social styles and individual styles. These parallel styles will all display their respective modes of expression, called "expressive styles": bold and uninhibited, or gentle and sweet-toned; complicated and high flown, or simple and concise; temperate and refined, or lucid and lively; embellishing, or plain; serious, or humorous; elegant, or popular; compact, or unconventional. Here, we present a figure about the system of styles.

With a strong sense of language styles in mind, we can communicate on a range of subjects, with persons in various walks of life, and show our appropriate linguistic "manners" for various situations; we can heighten our understanding and appreciation of literary works—the art of language, and can often find some hidden meanings conveyed by the subtle working of styles, and we can improve our language teaching, literary creation, and translation.

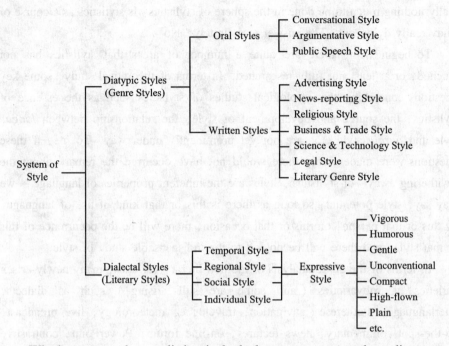

What's more, when stylistics is looked at as an approach to literature it displays an ever-indepth exploration of literary texts. It not only tells what use is made of language in the text, but more about why and how. Why does the author choose to express him-/ herself in this or that particular way? How is such-and-such an aesthetic effect achieved through language? The aim of literary stylistics is to relate aesthetic appreciation with linguistic description. It is not to provide a hard and fast technology of analysis, but as Spitzer put it, a "philological circle", "a cyclic motion whereby linguistic observation stimulates or modifies literary insight, and whereby literary insight in its turn stimulates further linguistic observation" (Leech & Short, 1981: 13). According to me, this cycle is spiral in nature – winding continuously toward a deeper understanding and rich interpretation of literary texts.

This spiral motion guarantees the indepth analysis already. To say nothing of the constant adoption of new frameworks provided by related disciplines in raising the explanatory power of literary stylistics in the interface studies between language, texts and literature.

Now let's come to the question of the future prospect of stylistics. Is there really nothing much to be done in the sphere of stylistics? Is stylistics as a course of study really dying out? The answer is definitely "No".

To begin with, there are quite a number of areas that stylistics has not touched, or at least not fully researched. In terms of theoretical study, some key questions concerning the ontological studies of stylistics such as the essence of stylistics, the source and development of style, the relationship between *langue* style and *parole* style etc. are not yet prominently under way. To me, if these questions were made clear, there would not have occurred the remark about the "withering away" of stylistics. Styles are the inherent properties of language – we may say, style potential; so long as there is this or that kind of use of language, by this or that person, on this or that occasion, there will be the occurrence of this or that style, and there will be no end to the indispensable study of style.

In terms of the genre analysis of the non-literary varieties, many newly-arisen varieties or subvarieties (and some are still arising!) such as dialects, interlanguage, motherese, navigation, travelogue, meteorology, live broadcast, on-the-spot commentary, news features, on-line forum, PowerPoint, contrastive study of varieties between, say, English and Chinese etc. need us to take care of.

The analysis of literary texts and authorial styles are indeed a vast area for stylisticians to give a full play of themselves. Compared with English and American young scholars, not many Chinese young scholars are making a systematic and comprehensive study of individual authors (see Hu, 1996) though some ph. D candidates have begun to delve into some famous writers. Besides this, we can also make a study of the sum total features of literature of a period of time, or of an ethnic group, and make a contrastive study of the styles of different nations.

In terms of the application of stylistics in the field of EFL teaching, there are many things stylistics can do: help students in their study of reading and writing in English, and in their translation.

Therefore the worry about the prospect of stylistics is ungrounded and unnecessary.

References

Hasan, R. 2004. Analyzing discursive variation. In *Systemic Functional Linguistic and Critical Discourse Analysis*, ed. by Young & Harrison. London & New York: Continuum.

Leech, G. N. & Short, M. H. 1981. *Style in Fiction: A Linguistic Introduction to English Fictional Prose*. New York: Longman.

Swales, M. 1990. *Genre Analysis: English in Academic and Research Settings*. Cambridge: Cambridge University Press.

胡壮麟(Hu, Z.), 1996,《我国文体学研究现状, 中国语言学现状与展望》。北京: 外语教学与研究出版社。

申丹(Shen, D.), 1998,《叙事学与小说文体学研究》。北京: 北京大学出版社。

王佐良(Wang, Z.), 1980,《英语文体学论文集》。北京: 外语教学与研究出版社。

王佐良、丁往道(Wang, Z. & Ding, W.), 1987,《英语文体学引论》。北京: 外语教学与研究出版社。

徐有志(Xu, Y.), 2000, 现代文体学研究的 90 年,《外国语》(4): 65-74。

徐有志(Xu, Y.), 2003, 文体学流派区分的出发点、参照系和作业面,《外国语》(5): 53-59。

编 后 记

由中国文体学研究会主办、清华大学、北京大学承办的首届文体学国际会议暨第五届全国文体学研讨会论文选集《文体学：中国与世界同步》终于即将面世，我们有幸能够为中国文体学的发展做出一份贡献，感到无上荣光。许多师长、同仁为文集的出版做出了无穷努力，谨在此向他们表示衷心的感谢！

中国文体学研究会名誉会长胡壮麟教授、中国文体学研究会会长申丹教授非常关注本书的出版，申丹教授亲自审定了目录并撰写序言。《中国英语教学》常务副主编刘相东先生和外语教学与研究出版社有关领导对本书的编辑进行了指导并承担了本书的出版事宜。

清华大学外语系领导罗立胜主任、王瑞芝书记大力支持中国文体学研究会秘书处的工作，动员全系师生筹办会议，保证了会议的成功举行。秘书处工作人员刘楠楠老师、卢秀霞老师、李舒曼老师等做了大量的日常工作，保证了会议的召开和论文集的出版。

编 者

2007 年 8 月

清华大学外语系